Praise f

"*Evocative and poignant, this book is a worthy companion to Karen Heenan's enthralling novel 'Songbird'. Highly recommended.*"
—Tony Riches, author of the Tudor Trilogy

"*[A]n intimate look at aspects of Tudor history that too often get glossed over or relegated to footnotes...
a joy to spend time thinking through their complexities with people that either were real or felt real on the page.*"
—Allison Epstein, author of A Tip for the Hangman

"*Heenan's storytelling is crisp, authentic and addictive.*"
—Judith Arnopp, author of Tudor fiction

"*[N]ot only a different look at Tudor history, but...one of the finest character studies I know.*"
—Marian L Thorpe, author of Empire's Legacy

"*A wonderfully realistic Tudor world.
Songbird was a confident and excellent debut and Ms Heenan goes from strength to strength with this new book.*"
—Annie Whitehead, author of Alvar the Kingmaker

"*A wonderfully-written tale, and cleverly done, to deal with such heavy themes with a lightness of touch.*"
—Mary Anne Yarde, The Coffee Pot Book Club

E-book ISBN: 978-1-957081-02-1
Paperback ISBN: 978-1-957081-03-8
Audiobook ISBN: 978-1-957081-06-9

Cover design and illustration ©2020 Anthony O'Brien. Image used under license from Shutterstock. All rights reserved

Interior layout ©2021 Eva Seyler.
Typeset in Adobe Garamond Pro and Gondola.

A Wider World

KAREN HEENAN

Table of Contents

"He that is discontented in one place
will seldom be happy in another."

~Aesop

Chapter 1

"THEY SAID I WOULD not end well."

"And so you have not." The young man has an air of self-importance, something he should have outgrown by now—but perhaps not. He has, after all, arrested me; mayhap he should feel arrogant.

I walk toward the fire, smiling as he moves out of my way. "I did not begin well, I will grant you that. And my middle was... middling." The heat warms my face, masking any flush of anger. "But my end is not yet accomplished."

He speaks again, his confidence recovered. "For your nefarious history with Thomas Cromwell, for your role in the destruction of the monasteries, and your attempts to dismantle the one true church, for promoting Luther and the English Bible, Her Majesty charges you with heresy."

I ignore him. "You, who have interrupted my supper with your warrants and demands, who are here to see me to that end—you have no idea of my beginnings."

Mongrel, they called me. Bastard. Unloved, I should have withered. I did not. I forced myself to flourish, to prove the world wrong.

"The world did not, early on, consider me of enough importance to care whether I lived or died. Now, I have achieved importance in the eyes of some—though only some see my true value. Whether you come to see it remains to be seen."

The young man—William Hawkins—snorts. A laugh? A sound of disbelief? He drops into my empty chair, his black boots stretched toward the blaze.

I watch him in the small convex mirror, which stands on the

cupboard, a memento of my Venetian travels, just unpacked. "You were told I was clever, to beware my words. I do not appear dangerous, do I?" A man of fifty-odd, dressed in clerical black. Thin to the point of gauntness, though seemingly healthy. A man with few attachments in this life, and those well concealed. "I can see you are interested."

Hawkins demurs, but his eye stretches at my words, and I continue, "The storm will not abate before morning. It is not solely in my own interests that I suggest you ask your men to stand down."

Hawkins is unwilling but sees sense in the end. I try not to listen as he speaks to his men. Nine of them—as if I require an army to be brought to justice. They shed their wet cloaks and settle themselves in the hall. I'll have ale brought out; their goodwill will be more easily won than my captor's.

I look at him again. He gives the impression of wearing armor, but in truth, he has nothing more than layers of damp wool, like the rest of us, with a well-cut doublet on top to show his status. "We may as well pass the evening in conversation."

Chapter 2

IT IS DIFFICULT TO determine the truth about my parents from what I was told during my childhood. I believe, for example, that my father was a priest who did more than give penance to the young nun who bore me. I know for fact that I was born at Wardlow Priory in Yorkshire. There I was housed with other foundlings and cared for by the nuns. When I was four, I was given over to a family who had lost two sons to the sweat and were willing to raise a boy of dubious parentage—and, if I am honest, of dubious physical charms, as well.

I was a sturdy child but not inclined to work. By six, I had discovered that the church was a haven where I could hide from my father's temper. The priest found me one day, sniveling in a corner. He dragged me out, stopped my bloody nose with his kerchief, and asked my name.

"Robin."

He cocked his head. Under his thick black brows, his eyes were gray—nearly the same shade as my father's—but kind. "Who are your parents?"

My nose tickled as more blood made its way down. "We live top of the hill, the falling-down alehouse." Most of the houses in the village looked to be falling down, but I knew no other way to describe my home.

"Wythe?" he asked. "Your father is Timothy Wythe?"

I nodded.

He led me outside to the well, his dusty black skirts flapping around his legs, and brought up the dipper. "Why have I never seen you at school? Or at mass?"

The water was so cold, it pained my eyes. "I'm not meant to," I said. "I help with the brewing." I was usually tied to a post in the brewing shed; as little as I liked it, it did not seem worth mentioning.

Father Gideon considered me. "You're a well-spoken lad. You should be in school, at least for a few years."

My eyes grew large. The idea of telling my father, who loomed enormous in his tattered smock and equally frayed temper, was terrifying. I handed Father Gideon the dipper and sprinted down the lane toward our falling-down house.

It was more than a week before Father Gideon turned up at the alehouse door. Mother was tending a pot over the fire, and Father sat on a nearby bench with a mug of ale. My sisters—two older and one younger—were sewing by the window in the fading light. There were no customers; after an outburst, the men stayed away for a day or two but were drawn back eventually by the lure of cheap drink.

"He's going to want feeding." My father shoved back the bench. "Hide the meat."

One of my sisters scurried to do his bidding, and then the four of us retreated into the shed.

"Will he eat all our food?" little Mary asked. "He's almost as big as Father."

"Worry more that Father will fight him." Esther was my middle sister, almost ten, and she was the only person in the house whom I loved. She had long brown braids that got covered in burrs when we went foraging together, and she let me pick them off.

None of the others liked me to touch them; Dorcas, the eldest, tried never to look at me. Was it because she missed her brothers? I had never asked.

We huddled in the fetid straw, listening to the murmur of adult voices, smelling the food we could not eat. Finally, Father Gideon passed by in the lane, and we shifted our cramped limbs. Dorcas picked up Mary, who had fallen asleep, but before she could pass into the house, Father's bulk filled the doorway.

He hauled me up by my shirt. "The priest says you're to go to school." His sour ale breath filled my senses, and I was afraid he would beat me so that I could not go to the school. Instead of striking me, he shook me like a rag and threw me to the ground. "You'll go, but you'll earn the privilege. No supper for you. Stay out here, and think about your fine chances!"

I stayed in the cold shed all that night, my stomach rumbling, wondering what Father Gideon had gotten me into. Did I need another reason for my father to abuse me? What chances did I have? And why did I deserve any? My mother told me often enough that they'd gotten a bad deal when they took me, wanting a strong boy to replace their dead sons and getting me instead—a lazy, disappointing dolt only fit to fetch water and stare at barrels.

I dozed near dawn and was awakened by a chicken that had found its way inside. It fluttered and clucked, then burrowed into the straw. I listened to the familiar sounds, and when it squawked once, loudly, I reached out and snatched the egg. The shell was warm, and the egg, which I cracked straight into my mouth, was hot and greasy, but it took away the worst of my hunger.

Chapter 3

HAWKINS STILL WEARS HIS sword, but he has left his cloak and hat downstairs. There is a very fine dagger at his belt.

I have decided to placate him. "As much as I dislike your errand, I'm glad you got here before the storm struck." I would not want anyone out in such a gale; the weather on the coast was extreme— our brief summers were glorious, but winter started earlier each year. "Your men are comfortable, bedded down in the hall?"

He nods, his expression less cocksure than earlier. Spending the night was not part of his plan. "They are well enough."

"I am glad of it." They are young and have ridden far; they will sleep. We are not likely to, not with the rain lashing the windows so they rattle in their frames. Not with the threat of execution banging around in my brain.

Settling into a seat across from me, he says, "This is severe for November."

"We get the sea storms." When the wind subsides, I can hear— just faintly—the crashing of the waves. "I'm expecting my wife any day. I imagine the storm will delay her, as it holds us here." I estimate how far he can be pushed. "I don't suppose you'd consider waiting?"

"No."

"I thought not." I cannot just vanish; I will write a letter once he falls asleep.

He looks around my bedchamber, where we have removed to get away from the snores and mutters of his men. "This is a small room."

"In a northern house, warmth is more important than show," I say. "It contains everything I need to make a life, if I am permitted one."

Those last few days on the *Unycorne*, I dreamed of this room.

I rarely remember my dreams, but these were clear yet so very ordinary: dreams of my bed, with its heavy green curtains, a fire in the hearth, and a bowl of late apples on the table, lending their cider scent to the air. My tastes, despite appearances, are simple.

"If we cannot sleep, we may as well drink."

Hawkins looks in dire need of something, presented as he is with a willing captive but weather that bars the door.

"May I call for my servant? Sebastian only sleeps when I go to rest."

He nods.

I decide to push him, just a bit. "You have the look of your parents about you."

His blue eyes widen. "You know them?"

"I knew them both. In his youth, your father was strong for Queen Anne. Did your mother convince him to change sides, or did he simply dance to the king's tune, as we all did, and end on the right foot when the music stopped?"

Even in the dim room, I can see him flush. He's got her skin, as well as her eyes. "My mother is dead. Don't slander her."

I hadn't heard of her death, but why would I? For the last few years, I only kept up with news that touched my own life and my eventual return.

"She was a fine woman," I tell him. "Give your father my condolences. I doubt I shall see him myself—unless he has become Constable of the Tower, which I do not think is in his remit."

He's probably here in Yorkshire or at one of his other manors, waiting, with his head down, as all sensible men are, to see what happens next.

Sebastian appears. He's been outside the door, waiting for my call, hoping to defend me from this undangerous young man.

"Bring us some wine, will you, Seb?"

My captor looks away from the fire. "I don't want wine."

"I hope your men have left some ale, then. My uncle keeps a stock of perry, if you'd rather." I look to Seb for confirmation.

"I drink wine." His lip comes out, truculent. "I just don't like it much."

Was I this callow and easily offended at twenty-five? "We all have our preferences. I had no intention of slighting you—certainly, you're accustomed to wine; we've just discussed your bloodline."

Seb shuffles his feet in the rushes; he will toss Hawkins through the shuttered window at a word from me.

Instead, I say, "Bring a jug of wine for me, and some bread and cheese to toast over the fire. And some ale for my friend."

With a disappointed glance, he disappears.

"I'm not your friend."

I do not rise to his bait. "You object to the term? How then should I address you? As my enemy? My adversary? You are young, but I would not call you my inferior." I stretch my hands out toward the fire; the damp makes my joints stiff. "I prefer 'friend.' I've had few enough of them in my time. I'm trying to improve my standing in the eyes of God as I get closer to meeting Him."

Chapter 4

THE DISCOVERY OF BOOKS, and the worlds contained in them, was worth the price I paid at home. I turned out to be a clever child, which did not endear me to the other boys. I cared little for their opinions; all my energies were put toward completing my morning chores to attend school, running home during the break for more chores, finishing my lessons, and running home again to work into the evening.

I no longer ate with the family; a crust of bread and a chipped cup of pottage were left in the shed, and eventually, I took to sleeping there for the sake of convenience. It was no colder than the house, and often I could convince a stray dog to venture inside so I could huddle in its warmth. On the worst nights, I settled in the straw near the cow, whose ribs stuck out as sharply as mine.

Father Gideon was a strict teacher but a kind man. At school, I was expected to pay attention and answer correctly, or face the same stripes across my palm as my fellows. After school was over, he would talk to me about my lessons or recite a poem he'd memorized.

He also taught me to write and bade me practice often. I scratched my letters into the dirt floor of the alehouse, knowing even if I were caught and punished, no one in the place could understand the words "Tim Wythe is a pig."

As the year wore on, and I proved that I could go to school and do my chores with no less skill than before, my father settled down. When Father Gideon borrowed me for a task and sent me away with a penny in my fist, my father saw a useful child whose inconvenient brain might turn a profit.

It was a hard existence, but I'd never known better, and I was content. Until I spoiled it all.

Then, as now, it was something I said. Or rather, something I sang. In addition to school, Father Gideon trained me to assist at mass. Though he knocked me about for it, it was an honor my father couldn't fault; in the alehouse, he bragged that "his boy" had been chosen by the priest to serve at the altar.

I took no pride in his words. I was not his boy, but if I could make him money or raise his status among the villagers, he would claim me.

For myself, I liked helping Father Gideon. Because of my lessons, the words of the mass were more than rote memorization, and I liked the clean smell of the wax tapers and the sparing use of incense. It was special, separate from the smells of ordinary life. Having a robe to put over my filthy clothes made me feel important—full of myself, one of the boys told me as they cornered me outside the church to teach me a lesson.

I couldn't duck and run at home—Father would only catch me and hit me harder—but I could fight my peers. I threw myself into their midst, shrieking and striking out on all sides, more like a devil from the faded fresco above the altar than a human boy. My fists connected a few times, and when Father Gideon dragged me off my antagonist, we had bloody noses and eyes beginning to swell shut.

He swatted the other boys and sent them off, then lectured me. "I expect better from you than this type of brawling."

"Joseph made fun of me for serving in the church."

"That's because he wants your position," he said. "But Joseph isn't smart enough, and he would drink the wine." He shook his head. "You're determined to ruin what looks you possess, aren't you? Clean yourself up, and go home. I'll see you in the morning."

The boys kept their distance after that, and even my father smiled faintly when I told him that I'd beaten three of the village boys for making fun of me. His smile chilled me; I didn't want his approval if it meant acquiring his violent ways.

As Christmas approached, my sister Dorcas prepared to leave, given in marriage to my father's competitor in Bolton, the next village over. Because of her proficiency with brewing, she was taken with no dowry but her green eyes and her assumed possession of my father's recipes. I served at her wedding, watching as she stood like a startled deer between our father and her new husband, who was built like one of his ale barrels and had a red face from decades of sampling his own wares.

I could see that my fourteen-year-old sister was frightened by her husband. Would he treat her the way Father treated Mother when he learned she had no special talent for brewing beyond the skills of any brewer's daughter? Dorcas was not a kind girl, but I did not wish that upon her.

I was huddled with my sisters—Essie and Mary were crying, and our parents were being no comfort—when Father Gideon called to me. I cast a regretful glance at the girls but ran to the priest as I would run toward my future. "Yes, Father?"

"A friend is visiting at Christmas," he said. "I will need you on your best behavior."

"Yes, Father."

He meant no fighting, no slacking, everything polished and perfect. I could do that. I did that every day.

"I've heard you sing," he said, sitting down in the first pew and gesturing for me to join him. "I'd like you to sing for him."

My face grew hot. I did sing, sometimes, when I believed myself unobserved, trying to copy the words that Father Gideon sang at mass. "I don't know any real songs," I said. "Just what you sing in the church."

"That will do, for a start," he said, "but I'll teach you something new. There's a lot of music you'll not know, since we have no choir."

"A choir?" I turned the new word over in my mind.

"A group of singers," he explained. "Large churches have them to sing during the mass, to bring everyone closer to God."

Could anyone join a choir? Was I too young? Was my voice even good enough? As these questions and more swirled in my mind, I saw something before me—a door swinging open, with a road just visible outside.

Brother Anthony was older than Father Gideon and not much

taller than me. He wore a hooded black robe and leather boots, which he traded for sandals once inside the church. His hands were spotted and gnarled, but his mind was agile. He grinned like a boy as he quizzed me on Latin. "Gideon, you've done well with this one."

"Most of it's not my doing," Father Gideon said. "He's a bright child, especially considering his origins."

Did he mean my family at the alehouse or my true parents? Did I care? Praise from these two men had physical weight; I wanted to stay at the church, or Father Gideon's small lodging in back, and let the alehouse fall to ruin.

I busied myself with polishing the chalice and cocked an ear in their direction, hoping the ale in their cups—sent by my father in a surprising gesture—would loosen their tongues and cause them to forget my presence.

Polishing was hypnotic, and I was lost in a dream when Brother Anthony said, "The boy deserves better than this, especially if his voice is what you say."

"It is," Father Gideon said. "And if it weren't, I would find another way to save him. His foster parents run the alehouse up the hill, and while their ale is good enough,"—he tipped his cup to Brother Anthony—"they're not fit parents for a cat, much less a boy like Robin. They just married their oldest girl off to a man of forty. Poor mite was near tears at the wedding. Not a thing I could do."

The monk rubbed his tonsure and sighed, dropping his head back. "There often isn't, Gideon. That is why we pray."

"What about the boy?"

I edged closer.

"I'll listen to him tomorrow. If he suits, I'll take him with me."

Father Gideon topped up their cups, clunky wooden things made by Eamon, the woodturner. "I will miss him sorely," he said, "but he is wasted in this place."

Brother Anthony placed his hand over the priest's. "So are you, my boy."

I crept out, buzzing with their words. I knew nothing of monasteries and less of choirs, but Brother Anthony was a kind, learned man, beloved of Father Gideon. If Father Gideon wanted me to go with the monk, I would go.

But how would we tell my father?

I tried not to watch Brother Anthony when I sang at Christmas Mass, but he was hard to miss, assisting Father Gideon in my place and clasping his hands together as I sang "Jesu Corona Virginum," which I had only learned two days before. Short on time, Father Gideon had taught me the words, but I was working out the translation on my own with his Latin grammar. "*Jesus, crown of virgins...*" Finishing that would take me most of the winter.

Mass ended, and I ducked behind the nave to remove my robe. My family had attended, to hear me make a fool of myself, as my father said. When I met them at the door, they just stared. Even my father was quiet, and Essie—dear Essie!—put her arm through mine.

"Wythe," Father Gideon said, "your son has done you proud today."

"'Bout time he's done something," my father muttered. He looked at me, squinting, as if he didn't recognize me. "Good for nothing boy."

Father Gideon put his hand on my shoulder. "He's my prize student and an accomplished singer."

"Indeed he is." Brother Anthony came around the door. His robes flapped in the stiff wind, but he held fast. "I've not heard his like in many years."

"It will do him no good in the alehouse." My father's hand closed on my upper arm, the fingers biting deep. "You've wasted enough time today."

Anger flashed across Father Gideon's face, so swiftly I might have imagined it. "Time spent with the Lord is not wasted," he said. "In what state is your soul?"

My father sputtered and hauled at me, but Brother Anthony

seized my other arm and, consequently, Essie, who still clung to me. "This boy is special," he said. "I would speak to you about him."

"Not now." Once mass was over, men would start trickling into the alehouse, and he would miss no customers because of me.

"You'll not take the boy." My father had been drinking before Father Gideon arrived and was in no mood to be pushed.

Father Gideon pushed anyway. "You don't want him."

There was a dragging sound as if a bench had been shoved back. "We took the bastard so he could work, and work he will."

"But will he?" His voice was soft, persuasive. "Find another boy; a strong, stupid boy who will see the alehouse as an opportunity. Robin will never do the work properly."

"I'll beat it into him."

Father Gideon was doing me no favors getting him riled up. I should go in and apologize for my aspirations, beg forgiveness, and promise to work in the alehouse until I was as old as Brother Anthony. I couldn't do it. This wasn't my work. I didn't know what my work might be, but it was not brewing or hauling barrels, nor was it serving and drinking with the men of this village—men who would never respect me.

I had never before dreamed people might respect me, but now I craved it. I wanted to be worthy. Perhaps I could be respected as a brewer, but that wasn't enough now.

There was more speech, too low for me to hear. Just Father rumbling and Gideon's quieter responses.

Where was Brother Anthony? Perhaps a stranger would have been more persuasive? No. Father would make up his own mind. Another man, strange or familiar, would make no difference in the end.

My fate was in his hands.

"Timothy," Father Gideon said urgently, "Brother Anthony is from Hatton Priory. They often have boys there, same as you got Robin from Wardlow."

There was a long pause. I crept closer to the door.

"Let him take Robin, and he'll send you a strapping boy, one more willing to help you. Not a son," he said, "but a boy so good, you'll wish he was yours."

My father got up, and liquid sloshed into their cups. "No boy is that good."

I could hear the smile in the priest's voice. "Wouldn't almost any boy be better suited than Robin?"

A small, cold hand touched my arm. Essie's eyes gleamed in the dim light. "You'll get beaten if he catches you."

"You think I don't know that?" I moved over so she could sit beside me. "So will you."

"What are they talking about?" Her feet were bare, and she scrunched her toes in the straw, trying to find warmth.

"Father Gideon wants me to go with that monk, and he's promising to send a boy in my place."

"They couldn't do any worse."

"That's true." I could hear no more conversation. The men were quietly drinking, leaving my life to hang in mid-air. "Would you miss me?"

Essie laughed softly and poked my ribs. "What does that matter? I won't be here forever. They'll find a match for me like Dorcas, and off I'll go."

I hated the idea of Essie with some fat old man. "Maybe you could come with me."

"To a monastery?" Her voice lilted upward. "Maybe the new boy will be nice. Maybe Father will like him so much that he'll let me marry him, and I won't have to go away."

"If I stayed, would you marry me?" I'd never thought of marriage, but I was jealous that Essie might want to marry my replacement.

Her warm breath made my skin prickle. "Of course not," she said. "I love you, Robin, but you're far too ugly."

I was asleep when Father Gideon stumbled into the shed.

"We've won," he said. "Anthony and I will be back for you before noon. Pack your things."

His eyes were red, and he smelled of our strongest ale. Had he drunk Father under the table?

"How?"

"By the Lord's grace," he said, "I'm not sure. But he said yes, and I will hold him to it." Stepping past me, he pushed open the door to the side yard and stood blinking at the stars, the cold air jostling against the ale in his system. He exhaled a cloud of mist against the dark sky. "Sleep, Robin. Tomorrow will not be an easy day."

I caught his hand. "Thank you, Father."

"Thank Brother Anthony. He sees a bright future for you."

Back in the straw, I pulled the blanket around my shoulders and propped myself in the corner. I whistled for the dog, but it did not appear, and I resigned myself to a night with the cow.

Chapter 5

HE'S DRIFTED OFF. It's hard to believe my words are the weapons they use against me, when I cannot even keep my captor awake. I'd hoped to talk with him of fathers, but no matter; there will be plenty of time.

Seb leans toward my ear. "I have given him your uncle's bed."

I want to ask where that bed's occupant will sleep, but Hawkins stirs. "Seb, please show our guest to his chamber."

The young man staggers to his feet. Afraid of my wine, he drank far too much ale.

"You needn't worry, Hawkins, I won't escape into the night."

He looks as though he would like to object, then stumbles and leans hard on Seb's shoulder.

"Have a look out the window before you retire," I call after him. "It's still blowing a gale, but the rain has turned to snow."

Sworn to his duty, he will want to attempt our journey in the morning. I doubt the roads will be passable—not that the roads in England are ever passable. It's one more thing the French and the Italians have on us, other than drinkable wine.

"Sleep well, my young friend," I murmur after him. "Dream of fair skies, for I do not believe you will see them on the morrow."

The creak of the shutter wakes me, then the sudden glare when Seb throws open the bed curtains. I have spent the night in a fug of warmth, and the chilly air is like a blow to the face. "What a blessed morning." A glance at the window shows snow edging the sill, more than the night before. "Has our guest arisen?"

"Aye." His mouth curls at one corner.

"A more pertinent inquiry—has he opened his shutters?"

This time, Seb breaks into a grin, his teeth gleaming white against his dark skin. "He has indeed."

"I thought so, else he would have been in here already, clamoring to depart."

Seb hands me my stockings before my feet can touch the floor.

"Such a convenient storm. One could almost believe the Almighty had a hand in it. Have you been at your prayers again?"

"Not me." He tugs my shirt off and leaves me shivering for a long moment before returning with a bowl of warm water and a linen cloth.

"I wore myself out last evening talking to that fellow." Talking about my life—why had I done that? I can't remember the last time I spoke about my parents, neither my foster parents nor my real ones. I try not to look back.

"Was it talk or drink?" Seb shakes out a fresh shirt as I rub myself with the cloth. "It was certainly drink for him."

"A bit of both." I dry off and reach for the shirt. "I will save my stories for our guest." Seb knows most of my tale, one way or another. Servants always do.

I am certain we will not leave this day, but nevertheless, I dress for the outdoors: woolen hose, my heaviest stocks buckled over them; a white shirt, with my black wool broadcloth doublet, and a small knife—a trick learned in Italy—tucked into an inner pocket. My hair is combed, my beard trimmed. I think to ask Seb to shave it, but reconsider. It will be cold, riding.

Instead, I go downstairs and take my morning pottage and ale into the library. I will enjoy my routine while I can. Seb joins me, amusing himself with a book of maps while I address almost five years of neglected records.

A fist is applied, none too gently, to the door. I consider the benefit of silence, of pretending I have gone, but it would prove nothing. I shrug. "Let him in. He'll come anyway."

Hawkins looks tired, his eyes puffy and his expression irresolute. His dark hair, uncovered, hangs in his eyes. He is, however, fully dressed, with his hand, yet again, on his sword. Tiresome boy.

I greet him like the May. "You catch me at my desk. Fear not, I do not seek aid and comfort from abroad. I am beyond their help. Here, you may see—I am reviewing the household accounts." The letter to my wife was finished last night and given to the cook for safekeeping; I do not want young Hawkins to read my words to her. "Don't treat me as Cromwell did Thomas More, taking away my books and paper. More suffered as much from that as he did the separation from his wife and daughter."

"I care not for your tales, old man." He turns on his heel, striking a pose for an unseen audience. "You attempt to distract me from my sworn duty."

"I do not," I assure him, but the words sting. Old man, indeed. "I but try to pass the time."

Hawkins drops heavily onto a stool, his sword clanking. "Did Cromwell really take his books?"

"He did indeed." I saw it myself, the stack of material brought from More's cell in the Bell Tower. "King Henry rid himself of that turbulent priest, but like his predecessor, he was haunted for the rest of his life by his actions. More's ghost no more resides in the Tower than Becket floats in the rafters at Canterbury. I believe souls which depart this life at the whim of their masters follow not their executioner but he who gave the order."

"Speak you of the queen?"

"I make no reference to Her Majesty. I speak of her father and of Henry II." I stretch and settle my black bonnet on my head. Captivity is no reason not to look like a gentleman. "The problem with being so many years at court is one cannot make a reference without being accused of directing it at the wrong person."

I wonder where Becket resides now, since my combined masters saw fit to relieve him of his shrine. Perhaps the poor man is finally at rest.

"I hope you were comfortable last night," I say. "The house hasn't been fully occupied in some years. It's an arduous journey from London, and sitting by the fire and listening to me must have been wearing. You shouldn't feel bad for dozing."

"I didn't doze."

He is like a child, contradicting me as a matter of course. "As you will. But I shall keep my words to myself today and bore you no further."

Sliding down in his seat, he plays with his sleeve, pulling a bit of lawn in and out of the slashing. "You were talking about the monasteries, weren't you?"

"The monasteries?" Yes, I'd gotten as far as mentioning Hatton before he fell asleep. "Yes, I was."

"You helped destroy them." Obviously, he knows that, considering the charge against me.

"I was…involved in the dissolution, yes." I look at my hands. "But I have not reached that point in my tale. We are approaching a monastery, yes, but I was still a boy when I caught my first glimpse of Hatton."

Chapter 6

FATHER GIDEON CAME FOR me at noon, as promised. Too excited to sleep, I'd set myself the task of cleaning the alehouse before the family woke. Empty cups still littered the tables. I washed the cups, swept the worst of the rushes to the far corner, and laid a fire before retreating to the shed to gather my belongings: a hairy frieze coat and a wool cap. Those, along with the clothes on my back, were all I owned. I had come with nothing, and I would leave in nearly the same state.

When the fire was crackling, Mother came in to prepare breakfast, followed closely by my sisters. It was only the usual pease pottage, but it was warm and filling. I hunched around the emptiness in my middle.

"Mother says you're going." Mary reached for her wooden spoon.

"I am."

"Where?"

"To some fine monastery, to live among the priests," Mother said. "Back to the filth that spawned him." She dumped the pottage on a trencher of stale bread, and the girls started shoveling it in.

"May I have some?"

"Let your friends have that honor," she said. "We'll waste no more food on you."

Essie's eyes conveyed the message that I could have her breakfast, if only Mother would turn her back. Mary passed me a bit of bread under the table, and I tucked it into my sleeve.

"Where is Father?"

"Gone to the smith. The kettle has a split. He'll not be back before you leave."

I permitted myself a sigh of relief. I might leave hungry and unloved, but at least I would not leave bloodied, or blamed for the broken kettle. "Please tell him I thank him for all he has done for me, and I hope the next boy is more worthy of your care."

I was being polite to earn my breakfast, and she knew it, but with an impatient sound, she threw another spoon on the table.

"Here's Father Gideon!" Mary stood on the bench, looking out the window. "Where's the other one?"

"Mayhap he's gone," Essie said, the tip of her braid in her mouth. "You'll be stuck here forever."

I would not be stuck there forever. If Father Gideon and Brother Anthony did not come for me, I would bide my time until I was old enough to run away.

Father Gideon entered, ducking his head under the lintel. He greeted my mother and the girls, rubbing his hands and extending them toward the fire. "Are you ready, Robin?" he asked. "Have you said your farewells?"

"He has," Mother said. "You can take him."

"Where is Brother Anthony?" I swallowed the last of the bread.

"At the church. You have a long ride ahead; I thought to save him a little of the cold."

"Well, boy, do better for them than you have for us." Mother turned away and began poking at the pot over the fire. Mary joined her, clutching a handful of her skirt.

"Bye, Robin." Essie showed no sadness at losing me, but I still took pleasure in her pink cheeks and brown braids. She was the only kindness I had known in this place.

Father Gideon guided me out to the windswept road.

I stopped. "One moment." I darted through the side yard and reached into the shed, retrieving my blanket. Wrapping it around my shoulders, I rejoined the priest, and together we turned on to the lane that led toward the church.

When we crested the hill, I took a last look at this place, which had never been my home. The church, with its mongrel combination of stone and harled plaster, stood opposite the small market cross. Across from it, a scattering of houses, no more than a dozen, were arranged in a semi-circle. On such a cold day, there were no signs of life other than two dogs mating by the cross, and the diminutive figure of Brother Anthony, waiting at the church door.

Before we joined him, before I was separated from Father Gideon, possibly forever, I had a question I must ask. "Do you know who my parents were?"

"Before the Wythes?"

"Yes. My real parents."

He stopped, and his big hand rested on my shoulder. "Some things are best not looked into, Robin. I don't know who your parents were. There may be a record at the priory where you were brought up, but there might not."

I scuffed my feet, sending clouds of dust up around our legs. "You mean, if my father was a priest."

Father Gideon resumed walking. "It may be true, but you'll do well to remember that priests are but men. And men may fall. If he's made his peace with God, all will be well."

"Well for him," I said.

He did not scold me for my tone or my uncharitable thoughts about my father. I did not assign as much guilt to my mother. Living in small spaces, I understood how babies were made, and it seemed to me the woman had less part—and less say—in the business than the man.

"Forgiveness is as much for your benefit as for the person who has wronged you. You would do well to remember that."

Our journey took three days because Brother Anthony was an amiable man who slowed his mule at every likely place, teasing news and gossip from townsman and peasant alike. When he met a fellow churchman, I knew to sit tight in my blanket because they could talk for hours, beginning with church matters and ending well into the secular realm.

It was an education, that journey. I hadn't been out of Hawley since my arrival, and before that, the only place I knew was Wardlow. England was something my mind could not encompass—already the landscape had altered from the dales around Hawley to the stark beauty of the moors leading to the monastery. My next home.

Brother Anthony, seeing my interest in the scenery, told me that Hatton was less than five leagues from the coast. I developed an immediate desire to travel there. "Someday, I will cross the sea."

"I've no doubt." He looked over his shoulder. "We should be there by vespers. I'll hand you over to the sub-prior, and he'll see you settled in."

"I've heard that before." I did not mean to sound ungrateful.

Brother Anthony laughed. "On its worst day, Hatton will be better than that muckhole you've just escaped."

I had an idea. "Brother Anthony?"

"Yes, child?"

"Do the monks have to know where I'm from?"

He reined the mule into stillness. "What do you mean?"

"Do they need to know who my first parents were?" I wanted to start fresh in this place, without the ghosts of my scandalous parents dogging my steps.

"No," he said slowly. "We accept a man—or boy—for who he is. Blood only matters when a novice can bring his fortune with him."

"Then I would be someone new," I said. "What is Father Gideon's given name, before he joined the church?"

The mule lurched, and we began to move. "He was Gideon Lewis. I've known him since he was a lad your age."

"I will be Robin Gideon Lewis, if you please. My own name, but his too, since he treated me so kindly."

Brother Anthony's eyes gleamed, and he wiped his sleeve across his face. "That is a fine name."

Robin Lewis. A new name for a new existence. Should any of my parents ever attempt to find me, the trail would dry up in Hawley, and they would find me no more easily than I could find them.

Brother Anthony was correct: we arrived at vespers. Already it was so dark that I could not make out the buildings clustered beyond the church, but the priory seemed like a village all its own.

A servant came to take the mule, and another relieved us of our bundles.

The unearthly sound of the psalmody reached through the doors, and my heart thudded in my chest. Soon I would be able to sing like this and sound like one of God's own angels.

Brother Nicholas, the sub-prior, showed me to the dorter and told me what was expected of me. While I did not have to observe the divine office as the monks did, I would be expected, once I was part of the choir, to sing mass daily, in addition to my studies. "Brother Anthony tells me you have a fine voice and a sharp mind," he said. "God shone a light on you, boy, so that you could be found and brought to us."

The brothers of Hatton were as varied a group as you would find anywhere, from Brother Martin, who kept the choristers under control and made me stretch my voice, to stern Brother Anselm, the librarian, who stretched my mind to encompass Greek, Latin, and French. Prior Richard was kindly but distant. Brother Nicholas was pleasant enough so long as the discipline of the priory was not disturbed. Brother Rufus was a bulky, impatient man, tasked with keeping an eye on the students.

And students there were, for in addition to boys such as myself, placed there by good fortune, there was a population of perhaps thirty more, sent by their families to absorb the monks' excellent education.

This place would not hold me forever. Listening to the vocabulary and intonations of my elders, I understood that my Yorkshire accent would not serve me in the future I envisioned. Within months, I had lost the broad accents of the West Riding and its limiting dialect.

As at Hawley, I made no friends among the other students. They seemed to possess secret information about friendship which eluded me; they were open with each other, and I preferred to keep close, which brought the usual accusations of snobbery and pride.

What did I have to say to these boys? They were another breed, most with no ambition but to serve their time at school and return to their families. Having no family, I would have to make my own way. That knowledge set me apart.

The years I spent at Hatton were the happiest of my childhood, and over time, the monks became my family. The library was my refuge, and Brother Anselm's solid presence was a comfort when I retreated from the taunts of the other students.

"You must learn to get along, Robin." Brother Rufus repeatedly pulled me aside, trying to teach me the ways of boys. "Play their games when you are not reading. Talk to them."

I vowed to be quiet and obedient, to get along and draw no attention to myself, so that I would not find myself again on the back of a horse or mule, being sent to a new destination, but it was easier promised than accomplished. My mouth was ever my undoing, in one way or another.

Chapter 7

"REALLY, THE LESS SAID of my time at Hatton, the better." We have come in from checking on the horses, and the sudden warmth of the hall, after the driving snow, is a welcome respite.

It was to Hawkins's credit that he did not leave this chore to his men. As his host—and his prisoner—I accompanied him. The cold mattered less than the opportunity to observe him; a good understanding of this young man could only benefit me.

"It ended, of course, when Cardinal Wolsey heard me sing. Brother Anthony and Brother Anselm, my particular favorites, were sad to see me leave. I cried, in a most unmanly fashion, but even Prior Richard could not countermand a request from the cardinal."

It hurt, still, thinking of it—the stoic faces of the brothers, my own sobs, the road stretching out between me and my next home.

"I was transported this time not on the back of a horse, but in the back of a cart. A slight improvement in my situation, but the only one."

Chapter 8

THE CARDINAL'S CHORISTERS WEREN'T students; they were a mob of talented children who, when they weren't singing like angels, rampaged around their confined area like wild beasts. Hampton Court was an improvement in name only. I missed my schoolmates—something I hadn't expected. I missed Brother Anselm. I missed learning. I missed *books*.

I would rot there.

Quite early on, hiding from the other boys, I discovered the cardinal's vast library. The great man found me there several times and scolded me, but it never stopped me from gaining entrance. When he saw my reverence for his books, he let me be and ignored my presence. It happened rarely enough; choristers were kept close.

The other boys were happy to be clean, warm, and fed, as I should have been. But I missed the austerity of Hatton, where there was kindness, and where God didn't seem lost in pageantry. Wolsey was the highest prelate in England, yet there was no sense of holiness about him.

I was too unhappy to care how I was perceived, which brought punishment from the choirmaster. My silence was taken as superiority, and nothing would convince him otherwise. He shouted at me, his face red, but I had been shouted at by far worse. When I was not sufficiently cowed, he bent me over a table and took a strap to my bare buttocks.

Eyes swollen, I returned to the choristers' rooms to be met by a dozen jeering boys. "Did the master teach you you're not so high?"

Their words smarted more than the strap. I took a sharp breath. "It will take more than a beating to make me believe I'm not better than you."

Another mistake.

One of the boys planted a foot on my recently whipped rear, and I turned and threw myself at him, spitting and clawing at his eyes. I had never learned to fight properly, with fists; I fought like the mongrel children at Hawley, to maim and injure. It earned me another beating, and confinement when not singing.

I quickly learned that fighting only bloodied my nose and blacked my eyes. Words could do far more harm. Not the foul words of my foster father, which came back when I was tormented, but clever remarks gleaned from observation of my adversaries. My tongue became feared, and the others began to avoid me.

At eleven, I was handed over to the king's choir, the prize in a ridiculous contest. King Henry got the notion that the cardinal's choir was superior to his—which it was—and Wolsey offered him any chorister who would improve the royal choir. I was the chosen one, the king exclaiming about the purity of my voice. It stayed thus for five years.

The king's choristers were, if possible, worse than those of the cardinal. They mocked and sniped and hid my robes, and on one memorable occasion, they hid me. It was my lowest moment, being manhandled by a pack of boys and crammed into a cupboard, knowing the choir was due to sing mass. I shoved against the door, but the lock held against my battering, and eventually, I shouted for help.

Footsteps sounded on the floor, and the door rattled. "Robin?"

"Yes, sir." It was Master Cornysh, the last person I wanted to find me in such a state. "I'm locked in, sir."

"I know that." The king's choirmaster was not patient on a good day. Moments later, a key ground in the lock, and the door was yanked open. "You're not late yet, boy, but you'd best run."

Mounting the stairs to the robing area behind the Chapel Royal, Master Cornysh opened the door to gleeful chatter about the prank. "Boys, see what was found locked in a cupboard downstairs."

I grabbed the nearest robe. It pulled across my shoulders and ended above my ankles, making me look more the fool than usual. "Where is my robe?" I asked. "And how were you planning to explain my absence?"

"Bess was to sing in your place," one of the boys said. "It is she who's wearing your robe."

Color rose to my face. Bess Llewelyn was a weedy girl of my own age, one of the king's personal minstrels. Her voice was nearly as good as mine, and it was this, as much as their rough handling, that made me look at her and say, "As if a girl could replace me."

Her dark eyes widened. We'd never spoken before, and it was not the best of introductions.

"We'll talk about this later," Master Cornysh said. "Come along now; you're already late."

They followed him like ducklings, those boys—the same boys who not a half hour before had pummeled me and locked me away. I ducked to the head of the line and turned on them. "I'll see that you pay for this, you misbegotten sons-of-whores. I will see to it."

Those words were not mine: they belonged to Timothy Wythe, and I hated hearing his words in my mouth. I also hated being made ridiculous. The king would not see me in my too-short robe, but I wanted nothing more than to hide myself away with the cardinal's parting gift, a small book where I wrote what I remembered of my Latin and Greek.

All the knowledge of the world was within reach, and I was trapped in this place, which thought of nothing but frivolity and music.

Master Cornysh later called me to task for my language as well as my temper. When I mentioned it was not an unreasonable reaction to being locked up, he said, "It's your own fault. I know you were probably happier in the cardinal's household, but you must make the best of it."

It appeared he was not going to beat me. I loosened my shoulders, which were hunched below my ears. "How?" My desperation shamed me. "I don't know how to get along. I never have."

He slumped down in his chair. "That much is obvious." Drumming his fingers on the table, he said, "The cardinal's choirmaster said you were both difficult and not well-liked. How is this worse?"

I cast my eyes down. "I had something there, sir, that I do not have here."

Cornysh looked at me. "And what is that?" His tone said: this is the king's court; everything is here. And it was, but not for me.

"The cardinal allowed me entrance to his library," I said. "I miss books."

The room was hidden away on the top floor where Cornysh could work at his music in peace. Though I was there for a lecture, I found myself savoring the quiet.

"You were educated at Hatton?"

"Yes, sir."

"Educated beyond your station." The words were harsh, but his tone was not. "And now you're trapped with this lot who want only to sing and be praised and earn their next meal."

That was a perfect explanation of my plight. "Yes, sir."

"They are boys," he said. "Normal boys. They do what is expected, until such time that they no longer can."

What did he mean? I was afraid to ask; he was being far more patient with me than I'd expected.

"When you become a man," he said, "your voice changes."

I knew that, but it hadn't occurred to me to wonder what happened to choristers who outgrew their usefulness. "What then, sir?"

His square shoulders, in a rumpled green fustian doublet, lifted. "It depends. Some are retired with a small pension; some stay on to sing a man's part. Others, if they have the aptitude, are sent to university, to return later in some useful role."

It was like knowing the sun would rise after a storm. Choristers who earned their keep, who earned the admiration of the king, were rewarded with education.

I smiled hugely. "I have the aptitude, sir."

"I'm sure you do," he said. "You also still sing like an angel, which is all that matters now. Find your place, sing when you're asked, and try not to make everyone hate you."

Chapter 9

"You couldn't manage it, could you?"

I'd not thought of William Cornysh in twenty years. I look up, almost surprised to see Hawkins before me. "Manage what?"

"To make them not hate you."

"Hate is a strong word. I've been disliked, despised, detested, loathed, slandered, and yes, hated. It's as unpleasant as you might think."

He looks skeptical. "You let your life be ruined by a bunch of children."

"I was a child myself, with no idea how to behave." I pause to listen to the sleet scouring the thick stone walls. It is dark again; the day has gone in drinking and conversation, and in watching Will Hawkins's repeated trips to the window. With any luck, he will retire soon and I can continue with the accounts. I've not been permitted to speak to my steward, so I must leave notes to be read after I have gone.

It is best to abandon these distressing thoughts and continue speaking. "His advice stayed at the front of my mind, but learning how to get along wasn't easy; never having had friends, I missed opportunities when they were presented, and for a year or more, I was mostly alone."

Solitude became natural to me. I am happiest alone, and yet, here I am, speaking to this young man as if my words are the only things standing between me and death.

Perhaps they are.

Chapter 10

THE COURT WASN'T ALL unpleasant; I liked the choir, when I didn't feel trapped, and Master Cornysh was kind. He sometimes brought the choristers to his comfortable house in London, where we were fed and fussed over by his wife, Jane, and where he left me alone with his few books, an untold luxury.

I was always well-behaved after a visit to the Cornysh residence, mostly because my mind was elsewhere, revisiting the words I'd read, the scant notes I'd written in my journal upon returning.

My tenuous situation came to a head one afternoon when Bess found me and tried to make conversation. I was having none of it. She had stirred up half the court servants against me; how dare she now ask if I missed my friends in the cardinal's household?

"I had no friends there. Nor do I need any here." The practice room had been peaceful until she appeared. The sun was sinking, and I wanted to lean against the open window and drift for a few moments.

"You've your voice to keep you company; is that it?" Her dark hair straggled from beneath her white coif. Did no one look after her? "What will happen when it breaks? Then you'll have nothing and no one to care."

I prayed for the day when my voice would break, when my real life could begin, but telling her would be letting her into my thoughts. "Perhaps it won't last forever," I conceded, "but whilst it does, I shall outshine you all. No one else can sing as I can."

"Am I not as good?" Her opinion of her own talent was as strong as my own.

I smiled. "Good enough, for a girl."

Cheeks red, Bess reminded me that she could have taken my place in the choir, and when I laughed at her, she challenged me to a competition.

Another competition! I was still raw from the contest that brought me to court. "No. You're a girl."

"Then what have you to fear?"

She would not leave it be, even after I pointed out there was no music. We did not need music, she said—at least she did not. "No one likes you now—they'll hate you for certes if you win."

Our competition—and my subsequent defeat—was overheard by almost everyone, and while losing smarted, my life became much easier. Bess's protector, a young lutenist named Tom, even thanked me.

"I did not let her win," I told him. "She is better."

Tom smiled, ducking his head so that his fair hair hung in his face. "Her voice is glorious."

Cornysh told me Tom had been in the choir, and I wondered that he could be so forgiving when one of his own was mistreated. Then I saw his face when he spoke of Bess, and I understood he could see nothing clearly but his feelings for her.

It was a long year before Bess and I made peace. Rapprochement was sudden: we came together by the river, both of us hiding from our responsibilities, and for a moment, we circled each other like dogs. Then the tension went out of us, and it became all ease.

I could not believe that friendship could be forged so quickly. By the end of the year, I had several friends in the Music, if none in the choir. There was Tom, of course, and a pale girl who had tried to befriend me before—Agnes, her name was, a girl pious as any nun and prettier than a painting of the Virgin.

Bess reminded me of myself. She had been sold to the court, and without family, she clung tight to those she cared about. She and Agnes were like sisters, and I believe she thought of Tom as her brother. He, on the other hand, would continue brotherly only until she grew up.

The problem with orphans, and children who are thrown into situations like court and choir—or monastery, for that matter—is they are so unaccustomed to love that they attach either to everyone or to no one. Tom, at fifteen, could not imagine his life without Bess, as I could not imagine my life forever in this place.

Chapter 11

"Why do you waste so much of your tale on a pair of minstrels?" Hawkins shoves his bowl away, his pottage half-uneaten. He is so young, in his opinions and in his willingness to turn away food not fine enough for his palate.

"One's story is not just one's own," I tell him, reaching over and scooping up the last of his meal with my spoon. Pease pottage flavored with bacon is still my favorite breakfast. "I mean nothing by that—the selfishness of youth makes us think that we are all, and we are not. When I was your age, I still believed myself central to my life, but I learned. Bess and Tom touched my life in many ways over the years. They touched many lives."

Hawkins drains his ale and fiddles with his dagger. "I'm certain they did." His tone is irksome.

"If you'll let me tell this in my own fashion, you'll perhaps see that your own life has not been untouched by them."

The men are still eating, heads down. Good lads. I wait for what I know is coming.

"Have your man make you ready," he says, pushing away from the board. "We can't linger here forever, living soft off a prisoner of the queen."

"I'm ready." I swallow the last of my breakfast. With his well-polished boots, he reminds me of his father: vain in the particulars of dress. "A bit of mud never hurt anyone."

Seb had barely begun to unpack when Hawkins battered down my door. Nonetheless, he has assembled a change of clothes, several shirts, and a half-dozen books in two packs, one for each of us. I hope it is enough to keep me in whatever cell I am housed, and for however long.

Conveniently, Hawkins has brought extra horses. I suppose he—or someone—assumed I might not have my own after so many years away.

"I hope you've chosen a decent beast. I may be no longer young, but I've spent a good part of my years in the saddle, and I require no toothless nag to carry me to London." I turn up my collar and allow Seb to swaddle me in my cloak. "Though a toothless nag might take a bit longer—may I reconsider?"

We leave the house with the cook and maids keening in the hall. Behind them is Fowler, my steward. He raises a hand.

The sleet turned to rain overnight, as often happens on the coast, and much of the snow is gone—enough, at least, to make our journey possible. All that remains are spare hard-hitting flakes, which sting the flesh and make a man crave his hearth. I eye the horses in the courtyard: one for me, and, thankfully, one for Seb. I would hate to leave him behind. He would only follow anyway.

My knee joint grinds as I walk carefully across the cobbles. One slip, and I'll be incapacitated, and I wish to be no more at his mercy than I am. "I move a bit slowly at times. My knee plays up in the cold and when I spend too much time on horseback."

At his shout, the horses begin to move. For a moment, I am taken up with the jingling of harness and the creak of leather, the age-old excitement of travel.

Not this time. There is nothing to anticipate in a journey toward one's execution.

Chapter 12

As THE KING AGED, so the court grew in importance. Looking back, we were a backwater country compared to the rest of Europe, but we knew it not—and if anyone did, they wisely did not speak of it.

In 1520, the cardinal arranged for a meeting to take place between King Henry and the French king. It was as much spectacle as summit, and certainly every noble with a guinea in his pocket to outfit his household was there, along with all the royal musicians and choristers and enough servants to keep the whole production running smoothly.

It was my first time aboard ship, and while the majority of the choristers hung over the rail or confined themselves below, I stealthily climbed to the crow's nest to catch my first glimpse of France as we crossed the narrow sea.

Calais looked no different than England, but it was. It was France. *Another country.* Where other languages were spoken and unfamiliar customs were the norm. It was like being handed an enormous, breathing book and told I had just over two weeks to learn it all. I determined to try.

Far too much of my time, it turned out, was devoted to music. There would be a final mass at the end of the visit featuring the French and English choirs, each singing with the other's organist. It was the sort of musical gymnastics the king enjoyed but which caused headaches for Master Cornysh. I disliked the competitive aspect—why *must* men turn everything into a contest?—but when I listened, it took me back to that first night at Hatton, when the psalmody reached out and snared my heart.

In the meantime, I reveled in the experience of being in a foreign land. England had become second nature, one palace looking much like another from my perspective. There was a wider world out there to explore, and this crossing and the weeks that followed were my first taste of that world.

I wanted more. I could speak easily enough with the French choristers and anyone else who addressed me, and I practiced my language skills by befriending the boys my own age. My fellows were confused: Robin, who only spoke when spoken to, laughing and carousing with England's enemies?

It was not them; it was me. I wanted to hone my French on native speakers and make friends who might someday grow into positions of power. England was a small country. It would not hold me forever.

Chapter 13

Wednesday, November 12, 1558
Yorkshire

ONE OF THE BENEFITS of my house is its isolation. It is difficult to reach and difficult to leave. I wonder if Hawkins will continue along the coast or turn inland to the packhorse route across the moors, where the wind can sweep a man from his horse. Neither is a pleasant option in this weather, but both will lead to York, where we will pick up the North Road to London.

I calculate the distance: sixty leagues, give or take, to reach London. We'll not manage more than eight leagues per day at this speed. The way the horses are sliding about, it would be dangerous to attempt more. Hawkins is eager but not stupid.

In fine weather, I've made the trip in five days. In the early winter we seem to be having, it will be closer to seven, even if Hawkins has arranged for frequent changes of horse. He's a young man trying to rise; there will be horses.

I need more than five days. I need more than seven. From my saddle, I say a quiet prayer. *Your choice, Lord: mud, snow, ice, a flood in the estuary. Anything to slow us down.*

Keeping my captor distracted is also to my advantage. He is, by the look of him, still thinking about the Field of Cloth of Gold—worth thinking about but nearly forty years in the past.

"In my sixteenth year," I tell him, "my voice broke. I'd been longing for that day, waiting for the voice of an adolescent boy, sliding up and down, awkward as a staggering babe, but mine broke cleanly, becoming—you will not reason it, hearing me now—an acceptable tenor almost overnight. I could have stayed on, and the Master of Revels did ask, but I wanted no more of kings and courts and cardinals, at least not as a musician."

"Were you not happy as a musician?" The question appears as

much to humor me as to amuse himself. He is impatient, but in addition to mud, there may still be ice in the rutted road, and he dares not attempt more than a ladylike trot.

"Not really." The court had been an education, but the kind of education I wanted could not be provided there. It could, however, be provided at the expense of the court, and in time, arrangements were made for me to attend university. "I wanted to experience the world outside the court. I wanted a larger life, and I got my wish." I look at him jogging along at my shoulder. Seb is somewhere behind me, no doubt making friends with our guards.

"You are here as a result. Be careful with wishes, my friend; they rebound."

Chapter 14

I RODE AWAY FROM Greenwich with hope in my breast. All my life, I had been less than nothing—bastard, orphan, chorister, performer—but now I was on my way to Oxford as a student. It was my first chance to control my destiny that did not involve singing for my supper.

Despite my attempts to remain aloof, I left friends behind, but none so close that I would miss them. Now, with my voice no more than average, I would be judged on the capacity of my brain.

My voice had gotten me this far, and for that I was grateful. From this point on, it would be up to me.

The Magdalen College term started after the new year. My fees were paid by the court, and I was given a small stipend for expenses. Inquiring at the college, I was directed to a house on the west side of the town, where I paid a pittance to share lodgings with three other students.

I spent a portion of my funds on a second-hand student's gown, the best I could afford. My status was known, but I saw no reason to look like a charity student.

Oxford had been my dream since Cornysh told me of its existence, but it did not take long for reality to set in. Not long after classes began, I learned that I was no one special in this place. There were students far smarter than me, possessed of a greater facility with languages, able to produce articulate, praise-worthy responses to questions in a blink.

It was infuriating and also challenging. Knowing I could at any time be shown lacking, I studied harder than ever. I made a bit of money teaching a fellow student to play the lute, grateful at last that I had been compelled to learn. I was by no means proficient, but Randall did not care. When he acquired a wife, he wanted to be able to serenade her. His coin paid for extra tutoring in Greek, which I required to catch up to my classmates.

I slept in snatches, never quite enough to get over the exhaustion of trying to learn everything I should have known prior to my arrival. I stayed at the library until the fellows ejected me, well after dark, inhaling books and exhaling knowledge. I bulged with facts and information that my fellow students found superfluous.

They were there to become lawyers or priests or to learn to do accounts and become stewards for some nobleman. I wanted to learn because the information was there and because many things interested me. I wanted no specific curriculum; I simply wished to be an educated man and to make my way in the world with that as a marker, but that was not how a university worked.

Realizing I would be happier if I were just given free rein of the library, I dedicated myself, education-wise, to the learning of modern languages and the law, believing those to be the most useful subjects for the future I had come to envision for myself.

Chapter 15

"Damn!"

The cry is behind us, and all must stop. One of the horses has stumbled into the ditch, and when they try to raise it up, it's obvious the beast has broken a leg. I turn when Hawkins retrieves a pistol from beneath his cloak and ends its misery, and there is a rest while the baggage is redistributed so the unhorsed man has a ride.

Swinging down, I land hard, and my knee nearly buckles. Seb is there in an instant, his arm around me. I lean against him, shaken by the scream of the horse, the ring of the shot, the snow in my face rubbing my eyelids raw.

"Are you all right, master?"

His constant care warms me. "I'll do."

We walk up and down a short stretch of the road, one of the guards following. My knee sings with pain, but it's an old tune.

"We're off," Hawkins calls. "We just need to get across the moor, and there will be a place to stop for the night. The beasts need shelter."

"As do we all," I return, letting Seb boost me into the saddle. "The roads are abominable, but I suppose if you're fortunate, we can make London in a week and you can present me to Her Majesty with a ribbon atop my thinning hair."

He looks at me from beneath his ice-brimmed hat. "My orders are to take you straight to the Tower."

"I suppose that is only fitting," I say. "Her Majesty has no time to trade quips with a foul traitor like myself."

"You've been charged with heresy, not treason."

That's right; I'd not really listened to him that first night, too busy trying to formulate a plan. "You still haven't properly shown me the warrant, you know," I say, waspish. "As someone formerly in a similar position, I should note you are required to do that."

He looks abashed. "Sorry. I'll take it from my bag at the next stop."

"At least I'll not be condemned as a criminal."

I've committed many sins in my life but few crimes, and all those at the request of my monarch. I've lied, and I've betrayed, and I've sold information for my own gain. I've swapped my religion so many times that God's head must spin. What does it matter in the end? God is God. My prayers reach Him whether they are in Latin or English, alone or through a priest.

We ride in silence for a while, the snow turning again to rain. The Yorkshire moors are some of the most beautiful countryside on earth, but I'd not choose to cross them in winter. They stretch ahead of us, endless, covered in snow and mud, with a myriad of hazards beneath the surface.

I close my eyes and let the rhythm of the horse lull me into something resembling sleep, if a man can be said to sleep when he's wet through and threatened with imminent death. At Winterset, I would be before my fire, with a book on my lap...

The horses' hooves make sucking noises in the mud, like a hungry man drawing marrow from a bone. At last, to cover the sound, I say, "I'm curious about one thing. How did you—how did the queen hear of my return? Very few people knew my plans."

"You've no need to know that."

I nod, then— "It does no harm to tell me, it's not likely I'll be able to revenge myself upon them from the scaffold."

"Your steward, from what I've heard."

I don't believe for a moment it was Fowler. He's loyal, or at least disinterested, and he showed no sign of fear when we spoke on my return. But he did know I was coming, so it could be servants' gossip that grew legs and ran over the moors.

There is one man who would be very interested in my return and who would have had an ear open for such gossip. If—somehow— he caught wind of it, then I knew how this came about. I accept

Hawkins's claim, for now. "So, I am to be brought to justice on the word of my steward?"

"His word is as good as any other." He does not look at me; he is uncomfortable with a gentleman being arrested on accusation by a servant. Interesting.

"Justice. That's quite a word, isn't it?" I play my favorite game, hoping he will join in. "From the Latin *justitia*, righteousness, from *justus*, upright or just. Now it is the exercise of authority in assigning reward or punishment. To tell the truth, I prefer the Romans' interpretation."

My captor speaks, and by his words, he has been listening. "But justice must be served," he says, "as queens must be."

Chapter 16

ONE OF THE THINGS I enjoyed most about Oxford was the lack of women. I had nothing against them, but not having to interact with them on a constant basis let me drift away from the question of whether or not I was actually attracted to any of them.

The young men with whom I shared lodgings, and some degree of closeness, liked women and talked about them incessantly. Roger, the eldest, who was studying to become a lawyer, was pledged to a girl in his village, but that did not stop him from blatantly flirting with our landlady's daughter.

John and Matthew, both from the south, spent their spare time in taverns and brothels. They had detailed discussions about the relative merits of the whores they visited, and frequently asked me to accompany them. I always refused, shrugging it off by saying I hadn't the funds for such extravagances.

"That leaves you with your left hand or your right, Rob," John said, bending double with laughter. "The right hand for every day and the left for Sundays!"

The others roared, and I looked down at my book to hide the color that mounted to my face. I was eighteen years old, and if not as experienced as my friends, the least I could do was not blush like a girl when they spoke about such matters.

Matt grabbed a handful of hair and tugged my head upright. "Look at how red he is," he crowed. "You've embarrassed him, John."

"I'm not embarrassed," I said, removing his hand from my hair and returning to my text. "It's warm in here."

"Right, that's what it is." Matthew pulled up a stool and sat beside me. He dropped his voice. "You can come out alone with me some night, if you like. It doesn't have to be the whole merry band."

"I don't have the money for such things, Matt. I'm here for an education." This was my chance, and I was not throwing away my future just because my so-called friends were obsessed with what lay between a woman's legs.

"Whoring is an education," he said seriously. "It teaches practical mathematics, negotiation, physical prowess, and if you find a girl near the docks, you might be able to practice your French or Greek with her."

"There are no docks in Oxford."

"Well then, let's go to the nearest port and find some." He turned and addressed the room. "What say you, gentlemen? Let's go on progress and find foreign whores."

"From foreign shores?" John bellowed with laughter.

The conversation was breaking down. The library would offer a silent place to study; I got very little done in our lodgings when the others were about.

I liked these young men as much as I liked most people, and better than some, but I couldn't understand how their lightness of mind didn't contrast with the goal—stated among us all—of educating ourselves for a future better than that we'd been born to.

Walking the narrow lanes between my lodgings and the Magdalen library, I considered this conundrum. They all made good grades. Matt, for all his drinking and licentiousness, possessed a brain purpose-built for the life of a scholar. He absorbed books and could spout them back, verbatim, in a manner that made me quite envious.

Even John had exchanged letters—one letter, actually—with the great Erasmus. I had been allowed to touch it after buying a round of drinks at the tavern. The cost was worth it, to touch paper that had been touched by the possessor of such a great mind.

Almost two years in, and I still had no firm plan of what I would do when I left Oxford. In addition to the required classes, I had taken classes in theology, but I was no priest. I studied law, but though I found it interesting, I did not wish to qualify as a lawyer. Men like Thomas More could be lawyers, but with my birth, I would be left with farmers' disputes about cattle or land rights.

Languages were my favorite subject: not just Latin and Greek, as all students were required to learn, but French and a bit of German. Everyone needed to communicate; languages were not only interesting but useful.

If my time with the king and cardinal had taught me anything, it was that my place was among the high-born, if only as a useful tool.

There were volumes in the library that were available to be freely handled, even borrowed, but those were never the books that I wanted. I took a seat at the lectern-table, where the interesting books were held. I shifted the chain to one side, opened the board cover, and disappeared into the histories of Herodotus.

A scrape of wood on the tiled floor penetrated my concentration and alerted me to the approach of the library fellow. Once again, I was the last person in the room. The fellow made his way down the central aisle, straightening books and checking the window latches. He stopped at my lectern. The light of our combined candles was nearly enough to clearly see the page in front of me.

"The doors are being locked, young sir." His voice, though low, echoed under the high beams. "Didn't you hear the bells?"

"No." I regretfully pinched out my candle and stowed it in my satchel, and followed him out to the cloisters. The temperature had dropped, and a breeze from the Cherwell found its way through the narrow streets. Ducking my head, I turned toward my lodgings, trying to ignore my hunger.

The glow from a tavern window drew me. It had been a long day, and I had eaten nothing since breakfast. My purse held only a few coins, enough for a meal and some beer. I would cut a corner elsewhere to justify the luxury, I thought, and pushed open the door. The room was mostly empty, only a knot of students arguing quietly by the window and one man slumped in a corner, unconscious.

I took a seat near the fire, letting its warmth bless my back. How long had I been hunched over that book?

A serving girl approached slowly.

"Do you have any food?" I almost hoped she would say no so I could save my money.

"Aye," she said. "There should be a pie or two left."

"I'll have a pie and a mug of beer, then."

She disappeared, and I took a book from my satchel. The words swam on the page already; beer was probably not the best idea. I wanted it, though, as a reward for my day of work, and for resolving a particularly tricky bit of translation.

By the time she returned with mug and trencher, I was staring into the fire, my book abandoned. My shoulders ached. I took a deep swallow and sighed, dropping my head back.

"Long day, sir?"

I started, not noticing she was still there. "Yes."

She was about my own age, with round cheeks and dark braids under a cap that had seen much laundering. Her hands, clasped in front of her apron, were raw and red. She looked as tired as I was but smiled at me kindly. "Are you one of them students?"

"I am at Magdalen College, yes." My status was obvious from my gown; she should have known that.

"Why do you do it? Reading and writing all day, you're as pale as a ghost."

"I've always been pale." The pie was steaming hot, filled with a flavorful but unidentifiable meat. The more I ate, the hungrier I became.

"Do they starve you at that college?"

"They feed me, but I missed my dinner today." I picked up the last crumbs of pastry with ink-stained fingers. "And the food's not this good."

She giggled, a bright sound in the gloomy tavern. "I'll tell my aunt," she said. "She does the cooking."

"This is your family's place?"

"My uncle's," she said. "I work here, sometimes down here, and sometimes upstairs."

"Upstairs…" Thankfully I was facing the fire, so my red face would not be obvious.

Her hand came to rest lightly on my arm. "I'm done serving for the evening, sir, if you'd like to see upstairs."

I spoke past the lump in my throat. "I'll just be finishing my drink."

The hand retreated. "I didn't mean to offend."

I didn't imagine her advances—if she had to make them—were often refused. "I'm not offended," I assured her. "I can scarcely afford this meal." I dug the coins from my purse and put them on the table. "That's all I have."

She scooped them into her palm. "You got the last pie," she said. "It was a little squashed. I feel bad charging you full price."

I waited for her to return a coin, but instead, she slipped them into her apron pocket and held out her hand. "That means you have a bit left."

It was as if the great Tom bell was pealing inside the confines of my skull. I stood on legs suddenly unsteady, hesitating beside the table. The door was to my left; the girl, with her cheeks and her braids and her small warm hand, to my right.

"Oh," she said, very quietly. "I think I ken the problem." Standing on tiptoe, she addressed her next words into my ear. "If it's your first, it's best to get it done with and have it out of the way."

Was my virginity as obvious as my red hair?

I followed her up the rough stairs and into a curtained-off chamber, its only furnishings a stool and a straw bed. I stood like a statue while she removed my student's gown, her fingers dealing surely with the clothing beneath. Soon the chill of the room reached my skin.

I opened my eyes. When had I closed them? She stood before me, still fully dressed. I wasn't certain of what we were about to do, but having her dressed while I was mother-naked made me feel more vulnerable than I imagined was possible. I covered myself with my hands.

"You needn't do that," she said. "You're perfectly fine."

"I feel naked."

"Well, you *are*, you great oaf." She giggled again, and I could see the child she had been. It was off-putting as I was trying very hard to think of her as a woman—and of myself as a man, instead of just a mind. I had a body, and it had ideas of its own about this girl.

"What's your name?"

"Rob."

"Well, Rob, do you want me to take off all this kit, or should I just raise my skirts, and we can get on with it?" Her businesslike words struck me. For all of the fine thoughts I was having, she was no different than the girls Matt and John talked about.

"Fair's fair," I said. "You've undressed me."

"Your turn, then."

I had as much experience with women's garb as I did their bodies. I raised shaking hands to her laces, and she let me undo them partway before she pushed me aside.

"Get on with you," she said. "I'll do it myself."

The stinking tallow candle revealed an angular, almost boyish body under its feminine garb. There was a dark bruise on one thigh and another high on her shoulder. From the tavern or from her work upstairs?

"Stop looking at me." She removed her cap and took the pins from her hair. Her braids fell to her waist.

I reached out to touch one of them. "I've never seen a naked woman before."

She blew out the light. "It's not about seeing, it's about doing." Her small hands were on me, and there was a sudden rush of blood from my head.

After the incident at the tavern, I threw myself headfirst into my studies, barely coming up to breathe and eat, much less venture out in search of fornication. I tried to convince myself I had not relished the act, that I had given in and gone upstairs in a moment of weakness and exhaustion, but in truth, I had taken much pleasure in what we'd done. I understood the urges that drove Matt and John to the brothels, though I had no intention of repeating the experience.

It was the release I had enjoyed most. It loosened my shoulders, cured my headache, and in some mysterious way, cleared my mind. With a wry smile, I thought that release could be accomplished without involving others. Although frowned upon by the church, John's recommended activity was less expensive and did not run the risk of disease—or becoming close to anyone.

The girl, Sarah, pushing me off her, had said, "Well, now, wasn't that nice? You come back anytime you like, sir. I'll be here."

That was the problem. She would be there. She had been there previously, and even if I wished to visit her again—which I emphatically did not—I was afraid I would find her already taken up with one of my friends.

No, women were not for me.

I began to question, as winter turned to spring, whether Oxford was for me. I chafed at the restrictions—except that I wasn't singing matins and lauds, I was as confined as any chorister. The desire was still in me to see the world, but the longer I remained, the more I understood how some came to Oxford as boys and stayed until they were doddering old men.

That was not the life I wanted.

My problem was, and always had been, that I only had a clear idea of the life I did not want.

Roger came in and found me staring out the window. "What, no book?"

"I'm bored." All the books were written by men dead hundreds of years or by others who were living lives in places I had never visited. Nothing suited me.

"That's not like you." He hung his gown on a hook and stretched. "You're the scholar of the lot of us."

"I'm not so sure about that," I said. "Look at what Matt's accomplished in these last months. He's going off to—"

"That's Matt," he said roughly. "I thought you wanted to go

back to the court someday."

When had I mentioned that? I spoke so little that hearing my ambitions aloud was disorienting. "I can't see a path from here to there."

"I'm leaving soon." He propped his feet on the table, a big man comfortable in his skin. "So is Matt. Do you really want to stay here with John and find two new students to share the chamber?"

"No." I was done with Oxford, done with school. I wanted to learn how to live in the world as a man. "But I don't know what to do next. I don't have the experience to get taken on by anyone at the court. I need to know more."

"You have half the plan, then." He drummed his hands on the table, closing his eyes in concentration. "Have you ever thought of traveling?"

Chapter 17

OUR ROUTE, I UNDERSTAND, will be the same as that taken by Cardinal Wolsey in 1530, when he was arrested by the Duke of Northumberland. Even the month is the same: a dreary November. But the cardinal perished in Leicester, saving the king the trouble of an execution, which would not have been popular. Wolsey was much loved here.

I have no intention of dying on the road. I'm quite hale, God be praised, and if Hawkins has patience with my stiff knee, he'll eventually reach London and be honored for ridding the realm of such a dangerous man.

But if he wishes to avoid Leicester, I will not object.

"You're in an awfully good mood." We are forced to share a chamber, and Hawkins doesn't much like the idea of sleeping beside me, but neither is he brave enough to ask me to sleep on a pallet.

"What of it? Is a condemned man not allowed to enjoy himself?" I am happy to see the end of the moors and the beginning of a proper road in this old market town, to have a belly full of food, and to have spent an hour in unexpected conversation with our host.

Seb undoes my points and carefully removes my doublet. He takes his time, enjoying our conversations. "I haven't seen Dickon Talbert in over a decade. He was always a decent fellow. As you see by my reception, the rumors that I am universally hated are not universally correct. That was a fine supper he gave us."

"It was." Grudgingly said, but every time I'd glanced at him, he'd had a bit of meat on the end of his knife.

I roll my neck, trying to loosen the stiffness caused by hours on horseback. Seb works his knuckles into my shoulders, and I force myself to continue. "It was surprising to learn of his loyalty to the queen, considering our service together, but it shows if I had played things differently, or been a bit more adroit four years ago, I might not have had to leave so abruptly."

I brush Seb's hands away and sit on the side of the bed. "And now, of course, you've made me leave again. I wish I'd had more than one night in my bed before you came bursting in—I feel as if this is some fever dream aboard ship."

"No dream," he says. His servant removes his clothes, taking less care than Seb. "You're here, and soon enough, you'll be in the Tower."

"I would have liked to have been there for my wife's return."

He holds up both hands. "Thanks be to God we missed that."

"You think she would have made a scene?" I ask. "Perhaps she would have. Women make scenes, particularly when their husbands are threatened. But she is an exceptional woman. She might wave me off from the courtyard and turn around to make a list of replacements." It sounded like a jest, but it was—I believed—entirely possible. "You're not wed, I take it?"

"No." Hard to tell from his voice whether he's happy about the situation or not.

"At your age? There's a match in the works, surely?"

"No." He gets into the bed with a thump and pulls the covers up to his chin.

I settle myself more slowly, as befits my age and dignity, and lean over to blow out the candle, admiring the pewter candlestick. "Well, don't rush the matter. You're young yet—not yet thirty, if I may guess. At your age, I had no plan to acquire a wife. Women rarely entered my mind.

Chapter 18

DILIGENT INVESTIGATION, COMBINED WITH eavesdropping and cultivating students I had previously ignored, revealed a divinity student with an uncle in need of someone to handle his correspondence during an upcoming trip to the Low Countries. I spent the last of my stipend bribing him for an introduction.

My new employer, Edward Campion, was a big man with light hair and a sunburned face, and an amount of bluster equal to his size. He advanced a portion of my salary prior to our departure. "Get yourself a decent suit of clothes," he said. "I can't meet the merchants of Bruges with my secretary looking like a ragamuffin student."

Bastard, orphan, fosterling, chorister, student…secretary.

I found a mercer who understood what I wanted and who took my student's gown in partial trade for cloth. I chose a sturdy gray wool for my coat and lawn for a shirt, which I had the tailor make up. Second-hand stocks came for a few shillings. My old flat cap would do, cleaned and re-trimmed, and my boots would survive another patching and polishing. Instead of replacing them, I bought a pair of leather shoes; only clods and those with no upbringing at all would wear boots to an indoor meeting.

Even as a child, I understood the importance of clothing. The poor wore whatever held together, rough canvas or frieze being the norm. Monks had their habits, and thus, their rank was always visible. It was the wealthy that interested me: their status was determined by what they wore. I could not wear a doublet above my station, but until I could afford black broadcloth, gray was indeterminate and easy to keep up. I did not need velvet or satin to pass among people of quality; if I wore good cloth—and the Low Country merchants knew cloth—then my origins could be concealed beneath my doublet.

Dressed in my new suit, with no gown flapping about me, I walked back along the High Street to my room. Passing by several students from Merton College, I nodded a greeting and was gratified by their response. I had been invisible to their kind before, unless they were drunk—in which case, they might well have hauled me into an alley or attempted to throw me into the Cher.

I still had a bit of Campion's advance left, and I decided to do something to celebrate my change in fortune. A different man would have collected his friends and taken the celebration to a tavern, perhaps upstairs afterward.

The evening with Sarah remained in my mind, but it was not something I wished to repeat, at least not anytime soon. That sort of distraction would be fatal to my chances; nothing could stand between me and my goal, which currently was to perform in excellent fashion for Master Campion and move on to a better employer after my return.

A lane led off the High Street, a narrow passage filled with the sort of shops I generally avoided as a priest would avoid a butcher on Friday. There was a shop there, a loud and clanging printer of the Worshipful Company of Stationers and Newspaper Makers. He specialized in broadsides and works for lawyers, but in the back, he kept secondhand books, if one knew to ask.

The chest was half-full, but the selection was not to be scoffed at: there were two books, well-worn, by Caxton himself, along with several volumes in Greek and Latin. I paused over the Caxton—he had started his printing career in Bruges, and it would be appropriate to purchase one of his volumes to read on the voyage. Ovid's *Metamorphoses* or Chaucer? I had read both, but this translation of Ovid was particularly fine.

A dream, shelved away in the back of my mind, was to someday have a grand library. I must be forgiven if I looked at the Ovid and saw it as the first step toward that dream. It was the first book I purchased with my own money. I had a few others: one a gift from Cornysh and another given to me by a fellow student because its binding had split—the wastefulness of the wealthy—but beyond that, I had only the journal given to me by Cardinal Wolsey and a shoddy replacement when the first one was filled. These volumes hardly made a collection, but it was a beginning.

When the *Primerose* departed Portsmouth, the skies were blue, the sun was high, and there was a mild breeze blowing us along the Solent toward Calais. It was perfect weather, but Campion, veteran of many voyages, turned green the moment his boots touched the deck.

"Don't bother me until the morrow," he said. "I'll be below."

I took myself off happily enough. I would find another place to rest; I had no desire to share a tiny cabin with him in that state.

Five years past, I had made this journey with the king, but this time, the journey was my own choosing. The future was mine, and I would see this wider world from the deck of a ship, the window of a coach, the back of a horse. I cared not for my mode of transportation, only that I was loosed from the bonds that tied me to England.

I was a free man.

By midday, the waves were rough under a gray sky. The deck lurched and swayed, and I shifted my weight to accommodate it, thinking how miserable Campion must be below. There was no cure for seasickness but time, and I was not the sort to provide sympathy, nor, I thought, was he the sort to accept it.

The sailors moved to and fro, climbing masts, adjusting sails, doing things mysterious to me but obvious to them. Education, for all its benefits, does not give a man the physical knowledge of a task. I would have been at a loss to do this work.

One young man in particular caught my eye whenever he moved in my direction. Graceful as a dancer, he could have passed as a gentleman of the court had he worn anything other than stained slops and a threadbare tunic, and had he been any color but shining ebony. He was tall—almost slender—but I could see the muscles in his back moving under his tunic.

He saw me watching. "Rain soon," he said. His accent was not one I had encountered before, and it made me want to talk with him.

"I don't mind rain," I said. "It's an improvement over my puking employer."

He burst into laughter, displaying a wide gap in his upper front teeth. It should have ruined his looks, but it somehow made him more appealing. "You must sleep eventually."

The first drops of rain spattered my face. "I'll find somewhere."

"There are hammocks for the crew," he said, grinning. "You'd be welcome."

He moved away, and my eyes were drawn by something I could not explain. He was not the first black man I'd seen, but they were not common outside the cities. On my wanderings in London, I'd encountered Moorish servants and sailors near the docks, and there had been a royal trumpeter who had retired while I was with the king's choir.

It was not his difference that drew me. It was something deeper, something I recognized in this young man that bore no resemblance to my pale, freckled, red-headed self. I blew out a breath and tilted my head back to the rain.

His name was Gregory, I discovered, spending my second day on deck, listening to the bantering sailors. They were a motley band, the crew of the Primerose, running the gamut from pallid Englishmen to men darker than Gregory. The span of languages was just as wide, and a small part of me wanted to remain on board until I absorbed them all. Suddenly, English, French, Latin, Greek, and a smattering of Spanish and German were insufficient.

Campion ventured up on that second morning, pale and tight-lipped, but upright and in his natural state of being. "Every time," he said in greeting. "Every time I set foot on a ship."

"And yet you travel so frequently." It was an odd choice of work for a man who could not keep his guts in his belly.

"The world won't come to me."

We breakfasted in the large cabin below, where I shoveled in porridge and ale, and my employer managed several bites before sitting back.

"Perhaps not quite yet," he said. "How did you manage yesterday?"

"I stayed on deck. I like sailing."

"Lucky," he said sourly. "Well, I have work for you today."

It was still raining. Being shut up below with his ledgers and correspondence was no hardship, yet the deck called to me. As we rolled from side to side, the entire ship seemed tensed, but in preparation for the storm, not in resistance.

After a plunge that sent the inkpot rolling, Campion gave up. "It's bed again for me."

"Shall I bring your meal down?" I stowed away anything that could fall or be damaged.

"No."

"Bread, at least. Better to have something on your stomach."

He shed his clothes as quickly as a man of his stature could undress. "Fine." He dropped his doublet on the floor. "And perhaps some ale." He kicked it aside and climbed into the bunk in his shirt.

I carried the basin to the floor nearby, wedging it close with the heavy bench. "Try to rest, sir."

Running lightly, I emerged into a gale stiff enough to tear the bonnet from my head. I caught it before it flew overboard, and stayed close in the doorway. Rain lashed the deck, running in streams across the polished wood. The very air was dense with water. It should have been disagreeable but instead was oddly thrilling. Storms were when I most experienced the power of God, something so much bigger than myself, something that could not be controlled.

"You should be below, sir." It was the first mate, emerging from the passage behind me. "Captain doesn't like passengers on deck during a blow."

I retreated into the passage, but I could not bring myself to leave the scene entirely. The air crackled with energy, and I crackled along with it; I was released from my bonds—anything was possible.

"You'll be wet through."

I did not have to turn to know that Gregory was behind me. The words, spoken in my ear, caused a shiver to run down my spine.

"I told you, I don't mind rain." I turned, brushing against him in the narrow passage.

He was drenched, yet I could feel the heat coming off him. "You make a fine sailor." He looked on the verge of laughter again.

I smiled. "A tolerance for rain does not make a sailor. I could not climb a mast as you do, nor do I know how to reef a sail."

Gregory leaned in, so close I could smell the ale on his breath. "I could show you. You should see the ocean from above. It's like being God on High."

His blasphemy made him even more attractive. I thought of what I had done with Sarah and wondered how much different it was with a man, beyond the obvious similarity of parts. Hot blood colored my face, and I ducked my head.

"I have work to do." Gregory laid a finger on my bottom lip. "I will find you later, if you want."

The storm pushed us back toward England before it blew itself out. I told Campion that we would be one day behind, perhaps two. His response, and his continued vomiting, sent me back up on deck, where I found a quiet place to sit down with Ovid and lose myself for a few hours.

Bells rang, and men moved back and forth outside my field of vision; I paid them no mind until a shadow fell across my page. The sun made Gregory no more than a silhouette before me, but I could see the flash of his teeth and smiled in return.

"You read. You are important?"

I closed the book and pushed myself upright. "I hope to be."

His smile was glorious. I nearly swayed from the power of it. "My watch is done."

"Already?" I asked. "It's still daylight."

"A watch is six hours," he explained. "I'm off below."

I hated to see him leave. "To rest?"

He cocked his head. "If I must."

I stowed my book in a pocket and followed him through the door and down the passage. Instead of turning toward the cabin where Campion groused and slept or the area where the sailors' hammocks hung, Gregory unlatched the door to the hold and drew me into the darkness, leading me surely through a maze of crates and trunks to a small open area.

There was a blanket on the floor; I could feel it beneath my feet. This was a place he—or other sailors—had used before. Did I want to be here? Did I want to do whatever it was that men did with each other? I drew back and banged my shoulder, gasping with the sudden pain.

"Hold still." His accent was more pronounced when I could not see his face. "You will hurt yourself."

"I shouldn't be here." I had gotten turned around. Which way was the door?

His fingers gripped my shoulder but with no force. After a moment, they slid up to my neck and tangled in my hair. "You can leave, if you like." His breath was warm on my face, and after a moment, his lips lightly touched mine. "Or you can stay."

Was it minutes or hours that I was in the hold, having my world turned upside down? I only realized it was dark after Gregory led me to the door and bade me wait a few minutes until he was away. I used the time in tidying myself to what I hoped was a respectable condition, and then I made my way back to my cabin.

Campion was sitting up in his bunk with a surly expression. "Where have you been? I sent someone up after you an hour ago!"

I feigned surprise. "I was reading on deck, and I must have fallen asleep." The remains of his dinner made me realize I'd missed a meal. "I'm glad you were able to eat." I cleaned up the mess, pouring another cup of ale. "I'll take these away and come right back."

Once the door was shut behind me, I shoved the scraps of his food into my mouth, almost choking on the cold, greasy beef. The ale I drank straight from the jug, wiping my mouth with my sleeve.

My sleep that night was thin. I awoke to every movement from Campion and eventually got up, shifting from the bed to the table. This would not do; if I could not master myself, he would see that something was amiss. I could not lose my place.

I thought about that nook in the hold, with its well-used blanket. When I asked, Gregory laughed. "You are not the only passenger to have come here, and I am not the only sailor to bring someone."

What we had done was different than the act with Sarah, but only in its essentials. It was still distressingly physical, but the release was the same, gratifying and mind-clearing. If only one could be accomplished without the other.

We dropped anchor the next morning, unloading cargo and passengers and taking on more. I remained in the cabin, catching up on work before we reached Damme. I ventured above only once. I did not see Gregory and was not certain if I was disappointed.

The wind pushed us into port early the next morning. Gathering my things, I made certain Campion's affairs were in order. He was beginning to feel better and looked around the cabin as I stowed the last of his papers into a leather folio. "Another wasted voyage," he said. "Someday, the physicians will invent something for seasickness."

"When is your first meeting with the merchants?" I asked. "How much needs to be completed before we reach Bruges?"

"Everything is in order," he said. "I like to be ahead of people—sharp, these merchants are." He gave me my instructions: while he made arrangements for horses, I would see his goods transferred to a smaller boat that would bring them up the Zwin to Bruges. Campion sold cloth, and we carried with us crates of samples with which he would hopefully stun and impress buyers in the Low Countries and Italy.

We could, of course, travel with our cargo, but Campion did not wish to arrive at his destination green and heaving; a day on horseback, in the fresh air, would restore him.

Emerging on deck under blue skies, I saw a landscape similar but somehow very different from England or Calais. Here it was: the world, at last, come to fruition.

Campion moved to greet the captain. "As you see," he said, "I have recovered, just in time to leave you."

The captain laughed. "This is not our first voyage. I expected nothing less."

We moved through the cluster of men, and I caught sight of Gregory. "*Adios.*" I read the word on his lips and offered a quick wave, hoping Campion hadn't caught the exchange, then wondering why I cared. What if I struck up an acquaintance with a sailor—what else had I to do while he was abed?

Making our way down the gangplank, Campion spoke over his shoulder. "I hope you weren't bothered by that lot while I was below."

"I don't know what you mean." We reached the dock, and I staggered slightly on the solid ground.

"Filthy sodomites," he said in a conversational tone. "All of them. I should have warned you."

Chapter 19

"I've shocked you, haven't I?"

Hawkins's neck is red. Embarrassment, or horror from having spent the night in the same bed as a confessed lover of men? I nudge my horse closer, but he refuses to look at me.

"It's not as if there haven't been rumors before—I started some and squelched others; I know what's out there, young man."

He kicks his mount to ride ahead, leaving me to our escort.

I obligingly touch my heels to my gelding and catch up to him. "You needn't draw away like a fainting maid, you know. You're not that pretty." I was never one for seductions anyway. Relationships were too complicated, too mysterious. It was what I appreciated most about what occurred in that dark hold with Gregory—the directness of it all.

There's something to be said about getting straight to the point.

Chapter 20

I FELL IN LOVE with Bruges as soon as we arrived: the fanciful buildings and narrow lanes interlaced with canals made me feel I was getting a taste of Venice. Its presence on Campion's itinerary had been the deciding factor in my taking the job.

The job was going well enough. I found the work interesting, though I would never be a man of business; it involved far too much time in society. On most days, we had meetings with one or another—or several—of the merchants and wealthy men with whom Campion was trying to curry favor. I took notes of their conversations, drafted contracts, and back at our lodgings, turned the words Campion flung over his shoulder into legible correspondence.

"Add in the language about the schedule of delivery; it's in your notes," he said. "That will do for now. Make three copies, one addressed to each of the houses we visited today, and one for my records." He looked around the small chamber we shared. "I'm off with van Spiere this evening. I'll be back by curfew. Have those done."

The door slammed as he went off to his evening of business, which involved eating, drinking, and whoring. I had come quickly to loathe him: not his habits, which were typical, but his manners, his very person. He was coarse not only with me but with all those he considered lower than himself, while fawning in ridiculous fashion toward anyone above him. Some of the merchants did not even bother to hide their contempt.

The next day, having delivered our letters, we set off for the house of Jan van Praet for one final meeting.

"These Dutch are wily." Campion had been saying this since our arrival, and I had seen it proved by how easily they took advantage of him. "I will want you there for the morning, but only I shall stay to dine. You may amuse yourself until I return."

"I shall endeavor to do so." I smiled inwardly at the idea of an afternoon to myself in this fascinating place.

"For God's sake, Lewis, try to enjoy yourself. I certainly pay you enough." He reached into his pocket, flipped a coin at me. "Whores work during the day, you know. Have one on me."

My first instinct was to throw the coin back in his face, but he didn't pay me well enough for that. I slipped it into my own pocket, muttering my thanks. Why was it assumed a man's first destination in a new town must be a brothel?

Several hours later, having at last been dismissed, I made my way along the main canal to the market square, dominated by its enormous belfry. At this time of day, the square was full of people, men and women of all status. Children raced around, shrieking, as children did everywhere. Dogs scavenged for scraps in the gutters, and overhead, gulls screamed, circling from the nearby harbor. There were horses, stamping nervously by their riders or harnessed to carts full of goods.

I admired the houses with their stepped rooflines and the convenience of the town, both cobbled streets and canals being available for residents to move about. It was a far cry from London and its narrow, filthy lanes.

Moving from the market square to the nearby burg square, where the town's business was carried out, I continued my wanderings. A powerful smell called me, and despite my usual tendency to spend money on nothing but books, I took a seat at a table with a mug of beer and a bowl of small black shellfish. Their strangeness lasted but a moment; before I left, I had devoured the entire bowl, swallowed a second mug of beer, and avoided the friendly overtures of the serving girl.

I found the bookseller after a pleasurable interlude of being entirely lost in a strange place. Several hours were spent in browsing books old and new and in halting, multilingual conversation with the shopkeeper and several customers. My visit ended with the purchase of Luther's German translation of the New Testament.

Luther's theses and his break with the church had caused an

upset at court. Despite my curiosity, I had thus far had not been able to lay hands on a copy. Even the libraries of Oxford, with their exhaustive collections, appeared not to have it—though that could be politic on their part, to not give the appearance of promoting Protestantism.

To find his translation was an amazing piece of luck. It had only been published a few years ago, and it was still illegal in England to possess a copy. My German was not equal to such a job of translation, so I also acquired a German grammar to assist in my reading. This took every coin in my purse, but it would provide far more long-term satisfaction than Campion's recommended activities.

My employer grew more tiresome as we traveled. His bluster and faulty judgment made our business more difficult than was necessary. He continued thus from Bruges to Frankfurt to Strasburg, where he not only lost an important customer but a significant amount of money at cards.

After what felt like years, we reached Milan. My early grounding in Latin made French come easily, but I found Italian difficult—perhaps not so much the words as the speed at which they were spoken. My first weeks in Italy were spent drowning in a language which would have been familiar, if only I could pin it down.

I was grateful that Campion spoke the language not at all, so my halting attempts were not as obvious. He grew impatient that I did not translate as quickly as before, but the work got done.

The Italians, in Campion's opinion, were no better than the French, the Dutch, or the Germans. Slippery, untrustworthy business partners, but what could one do? How could he be so blind? Speaking of himself as a successful merchant, a skilled negotiator, did not make it true.

It was always the fault of the other party when a contract was drafted away from his best interests, and I was glad I did no more than write down the terms, for if I had any hand in the negotiation, I would bear the blame when he came out on the losing side, as he would.

I bore some of it anyway, and as we rode from Milan toward Padua, our much-diminished stores rattling in a cart behind us, I could not tell if it was the sun, his constant complaints, or something else that made my head hurt so dreadfully.

Chapter 21

THE WEATHER TURNS AGAIN. A hard rain starts mid-morning, making the landscape gray and dreary as dusk and doing nothing to ease our fording of the Rye. Just past midday, we see a building rise out of the blanketing fog. There is a general sense of cheer as we head for a warm place, food, and a change of horse.

Wet through and bespattered with mud, we look like a band of ruffians, and the innkeeper sensibly bars the door. Hawkins drops his hand to his sword and reminds him of his purpose with a few quiet words, and we are suddenly invited in and given a table before the fire. There's hearty ale and a rich stew and bread, a sturdy loaf of mixed grain: the kind of food that will keep a man alive on a winter's ride near the length of the country.

Seb is at the far end of the table. He's befriended the younger guards; they are fascinated with him, as if they'd never seen a black man before. Perhaps they haven't. I have no idea who's allowed in Her Majesty's presence—for all I know, they may all be white as milk, in addition to being pure as the Virgin.

"You're wondering about my wife," I say to pass the time.

He tears off a handful of bread, dips it in the stew. "No."

"You are." I watch him eat, to make him uncomfortable. "I can feel your judgment from across the table."

Resting his hand on the table, Will Hawkins looks me full in the face with his mother's eyes. "Fine. So I'm curious."

"Isn't that better to admit it?" I carve off a piece of bread and fastidiously wipe my bowl. "I never intended to marry—and not just because of my habits. I'm not an easy man to live with, and my work would not be improved by a wife. Some men need a comfortable home, with a woman to warm their bed and serve their meals."

My friend Ned was such a man, happy in the bosom of his

family after a tempestuous and prolonged youth. "I've been forced to share a bed far too often at court, and I've lived in lodgings the rest of the time. A landlord only expects so much. He doesn't want affection. Or constancy. Or even conversation."

I never believed myself capable of those things. That I have in recent times acquired a wife tells me only that I was wrong or that men are capable of change. I prefer to believe the latter, as I have seen men change over time when presented with circumstances beyond their control. You can either dash your brains against a stone wall or learn to live with it.

Chapter 22

THE CAVE WAS VERY cold and filled with birds. They made no sound, but every so often, their light feathers would brush my face. Was I never to be found in this icy darkness? And how had I fallen into a cave? I summoned my last clear memory: riding toward a city with Campion. I could see it in my mind but could not put a name to it.

Was it Venice? I was certain we were in Italy, though my thoughts were jumbled. I remembered leaving Oxford, a ship, blinding sunshine. And a dark place. I was in darkness before, with someone touching my face.

Was I still there? Was it the same cave, and all these memories, were they the dream? The harder I thought, the more my head ached.

I sank back into the dark.

The wings brushed my forehead once, then again. I pushed myself toward consciousness and began to hear sounds. Voices.

I opened my eyes to a hand, its fingertips just brushing my forehead. These were the feathers I felt while unconscious. When I tried to speak, a searing pain in my throat echoed the pain in my head. I made a strangled sound and winced.

"*Tu sei sveglio!*" The man was dressed in a Benedictine's rough black. He spoke again, a disconcerting flood of Italian. I recognized few words and succumbed to unaccustomed panic—I, whose talent and purpose had been languages, was at a loss. I could not speak, let alone speak Italian.

The monk understood. He smiled, the sweetest expression I had ever seen on any face. "*Inglese?*"

I nodded. The inside of my head was filled with a carillon of bronze bells colliding. I closed my eyes, suddenly dizzy.

"My English," he said, "she is small. You *capisci?*"

Did I understand? I blinked and tried to nod again, but it was impossible.

"Rest now." Again, that gentle hand. "Talk later."

When I next awoke, I was in a different part of the infirmary. The warmth of a nearby fire seeped through my blankets.

Tentatively stretching, I took inventory of my ills. My chest was tight, and my breath shallow. My head still ached, and my eyes sealed themselves against the light. My throat felt as if I'd swallowed glass.

As if sensing that I was awake, the same monk appeared, bearing a tray with a small jug and a cup.

"You look better." His English was halting but better than my Italian. "This is for you." He sat down on a stool beside me, placing the tray on the floor, and held the cup to my lips.

It was vile, a bitter, pungent brew that burned all the way down. I gasped, raising a hand to my tortured throat.

"Is awful, I know." He put the cup aside. "But is for the pain. You will drink more."

I would drink more, if it helped with the shredded, bloody feeling in my throat. I tried to raise myself on my elbows, but the weight of my skull would not allow it. The monk snatched a pillow from the next cot and propped it behind me. "You are still weak," he said. "You were very sick."

I caught his sleeve in my fingers and tried to convey a message with my eyes. *How long have I been here? Where is Campion? What is this place?*

He sat down again, wanting to help but limited by language. His expression brightened. "Do you have the Latin?"

I smiled. I might not be able to speak, but at least I could understand him.

"*Grazie Dio.*" He measured out another small portion of medicine. It was the price, obviously, of speech.

I drank, making a face, and sagged back against the pillow.

"You have been here six days," he told me. "Most of that time, you were either unconscious or raving. Your fever was very high. Is still high but better."

"Where?" I tried again to speak, but no sound issued forth. I made the word with my lips. "*Dove?*"

"You are in Padua. This is Santa Giustina. Your friend brought you to us. He was frightened."

I remembered Campion's fear. It was impersonal: not fear of contagion, but fear occasioned by inconvenience, of being trapped with a sick man to care for. "Where is he?"

The monk reached under my pillow and brought forth a letter. "He left this for you."

In a few lines, Campion severed our connection.

> *I hope this letter finds you recovered. I have continued on as my business requires. Do not concern yourself. I have donated to the abbey for your care.*
> *EC.*

Dropping the page, I closed my eyes in defeat. Less than four months into my new life, I was stranded in a country where I did not speak the language, too weak to move, and with no means of returning to England.

I relapsed and spent a few more days in the cave. When I emerged, my fever broken at last, I had lost all sense of time. Some days had flown, some crawled, and others disappeared entirely, lost in the fog of my illness. I was clear-headed but exhausted. Even sitting up made me short of breath. The monks gave me broth and more medicine and left me alone.

There were three infirmary monks to care for perhaps a dozen patients. Each was kind in his own way, and all learned to address me in Latin, which made my days less silent. The brother who first tended me appeared in the late afternoons, and when not called to other duties, stayed nearby and talked to me.

In this way, I learned the history of his city and that Venice, the place I dreamed of reaching, had been formed in centuries past by men of Padua fleeing siege. It was also just a day's ride from the abbey.

When Brother Salvatore—for that was his name—left me at compline, I drank a bit more of the foul medicine and lay back, dreaming of a city improbably built upon water, wondering if I would ever reach it.

But for my inability to speak or move about, my time in the infirmary was peaceful and familiar. I lay, my feet toward the fire, and listened as the divine office, beautifully sung, floated up from the chapel.

Brother Salvatore returned to check on me, his finger across his lips to remind me that it was the great silence. Trapped as I was in my own great silence, it made no difference. Before he retired to his own cot, I gestured for him to come near, making the signs of writing and holding up my hands in supplication.

Comprehension lit his face. "Sleep," he mouthed. "Tomorrow."

When I awoke, there was paper, a sharpened quill, and a bottle of ink at my bedside. Seeing the familiar implements made me feel better, though I wondered why I had requested them. I had no one to whom I could write; I couldn't even tell Campion of my recovery, because I didn't know where he'd gone.

Breakfast arrived: pottage so well mashed, it did not pain my throat. Afterward, I decided to test my strength. The wooden floor was cool and smooth under my bare soles, and I pushed myself upright, holding the wall for balance. My legs bore my weight, and I made a slow trek to stand before the fire.

"You should not be up."

I turned and toasted my backside. "I feel stronger," I said, but the words were only a whisper. Somehow, I had assumed my voice would recover as quickly as my body.

Brother Salvatore led me back to bed, and pointed to the pen and paper. "You have not tried them."

"I have no one," I said, straining to make the words clear.

"Write to me," he said. "Tell me who I have been praying for."

When he returned that evening, I handed him a closely-written page. "My life," I whispered, and lay back.

He began to read and laughed almost immediately, causing me to open my eyes. Nothing in my sketch had been at all comical.

"*Pettirosso.*" He waved a hand over my hair. "That is your name." Ah. Redbreast. Or, in my case, redhead.

The light faded as he read. Soon, only the glow of his candle lit the room. At last, he folded the letter. His eyes, so dark as to be nearly black, were filled with a lively sympathy. "I know you now," he said. "I know your heart, and I can pray for you."

It was one-sided. I didn't know a thing about him, other than that he was a monk and appeared to be a few years older than myself. Not bothering to try to speak, I put my hand on my chest and then gestured toward him. *What about you?*

He had a boy's smile. "Tomorrow," he promised. "We will see if you are strong enough to go outside."

Light streamed through the narrow infirmary windows. God had granted a bright, clear day for my emergence from the captivity of illness. I broke my fast and waited. I was able to sit at the table for my dinner, a flavorful soup that was the first real food I'd tasted in weeks. A mug of beer, differently flavored than English beer, was a welcome addition. I signed my gratitude to the young novice.

Brother Salvatore arrived in the afternoon, moving as quickly as his training allowed. He apologized, first in Italian, then in Latin, explaining he had been caught up first in an extended chapter meeting, then in a project for the abbot. "But I am here now," he said, "and look, I have brought your clothes."

It was uncomfortable being dressed by him, but I wanted to go outside. Brother Salvatore affected me much like fresh air and sunlight, an unceasingly cheerful presence in my stone-walled prison.

The broad stairs were maneuvered one by one, with me clutching the rail and Salvatore holding my arm on the other side. We ventured into the shelter of the cloister, and I stopped at the first touch of the breeze on my skin. Beyond the cloister, the ground ran down to a swampy expanse, a landscape unfamiliar but strangely attractive.

"Is beautiful, no?"

"Beautiful," I said without thinking, and the word emerged from my throat, strangled but audible.

We looked at each other, delighted.

"Do not overdo," he warned.

Together, we walked the length of the cloister and back until the bell rang for vespers.

Faced with climbing the stairs to the infirmary without him, I pointed toward the chapel. "May I listen?"

He put his finger to his lips, leading me to an empty stall, while he took his place with the others. Their voices, rising and falling in the familiar hymns, took me straight back to Hatton. I wished again that I had found some vocation there or had at least lacked the ambition to go beyond that good place.

This was another such place. I would not be strong enough to leave for some time yet, but I resolved to make myself useful.

My offer of help was accepted once my handwriting was scrutinized, and I was placed in the scriptorium. Though I was but a guest, the prior requested that I wear a novice's habit while I worked. "Brother Ludo is quite old," he explained. "His mind is sharp as concerns God and books, but he grows forgetful in this mortal life. Dressed as a novice, you will not trouble him."

The rough wool was more comfortable than my own clothes, and I was happy to accommodate them as they accommodated me, joining them for meals at the refectory table and absenting myself to the library during the divine office and the chapter meeting. I met Salvatore each day before vespers to practice my Italian.

My voice slowly returned, though it was no longer a voice that I recognized as mine. It was deeper and occasionally slipped out of my control, making Salvatore laugh.

"You sound like *un oca*." He honked at me, an impish smile showing beneath his hood.

"A goose," I said. "I sound like a goose."

He honked at me again.

"It is good that I like you so much." I took an odd delight in his teasing.

"I like you too, Brother *Oca*."

"*Oca Rosso*," I corrected, and he dissolved into laughter. I told myself that I was learning Italian and teaching him English. I would not consider any other motive in our daily meetings and the pleasure I took in his company. "Tell me about yourself." We were putting the abbey's herb garden to rest for the winter. "There's so much I don't know."

"I have told you already." He plucked a leafy green herb and placed it neatly in a basket for drying.

"Not in English." I followed his movements closely. I had no experience with herbs, but since his work took him outside, I would accompany him.

He sighed. "In English. I was born here, in Padua. My father, he was…a smith, you would call it. I have six sisters and three brothers. Two of my sisters are at Santa Vincenza."

"Are you the oldest, the youngest?"

"I am middle," he said. "I learn my father's trade, but I have no love for it. From an early age, I wanted God."

We all had our early ambitions. Mine had taken me from Hawley to London, from Oxford to Padua, while his had taken him no further than outside the city walls.

"Is Salvatore your real name?" The brothers at Hatton took new names upon joining the order; I assumed it would be the same in Italy.

He shook his head. "My birth name is Antonio."

"For the saint." Saint Anthony was so prevalent in Padua that he was referred to simply as *the saint*.

"Just so. And you have always been the robin?" He spread more herbs in the basket and discarded a few of mine.

"My name is Robert. Robin was what they called me as a boy," I said. "I took the surname Lewis in honor of the priest who rescued me from my foster parents."

Salvatore picked up the basket. "So, you have always had a fondness for priests."

Horrified color rose to my cheeks, and I promptly changed the subject. "You never wished to marry?"

Salvatore shrugged, the movement fluid beneath his black cowl. "I thought of women as any young man might think, but then I thought of my father. No matter how hard he worked, he could never provide for us." He cast his eyes upward. "Here, if I fall short, only God is disappointed, and no one starves."

As I followed him back to the cloister, he turned. "What about you, *Oca?* Do you have anyone?"

My thoughts turned to Sarah, who initiated me into the fleshly arts, but then I thought of Gregory, his dark skin gleaming in the sun, his hands on my body in the black hold of the ship.

"No."

My stay coincided with the season of Advent, and once I was sufficiently recovered, I joined in the fast. Meat, cheese, and eggs were held for the Christmas feast, yet I was never deprived, for food at Santa Giustina was plentiful and well flavored. Also, I was fed on a different plane, beyond food, by my days in the library.

I could imagine staying there. I did imagine staying there most mornings when the bells woke me. The sound of the lauds made me smile as I said my own prayers. The abbey was a place of order and calm but also excitement, for when I sat down to test my ideas against Salvatore's or one of the other brothers', I was more alive than I had been since my arrival at Oxford.

A wider world was what I had craved. I thought that meant travel, but perhaps instead it was a life of the mind. Finding a community which treasured learning seemed more important than far-off destinations.

Too, there was the restfulness of Catholicism. Even before Oxford, the views of Luther and the other evangelicals had interested me. Deep in my bag was the New Testament I acquired in Bruges. Would the abbot expel me if he knew? I wanted to discuss the new religion with the brothers, but I was afraid. They joined the order because their love of God went deeper than their bones, and here was I, a stranger in their midst, wanting to discuss heresy before dinner.

Was I a freak that I could see both sides? I understood Luther's objections to the church as it currently existed. I didn't believe that anyone, king or commoner, should purchase his way into heaven or out of hell.

But could I look at any one of these men and tell him that he could only be saved through faith or that his penance did nothing to redeem him in the eyes of the Lord? I couldn't believe that either. Faith was primary. All goodness flowed from that faith. Penance for one's misdeeds, if done in faith and not fear of hellfire, should still be worthy of note.

I grew weary examining my own situation. I did not doubt, yet I was not always a good man. It was a failure of my faith that I was not the best version of myself. If I truly believed, I should be better.

Treading my dual path, I went to mass that day and prayed fervently. When I rose from my knees, I felt the usual clarity which came from prayer.

Salvatore met me outside the chapel. "You seem deep in thought."

"I have much on my mind," I said. "Would you walk with me?"

He waited while I fetched my cloak. Though there was a knife's edge to the wind, he did nothing more than pull up his hood and tuck his hands into his sleeves. My years at court had made me soft; as a boy, the winter gales meant nothing, but now I shivered.

"What is bothering you?" he asked once we were outside. "You have been less yourself lately."

I had been either ill or unable to speak for more than half of our acquaintance, yet he judged me correctly. I struggled to find the words to frame my thoughts. "It is a matter of religion," I said at last. "But I do not know how to speak of it with you."

We walked to the edge of the marsh, skirting around the crusty silvered edges. Farther out, it was unfrozen and could draw a man in to his knees.

"If you cannot speak of religion to a monk, I assume you speak of another religion." He looked at me candidly. "Do you have sympathy for the reformers, *Oca?*"

I was exposed. And seen. "Not totally—I have told you how I was raised, and I see the good such places do in the world."

"But you doubt." It was a statement, not a question.

I explained what had brought me to mass that day, watching his face carefully for judgment, seeing none. "Faith must be at the heart of it."

"Without faith, religion—any religion—is meaningless." He spread his hands. "I am sure there are many here who agree with some points of Luther's doctrine, but you will never hear it spoken. When someone proposes to destroy the structure of your life, you do not admire the tools he will use to do it."

"But you speak of it." It heartened me to know that he agreed with at least some of my thinking.

"I am not within the precincts of the abbey." Salvatore smiled at me. "And you are a special case, my friend. I can speak to you because you are outside all this."

"I don't always feel outside."

Salvatore turned toward the abbey. "But you are," he said. "Thank you for making me exercise my limbs and my brain."

Chapter 23

WELL-WATERED AND FED and dried by the fire, we set off again. My mount this time is a thickset gray with a smooth gait; perhaps I will not wake on the morrow with my low back in agony. Our next stopping place is a manor outside the walls of York, held this time by someone firm for Queen Mary. It will not be as congenial an evening, and I am certain Hawkins and I will, again, be chambered together. I will undoubtedly be bedding down on the floor.

"How did you dare talk to a monk about such matters?" he asks, proving he has been paying attention in spite of himself.

"It was different then. A man could still hold the tenets of Rome and Luther in the same way he could be a friend to both Thomas More and Thomas Cromwell. It changed soon enough. I drifted further toward reform, both from genuine belief and from expediency. I could see which way the wind was blowing."

"Not always," comes his response.

I raise a brow. "Not always, else I would not be traveling in your very pleasant company. But I received word in France that the wind was changing. Perhaps I am not wrong; perhaps I am simply early."

He snorts.

"What will you do, young Hawkins, if the wind changes? How deep are your footprints on the wrong side of the fence? Could you blame them on a brother with a similarly-sized foot? Or are you not that attached to your own head?"

"Of course, I am." His hat is pulled low over his face, dripping water on his horse's neck. "I'm not a traitor."

Youth is truly wasted on young men such as these, unable to think beyond the ends of their aristocratic noses.

I sigh. "You look at me and think I have betrayed Mary because I supported Jane Grey and because I now support Princess Elizabeth. I tell you, Jane would have been no better than Edward or Mary—her heretics would have been Catholic, but she would have burned them just as merrily. I supported Jane because my beliefs are well known, having served Cromwell and continued to hold office under Edward. A sudden swing toward Rome would have only drawn attention. Attention was drawn anyway, by the same person who called me to your attention—"

"It was your steward," he says doggedly. "I told you."

"As you say. I thought it best to take myself out of England for a time."

He shook himself like a dog, water flying everywhere. Would it never stop raining? "You'll feel the fire soon enough."

Again, the arrogance of youth. "Have you ever seen a burning? I imagine you have if you're riding about the countryside collecting heretics like a child chases butterflies. You know what it's like, then. The condemned is tied to the stake—in several places, to ensure they don't break free. Faggots are built up around their feet, and a fire lit. It's a slow fire. You're roasting a significant piece of meat."

I catch a look at him. His lips are a thin line: perhaps he's not witnessed one after all.

"I heard tell of a man who recanted on the pyre," I continue blandly, "but he was so badly burned that he died anyway. He should have changed his coat earlier."

For a moment, it appears he will answer, but then he jogs his horse sideways to confer with one of his men.

I would tell him, if he'd stayed, that what I hold most against Her Majesty are the burnings of the women. Knowing the yearning for a child, she burned mothers. She burned pregnant women. The God I serve does not require judgment to be rendered first on earth. If a priest cannot stand between man and his God, neither can a queen.

Chapter 24

THERE WAS NO REASON for me to stay on, beyond the difficulties of winter travel. I ignored the prior's questioning glances and kept to my duties in the library. I was there so much that Ludo began to refer to me as his young brother.

The library was a place of wonders. I loved to sit on a high stool, reading an ancient text or copying a borrowed manuscript for the monastery's collection. My secretarial hand grew neater still, and I expanded into a swooping italic that looked like music on the page.

On replacing some books in a storage crate, I came across a worn copy of Plato's *Phaedrus*. My Greek was never strong, and I'd had no occasion to read or practice it since Oxford. "May I borrow this, brother? I would like to try my hand at translation."

He looked at the volume, then at me. "In here," he said. "Not in your cell."

As it could not interrupt my duties, the translation went slowly. I was much taken by Plato's language and ideas and mulled them over in the darkness of the great silence. His allegory of the chariot was fascinating. The chariot of the gods was drawn by two winged steeds, but the soul of man was pulled by less noble animals, one a horse, which pulled toward heaven, and the other a wayward beast, which leaned toward adventure and desire.

The more I read, the more I recognized that division within myself. I wished to be good; I wanted to achieve heaven someday, when I was old and tired of life. But a part of me craved that which would keep me from my ultimate goal, the love which Plato also described and which the noble steed would strive to avoid. I rubbed my forehead and continued reading.

Now when the charioteer beholds the vision of love—

"*Oca*, can you come?"

I slammed the book shut. "What is it?"

"Brother Giovanni has been injured."

I looked back at *Phaedrus* and hoped Brother Ludo would not come along and tidy away my work before I could finish. I also hoped I would be able to meet Salvatore's gaze without blushing.

By the time we got Giovanni up the stairs—carrying him between us like a sack of grain, if grain wailed volubly in Italian—my pulse had returned to normal. What was I thinking, letting an ancient Greek speak to me of love?

Salvatore dealt calmly with his patient, smoothing his brow and giving him poppy syrup to ease his pain. He asked again for my help when he splinted the leg, and Giovanni thrashed and cried out.

"Another spoonful," Salvatore said tersely, unable to leave his place. "No more."

When it was done, Giovanni was dull-eyed and ready for sleep.

Salvatore put a restraint across the bed to keep him from rising. "I should have found someone else. You are only just recovered yourself."

His gaze made my flesh prickle. "It doesn't matter."

Looking at the light, he said, "You have an hour before dinner, if you wish to return to your book."

The desk was bare when I returned. I found my papers piled on a chest far from where *Phaedrus* had been relocated. Brother Ludo was dozing on a stool.

An hour was not much time, but I was determined to get through the rest of Plato's speech, and then put the book—and its disturbing ideas—to rest. I opened the delicate, closely-written pages and began the laborious cross-checking of words.

The bell rang for sext, and Ludo's eyes popped open.

"I will be along after," I said, though I often joined the service before dinner.

On it went, allusion and allegory, horse and chariot, desire and shame. How could a man from ancient times speak in my ear in such an intimate manner?

> *After this, their happiness depends upon their self control;*
> *if the better elements of the mind which lead to order and*
> *philosophy prevail, then they pass their life in happiness and*
> *harmony, masters of themselves.*

There was more, but here I stopped, shutting the book and dropping my forehead upon it.

Perhaps self-control was easy for Plato, but seeing Salvatore across the refectory brought a tightness to my chest that made it hard to breathe.

I didn't pray to be free of temptation; I prayed that my affection was mutual, that my feelings—however wrong—were reciprocated. Plato understood, but the modern world did not have a high opinion on love between men. Campion's contempt when he had spat the word "sodomites" was never far from my mind.

My sleep was shallow, interrupted with images of Salvatore by the infirmary fire, his olive skin awash with light. His smile. His laughing voice calling me *Oca*. His eyes, so nearly black, in which I could see a new version of myself.

Avoidance was impossible, but for several days, I arrived late and did not take my accustomed place at the table. Meals were silent, only the singsong voice of a brother reading from the Rule. Any speech afterward was in Latin.

I missed my Italian lessons, and I missed my teacher. He was my only friend in this place.

At night, I tried to find a solution to my problem. I had planned to return to England, to build a future there. But this unexpected love—I would let it wreck my plans, if only it would come to something.

But what could come of it? This was Salvatore's world, and it fit him. It did not fit me. Monastic life, with its peace and learning, was attractive, but obedience had never been my strong suit. Poverty I did not mind; despite my ambitions, I never expected to be rich.

Chastity…that had been the least objectionable restriction until now. I thought of the crass terms I'd heard for love: swiving, bed sport. Did they even apply to what I felt?

The act with Gregory aboard the *Primerose* took on new significance. I pushed away my shame and tried to imagine myself with Salvatore in such a way. It brought a rush of blood to my loins, and I caught up my cloak and took a long walk by the swamp until I mastered myself.

Salvatore sought me out after a week of distance. "Walk with me?"

"Brother Ludo is waiting."

"Brother Ludo will talk to the angels until you arrive."

The day was cold but bright, and the wind, which bent the tops of the trees, did not touch us in the secluded cloister.

"You are sad, *Oca?*"

"Not sad," I said. "But I have much on my mind."

I had slept little, arguing with myself, listing all the reasons why I should leave and the one reason that made me wish to stay. I sat on the wall, hoping he would join me. This was not a conversation I could have without seeing his face, and walking side-by-side gave me only his hooded profile.

He sat gingerly on the cold stone and placed his hands on his thighs. "What is it?"

"I have been here three months now," I said, knotting my hands together on my own black-clad legs. "A quarter year."

"You have made a good recovery."

"I want to stay here." I hesitated, then spoke my heart. "I want to stay with you."

"I would like you to stay, my friend." He smiled, but it was a sad smile. In his beautiful eyes, I saw something that resembled understanding. "But this is not the life for you."

"I've never found the life for me."

"You are young still." He made the five years between us sound vast. "You will find your place."

"But what if my place is with you?" My voice shook at my boldness.

He leaned back, and I could see the thoughts as they flashed across his face. I liked none of them. "Robin, you feel this way because I cared for you. You have not been treated gently by the world, I think, and you mistake gratitude for something more."

That was not what I expected, and it struck me like a blow. "Do not tell me of my feelings." I held his eyes until he looked away. "Do you think I do not know my own heart?"

"I think you are young." His voice was very quiet.

"You nursed me and treated me with kindness, but there is more than gratitude in my heart." I touched his hand, retreating before he could push me away. "And I believe you know that."

"Perhaps," he said after a long silence. "But as you say, I am a man of God, and these feelings are not for me. If I am not chaste in my heart, it is the same as being unchaste in my body. It falls under disobedience to the Rule."

"So, all you have left is poverty." I tried for a light tone.

His eyes crinkled. "And poverty is one of the reasons I joined the order." He reached across and took my hands. "It is time for you to go."

"I will never look at a goose in the same way again."

"Nor will I."

Chapter 25

THE KEY TURNS IN the lock, the tumblers falling. "Hawkins got his way."

"How do you mean, master?" Seb gives the door a black look. He doesn't like locks, particularly when he's on the wrong side of them. "Because we're in here?"

"And because he's out there."

I look around the small chamber. We've both slept in worse, and after a day of wet and cold, it will do. There is a small iron brazier and a tallow candle, which almost makes up for the lack of wine. If I'd known, I would have drunk more at supper.

Peeling off my still-damp doublet, I shake it out and debate how best to dry it. The decision is taken from me as Seb snatches it away, shakes it again, and drapes it on a chest facing the fire. "Let me do my job."

Soon the room is festooned with steaming wool, and my servant and I are sitting by the brazier in our shirts.

"This is not so bad," he says. "Hawkins's men snore worse than you."

I rub my hands together over the coals. "You've been making friends among them?"

"No more than you have," Seb says, yawning hugely. "Talk, talk, talk. Are you trying to deafen him or just confuse him?"

"I am trying to remind him of my humanity," I try to explain. "Do you remember that book I borrowed from Signor Grimani in Venice?"

"The one you and the Signora were translating?" He is more awake now.

"Yes." I remind him of the Eastern princess, Shahrazad, who

told her murderous husband a new story each night, stretching it so long that dawn came before she finished the tale, postponing her execution.

"You're not married to William Hawkins," Seb says. "And he doesn't have enough power to save you."

"That's true, but I want him on my side. And I want him to take his time about getting to London. Ned's information wasn't wrong, just his timing."

Seb squats, fluffs the straw mattress, lays two blankets on top. "How long do you think?"

"Until she's dead?" I stretch out on the makeshift bed. "Not long, I hope—for my sake."

"For both our sakes." He gets in beside me, radiating heat.

"There's no warrant for you." I lean over to blow out the candle. "You'll be fine."

"If you are dead, what happens to me?"

"You see me off and ride for Winterset."

"I'm not telling the mistress you're dead," he says. "You'd best find a way to survive."

The floor is hard beneath the straw, but it's not a horse, it's not moving, and it's not raining. For the moment, it's enough.

Chapter 26

FROM PADUA TO VENICE, and then aboard the *Jane Frances* bound for England. I saw none of it, completely bound up with Salvatore. In my heart, I knew he was both completely right and utterly wrong. Perhaps I had fallen hard because I'd been treated with such kindness and grace, but there was more to it than that. There was physical desire, of course, but at the center was the simple need to be in his presence, to know he was there, wanting to spend time with me.

When I came to breakfast that last day, dressed in my own clothes, Salvatore was already gone. A sick call at one of the monastery farms, I was told. I lingered, but when he did not return by early afternoon, I walked into Padua and sold everything I owned, except my books, to buy passage home.

If we'd been able to say goodbye, what would I have said? Would I have told him I couldn't imagine my life without him? It was so far from my image of myself as an island, needing no one, and yet it was true. For the first time, I needed someone, and I could not have him. Missing him caused actual, physical pain, my muscles aching as if I'd been beaten. How did one live after such loss?

I put so much effort into managing my feelings that I took no notice of my surroundings. As before, I was resistant to seasickness, but I stayed below to avoid conversation. I wanted nothing to take my mind off my misery. The *Jane Frances* put in at six ports, but I remained on board, even when time permitted.

"England," I'd said, "just get me to England." Now, seeing the sandstone cliffs, it occurred to me to wonder: to what part of England was I returning? I put the question to a passing sailor.

"You don't know?"

I shook my head.

"We put in at Whitby."

Whitby. After all my travels, was I to return to Yorkshire?

My home county was more than Wardlow or Hawley. It was also Hatton.

The cart reached the market square by noon. "This the abbey you're wanting?" the driver asked as he guided his mules into the open square below looming Whitby Abbey.

"No." I hopped stiffly down, my legs unsteady. "But it's not far. I shall walk from here."

It wasn't far; it wasn't near, for someone who had been ill and then kept close on board ship for weeks. Walking to Hatton took me the better part of the day. I was lucky winter was past, else I would have arrived near dark instead of in the slanting, still-bright sun of afternoon.

The land flattened near the coast, saving its drama for the cliffs, but there as I walked farther inland, the moors tested my strength. I made it to the top of a rise, thinking I must be close, and put my pack down to catch my breath. When I looked up, Hatton was there at my feet, a modest cluster of gray stone buildings circled by a ragged wall, its farm holdings and meadows sprawling out behind. Sheep dotted the green hills, and their bleating carried faintly on the breeze.

My energy returned. Even if no one there remembered me, which was unlikely, it was their duty to take in a stranger. I could stay for a few days while I gathered my wits and decided what to do with myself.

I rang the bell at the gatehouse and waited, my forehead resting against the rough stone. The April air was soft on my cheeks, and in the distance, I could hear the slapping of sandals as the gatekeeper hurried out.

"Can I help you, my son?" A face peered through the grate, breaking into a smile of recognition. "Robin!"

The key ground in the lock, and the gate swung wide.

"Brother Anthony." His wiry arms went tight around my midsection, and I rested my chin on the top of his head. "I am home."

I let the healing stillness of the priory close over me like water. At first, I slept and listened to the sound of the office drifting through the building, but soon I joined the monks in the high-ceilinged refectory, eating in silence with men who had known me from boyhood.

My fear of being unknown was groundless. Prior Richard was dead, replaced by Brother Nicholas, and Brother Rufus was now sub-prior. Brother Anselm held sway in the library, and there were other familiar faces who had been novices when I left.

Given a cell in the dorter, I sat down on the hard cot and closed my eyes. I was in a safe place; I was with friends; I could rest and begin, slowly, to make a new life for myself.

Falling in love had thrown me off balance. It was like the dream of opening a door and discovering a new room, unknown yet strangely familiar. I wanted to sit in this room with its beautiful light and think about Salvatore and what could have been if we were different men, in a different time. Those thoughts were sharp as broken glass.

It was too much. I put his memory in a box, high up in my mental cupboard, and locked it away. Except for Brother Anthony, the monks were discreet, never asking about my plans and frequently sending me outside on small tasks. For the first weeks, I was only indoors for meals and mass, spending my days in the hills. I built up muscle that had weakened during my illness, and the air blew the cobwebs from my mind. I found myself again in the golden peace of Hatton.

Brother Anselm welcomed me into his world of books and treated me gently. He had been my favorite when I was a child, and it was interesting to meet him as a man. He'd always seemed bigger than the others. I saw now it was not height but breadth, as if his body had been shaped by his past labors. His shoulders strained beneath his habit, and he was able to move the heaviest chests without asking a novice to help him.

"You wanted to travel," he said one afternoon, catching me perusing a map. "Did you see the world?"

"Enough of it," I responded. "I left Oxford for the Low Countries, and I saw some of France and Germany on the way to Italy."

His smile widened. "Italy…that was where I'd have wanted to go."

I didn't want to speak of Italy and changed the subject, questioning him on a beautifully illuminated manuscript open on the lectern.

"It's borrowed from Whitby," he said. "I'm copying off part of it—not the pictures, mind, I'm not that good—for our history."

This was a topic in which I could get lost. "I'd be pleased to help." It reminded me of helping ancient Brother Ludo in the library. Was my life doomed to repeat itself, over and over, journey after journey, library after library, until I took leave of my senses? "I've a very good hand."

I spent my days now in either the library or at the gatehouse with Brother Anthony. At most priories, this job would have belonged to a servant or a novice, and indeed a servant did stay there during the great silence, but the prior had decided that Anthony's gifts were best used in welcoming others to the community and presenting a cheerful visage to the outside world. It surprised me that such an outgoing man had chosen a cloistered life, but when I observed him at prayer, I understood his love of people was part of his love of God.

He was restful in a different way than Anselm; instead of slow, contemplative conversations and long silences, Anthony bobbed around like flotsam on waves, telling me everything that occurred during my years away. It was the first time I'd laughed in weeks, and I was grateful for his company.

We were settled on stools, looking out at the road. A storm had swept in, and the track transformed quickly from dust to mud. I was happy, knowing it would mean no visitors for the rest of the day.

"You'll be off to your books later?" Anthony rubbed his nose and squinted out at the downpour.

"Most likely."

"Anselm's a good man." He rocked on his stool and bumped shoulders with me. "He came here like you, many years ago."

I turned to him. "As a child, you mean?"

"As a wounded man." Anthony cast his eyes over the road, his thoughts far away. "He was a soldier who'd seen things he could not abide, and he left the world."

This was news but unsurprising. Soldiering might explain Anselm's physique. "How long ago was that, brother?"

Anthony's face screwed up in concentration. "He arrived a few years before you did. He was in the Scottish war."

That would be Flodden, the war conducted by Queen Katherine while Henry was in France with his *other* war. The Scots king had died, widowing King Henry's sister. It was a wasteful, bloody business.

Later, I made my way to the library and found the book I was copying waiting for me. I sharpened a quill and began, waiting for Anselm's return.

He generally worked alongside me, and so it was today, until he finally put down his pen and looked at me. "What's on your mind?"

I started and blotted the text. Now I would have to wait until it dried to scrape off the ink and begin again. "I was at the gate with Anthony," I said. "He was telling me—"

"He was gossiping," Anselm said calmly. "About me? You've not looked at me since I came in."

My face grew hot. "He mentioned how you came here."

Anselm put his quill aside. "It's no secret," he said, "among the brothers. It's not something I care to remember, other than when I need reminding that this is the place for me."

"Flodden, was it?" I blew on the ink, which remained stubbornly wet.

He nodded. "I was a stupid boy, but the men I followed were no smarter, looking back upon it all." Rubbing his temple, he said,

"I still dream, some nights, of the slaughter."

"How old were you when you came here?" Young Anselm, scarred by war, was unimaginable.

"Twenty-two." He slid a blade across the table. "The ink is dry."

It was a kind way to tell me he was done speaking, and I took the blade and began to work at the blotted parchment in silence.

The brief Yorkshire summer was upon us, and I spent more time than ever in the hills. Even the library felt like a confined space, yet I could not envision leaving.

Flat on my back in the sheep meadow, my eyes shaded by a nearby tree, I considered my options. I'd sung for royalty; I'd been educated; I'd traveled further than anyone I knew; I'd had my heart broken. There was nothing left to experience, but I was not so stupid as to believe I knew all of life by twenty.

I needed something to which I could dedicate my energy and my intelligence. Wherever I washed up, it would have to be near books. Hatton's library healed me as surely as the attentions of the monks.

I had taken to participating in the divine office with them, though I was excused from singing when Father Nicholas heard my poor attempts.

"Does it hurt?" he asked. "You sound like a strangled goose."

I closed my eyes at the reference. "It does, a bit. The infirmarer in Padua wasn't certain I'd regain it at all."

He put a light hand on my forehead. "Then I would not have you risk it further. Your prayers are enough."

Were they? I pushed myself up from the grass as the sound of the bells echoed over the hills. It would soon be time for dinner, and there would be enough light after so that I could retreat to the library. Perhaps Anselm would be willing to discuss my future.

He was, and he did, but we did not agree about it at all.

"You need to leave before you grow moss," he said. "I can already see it—some part of you thinks it would be best to stay here, away from the world."

I met his eyes. "What's wrong with being away from the world?" I asked. "It has served you well."

"I had seen more of life by then than I cared to ever again. It was the right choice for me." He looked up from his script. "I know you've been through something, Robin; it's written all over you. But you're still whole, under the pain. You can make a life for yourself outside this place."

How could he say I was whole when I had left a part of myself in Italy? I could not tell him that and resorted to ducking my chin and muttering like a sullen child, "You don't know that."

Anselm sighed. "You're right; I don't. But if I had to hazard a guess, I'd say you're stronger than you believe, and you should try."

I had no doubts about my abilities, but he had seen to the center of it: I was not certain I could face the world again. Hatton cradled me in familiarity; I was safe there. But was safety enough? "I can't see a way forward." My voice was tinged with desperation. "All I can see is gray."

"You were never a boy not to know what you wanted," Anselm said. "What happened to throw you so far off course?"

"Nothing." I paced the stone floor, unaccountably close to tears. "I've just lost my way, that's all."

He clapped a hand on my shoulder. "When something burns, there's no point in sifting through the ashes. You can't rebuild what was lost. See it for what it could be, Robin, instead of what it was. Something new may come of it, but what? You get to decide."

"I can't think."

"That's what this place is for," he said. "Quiet your mind, and you'll soon hear the voice of God."

A few days later, Father Nicholas summoned me. We had spoken on several occasions during my stay, but he was too elevated—and too busy—for the likes of me. Perhaps he, too, had an idea of what I should do with the rest of my life.

"Brother Anthony tells me you're thinking of staying on."

"I am considering it." Anthony and I had discussed it in

confidence during our last stint at the gatehouse. "But—"

"It won't do," the prior said. "It's a bad use of a house of God, to hide from the world. You must be here from sincere love and because you can imagine no other place to be."

"I know that, Father. I have decided that my place is not in holy orders. I must find a way to serve outside these walls, though I love them for the shelter they have provided over these last months."

"Good. You always were a sensible lad." Father Nicholas waved me to a bench near the window. "You left here once with Cardinal Wolsey. How would you feel about returning to his service?"

I turned to look at him. "You know I can no longer sing."

The prior laughed. "The cardinal has other needs. He's lord chancellor, the highest man in England, excepting the king. He has constant need of educated, trustworthy men to act as secretaries and clerks."

I let the suggestion sink in. My time with the cardinal had not been unpleasant; I remembered him fondly for not evicting me from his library. His library… "Perhaps that would be a good fit."

"I shall draft a letter to him this day," Nicholas said, the decision made, "and you can set your affairs in order, say your farewells, and be off to Hampton Court by Saturday."

Chapter 27

Friday, November 14, 1558
York

HAWKINS RELEASED US EARLY, but we have not yet started: something about another lame horse, Seb whispered, and I am glad of it and gladder still to know, since we were locked in together, that he was not the one to cause the lameness.

"I thought you weren't going to talk about the monasteries?" Hawkins does a credible imitation of me.

I give him a sour look. "I know what I said. I have not planned my tale." I am no Shahrazad, despite my affinity for her story. "I returned to Hatton because I knew, of all places, I would be welcome there."

My dreamed-of world was wide but not always welcoming and not always easily understood. I understood Hatton in my bones— its purpose, its discipline, its brethren.

Chapter 28

I DECIDED, DURING THE week-long journey to Hampton Court, that I would try my best to be amiable in my new situation. I did not intend to make friends, but unnecessary enemies made for a difficult life. My solitary nature provided a kind of freedom; no one would know anything of me beyond what I told them. I was being given a chance to prove myself more than a voice, and I would make the most of it.

Advancement at court frequently depended on connections, of which I had none. The prior had convinced the cardinal to take me back. I vowed that I would make him—and myself—proud. Friends, much less relationships, were distractions.

I would not allow myself to be distracted. Or hurt.

Being an under-secretary was vastly different from being a chorister. I was still a servant, sharing a chamber and a bed with several others, but our quarters were better and more conveniently located. The other young men were agreeable enough, but after a few attempts to befriend me, they drifted away.

I looked up my friends in the Music and discovered that I had been missed. I'd liked them well enough, but had all but forgotten them upon leaving court. How strange to have remained in their minds when they had vanished from mine.

My new life exposed me to many new people, as the cardinal had business with every level of society. I had encountered Sir Thomas More in my previous years at court but would have never been permitted—or had occasion—to speak to such a gentleman. Now I saw him often in discussion with Cardinal Wolsey. I learned some of the cardinal's young men ventured into Chelsea in the evening to drink More's beer and listen to him talk, and I determined to attend one of these gatherings, despite my general avoidance of my fellows.

I had read More's *Utopia* while at Hatton, and it made an impression. I wanted to meet the man who could write such a book, and I soon inserted myself into one of those evening visits, with results that reached far beyond what I intended.

More and his family sat among retainers and hangers-on at the board, so that first night, not only did I speak to the man himself, but I sat across from his daughter Margaret Roper, as highly educated as any woman in England and her father's darling.

Sir Thomas's wife, Alice, retired early, but Margaret stayed on, taking a seat near the fire with a cluster of young men around her. She was a handsome woman a few years older than myself, who, though married and with two small children, was yet the center of her father's household.

"Translation is the best way to learn a language." The young men leaned in to listen to her pronouncement. "That is how I learned; my father set me to translating from the Latin as a girl."

"You've translated Erasmus, have you not?" Stephen Wingfield sounded in awe, whether of Mistress Roper or Erasmus, I could not be sure.

She lowered her eyes, giving the appearance of girlishness, but her voice showed no false modesty. "It is titled *A Devout Treatise Upon the Paternoster*."

"*Precatio Dominica*." There was only one other woman in the chamber, and I turned to look when she spoke. She was older, clad in widow's black, and appeared to be attached to a swarthy gentleman who had been introduced to me as Signor Bonnato.

"You have read Mistress Roper's book?" The young man's tone dared her to refute him.

"I have read the original Latin," she said. "I do not read well the written English."

Her accent made me yearn to try my Italian with her, but it did not seem polite to abandon Sir Thomas to practice my language skills with a guest to whom I had not been introduced.

As we gathered ourselves to leave, nearing eleven of the clock, I found myself face-to-face with the Italian woman. "I too have read Erasmus in the original," I said, "though I would like to try Mistress Roper's translation."

"I believe Vincenzo has a copy." She touched his sleeve, and a stream of words flowed between them.

I found myself adrift. So much for my vaunted language skills if a few short sentences about literature could befuddle me.

"You are Master Lewis?" Signor Bonnato asked, his forehead creasing in his attempt to place me.

I bowed and explained myself. "I am a secretary with the cardinal's household."

"My sister says you were asking about Erasmus."

I had somehow assumed, despite her mourning, that the woman was his wife. "Yes, I've not read the translation yet."

Signor Bonnato took my hands in his. "You may borrow it from my house," he said. "Gladly will I share my books with one of the cardinal's men. It will be an honor to have such a connection."

Perhaps I should have stressed that I was an under-secretary, but a part of me was warmed by his respect for Wolsey, who did not inspire much love these days among Londoners. "I would be pleased to borrow it, sir."

"You will arrange with my sister," he said, handing me off. "I must say a final word to our host."

I found myself facing the woman again. "I'm sorry, signora, but I haven't had the pleasure of an introduction," I said. "I am Robert Lewis, under-secretary to Cardinal Wolsey."

She curtsied in a sweep of inky skirts. "Bianca Turner," she said. "I keep house for my brother. Please, come any afternoon to get the book. We are also here in Chelsea, just down the road."

"A few of us are going to a pie shop after we're done here," a voice said over my shoulder. "Join us?"

It was Ned Pickering. Again.

Ned was a clerk in the cardinal's service, and he had been trying to befriend me since my arrival. He continued to try, as I continued to shrug off his attempts.

"I have work to do."

"We're done soon," he said coaxingly. "You're not that important."

"I have something to finish." I didn't look up. "And I will eat in the hall. My salary doesn't run to pie shops—of whatever sort you had in mind."

Ned's hoots of laughter showed that in this instance, pie shop did indeed mean brothel. Why couldn't people just say what they meant?

"Fine," he said. "We'll go for pie first; then you can leave before we go for more pie."

"I'll eat here." Why couldn't the tiresome man comprehend that I didn't want to spend time with him beyond that which was required by our employer?

He leaned over, his broad, smiling face just inches from my nose. "Too much bile in your system," he said. "Gives you a short temper."

"And what's to be done about that?"

"Ale," he advised cheerfully. "It balances the humors."

I finished my letter and waved it to dry the ink. With luck, Ned would take the hint and leave. Instead, he seated himself on a stool and busied himself with counting the coins in his purse. At a glance, he carried more than I currently possessed.

"Don't do that."

"Come out with us," he wheedled. "All work and no play…"

"Makes my career progress," I returned. "While yours—"

"Is doing just fine." He worked a coin between his fingers, back and forth. When it made two circuits, he dropped it on the desk and spun it in an irritating fashion.

I snatched it up. "Will you stop that?"

"Now you have enough for a drink and a pie!" he crowed. "Come on."

Maybe if I went along and made myself disagreeable, he would stop asking. "Fine," I said. "Don't you ever give up?"

Pickering bounded from the stool and knocked my cap off my

head. "No, because people tend to give in."

As I gathered my things, I asked, "Why are you here? You don't need to work in a place like this." Ned was from an old Surrey family; he would fit in better with the young courtiers who hung about Greenwich, hoping for crumbs.

"There's only so much to go around." His shrug said much about his family situation. "My brother will marry and do all the expected things, and I will get on as I see fit." He smiled at the gulf between their lives. "Being a younger son has its privileges."

"I wouldn't know."

"Of course you wouldn't," he said. "Everyone knows you're self-made, sprung from the Yorkshire soil, able to read Latin at four, translating Greek by six, and finding the king's favor before you found your own fist."

I survived the pie shop—the first half of the evening—and from then on, I was the target of a sustained assault. Ned Pickering was going to be my friend, whether I liked it or not.

"Why do you keep trying?" I asked after the third time he invited me out. "I'm not good company."

Ned grinned. It was his most common expression, a genial, somewhat vacuous happiness that concealed a surprisingly sharp mind. "I like a challenge."

"I don't understand why you spend your evenings in such frivolous pursuits. You're very good at your work, and yet you spend your nights roistering in taverns."

Ned spun his cap in the air. He always had to have something in motion: if it wasn't his mouth, it would be some inanimate object. "The appearance of stupidity is very helpful," he said. "All my life, people have underestimated me because I'm such a jolly fellow."

"Well, aren't you a jolly fellow?" It was one of the few things I thought I knew about him.

"Of course I am," he said. "But I have hidden depths."

His friendship was unavoidable. After I grudgingly gave in, life became quite pleasant. I took him up to court on a free afternoon and introduced him to the Music. Of course, it turned out that he played the shawm and the recorder—badly—and knew rude lyrics to every song.

"I'm not sure how you ended up with him, Robin," Bess said, "but I like him." There was a shout, and all the men burst into laughter. She smiled indulgently. "He brings out the boy in them."

"That's because he is a boy," I said ruefully.

I liked him too, but I wasn't ready to trust him with my secrets. "I don't know your entire history."

"But you could," Ned said. "I'm an open book."

"And I am a closed book. With a lock." I met his merry blue eyes and shook my head. "You have seen some pages; be content with that."

"I am content with everything." He shoveled food from his trencher, eating like a man who had not seen meat in a month. "I'm going to be extremely content later when I go to Southwark with the boys. Are you sure you won't join us?"

"I think not." The idea of actively seeking out physical relations made my skin crawl. I remembered Sarah, but that had not been a straightforward transaction; I hadn't gone looking for a woman, while Ned and his friends spent much time doing just that.

He topped off his ale and sloshed more in my cup, spattering the table. "Even the cardinal is not so prudish as you."

Prudish, indeed. While they went out to spend hard-earned coin on quick, impersonal congress, I had known love. It was no less genuine for being unconsummated.

I would never be an open book to Ned, even though—apparently—I would be his friend.

Some time passed before I was able to escape my duties to travel to Chelsea. I made room for myself on a barge stopping at Thomas More's and made my way through his orchards to the next property.

The Bonnato house was about half the size of More's Thames-side manor, but it was still larger than I expected. I knew, from discreet questioning, that Bonnato had been a partner in his brother-in-law's shipping business, and that upon Turner's death, all had come to him.

I wandered through a small formal garden which stretched between the house and the river. Though the design was sound, the garden appeared neglected. Did Signor Bonnato not employ a gardener? Making my way up the stone path, I scanned the windows. Most of the interior shutters were closed. I hoped I had not come all this way for nothing.

I let fall the ornate knocker.

After a time, the door opened partway, and a small servant peered around it, curtsying to me. "Good afternoon, sir."

"Good afternoon," I said. "I am here to see Signor Bonnato."

Her eyes widened. "Master Bonnato is not here," she said in a near-whisper. "He has gone to France."

I nearly sighed with relief. I wanted the book; I did not want to spend the afternoon drinking and chatting with the Italian. He was congenial enough, but my time was limited, and I was already worried about how long it would take to return to court and how many pages I might read during the journey back.

"Is Signora Turner at home?"

Another curtsy. "She is, sir." The door opened wider. "Please come in, and I will call her."

Left alone, I examined my surroundings. It was obvious that Bonnato and his sister were responsible for the decoration of the place; nothing in the way of art or furnishings showed the tastes of an Englishman named Turner.

I was happily absorbed in a tapestry of Bacchus drinking from a fountain when a light step approached.

"Master Lewis, how good to see you again. You honor us with your presence." Signora Turner still wore black, but this time, her hair was covered by a simple white coif.

I bowed. "I am sorry it took me so long. My duties keep me with the cardinal much of the time."

She led me toward an inner room. "It is of no matter, sir. I am always here."

"Not always," I said. "After all, we met at Sir Thomas's house."

She acknowledged my comment with the smallest of smiles. "I was compelled to accompany my brother. I do not leave the house on my own."

My mouth opened.

"*Mi dispiace,*" she said. "I have made you uncomfortable."

"No," I protested. "It is just—"

"I have made you uncomfortable." She gestured toward the door. "Please come through to the library, and we will find your book." The servant still hovered in the doorway. "Jane, please bring wine for us."

The library was a small room on the north side of the house. The shutters were open, but the afternoon light barely filtered through a thick screen of trees outside. Signora Turner lit several candles on a branched holder, and the books came into view.

It was not a large collection, but as I skimmed them, looking for Meg Roper's translation, I noticed Greek and Latin philosophers, eminent historians, Erasmus in the original, and several volumes of Caxton, including the one I had almost purchased in Oxford.

"You like books." She stood behind the desk. Candlelight fell on her skin, which had the sheen of a marble statue.

The unlikeliness of the image stopped me. She was a woman, no longer young, standing with her back to a window, light falling on her face. There was nothing more to it than that.

"I do." I slid a volume of Livy from a chest. The scent of old paper tickled my nose. "I spent some years in a monastery as a boy. A library feels like home to me."

"I spend much time here myself when my brother is away." She removed a book from another chest and offered it to me. "Mistress Roper."

There was a scratching at the door, and the maid entered with a tray.

"Please put it on the desk, Jane," she said. "I shall pour."

"Yes, madam." The girl straightened the bottle, placed two

extravagant glasses beside it, and disappeared.

I accepted the glass Signora Turner pressed into my hands. Taking a sip, recognition flooded through me. "It's Italian."

"Of course."

Of course. Despite its unassuming exterior, the house was a portal to another land. "In what part of Italy were you born?"

She seated herself in a rustle of skirts. "The most beautiful city on earth," she said. "Venice."

I had wanted to see Venice so badly, but I had seen it only through a fog of loss when I departed for England. "Is it as beautiful as they say?"

A transfiguring smile lit her face. "It is unimaginable. To think that men built a city that floats upon the water… I see it, even now. As a child, they could not keep me in the house. I would wander the calle, in and out of the churches, through the squares. I knew every inch of my city."

"How could you bear to leave?" I'd never had that kind of attachment to a place, possibly because I had never been in one place long enough.

"I had no choice," she said simply. "When I was too old to go out alone, I refused to stay with my chaperone. I would wear my brother's clothes and take a boat into the lagoon, sometimes to the far islands. I don't know what I wanted to accomplish. I could not escape my sex."

Her voice trailed off, and I tried to imagine this stern woman as a girl, in hose and shirt, rowing out into the great lagoon of Venice. A fearless girl, I thought—attractive to men and a nightmare for her parents.

"I was found, of course, and brought back. My father beat me and took away my books, and I was locked in my chamber for so long, I considered throwing myself into the canal."

"He let you out eventually."

Again, the small smile. "For my wedding to the merchant Turner," she said, "to whom he owed a debt he did not wish to pay."

I took a mouthful of wine while I processed the idea that a

troublesome daughter could be traded like goods. "Had you met him before?"

"Once or twice." She refilled my glass, and our fingers touched when she handed it to me.

"These are beautiful." I held the glass up to the light. Accustomed as I was to wood, pottery, or metal, the clear glass coiled and flowed in my hand like a live thing. The wine was also a live thing, bringing every sense in my body to a higher pitch.

"They were part of my dowry," she said. "There are only a few left. I dread the day when they are gone."

"You had only met your husband once or twice?" I returned to the subject, as much to listen to her voice as to hear the rest of her story. If I closed my eyes, I could believe myself in Italy.

"I was fourteen," she said. "I had not been out in society before that. I knew him only from my parents' table."

What sort of man married his fourteen-year-old daughter to a foreigner, no matter how much trouble she gave? And how had the very young Signora Turner managed? I had many questions, all of which would be considered rude.

My silence lasted too long. Signora Turner broke it by saying, "I was fortunate. My husband, he was a good man. When he realized how homesick I was, he sent for my brother and brought him into the business."

"And your brother inherited the company?"

"On my husband's death, yes." She spread her hands, which I noticed were bare but for a marriage band. "We had no children, so Vincenzo—Vincent, I must say in English—was his heir until such time that we had a son." She sighed. It was a surprising sound from a woman so controlled. "But he died within three years, and the only child I bore died with his father."

"I'm so sorry," I said. "What happened?"

"The sweating sickness took them both, and the servants. When my brother returned, I was the only one alive in the house."

I tried to imagine her, still just a girl, alone in a strange country. "Most women would have gone mad."

"You assume I did not." Signora Turner's eyes were dark and deeply set. "I believe I was, for a time. I could not see my way through the grief."

Her words touched something deep inside me; I understood that type of grief. "Losing everyone, being left alone in an empty house, in a country not your own."

"It is still not in my country. Twenty-three years I am here. I speak the language, I have met people, but I am as confined as I was in my father's house."

I calculated: had she not gone out in twenty years other than on visits with her brother? That seemed unlikely, though I didn't know her relations with Vincent Bonnato. The idea that she had spent two decades inside these walls disturbed me.

The wine was unwatered and far stronger than I was used to. Draining the second glass, I regretfully placed it on the table. I would need a clear head for the cardinal.

I had no idea of the hour, or whether I would be able to make my return journey by river as I had planned. Instead of asking the time, I turned back to my hostess. "How is it that you are confined?"

"My brother prefers that I not leave," she said. "He is older and remembers how my father dealt with my transgressions."

"What is he afraid you will do?" My rudeness surprised even me. "I am sorry, signora. That is not my affair."

She placed her glass beside mine. "It is no matter. I have no desire to explore London as I did Venice." Her hands twisted together. The frill of lace at her wrists was exceptionally fine. "I still walk Venice, both waking and sleeping. Only this morning, I woke from a dream that I was lost in the mist."

"How frightening."

"Not frightening," she corrected gently. "The mist in Venice is a welcome friend. It softens the stone and lays a hush on the air. A gondola moving on the canal is barely audible. Voices are flattened, so you cannot track their origin. Nothing is wholly real in the mist, and when I dream of it, I feel I have been given the opportunity to return home for a little while."

Her expression was distant. I hated to intrude, but I feared I'd spent far too long in this house.

I must have moved, for Signora Turner's attention snapped back to me. "I must not keep you. I am selfish in my loneliness."

"It has been a pleasure," I said truthfully. "Both in seeing your library and in speaking with you. We are much alike in one respect: while I am constantly in the presence of people, there are very few with whom I can speak." I bowed to her. "I cannot tell you how much I have enjoyed myself."

"I am glad of it," she said. "Please do come again, if you would like. Do not wait until you have finished the book. Mistress Roper is a competent translator, but I prefer the original."

Chapter 29

"I HAVE A STRANGE variety of friends, as you can see. Italians, musicians, merchants. My colleagues in the cardinal's household. And others."

Hawkins keeps his eyes on the road. The day is cold, but blessedly, the rain has ceased. The wolds and hills of Yorkshire are, in the other seasons, beautiful to behold, but now they are bleak fields of mud and snow, scattered with clumps of trees and the ruined husks of monasteries.

I turn my eyes away and elaborate. "I was a useful sort of person. I knew people. I heard things. I could accomplish small tasks for my betters which might enrich me."

This makes him turn his head, and I can see he wants to speak, but holds his tongue.

"You've never had to scrounge for coin with which to make your life more comfortable. If you are uncomfortable now, it is your own doing—you could be in a number of manors, doing any number of comfortable things." I touch the horse with my heels and canter ahead, making him chase me. Over my shoulder, I say, "Any discomfort you feel now is not my doing, but your own."

He was soon beside me again. "You speak as if I chose this errand," he says. "You know what it is to be at court. You look for opportunities; you work hard."

I give him Thomas Cromwell's unnerving smile. "Indeed, young Hawkins. If you keep your head down and work hard, you can become anything in this world. Even a dangerous heretical traitor, like me."

Chapter 30

"I WANT HER BACK," he said. "I want her back, and I want him gone."

When Nicholas Hawkins summoned me to his apartments, I assumed it would have to do with Bess—he had no interest in my work, caring only for his own pleasures. My friend had been one of those pleasures for a time. I knew not how they parted, but now, it appeared, Hawkins regretted his loss.

"Why do you think I have influence over either of them?"

His lip curled. "For some reason, they seem to like you. I can't understand why, but there it is."

"What do you want me to do?" It never hurt to have a man like Hawkins in your debt.

"I don't know," he said. "But you'll find yourself well compensated should you carry it off, Lewis. I'm more generous than the cardinal."

It wasn't difficult to arrange a place for Tom among the cardinal's minstrels and less difficult still to convince him to take it. Hawkins had produced from somewhere an exceptional Italian lutenist who had become the king's pet, and between Tom's feelings for Bess and his loss of stature, the court was an unhappy place for him.

I cared about Bess, but my sympathies were with Tom. While she and Hawkins had been making love in corners, Tom had been eating his own heart in small bites for sustenance. She wasn't stupid; she knew Hawkins would never marry her, yet she threw away happiness with both hands. I felt for them both, so obviously meant to be together and yet at such cross-purposes.

I did nothing to further Hawkins's other request: the return of his former mistress. He could manage that on his own.

Tom settled in at Hampton, making friends in his enviable way and causing the cardinal's minstrels to work a bit harder to keep up.

It seemed all was well; I had done the right thing—for Hawkins and Tom, anyway—and enriched myself in the process.

The money was spent, as all money was, on books. I left York Place for St. Paul's, where there was a cluster of excellent booksellers. I went there but rarely because it was impossible to browse and leave; a visit to a bookseller, much less several, would require most of the day and all of my money.

My first stop netted me an excellent Livy and a copy of Erasmus's *In Praise of Folly*. I could have stopped then, for that was certainly enough, but instead, ignoring my grumbling stomach, I ventured into a dark hole of a shop with barely enough light to read the titles on the spines.

The place smelled powerfully of leather and paper and printer's ink, heady scents far superior to the expensive rose oil worn by nearly everyone at court. After a leisurely perusal, twice having to carry volumes to the window to see them properly, my eye was caught by a copy of Dante's *La Terze Rima*, sometimes called the *Commedia*. I had attempted it before, but my Italian had not been up to the task.

Translation is the best way to learn a language. Margaret Roper's voice echoed clearly in my mind. Opening the book at random, I tried to read but understood perhaps three words in ten. If I worked at it, context would enlarge my vocabulary. I looked at the title page and saw that the small volume had been printed in Venice.

That decided it. I took the book to the counter and handed over the last of Nicholas Hawkins's money. I felt lighter as soon as it was out of my hands.

Chapter 31

"You seem unwell, my friend. I should have considered your feelings before I spoke thus of your father."

Hawkins is thin-lipped, one gloved fist tight on the pommel—to keep from reaching for my throat, no doubt. I shouldn't tweak him, but it's difficult not to, with his sire.

"You can't have reached this age without hearing some of the stories, man. He was no child when he married your mother, though she certainly was." I cast back to little Elinor Hawkins, floating through court like a dandelion clock, bewildered by the place that marriage had got her. "When he first married her, she was barely old enough to put up her hair, much less be yoked to one of the most licentious men of Henry's court."

He turns to me. "There is no reason to be insulting, Lewis. I've been doing the best I can for you during this journey; you know that."

I did know that, and I am appreciative, but I have not been forthcoming with my appreciation. "I offer no deliberate insults, but I shan't spare your feelings, not if the tale warrants. My friend spent time as his mistress, and he made her, on the whole, dreadfully unhappy. She would probably defend him—she did things like that, defend the indefensible—but he was not a kind man, and he wanted her because she didn't fall at his feet like all the others."

Did women fall at the feet of Nick Hawkins's son? I thought not. He was pleasant-featured, but he had none of his father's dangerous beauty nor his arrogance and none of his mother's innocent sweetness. How two such beautiful people had made such an ordinary young man was beyond me.

Chapter 32

IT SOON CAME ABOUT that I spent most of my free time in Chelsea, translating Dante with Bianca Turner. She claimed it helped her English, and I know it helped my Italian, but there was more to it than that.

I began to feel that the only time I was awake was when I was translating those dead words into a living language while seated beside a woman who inhabited a space somewhere in between.

"We are almost done with *Inferno*," I said, looking at the scant few pages left in the section.

"Next is *Purgatorio*." She sounded almost happy.

"I must admit, I am looking forward to *Paradiso*."

"This is *paradiso*," she said, putting her hand on my sleeve, "to read my own language again, to read Dante again, and from a book printed in my own Venice—you cannot know what this means."

I had begun to think of our chairs, side-by-side at the desk, as a form of paradise. If, indeed, paradise was equipped with Italian wine, pots of ink, and endless freshly-sharpened quills.

"I wish to repay your hospitality," I said. "I have no home of my own, and this place has become dear to me."

Candlelight still made her skin glow. "There is no need to repay anything. You have brought the world inside this house."

"I would take you out of this house if I could." It was a beautiful afternoon, and I could hear the river from the open window. "Even a walk along the bank, that would be better than you being shut up in here all the time."

"It is a cage," she said, "not a prison. I have the keys. I choose not to use them."

"It is a beautiful cage, but it is still a cage." I plucked at the slashing in my sleeve where her fingers had rested. "What happened to the girl who sailed the great lagoon?"

"She had her wings clipped," she said. "Shall I send Jane for more wine?"

I did not want to leave. I was happy in this house, with these books, yes, but also with a woman whom I barely knew. "I should not."

She nodded demurely. "I understand. Someone who flies free has no need of a cage."

I closed the book, leaving the final stanzas of *Inferno* for another day, and this time, put my hand on her sleeve. "My world is as proscribed as yours, signora. It may be larger, but I am no more free."

"But you are here." Her voice was soft. "Do they not wonder where you go?"

I looked down at the desk. "I come when I am not needed elsewhere," I said. "Today the cardinal is at York Place, so I have a few hours that would be spent on the river if I had to come from Greenwich."

"You go to much trouble to come here." The candles reflected in her eyes, tiny flames dancing in her pupils. Her hands were folded neatly on the desk, contained as always.

I hesitated and put my right hand over hers. "It is not too much trouble," I said. "I am very happy in this place."

She pulled away, leaping from her seat. "Master Lewis!"

Blood rushed to my head. What had I been thinking? This was a woman of nearly forty, a widow with dignity and position, who had a brother who could probably make me disappear into the Thames. "I'm sorry," I stammered. "I—it must be the wine."

Signora Turner leaned against the window behind the desk. "It is of no consequence," she said. "I do not know your English customs, perhaps I overreact."

"I believe our customs are the same; I overstepped in my gratitude."

Her face was still turned to the glass. "I cannot remember the last time someone touched me."

Twenty years was a long time without human contact, if one wanted it. My feelings regarding the physical plane were still confused, despite—or perhaps because of—my experiences. But I could see that Signora Turner was, beneath her abundant skirts and elaborate bodices, an attractive woman. A woman with desires that had been unmet for nearly all the years of my life.

"I am sorry if it was unwelcome, signora." The space between us suddenly felt thicker, as if the air had changed its composition.

She turned. "Would you call me by my name?"

"Of course." It did not appear she was offended by my behavior, only shaken.

"Then say it, *per favore*."

She looked like a statue. Not a saint, but one of the older statues I had seen in Italy, the ones carved by the ancients, representing some pagan goddess. There was a wildness in her, despite her black gown and starched white linen. Those were a costume, in the same way that men dressed up for a masque as dragons or demons.

"Bianca."

She exhaled. "*Di nuovo.*" Again.

"Bianca."

Her lips were parted. She looked younger, as if hearing her name had pared years from her age. "And you, Master Lewis?"

"Robin," I said in a voice suddenly rusty. These days I was Rob, or more commonly Lewis or Secretary Lewis. Only Bess still called me Robin.

"Robin," she said with a lilt in her voice. "No wonder you do not like cages."

We were standing in the center of the triple window. I knew not how we came to be there; I didn't remember moving. My heart was pounding. "Should I go now?"

"I would not have you leave." She was perfectly still, her bodice barely rising and falling with each breath.

"What would you have of me?" I could barely find my voice.

"I would have you touch my hand again." She raised her hand, palm outward, and I matched it with my own. It was as warm as mine was cold. Just the slightest movement brought my fingers between hers, and I could feel her reaction, as if lightning traveled between our skins.

I stepped back, my breath coming faster. I had not felt such a surge of lust since the *Primerose* when Gregory touched my lip.

I did that now, touching Bianca Turner's full lower lip with one finger. She gasped, and I could see clearly what years of deprivation had done to her spirit.

"We cannot go upstairs," she said. "My brother would be informed immediately."

I hadn't progressed to the idea of kissing her, and I was already being deprived of her bedchamber. "That's all right." I drew my finger from her mouth to her pointed chin and then along her jaw before dropping it to the coil of pearls at her neck.

She vibrated like an instrument beneath my hand, and when I slipped my finger beneath the pearls to the hollow of her throat, a small sound escaped her lips, a sound that nearly undid me.

Her eyes were closed, the deep sockets stained with shadows. Her lashes lay against her cheek, delicate as the feathers of a quill, or a line of music. "I did not know skin could hunger," she said. "It has been a long time since a man touched me."

Her bluntness only whetted my desire. It was a heady thing, desire—as unfamiliar as the undiluted wine served in this house, and as potent. "Bianca—"

The library door opened with a bang, and Vincent Bonnato strode in, flinging a satchel onto the nearest chair. "*Sorella*," he bellowed.

"I am right here." Bianca stepped around me. "There is no need to shout, Vincenzo."

Taking a deep breath, I discreetly picked up the Dante. "You have arrived in time to hear our latest work."

Vincent showed no interest in the *Inferno*. "You are here again, Secretary Lewis? Does the cardinal never require your presence?"

"Don't be rude, brother." Bianca filled a glass with ruby liquid. "Have a drink, and tell us of your travels. How were the Lunardis? Did they buy as much wine as you intended them to buy?"

At Vincent's insistence, I dined with them that evening. After wine and food and flattering questions, his mood improved, and he became expansive. He teased us about our translation and, at one point, would speak to me only in Italian. I was grateful for my quick memory and for the vocabulary built by tossing words back and forth with Bianca.

Sitting across from her at table was an interesting experience. I tried to concentrate on Vincent's stories, but then I saw her slender fingers pick up a glass or hold a knife, and I remembered the feel of those fingers between my own.

What if Vincent hadn't returned when he did? What if, God forbid, he'd returned just a few minutes later? If he let me live, there was still no doubt the cardinal would be informed, and I would be sacked. Wolsey was no prude, but he was discreet.

Being caught *in flagrante delicto* with a gentleman's sister was not discreet.

I busied myself with work, traveling to France with the cardinal and spending time with Ned and his friends. In the end, though, I couldn't stay away from Chelsea. When I appeared late one afternoon, I was welcomed as if I'd been there only the day before, with the maid bringing wine and sweetmeats to the library and Dante lying open on the desk.

I looked at the page. "This is where we left off."

"I waited," she said simply. "How much time do you have today?"

I took a healthy draught of wine, feeling it bloom in my mouth like ripe fruit. "I'm not expected back until late," I said. "Or even tomorrow."

"I will have your bed made up and make sure there is supper enough to please you."

"Anything you have is fine." I wasn't certain what I was saying. "Let us finish *Inferno*, shall we?"

We did, in fact, complete *Inferno* that afternoon and made a start on the first canto of *Purgatorio* before supper was laid in the hall, and I discovered that Vincent Bonnato was away again.

I am sure the food was delicious; it always was. I do not remember what was served, only that we sat at the table until our places were cleared, and talked of this and that, and drank more wine—both of us, I think, trying to put off the inevitable.

"I am in no position to make promises." I barely remembered forming the words in my mind.

Her skin was like gold in the firelight. "I have been married." Her fingers strayed to my sleeve, played absently with my cuff. "I do not miss marriage, but I miss...touch."

For most of my life, touch had been a fearful thing. Even when I had found release before, with Sarah and with Gregory, there had been an element of discomfort. Of shame. But I hadn't known them; I'd simply answered the call of my body. With Salvatore, there had been an element of physical comfort but never a mutual attraction. If there had—

I did not want to think of Salvatore in this house.

Bianca was different. We were comfortable with each other after months of translation. I trusted her, and I believe she trusted me. That was more important than any physical yearning, though, at the moment, my yearnings were rather insistent.

"I will go up now," she said. "Finish your wine. There is a door in your room that connects to my chamber. I will leave it unlocked, should you choose to join me."

Scarcely acknowledging her departure, I sat back, the expensive Venetian glass tight in my grasp. I knew what I wanted—what she wanted of me—and I was afraid. Afraid I would ruin a friendship that I valued. Afraid Vincent would find out and bar me from the house. Afraid, most of all, that my body or my nerve would fail me, and I would humiliate myself and be unable to return to this happy, comfortable place.

The wine was gone. I put the glass gently on the table for Jane to collect in the morning and made my way upstairs. Once before, when a hard rain came up, I had stayed overnight in this room. I hadn't known it connected with hers.

It was a small room, very foreign in its decoration, containing a curtained bed, a carved cupboard, and a prodigious number of candles. On one wall was a hanging I had admired before, featuring

Diana in a grove of cypress. It drew my attention again, and when I raised the edge, I saw the door. It swung inward at my slightest touch.

Bianca sat on the bed, still fully dressed. Firelight shimmered on her skirts. The rest of her was in shadow.

Two steps, and I was beside her. "I never knew that door was there."

"I was not ready for you to know then." She placed her hands on my chest. I could feel them, delicate and long-fingered, through my clothing.

"And now?"

"Now I am." She looked at me. "Are you, my Robin?"

By way of answer, I leaned down and kissed her, taking my time about it, getting us both used to the idea of intimacy. It took little getting used to. The fire in her touched off something dormant. I could feel it racing through my veins, like the lit charge to a keg of explosives.

Pins and points, sleeves and stays, shirt and chemise. Undressing was a slow business, made slower by repeated pauses to kiss and caress. When at last I undid the ties to her chemise, she drew back, holding the thin lawn close to her neck.

"I am not a young girl. I have borne a child."

"I don't want a young girl." I took a deep breath and peeled the chemise away, dealing with the surprising long drawers beneath—Englishwomen didn't wear those—and arriving at last at her naked body, clad only in black knitted stockings and ribbon garters.

Pressed close, we moved toward the bed, tumbling through the curtains and collapsing on the embroidered coverlet in a tangle of limbs. Lifting my mouth from hers, I spoke a single word: "*Paradiso.*"

Chapter 33

ANOTHER NOON, ANOTHER INN. This one, off the beaten track, welcomes our party and hastens to groom and feed the horses. We take over the large room, sprawling about, comfortable, while the innkeeper and his wife bring platter after platter of stewed meats and brown bread, and a bountiful supply of ale.

I keep an eye on Seb, who is playing at dice with several of our guards. He picked up the habit on our Italian travels, along with a pair of loaded dice. I wondered if they were in use this day.

Will Hawkins ventures outside to relieve himself, leaving me in the care of one of his men. When he returns, he sits across from me and downs another cup of ale. "So, you took the Italian woman as a mistress?" He grimaces.

"Does it make you uncomfortable," I ask, "the thought of making love to an older woman? Or is it that you cannot imagine me ever having been that young?" It is sometimes difficult for me, remembering a time when desire made my head swim like wine.

"Neither," he says. "Both."

I cannot help but smile. "You're still quite young. You'll learn."

I had learned. When I returned from Italy and put away my feelings for Salvatore, I hadn't expected to become involved with anyone, not ever again.

His mind runs along similar lines. "Was it because of your monk that you took up with her?"

"There was far more to my relationship with Bianca Turner than the memory of another." I find myself unable to speak his name, though I could easily enough when telling my story. "My feelings for her stood on their own. It would have been an insult to judge her against anyone else. She has no peer, neither among the women of my acquaintance then nor any I have met since."

"Hmm." He gestures for another pitcher. This dinner is becoming quite leisurely; if my captor has much more to drink, he's going to require a nap, and we will arrive at our next destination in the dark. "What about your wife?"

"What about her?"

He shrugs. "You've not met anyone like the Italian woman. Even your wife?"

I consider his question. I consider my wife and conclude, "Even her."

Chapter 34

THE KING'S DESIRE FOR an annulment of his marriage caused the cardinal, and thus his clerks, to journey frequently to wherever the court was lodged. The king shouted and rampaged; the cardinal soothed and cajoled. The king publicly caressed his not-yet-mistress; the cardinal pretended not to see and made promises that made him sweat and, later, pray aloud in his quarters.

I felt for him. All he had wanted was to secure an alliance with France, which he'd accomplished in April, but with the king lashing out in all directions, it—along with the cardinal's other plans—was constantly in jeopardy.

We were often at Greenwich, my favorite of the many palaces. This was good and bad, because as I escaped Hampton Court and Tom, at Greenwich, I was faced with Bess.

She cornered me in the hall and sat with me at a table. The room was packed, and I pretended not to hear her question until she repeated it. "You're hiding something, and I would know what it is."

I tried to put her off. "I know not how to dissemble, Bess."

"By all the saints," she said, her voice mocking, "if there is one art you have learned in that household, you have just named it." Her hand tightened on my forearm, making me put down my knife. "You will tell me, or I will go to Hampton myself. Is he not well?"

Despite my recent adventures, I was uncomfortable speaking of romantic matters, and I believed Tom deserved privacy. But Bess would not be put off. "If you must know, he has a woman."

She looked as if I'd struck her. "Who is she?"

I watched her face as I told her what little I knew. "Bess, are you all right?"

"Yes." She sounded not at all right. "You've just given me a shock. You tell me that the world is ended and then ask if I'm all right."

"It's your own fault, prying it out of me in a room full of

people." I handed her a cup. "Take a little of this; it will clear your head."

We walked about the great hall after we left the table. She had taken the news badly, and I didn't want to leave her alone to brood. We'd made one circuit when Nick Hawkins approached. Tucking my hand under her elbow, I turned so we walked away from him, forcing him to either wait or chase us down.

Within moments, he appeared before us, his effortless bow making his short cape swirl. "Secretary Lewis," he said, "I have not yet had an opportunity to welcome you back. The cardinal keeps you busy, I fear."

"I would fear if he did not." I was reluctant to speak with him. "You are well, sir?"

"Well in all but one respect." He gave me the wolfish smile that women inexplicably found attractive. "I have a great desire to speak with Mistress Bess, if you would but relinquish her."

I hadn't expected to feel such wrenching guilt. It was bad timing to encounter him. Had he seen us and decided to manipulate her when she was upset? I wouldn't put it past him, but I also didn't believe she would return to him so easily when he was one of the causes of Tom's removal from court.

For the remainder of our stay, I kept my distance. The day before we were to depart, a page found me: Bess requested my company in the practice rooms whenever I could get away. I went slowly to join her, still uncomfortable in those areas of my former life, wondering if she had chosen the location to keep me off balance. I soon understood that my feelings weren't important enough to register.

"I won't keep you but a moment." She was on edge, pacing instead of sitting with me on the bench. "I've a few questions, if you'll answer them."

"If I can."

"Is Tom in love with that girl?"

Damn. "I wish I'd never told you."

She looked calm, but I could see her fists clenched in her skirts. Energy crackled off her like lightning. "Is he in love with her?"

There was no point in giving false hope. "I think so. He's happy with her; I know that much."

She turned away. Years of performing had given her mastery of herself, but this was a struggle. Even the line of her back showed distress. "And has he taken her into his bed?"

"Bess!"

"Tell me."

"Yes."

A long silence. Another man might have tried to comfort her. I was not that man, even without Hawkins's money, and it disturbed me. Was I incapable of human warmth, but for exceptional circumstances?

"Thank you." Her voice held no hint of a quiver. "That's all I needed to know."

I rose then and took her hands. "Life gives us all hard decisions, Bess. If you need to speak again, I'm here."

She shook her head. A few wisps of hair had escaped her coif and curled around her temples. It made her look like the girl I had once so disliked. "I must go, Robin. If I do not see you before you leave, I thank you again."

I walked with her, down the stairs from the practice rooms and toward the more public area of the palace. When she turned away, I took her arm. "I shouldn't tell him so soon." I knew where she was bound; she'd learned what she needed to make her decision. "Make him wait."

Returning to Hampton, I was unlucky enough to encounter Tom straight from the river. I greeted him and kept walking with the others, a line of black-clad ducklings following the cardinal, but when he called to me, I stopped.

The pallor and sadness that had dogged his handsome face for the last half-year was lessened, if not gone entirely. "How was the court?"

I was not being drawn into another such conversation. "Have you written any new songs recently?" He played when called upon, beautifully, but he was not the musician he had been.

"A few, but…" His eyes went distant. "I still write for her voice. I can't imagine anyone else singing them."

I wanted to shake him—to shake them both—for the pain they caused each other and for the inconvenience to all of our lives. If they could just admit they cared! I thought Tom might have done that, and Bess had run like a deer because she could not see that the pretty thing upon which she had set her heart was not for her.

"Keep writing," I advised. "You'll find another voice eventually." It was all I could think to say.

He raised his hand, still holding the lute. "I'll try, Rob." Remembering his original mission, he repeated, "How was the court?"

It was the same code she used. "How was the court?" meant no more than "How is the other half of me?" It irritated me to be their go-between, but even I could see that they could not speak and remain whole.

"She's fine." I shifted the cardinal's papers to my other arm. "I must be going."

He followed me. "Fine? What does that mean?"

"She is fine," I said, "in the same way that you are fine. How is Lucy?"

He made the connection, looking like a man who had suffered a mortal wound. "She returned to him?"

"She has done no more than you have." My patience was at an end. "If you cannot live together, there is nothing to say that you must live alone. Make the best of your lives, and please, for all that is holy—leave me out of them."

Chapter 35

"I PROMISE THAT WILL be my last mention of him."

Will Hawkins's color is high. He is very close to losing his temper, something he has managed to control thus far.

"You're very sensitive where your father is concerned. Most men your age would be proud to have such a rutting stag as their progenitor."

His hand flashes out before I see it, and I jolt backward, just saving myself from falling off the bench. There is a scuffle on the other side of the room; Seb is being held by two men with whom he had been dicing.

"What did you expect?" Hawkins shakes out his hand, no better prepared for blows than my face.

"There was no need for that." I rub my cheek. "Only stupid men resort to violence, and only women slap."

He pushes away from the table. "We have to go. You're trying to keep me in this place all day, telling stories, and we have miles to cover."

I swallow the last of my ale. "You've alarmed Seb," I tell him. "He'll ride at my heels for the rest of the day now, so you'll have to temper your actions."

"I could send him off," he threatens. "You don't need a servant."

Shrugging, I respond, "You'd have to allot someone to help me; you can't watch my every move. With Seb, you know where his loyalties lie."

As we gather ourselves, I continue, trying to weave a thread of doubt into his mind. "Have you ever thought about the difficulty of loyalty in these times? In my life—in the last twenty-five years, in *your* lifetime—we've had two kings, two queens—if you count

Jane Grey—and all six of Henry's queens drew breath during that period. We've had Catholicism, the break with Rome, Edward's further reforms, and Mary's return to the pope."

Hawkins blinks at me, registering the breadth of the history I've witnessed and, thus far, survived. "That's quite a list."

I pull on my cap. "It is indeed. How does a man choose his loyalties these days? Do you even know?"

Chapter 36

CARDINAL WOLSEY KEPT HIS many projects going like a street entertainer juggling balls or plates or flaming swords. Many were in charge of these undertakings, but Wolsey knew them all and their progress.

Until the coming of the so-called Great Matter, the cardinal had always pleased the king. He met his match in Anne Boleyn and in the king's pig-headed refusal to give up on the idea of an annulment of his perfectly-legal marriage.

It was ridiculous on its face, the annulment. He'd received a dispensation to marry Katherine, which made his current protestation—that his marriage was invalid because of the prohibition against marrying a brother's widow—a bit far-fetched. Even if the pope were feeling morally flexible, the proximity of Katherine's nephew, the Holy Roman emperor, would prevent such a declaration.

The cardinal squirmed. He'd always found a solution before; he would find one again and, meanwhile, pray that the king would lose interest in his paramour. It didn't seem likely; anyone who saw Henry with her would know he was besotted. So long as she kept him out of her bed, he would behave like one of her spaniels, wagging his tail and panting for treats.

I was often tasked with letters of diplomacy and translating documents as concerned the cardinal's French peace. He kept up a brisk correspondence with his counterparts, never completely giving up on the idea of a French bride—if only the king would rid himself of the Boleyn woman.

Thankfully, I was not much involved in the annulment, though speculation about it filled every conversation. I was fully aware of the cardinal's lack of progress, and if there was a detail I missed, Ned filled me in.

Wolsey had an array of suggestions, depending on the papal mood: first, that the original dispensation went against Leviticus and was therefore invalid; second, that if valid, the original dispensation was incorrectly worded and was, therefore, still invalid; and third, that the decision should be made in England, by the papal legate—Cardinal Wolsey himself.

To everyone's surprise, the pope offered to send a special legate to discuss the annulment and to help find a solution to everyone's liking. Cardinal Campeggio was an absentee bishop in England already, and Wolsey was optimistic that this would sway the Italian to his cause. The king certainly thought so.

Despite this positive turn of events, the household was unsettled. It had been a difficult summer—the sweat had come to England again, sickening many, including Anne Boleyn, her brother, and her father. It would have been too convenient if she had been taken, but she recovered, to plague my lord cardinal throughout that season and the ones to follow.

Wolsey was away with the king for at least another week, hiding from the sweat. During his absence, a Welsh courier had come to plead a minor case for his lord. He had become friends with Bess during an earlier visit, so I invited her to Hampton. I made it plain that I would keep her from Tom, and I did, until Bess and the Welshman combined to force a reunion.

I believe the shock weakened Tom, for on the day Bess was to leave, we learned he had fallen ill. The sweat had been at Hampton earlier in the season, and I'd kept myself distant from the sick. Being able to nurse them without fear was a holy endeavor, and I did not possess that strength. I chose, for many reasons, to not look back on my own illness.

I watched in awed surprise as my flighty friend dedicated herself to the battle for Tom's life. When a doctor could not be found, she cared for him herself, her only assistant an elderly monk who brought the herbs she requested. I stayed outside the chamber with Ewan and a few of Tom's friends.

When one of the household priests learned there was illness under our roof, he came to pray over Tom and to give him extreme unction.

"You won't have an easy time of it," Ewan said as the priest made ready to storm the doors of Bess's private sickroom.

"God's will must be served." He closed the door swiftly behind him.

Ewan turned to me. "God's will is being served in that room."

I wasn't so sure. Bess was doing what she always did—what she thought was right—and the consequences would be what they were. This time, the consequences could be Tom's life. The priest was trying to save his immortal soul as Bess was trying to preserve his body.

Within minutes, Father Francis emerged, his face red with fury. "That young woman has taken his soul upon herself," he sputtered. "Be it on her when he dies." He stormed off toward the chapel to pray away the sulfurous taint of a strong-minded woman.

Ewan reached for his harp and plucked a few notes. "This is all the religion they need."

I left as he began to play. He was right, of course: music was their religion. But I was unnerved by Bess's rejection of the priest. New religion or old, God deserved respect.

I prayed Tom would live, because I feared what would happen if he died.

The doctor came on the third day and succeeded where Father Francis had not. I'd called Bess selfish in choosing to nurse him herself, but when she stumbled through the door, clothes disheveled, her damp hair straggling in her face, I reconsidered. She swayed on her feet, and Ewan moved immediately to wrap her in his cloak. All I could do was stare.

God was on her side. Tom recovered, and afterward, they were tender and tentative and wary with each other, but they had mended what was broken. When he left his bed, Bess was by his side, and when the king came back to Greenwich, Tom applied to return to the Music and marry his love.

The king, in love himself and wanting to see love around him, granted both requests.

Chapter 37

"You may relax, Hawkins. I have done with slandering—or telling the truth—about your father. I am finished with talking of his mistress, and my friend. At least for the moment."

Hawkins rolls his eyes. "I never knew what a wide-ranging acquaintance he had at court."

Is it a sign? Have I reached him? "All men have a wide-ranging acquaintance, if they've a head on their shoulders. You never know who might be useful." Nick Hawkins—or Lord Kelton, the king having elevated him before his marriage—had a head on his shoulders, and once he stopped thinking with the one between his legs, he did quite well for himself. I stop myself. I would deserve another blow if I said that aloud.

A bawdy song breaks out behind us. Seb is teaching the guards a tavern song he learned in the Low Countries. I smile and let him have his moment. The more friends we have, the better.

When they cease, I ask, "Where is today's stopping point?" I tug off my gloves. The unceasing cycle of wet-dry-wet has made them stiff, and I fear they, along with my joints, will never recover.

"Kenwood House."

I know the name. It irritates me that I cannot attach a master to it, but I will find out soon enough.

Chapter 38

As the king's displeasure with the cardinal became more obvious, more men were pulled into the undertaking of the annulment. One recent addition was a London lawyer called Thomas Cromwell. The son of a brewer—or a blacksmith, depending on the speaker's opinion of him—he was in charge of funds for the cardinal's pet projects: the Cardinal Colleges and his elaborate tomb.

Among his methods of fund-raising were the closure of some small monasteries and confiscation of their lands. The project was undertaken with the cardinal's blessing, and apparently that of the pope, so any protests were put up to the usual anti-Wolsey sentiment.

Cromwell himself was a man some twenty years my senior, dark and a bit stocky, with a brisk, authoritative manner. He knew everything that went on, whether or not it pertained to his bailiwick. By all appearances, he had a great affection for the cardinal. The colleges, even more than the tomb, were Wolsey's legacy, and the fact that he trusted Cromwell showed the cardinal's high opinion.

He was, I thought, the coming man. He was like Wolsey in that he was able to handle many projects simultaneously, without neglecting any of them. I was attracted to minds that encompassed worlds.

We met briefly over the cardinal's business, but I never had a chance to speak with him outside of that until we met one evening at the Bonnato house. Needing to get away from my desk, I took the long walk from York Place to Chelsea, using a book I wished to loan to Bianca as my excuse. When Vincent saw me, he brought me into the hall, where he was hosting a rowdy group of merchants—and Master Cromwell.

Cromwell was seated near Vincent and across from Michelangelo Lombardi, a Genoese merchant whose firm met much of the court's endless requirement for black velvet. I did not mark Cromwell at first, for his Italian was as fluent—and as loud—as any other man at the table, but he noted my arrival without interrupting the flow of his conversation.

Vincent introduced me to the assembly, many of whom I had encountered there before. Despite my protests, I was encouraged to take food and join in the gathering.

I liked the chance to practice my Italian, but Cromwell's presence made me uneasy. He paid me no mind, talking to one of the other men about the commissioning of sculptures for the cardinal's tomb.

"He keeps you on because you can speak to us," Lombardi said with a sharp look. "He is afraid we will cheat him."

"He keeps me on because I'm an excellent lawyer," Cromwell returned, not at all insulted. "And also because he is afraid you will cheat him, you thieving bastards."

A wave of laughter swept the table, and the conversation moved from the cardinal's angels to stone-cutting generally, the quality of wine in the stony regions, and the quality of wine at the Bonnato table, which Vincent proclaimed to be superior.

"It is Tuscan," he said. "I am a proud son of Venice, but the south grows a better grape." He raised his glass to the entire table. "*Italia!*"

"*Italia!*" we chorused and downed another glass of that very excellent Florentine red.

As the gathering broke up, I found myself bundled into a wherry with Cromwell and another merchant, John Cavalcante.

"Shall we put in at York Place?"

"If it be not out of your way." I couldn't remember where Cromwell lived.

"We're at Austin Friars." He showed no sign of intoxication, though he'd consumed at least four unwatered glasses since my arrival. "It's no bother."

He and Cavalcante kept up their discussion in the bow while I sat behind, allowing the river breeze, scented with garbage, to clear my head. By the time we bumped up against the dock at York

Place, I was myself again. I reached into my purse for a coin for the boatman, but Cromwell held up his hand. "My pleasure," he said, "to assist another of the cardinal's men to his bed."

I bade them good night, and the swirl of Italian began before the boatman dipped his oars into the water.

As my friendship with Ned grew, we rearranged our quarters so that we slept in the same small chamber with only two others. Ned learned my quirks as I learned his. He could borrow my clothes—those that fit him—but it was worth his life if he touched my books or papers. In exchange, I could touch anything of his beyond a small bundle of ribbon-tied correspondence from his sister.

He teased me about my library, which could scarcely be hidden in the chest beneath my bed. "You can't need this many books," he said. "You'd have money for entertainment if you sold a few of them."

I whipped my head around to stare at him. "Sell my books?"

"You can't need that many, man." He threw himself on the bed, scattering the two volumes I had not yet put away. "There are other things in life, Rob—people, for instance."

"I prefer the people in here." I gestured at the *Historia Regum Britanniae* Ned had so nearly deposited on the floor.

"People exist outside books, you know."

"I know that."

"Do you?" His gaze impaled me. "Then that makes it worse when you treat people as less important than a block of paper and ink."

"They are more than that to me." How could I tell him what books meant? They had been the only source of truth my entire life. I had found myself—and other people—in books, explaining human behavior to me when my own limited experience would not allow me to grasp it. How could he say that a book was just paper and ink?

"Fine," he said. "How much more? Are they more important than people? All people or just some people? Just the people that you like?" He sat up, risking Geoffrey of Monmouth again. "Actually, do you like any people?"

Taken aback, I said, "Of course I like people."

"Name five," he said. "Five people you like more than your blessed books."

I could think of five people, but Ned did not know most of them, and I did not want to expose them to his gaze.

"See," he said. "Not one."

"My friends, Bess and Tom," I said. "The minstrels."

"I know them." He cocked his head. "That's two."

"I have a friend in Chelsea," I muttered. "Mistress Turner."

"Mistress Turner, eh?" He raised an eyebrow. "That's three."

Salvatore had been the first name to come to mind. So much of my relationship with him was bound up with books: discussion, disputation, genial wrangling. "Antonio," I said, using his birth name. "A friend from Italy. We've lost touch now."

"Four!" Ned crowed. "I didn't think you could do it. Who's the fifth, Rob?"

"You are," I said. "If you weren't important, do you think I would tolerate this kind of nonsense? And since I apparently cannot rid myself of your friendship, I may as well cultivate it. Would you like to come to dinner at Mistress Turner's this week? I think you would find the company most interesting."

Tom was late. I waited with Bess in the practice room, the location of our long-ago competition, which served them as an apartment when no one was using it. They had a private chamber on the top floor, but it was not large enough for guests.

Marriage suited her, which surprised me not at all; she had been made for the fate she resisted.

"You look happy."

She looked different, somehow—fuller—though I did not think she was yet with child. "I wasted so much time, Rob. I need to savor every moment we've been given."

"How is Tom?"

"He is a wonder. He plays better than ever. He's working on a new song for the Lady Anne."

That was a wonder, for I knew Tom's sentiments toward that lady. "The King will be pleased."

"He will." She lowered her voice. "Tom says he pretends he's writing about me."

We lapsed into silence, drinking in the peace of the afternoon and the sound of birds outside.

"Have you ever been in love?"

What had brought that on? I debated, then told her the truth. "Yes."

"And nothing came of it?"

"No." I thought of Salvatore's dark eyes, his crooked smile. "It was an impossible situation."

"That's why you are the way you are." Sitting in the window, with her legs tucked up under her skirts, she reminded me very much of the opinionated Bess of our youth.

"And how is that?"

"Stunted." She gazed at me with pity, wanting the whole world to feel as she did. "You must let yourself love people and let them love you."

I knew how to love. I just didn't know many people worth loving. "I am capable of love." This reminded me far too much of my conversation with Ned; why was it impossible for my friends to stay out of my affairs? "I love you and Tom."

"That's different," she said. "I asked you if you had been *in* love."

"And I said yes." Bess was like a dog with a bone when it was a topic she wished to discuss, slippery as an eel when it was not.

"Was it requited?" She was sharp, for all her dithering ways.

"In a way," I said, then, "No. It was not."

Salvatore cared for me, perhaps even loved me, but not in the way I wanted. His vow of chastity was not what stood between us; he loved me as I loved Ned or Bess, not as I loved him. He loved me as a friend, a brother.

She put her hand on mine. "It's not the same as having them love you back, Robin. I should know."

The door opened then to Tom, saving me from any further talk of my love life. "How now, Tom, I hear you've penned a new song for the lady!"

He grimaced and then straightened his face at Bess's cluck of reproof. "I write a love song to *my* lady," he said. "How it is taken when sung does not concern me."

They were babies, the pair of them, blind in love and oblivious to the world around them. If that's what love did, I was better off without it.

"I came to invite the two of you to dinner in Chelsea this Friday if you're able to get away." I looked pointedly at Bess. "I almost withdrew the invitation because your wife is so annoying, and she may only come if she promises to behave. Ned will be there, and it is difficult enough to keep him on good behavior."

I must have been mad, I thought as Ned and I made our way to Chelsea from York Place. Bianca had offered before to host a dinner for my friends, and I had always demurred, not wanting to put her to any trouble. Vincent cornered me one evening and said, "You insult my sister by not allowing her to give hospitality to your friends."

That was the last thing I wanted. "I've strained your hospitality enough by being here so often," I said. "I did not want to bother you further."

He put a hand on my arm. "This is the happiest I've seen her since we were children together."

It was difficult to resist such an invitation. My friends were few enough: Ned, Bess, and Tom, three people whom I could trust to not make a scene or ask embarrassing questions. I asked Tom to bring his lute so that we would have entertainment if the conversation dried up.

I need not have worried. Vincent had invited a few English merchants and their wives, and the talk before and during dinner was lively. Seated at Bianca's left, I could feel her pleasure. "My friends are to your liking?"

"The young couple are a delight," she said. "And your friend, Master Pickering, is charming."

He was very charming. Ned on his best behavior was a delight to anyone—he told stories fit for public consumption, imitated his betters amid general laughter, and flattered Vincent until he preened like a peacock.

Bess and Tom were quieter, but I had earlier seen Bess speaking with Bianca, and it made me happy. They both needed friends outside of their small worlds, and I was pleased that I could bring them together, even briefly.

After the meal was finished and the table cleared out of the way, I asked Bianca if she would like my friends to perform for the assembly.

"They are guests in our house," she said. "It would not be polite to ask them to entertain."

Tom overheard and stepped forward. "Please, Mistress Turner, allow us—we are entertainers, after all, and I would like to repay you for this wonderful meal. Bess and I don't get away from court often, and this has been a treat."

A stool was brought for Tom, and Bess stood beside him. She looked like a bird in her blue-green gown, her abundant hair tucked away beneath a matching French hood. She sang like one too: her voice had never lost its childlike purity, but it had a richer tone now.

Their performance stilled the room, as it did every room in which they had ever performed. Bianca's hands were clasped to her breast, the lace at her wrists trembling with suppressed emotion. Vincent's eyes were closed, and the merchants and their ladies appeared to know just what they were witnessing: two exceptional musicians at the height of their powers, performing for the love of it.

I had listened to them for years, yet even I was drawn into the beauty of it—Bess's sure voice, Tom's playing, the songs they chose to perform. Tom even resurrected one of the Italian songs his rival had introduced to the court, which astounded me. How could he bear to play it when the singer of that song had taken his place in the king's affections and in the Music?

But play he did, and as he continued, there came a rumble, which was Vincent clearing his throat and beginning to haltingly sing along. Bianca's eyes flew to her brother, and she, who preferred her invisibility above almost all things, sang with him.

Brother and sister sang the song through, and at a glance from Tom, did it again and better. When the music stopped, the hall erupted into applause—for our hosts, for Bess and Tom, and from the sheer joy of what we had experienced.

Music was no longer part of my life, but there were times that I missed it.

A constant low level of dread underlay everything. The improbable was now certain: Anne Boleyn would get her way, and the cardinal would be arrested. Wolsey had been at court since the time of the old king. He'd helped Henry become the monarch he was, yet that did not matter. One impossible task uncompleted was enough to undo decades of mostly unselfish work.

Selfishly, the men of his household worried about what would become of us. If the cardinal fell from grace, would we fall with him? I thought not, but I had also never expected to see Thomas Wolsey in such dire straits.

Charges were brought in early October, and by the middle of the month, Wolsey was dismissed as lord chancellor, replaced by Thomas More. His estates reverted to the king, and the cardinal himself was banished to his house at Esher. Only a few servants accompanied him, and none of his staff.

The Bonnato house was a refuge, and never more so than at this low point in my fortunes. Vincent and Bianca welcomed me, assuring me that I could stay for as long as I wished—permanently, if I chose. Living in their civilized home, with a place for my books and my lover in the next chamber, was tempting but unrealistic.

For the first few days, I entertained a series of visitors who came bearing information. Bianca called it gossiping, but it wasn't; we were trying to build a complete picture of what was going on, and there were many pieces missing.

Should I offer myself to Sir Thomas More? He rose every day in the king's opinion, but he had a select cadre of young men already, and they were all vocal anti-reform Catholics. I would not likely meet his standards.

I thought again of Cromwell. Certainly, he had been busy enough over the past few years. In addition to his work on the colleges and his involvement with the Italian community, he had contacts all over Europe due to his early career. He was careful too; after our single meeting, I had never again seen him at the Bonnato house.

Ned was in a similar situation. He retreated to his family's estate, not far from Esher, where rumors of the cardinal would easily reach his ears. He came to see me at Chelsea before departing, and his composure was only slightly ruffled. "I do not believe the cardinal will remain out of favor," he said. "Wolsey has been the king's dearest councilor since he came to the throne. No man could be so ungrateful."

I prayed he was right but decided to bide my time and see which way the wind blew before committing myself to a new master.

Chapter 39

Friday, November 14,
to Saturday, November 15, 1558
Kenwood House
Lincolnshire

DUSK IS WELL-SETTLED BY the time we reach Kenwood; we will be late for supper, if we are at all expected. We clatter through an arch and into a wide courtyard. Hawkins and his men have dismounted before the oaken door swings wide, spilling light onto the stones.

Several men come out, hands on their swords, until my captor calls to them, "I'm Hawkins. I was offered a night here on my way south."

A man steps forward. Torchlight gleams on hair the color of beaten gold, and I know, before I hear his sly voice, who the master of Kenwood might be.

"Congratulations on your quarry." Jack Darlington looks at me as if we've never met, but I see it in his eyes, the old loathing. "Why isn't the man bound, for Christ's sake?"

Hawkins looks from Darlington to me. "He's not likely to run."

I set my teeth and dismount. Seb holds the reins, and he takes my arm as I land, in case my knee gives way. I would not want to fall, not here. Sheltered by my mount, I straighten my hat and tug my doublet into a proper fit. "Jack." I force a smile. "It's been a long time."

He turns away, still bearing a grudge. "You've missed supper," he says over his shoulder. "I'll provide a barred room for the prisoner, and then you and I can sit down."

Hawkins looks at me.

I shrug. "That's a tale for tomorrow—if he doesn't kill me in my sleep."

He hastens after our host. "No need for locks and guards,

Darlington. I've my own men, and I've been sharing a chamber with him each night to make certain he doesn't escape."

I walk between two of those men, their grip firm but not ungentle. Jack is in the hall, speaking to Hawkins. On the far side of the chamber, beyond the fire, is a pale woman in a gray gown, her arms around two small children. At a look from her husband, she straightens and hustles the little ones up the stairs and away from the criminal in their midst.

"Orson, take him up and put him in the corner room. Set a guard outside." He turns back to Hawkins. "My men can watch him while you and yours have a meal."

"Am I to starve?" I look from Darlington to Hawkins.

"Fine by me," Darlington says, "except Her Majesty would have naught but a corpse to burn. You'll get what you deserve, Lewis, and no more."

His men catch me up and twist my arms behind my back until they threaten to pop their sockets. Seb gets in between and takes a punch to the jaw that lays him out on the planked floor.

"Hawkins!" I shout.

"Go quietly, Lewis," he says, reaching for the cup. "They won't hurt you."

Still struggling, I am dragged up the stairs.

Once we reach the landing, Orson pulls a dagger from its sheath and holds it to my throat. "The master would reward me if I stuck you." His breath is foul, all ale and rotting teeth.

I turn my head away, and the blade creases my neck.

"That's a pennyworth of blood!" The other man laughs, binding my wrists behind me.

After that, they amuse themselves for a good while, tossing me back and forth like boys with a pig's bladder. When I fall—as I must, because I cannot balance—they aim a few kicks at my ribs and low back. I cry out, try to scramble away, and land awkwardly on my bad knee. The pain makes me vomit, and they swear and kick me again. Orson drags me upright and tosses me into a dark room and slams the door.

I've always disliked the sort of men who attach themselves to Darlington.

I get up, bracing my shoulder against some large crate or piece of furniture. I try to keep the weight off my knee, which is sending streaks of fire up and down my leg. My stomach threatens to empty itself again, and I swallow hard.

The chamber is nothing more than a storage room, I discover by slow investigation. I settle myself against a chest and try to shake out my cloak so it rests around me. There is no light and certainly no heat.

It's not likely Hawkins will leave me here overnight, and if he does, I'll be no worse off in the morning, just a bit stiffer than usual. It's better than being in the hall, subjected to Darlington's smirk; I would do myself no good if I wiped it from his face, no matter how much better I would feel.

There's a scuffle outside, the sound of men fighting. A shoulder slams into the panel, shaking the frame. I hear Seb's voice. "Master, I'll see you free of this place!"

"I'm all right," I call. "Don't get hurt over this; we'll be gone in the morning."

"You'll be here as long as Master Jack wishes," another voice says, and I hear the sickening smack of fist on flesh and the sound of someone sliding down the wall.

At first, I don't worry, but as hours pass and my bruises make themselves known, I begin to wonder. Is Hawkins still my captor, or has he handed me off to Darlington? Was that always the plan?

Did I survive this long to be undone by that little shit? A shaking starts in my midsection and spreads outward. I am confident in my ability to manage Hawkins, stringing him along with stories and minor delays, but my tales will not deter Jack Darlington.

I spend an uncomfortable night. Trying to sleep with my arms bound is nearly impossible, but I need rest. I can't face him again without all my wits.

A rattling at the door makes me sit up, and I catch my breath as my bruised muscles try to move. The door swings open to reveal Hawkins, with Seb at his shoulder.

"Jesus!" He kneels beside me. "What did they do to you?"

"I told you." Seb unties me, rubbing the circulation back into my hands. His lip is split, and one eye is swollen and purpled, but he seems otherwise unharmed.

I begin to relax. I could not live with myself if something happened to Seb. With a stifled sob, I put my arm around him.

"Can you walk, master?" He looks doubtful.

"I can walk, or someone can carry me," I say. "I'll not spend another minute in this house."

Together, we make a slow journey down the stairs to the hall, where our host stands waiting for us.

"This man was your guest, Darlington," Hawkins says stiffly, "even if he is a heretic." He looks genuinely distressed. "You said he was comfortably housed."

Jack shrugs. "You were content to sit and drink my ale all the night long. If you were so concerned about your man, you should have gone up and bedded down with him instead of falling asleep in front of the fire."

My face grows hot, and I wait for Hawkins to respond.

"I believed you were a gentleman." His voice wobbles a bit. "We'll be off, but first I would have breakfast brought for Master Lewis."

"I won't take a bite under his roof." I meet those cold blue eyes. "He's probably shat in the pottage."

Darlington takes a swipe at me, but Seb and Hawkins block him. "You can say whatever you want now," he snarls, "but you'll sing a different tune when they light the pyre at your feet."

I'm thirsty, I'm hungry, and I'm bursting to piss, but I manage a calm tone. "I wouldn't be so bold, Jack. I'm not the only man alive who remembers who you were. You rode north to see Aske hanged, and you were quite the merry Jack about it, as I recall."

"Liar!" He swings again.

Hawkins catches his wrist.

"Queen Mary may burn me, but she'll find you out in the end."

Seb drags me bodily toward my horse. "Master," he says, boosting me into the saddle, "please shut your mouth before you get us all killed."

I open my mouth to speak and decide he is right.

The house has disappeared before Will Hawkins speaks. "I'm sorry about what happened back there. I didn't know your history, obviously."

"You'll hear it soon enough," I say. "If you're still listening."

"Oh, I am." He looks tired. "It appears I have much to learn about people."

Chapter 40

FIVE YEARS WENT BY, during which time my life was uneventful. This is worth noting simply because of the times in which I lived.

Along with Ned, I joined Cromwell's household in late 1529. He seemed the most likely to survive the constant storms at court, and like the cardinal, he needed many clerks to keep his works moving.

None of us understood how he transformed himself from a man with deep ties to the disgraced cardinal to the king's newest favorite. One day, he was supporting Wolsey and keeping his head down, and the next, he was the king's entirely beloved and trusted friend, while somehow maintaining his loyalty to the cardinal—while he lived.

Cromwell worked diligently on the issue of the divorce at which his predecessor had failed. Did he support Anne Boleyn, or did he simply favor her for her part in driving a wedge between the king and the church?

The king and his not-yet-queen went to France in the autumn of 1532, and it was during this trip that she finally gave way. Henry gave way in turn and married her while his first wife still lived, because of the child he'd put in her belly.

That child was born—a girl, alas—but everyone was certain the next one would be a boy. The superstitious part of me wondered if the king would ever get what he wanted while he taunted God with his bigamy, but I wasn't stupid enough to say it aloud. I barely permitted myself to think it.

Working for Cromwell, I learned that he was more of a reformer than he let on, truly devoted to the Lutheran ideals he'd picked up on his travels. He gently mocked me for my own divided loyalties and what he called my sentimental attachment to the monasteries.

That attachment became an issue in the autumn of 1535 when, as part of a scheme to finance the king's lavish spending, as well as to destroy the monasteries, a dual program of evaluations was begun: a public survey of properties owned by the church and a separate, private valuation done by the king's commissioners— Cromwell's men.

This brought me into eventual conflict with Jack Darlington, whose presence would dog me for the rest of my days.

Austin Friars, Cromwell's house and the place where he conducted most of the king's business, was full of young men, and new ones arrived on a near-daily basis. I was assigned three of them to assist with the evaluations, and it was apparent from the start that Darlington would be a problem.

Sent to court by his rich northern father, he was a pretty young man, and he knew it. His blond curls were covered by the neatest of bonnets, trimmed always with fresh feathers, and the shirts which protruded through his slashed doublet were of fine quality. He favored popinjay colors, all those allowed to him by law, and undoubtedly I looked a ragged crow next to him, yet I was his superior.

My seniority, due to my time with both the cardinal and Cromwell, was nothing when weighed against my background; Darlington, second son though he was, could not bear to be supervised by a bastard nobody, and yet bear it he must because Cromwell advanced on merit. Though I had no family, I had an abundance of merit.

The road wound through grain fields, filled at this time of year with workers bringing in the last of the harvest. I tried to ignore the fluttering in my stomach as we rode toward Morden Priory. Who was I to walk into such a place and make demand of the prior for his records and to inventory the possessions of his house?

I understood the program as Cromwell laid it out for us: a number of small houses across England contained so few members that they would be more efficient combined. Such consolidations had been carried out in the past, but I didn't believe it was our place to pass such judgments. Previously, these visits would have been made by the local bishop or a senior member of the order. For all the king's wrangling with the pope, monasteries still belonged to the church, and the church was, as yet, in Rome. The church did not care how many men or women were left in these houses, only that they remained, offering up prayers and taking in tithes; it was the government of England that looked toward efficiency.

A novice came to greet us as we trotted through the gate. He was followed by a tall, ragged boy who smiled widely and reached for our reins.

I dismounted, steeling myself. "Good afternoon to you both, and God be with you. We are come from the court to see the prior."

The boy led our horses away, and the novice gestured for us to follow him. "The prior is unwell," he told us. "I am instructed to take visitors to the sub-prior, Brother John."

"We're here to see the prior," Darlington said, edging ahead of me. "We'll have none of your excuses."

I shot him a look. "I would be pleased to speak with Brother John. He may determine whether our errand is important enough to disturb the prior."

Once in the visitors' room in the chapter house, I turned to the three newcomers. "You will follow my lead in this matter," I said, staring hard at Darlington. "None of this demanding to see anyone. How you speak to people is important, and a monastery is a different world from the court or Austin Friars."

"It's an old world." His tone was aggressive. "It's a world that should be burned to the ground."

I pressed my lips together, mastering myself before I spoke. "I am in charge of this excursion, not you, boy. You will do as instructed, or you will wait with the horses. I don't care if we stay a week; I will have them bring your meals to the stables."

Petrie and Conyng snickered, as boys do when a bully is brought low.

"Do you understand?"

He muttered an affirmative, but I would not let it rest. "I didn't hear you."

"Yes, Master Lewis." The words were forced through gritted teeth. Darlington and I had tangled once or twice before, but it had been over office procedure; this was something larger.

"God be with you, gentlemen." The sub-prior entered through a small side door. "I apologize for my delay. I was visiting with Father Theodore when I was told of your arrival." He was a man of perhaps fifty, of middling height but strongly built. "I am Brother John. How may I assist you?"

Bowing, I introduced myself and the others. "I am sorry to hear the prior is unwell. Is his illness serious?"

"He is in his eightieth year," Brother John said. "A long life gives more than its share of aches and pains, but he is steadfast in his faith, and our Lord will deliver him." He looked at me plainly. "What business do you have with us, Master Lewis?"

"I am here on behalf of the vicar general," I told him, using one of Cromwell's titles. "Members of that office are being sent to all the small religious houses."

"Another visitation?" His broad brow creased in confusion. "But we have already been visited by Sir Tobias Pinkney."

"That was for the *Valor Ecclesiasticus*." It was no explanation. "His visit was an examination of church property."

"How is this different, may I ask?"

"This is an inquiry into the health and operation of smaller religious houses across all England. A similar exercise was carried out under Cardinal Wolsey, and some houses were closed or combined at that time."

Brother John folded his hands, for all appearances calm, though I could see his knuckles showed white. "Several of our brothers came here then," he said. "Has it come again?"

"It is difficult to say. I am requested to find out your numbers, the extent of your lands, the rents—a general inventory of Morden and its holdings."

Through the small door came the boy I had seen earlier, carefully carrying a jug and a tray of cups. "Ale, Brother John?"

A wide and genuine smile lit his face. "Thank you, Simon. You play the host better than I."

"Father Theodore taught me." Pouring a cup for the sub-prior, the boy asked each of us, in turn, "Ale?" and then poured another brimming cup. He moved deliberately, and his round face turned frequently to the sub-prior for approval.

"That will be all, Simon." Brother John touched the boy's arm. "I will call for you if we have need."

I took a sip of the ale. "Brewed here?"

"Indeed," said the monk. "We also make a very good beer."

Darlington made a sound that I chose to interpret as a cough.

"Do you have a brother who could show my associates around and explain to them the extent and uses of the lands?"

"Yes, of course." He opened the door and called to one of the young monks, giving him my directions. When Darlington and the others went off with him, Brother John turned to me. "And what aid may I give you, Master Lewis?" He was already haggard, from worry over the prior or perhaps in anticipation of this visit, if rumor had outpaced us.

"I would sit down with you over the accounts, if you would," I said. "Or if there is another brother more familiar with them, I will work with him."

"I will take you to Brother Mark, the bursar," he said. "The accounts are his, and he can best explain them."

I followed him through the chapter house, feeling the calm of the priory settle into my bones. "I grew up in a place such as this," I volunteered. "I understand much of the workings. I am sorry to put you to this trouble."

Brother John grasped my arm. "We are a world unto ourselves," he said, "but we understand there is another world which sometimes must reach in to disturb our peace."

"I will endeavor to disturb it as little as possible."

The bursar's chamber was empty, but the sub-prior took the

account books from a chest and laid them out on the table. "I will send Brother Mark to assist you," he said. "If you need anything, call for Simon. He is always near."

"Who is he?" There were often servants in monasteries to handle public-facing duties such as the gatehouse or the stables, but I rarely saw indoor servants.

"A village boy," Brother John explained, "a holy innocent whose parents gave him up because they knew not what to do with him. They said he could not work nor listen nor go to church, but the prior took him in nigh on ten years ago, and with care, you see how well he does."

I did. The boy was not like others his age, but he knew well his duties and carried them out. It was good that a place had been found for him.

"Moonstruck, Father Theodore calls him. He himself had a sister born the same way, and he couldn't bear to see Simon abused."

Through the window, I could hear the chime of the bells from the Augustinian friary. *Four. Five. Six.*

Damn. I'd lost track of time. If I'd finished by five, I could have gone to visit Bianca and Vincent. There wasn't time now to get there, and I couldn't be away all night; there was far too much to be done.

I tidied away my papers and sharpened a few quills for morning, a habit instilled by Cardinal Wolsey, to end a day of work by preparing for the next. It stood me in good stead here in Cromwell's sphere, where everything moved quickly.

A knock showed Ned framed in the door. "I thought you'd be gone."

"So did I." I pushed my stool away from the desk. "Do you want to go to the Swanne for supper?"

He agreed readily, and we made our way through the warren of rooms that constituted the offices at Austin Friars. It was more chaotic than usual, as much of the work was relocating to the disused palace at Westminster. "Good work on Morden," he said.

"I saw it when Legh was compiling the reports. I wish I'd been part of the visitations."

"It was just a typical house."

"If that be typical, then no wonder there's talk of suppressing all the smaller houses." Ned closed his eyes. "And they call them men of God."

"What are you talking about?" My report was, on the whole, positive. I warned the prior of Morden that there might be some consolidation of smaller houses, but I'd heard nothing of suppression.

"Lax and licentious monks," my friend said, with vigor. "Treasure beyond what was reported at the last survey. Servants all over place, fetching and carrying for able-bodied monks too corrupt to do for themselves."

Servants? I remembered the moonstruck boy who had found care and usefulness in the priory. "Where are the reports?"

"On Legh's desk. Why?"

"I need to see something."

The reports, bundled together, made an impressive pile. The order was not alphabetical, but by county, and I located the section for Sussex, pulling it carefully from the stack.

The report on Morden Priory was there, but the penmanship was not mine, nor were the words. I scanned the pages, wondering what had happened to my neat listing of the priory's members, activities, and finances. The value of the land rent was doubled, and there were remarks of multiple servants. Note was made of divine offices left unsung and meat served on fish days. There was even mention of wax candles in the dorter, which was completely false.

I looked up at Ned. "This is not my report," I said. "It is an invention. A fiction."

His face showed confusion. "Who would change it? And why?"

I knew why, at least in a general sense. Cromwell assigned this project to Thomas Legh and Richard Layton, men who would do his bidding without question, and who undoubtedly knew his mind as well as anyone could. I handed over my report to Layton's assistant. What convolutions it had gone through since then I could only imagine.

I turned to Ned. "Let's get drunk."

It was not yet seven when I arrived at Austin Friars, but already I could hear Cromwell's voice echoing through the building.

Ned and I had indeed gotten drunk the night before. My head ached, and my stomach was in no state for food; my friend still slept, though I had shaken him several times. I left it with our landlady to throw water on him if he did not emerge within the hour.

I stared at my desk, trying to focus on the correspondence placed there before my arrival, but from the moment I walked through the door, the monastery report had been at the front of my mind. It had been at the front of my mind all evening, at least until I blotted it out with beer, but then, as I vomited in the gutter outside the Swanne, adding my swill to the general filth, the image of the moonstruck boy returned.

"Do you have a moment, sir?"

Cromwell was at his desk, with its massive piles of correspondence, letters that flowed to and fro across England, into Wales, over the narrow sea to the continent, filaments in the web of his network of information.

"Never and always." His fleshy face relaxed into a smile. "What's on your mind, Lewis?"

I locked my hands behind my back, looking past his shoulder at the window. "It's the report, sir, the one I submitted on Morden Priory."

He put his hand on the stack, which had moved to his desk. "I've read it. Fine work."

I hesitated. "It's not my work, sir."

Something flickered behind his eyes. "What do you mean?"

"It's not my report," I said. "Those aren't my words; it's not even in my hand. I found Morden to be a well-run house, with sufficient brothers to carry out their duties." My rough voice, never steady, showed my emotion clearly. "The facts have been changed to show the house in a bad light when there must be plenty of places to fit that description without manipulation."

Cromwell looked over his steepled fingers. "And why would someone do that?"

"To alter the perception of the priory?" I hazarded. "To convince people that any value contained therein is purely material?"

A sharp nod. "You've answered your own question."

"But it's not true." The prior, those brothers…the moonstruck boy…they deserved to be left in peace. "It's a small house, but there was no licentiousness, no slacking of their duties to God or the community."

"An isolated instance," he said blandly. "Most of the houses visited had long lists of excesses committed by the monks."

"But Morden did not." I pressed the issue. "Whoever wrote the report, and put my name to it, did not see what I saw."

"You are concerned that your words have been altered?" Cromwell looked from me to the report.

"I am more concerned that facts have been altered," I said. "What about other reports, other houses? How much of what is here is accurate?"

"It is *all* accurate." He met my eyes, and I understood the directive came from either him or the king.

"I see." Despite the risk, I could not bring myself to apologize or say that I understood. "May I be excused?"

"No." Cromwell looked out the window. "How is your French, Lewis?"

"It is excellent."

"Very well. From today, you'll be assisting me with my correspondence and interactions with the French ambassador. You'll remain here, rather than moving to Westminster." His mouth turned up at one corner. "You're a useful young man, Lewis, but I won't have you working on a policy which will aggravate your conscience. It makes you inconvenient."

I turned to go, then stopped. "Sir?"

"Yes, Lewis?"

"If I could make a suggestion…" It occurred to me that although I was uneasy with the monastery project, others were not. "My friend, Ned Pickering, would do well in my place."

"It was Jack." Ned directed the words at my ear. "He knew the purpose of the journey from the start and rewrote the report to Cromwell's satisfaction. And his praise."

I wasn't shocked. He was a grasping young man, more obvious in his ambitions than I had ever been.

"What's to be done?" Ned looked ready for action.

"There's nothing I can do." I told him of my transfer to French diplomacy, which put Jack Darlington out of my reach.

Ned frowned, an unaccustomed expression on his easy face. "He's not out of my reach. I'll make sure he has every bit of shit work I can find."

"That's not necessary." I was grateful for his loyalty, but if Jack had Cromwell's favor, I didn't want my friend dragged into my mess.

I kept an eye on the monastery project from a distance. In February, parliament passed an act shuttering all religious houses with an income of over two hundred pounds. Their lands would pass to the crown.

Not wanting to involve Ned, I acquired on my own a copy of the *Comperta*, the compilation of the reports, and learned that Morden had been dissolved. The brothers were either transferred to larger houses or, if they so wished, relieved of their vows of poverty and obedience and permitted to live a secular life. The vow of chastity remained; they could not marry.

Abbots and other senior monks were pensioned off, rather than transferred, which struck me as cruel. Morden's prior would rather die within the precincts of a monastery, even one not his own, than in a world which he had not known for five decades.

Then it struck me. The prior would accept the pension, because of the moonstruck boy, who could not follow him to another house.

The boy would look after him until his death, but what then?

I had done this. Darlington had submitted the false report, but I betrayed my upbringing by going to that house and in writing a report at all. I was as much the cause of Father Theodore's death as the age and disease which would eventually carry him off. I betrayed not only these monks, but the brothers who had raised me.

The Thames moved sluggishly through the thick reeds near the bank. I leaned against a gnarled oak and stared across at the water, my mind still working over the suppression of Morden.

There was nothing I could do. The priory was gone, its precious metals melted down, its lands leased to local gentry—including the same Tobias Pinkney who had done the earlier visitation. Its fences and bricks were scavenged by the local population for their own building projects. For the moment, even the poor benefited from the closure.

This good will would not last. When the monasteries were closed in years past, the church itself was involved, and Wolsey had used the bulk of the money for his colleges. The one in Ipswich had been closed, but Cardinal College Oxford remained, now called King Henry VIII's College.

The funds from these latest closures would not be allocated to anything so exalted. Cromwell's work was on behalf of one man only, and that man, the king, needed money for less godly endeavors. The offices at Westminster, where Ned now worked, were named the Court of Augmentations. He explained that they were so called because the money they brought in augmented the royal coffers.

Some three hundred houses were to be shuttered, and if each realized a value of several hundred pounds, the treasury would be significantly bolstered. How long would it be until the king eyed the larger houses: the abbeys and monasteries with their shrines and holy relics, the places of pilgrimage. What would happen then?

"Will you come in, my Robin, or do you intend to hold up this tree all night?" Bianca was wrapped in a furred cloak, her face shadowed by its hood. So lost was I in my thoughts that I hadn't heard her approach.

"I haven't much of an appetite," I confessed, but I let her lead me indoors.

Vincent was there with a few associates, and the table conversation was lively. At the end, as they began to discuss the effects of recent political activity on imports, I looked at Bianca. "I should go."

"Let them talk their business," she said quietly. "Come into my parlor. We have not seen each other in some time."

It was nine years since I'd found my way to this house, and in some respects, it was my home. There was a chamber always ready to receive me, and most of my books lived there, where they were safe. Sharing lodgings, or sleeping at Austin Friars or any of a half-dozen other places, never made me feel secure of my possessions.

I took Bianca's hands and brought her close. Her arms twined around my neck. Our physical relationship had subsided as I was less and less available, but our affection was deep, and there were still occasions when the door beneath the tapestry stood ajar.

"What is wrong?" She tilted her head back to look into my eyes. "You have not been here for weeks, and even now, you are not completely here."

A small fire crackled in the fireplace. I sat down on a padded stool, and Bianca settled herself on my knee, surrounding us in her skirts. I twitched the black bombazine away from drifting sparks. "If I want to keep my place at court, I may have to do things I would rather not."

"We must all do such things."

She would be one to understand that. "But there is rather not, and there is against my better judgment. Against my values. Against my heart."

"What do they ask of you?"

I explained it to her, all of it: the *Valor Ecclesiasticus*, my visit to Morden and its subsequent closure, and the act now passed by parliament which cast a shadow over all those houses that remained.

"I am afraid of what will come. The king needs money and support, and he obtains both by this measure."

"For now, it is only the smaller houses, which might be closed anyway."

I hated to douse the hope in her voice. "They might have been, but for attrition of members, not for false charges of corruption and indecency."

Such ungodly things likely did occur, especially in the closed houses which kept their wealth invisible. But at Morden or Hatton, open priories that spent their money serving the local poor, it would not have been tolerated.

"You need a distraction." Bianca reached for a book on the nearby table and showed it to me. "Boccaccio's *Decameron*. Why don't I call for wine, and we will read together until you have to leave?"

Chapter 41

WE PASS FROM LINCOLNSHIRE and turn toward Cambridge; we will, I note, bypass Leicester entirely. It seems a good omen after the night I have passed.

I am somewhat refreshed; Will Hawkins deviated from his planned route and stopped at an alehouse not far from Kenwood, paying for an enormous breakfast and as much ale as I could comfortably contain.

It's not his fault. Darlington has always convinced people of his goodness, as if goodness can be measured by pretty manners and a face to match. Hawkins has, as he says, much to learn.

"It sounds a rough time, the Anne Boleyn period." He looks off into the distance. "My father never really spoke of her. My mother once told me she pitied the lady."

She would have. Elinor Hawkins was a sweet soul. "It's difficult to convey the unease that pervaded everything. Not just Cromwell's staff and other court servants, but the nobles and the churchmen as well. Could the king put aside—kill—his queen?"

"Hadn't he already put one aside with a better claim?"

He had, and with Katherine went the church, though not all at once. It took a few more years to convince Henry of the rightness of a faith which was bendable to his will, and then he immediately made it less flexible.

Chapter 42

ONE DAY ANNE BOLEYN was Henry's cherished queen, and the next she was imprisoned, charged with crimes that would make a man blush. There was a feeling in the air that anything could happen.

I accompanied Cromwell on one of his frequent visits to Greenwich to meet with the king. We went by river, and I looked down as we passed under the arches of London Bridge. Despite the profusion of shops scattered across—and built up—along its length, the heads of the executed were still visible, and if they were not, I would know they were there by the circling kites.

We shot the rapids under the bridge with ease, the size of the barge and the time of day making it less risky. I'd seen smaller boats try the same maneuver during a high tide and capsize, and I frequently walked across to avoid an unnecessary trip on that section of the river.

It was more difficult to ignore the heads when I walked.

Cromwell was silent for most of the trip, riffling through the papers he carried in a thick folio. An attack of conscience? It could not be that; he had drawn up the warrants himself. Did the idea of her downfall start with him or with the king? He'd once been her champion, but the king was his master, not Anne Boleyn, and the king was convinced that only a new wife would give him a son. Cromwell had to help or be sucked into the maelstrom while someone else did the king's bidding.

As we entered the palace, he turned to me. "I'll meet with the king privately, Lewis. Find occupation as you will: I know you have acquaintance here. Meet me in the outer audience chamber at four of the clock."

Did he know I had acquaintance at Greenwich because of my history, or was there something ominous in his knowledge? Cromwell had spies everywhere, but I never thought to question whether he kept an eye on his loyal clerks.

Because of that, I kept to myself until after dinner, when I met Bess in the hall. We made our way to the suite reserved for the king's vicar general, principal secretary, and current favorite, all of whom were Thomas Cromwell. I felt a sliver of pride that she would see the oak-paneled room where I worked, with its windows overlooking the verdant lawns.

She noticed none of it, turning immediately to ask, "How is the queen?"

"I wouldn't know."

"How could they accuse her of such things?" Her brown eyes were bright with anger. "Unfaithful, with her own brother? It's madness."

I gave her a warning glance. "The king is not mad."

"He hunted her like a deer," Bess said, "and now he has his quarry, he is disillusioned and all out of love. That is no better reason to put her away than he had for Queen Katherine." Her feelings were evident on her face. "I love the king, but he should try to accept life as the rest of us are made to."

Such words could land her in a cell next to Smeaton. "There is nothing you can do," I said, "except remain quiet and follow my suggestions. I'll explain further when Tom gets here."

"He is off somewhere." She peered out the window, then settled quietly before me. "Tell me now."

"You are too close to the queen." It had come to me, while eating the king's dinner, that more people were at risk than just those currently imprisoned. "I am afraid for you."

Bess made the same impatient face I'd seen her make for nearly twenty years. "Don't be silly."

I sat down behind a desk, hoping it would lend me some authority. She took direction only from the master of minstrels, who was also her husband. "The queen is in the Tower," I said. "Very few people return from that place."

"But she isn't guilty." Bess popped from her seat and paced the floor. "None of them are. Mark is a stupid boy but not stupid enough to involve himself with the queen, even if she would be unfaithful to King Henry. Which she would not."

I gestured for her to lower her voice. "I know you have sympathy for both of them, but you must be discreet. There are more important things to think of right now." I looked pointedly at her belly, straining behind her front-laced bodice. "Young Harry and this one here, they don't care what becomes of the queen. They just want their parents."

"And they have them." She softened at the mention of her boy and the unborn little one.

"You should go away, at least for a while."

Bess laughed in my face. "This is our home."

I sighed. "Maybe it was, but the court has changed since you arrived, even since you were wed. The king will have his way, and if it kills the queen, Smeaton, and any other number of innocents, he will not care."

She sat down hard as if her knees had given way. "He wants Jane Seymour now, doesn't he?"

"He wants a son," I said bluntly. "If Queen Katherine had given him a living son—even one—she would still be queen, and we would still be tied to Rome. People forget the king's father took this throne. King Henry may look secure, but without an heir, anything could happen."

"But he has an heir."

I pressed my fingers to my temples. "No, he has daughters. No woman will rule England."

There was a knock, and Tom entered without waiting. "I'm sorry I wasn't at dinner," he said without preamble. "I tried to see Mark."

"How is he?" Bess reached out, and he sat on the edge of my desk, one hand on her shoulder. She relaxed at his touch. If I could get him to see sense, she would follow.

"I wasn't admitted." His face showed concern. "The guards said he's been racked. I imagine he told them whatever they wanted to hear, to make it stop."

Mark Smeaton was a stupid boy, as Bess said, and perhaps

bragged too often about being in the queen's favor, but he was no more her lover than was her brother George.

"I've been telling Bess—you need to get away before either of you are pulled into this."

"We are not in so deep as that, Rob."

"You are master of minstrels, Tom." I raised my brows. "Which means you supervised him and should have known his whereabouts. It might even be assumed that you were sympathetic." I looked at his wife. "It's well known how close Bess is to the queen. She may have looked the other way when Mark came to her."

Bess gasped, and Tom said, "You think they would go so far?"

"I think an outcome has been decided and all that's left is to build the case."

Tom's struggle was visible on his face; he supported Smeaton as she did the queen, but he more clearly saw the danger. "What do you suggest?"

"Do you still keep in touch with Ewan?" I hadn't seen him in years, but he'd been a good friend to both of them; Shrewsbury would be far enough to keep them safe, if it could be managed.

Bess's face lit up. "I had a letter from him not three months past."

"I think you should visit him and stay until the situation here calms down. I could write to you there."

A glance, eloquent as a conversation, passed between them. Leaving the court was not something they had ever considered. They had grown to adulthood, to love and marriage, within its precincts. But the royal lion was as dangerous now as any creature in his menagerie, and if they could not keep themselves from being aligned with those who need not be proven guilty, removal was the safest option.

"Is Shrewsbury safe?"

"It's safe—for now, at least," I said, thinking of the rich abbey there. "You can cross into Wales if you must. Give me a day; I'll work it out. Make a few quiet farewells, and get your things together."

I sent an underling to investigate if there were any departures for the west within the next days and was gratified to learn that a party would be heading for Ludlow the next afternoon. They were willing to take a few passengers, for a price.

"That will do," I said. "Please inquire if Lord Kelton has a moment for me this afternoon."

He sprinted off. Having young men to do my small tasks was the surest sign that I had progressed. My library showed my inward growth, but my minions showed my public stature.

Within an hour, I met Hawkins in the great hall. He was dressed in his usual finery, and though he was in his early forties, he still carried himself like the dashing courtier who had nearly stolen Bess away from Tom. "Secretary Lewis."

I bowed. "A fine day to you, sir."

"I cannot imagine this is a social call," he said. "We have little reason to speak."

That was true enough. Our past dealings had enriched me but made me feel less of a man in the end. "I would ask a favor," I said. "It is not for myself."

"Let us walk." He strode out into the warm May afternoon, and we turned toward the river. "On whose behalf are you asking?"

"On my own," I said. "But not for myself." At his quizzical look, I expanded. "You know, of course, that one of the Music has been pulled into the queen's…situation."

"Poor bastard," he said. "He'll die for it."

"We have a mutual acquaintance in the Music, you and I." He took my meaning. "I am afraid she could be drawn into this."

"Surely not?"

"She is less safe than her husband, and he had watch over Smeaton," I said. "You know her history with the queen and her tendency to speak her mind."

Hawkins's mouth opened, then closed. He was a family man these days, with a half-dozen children and a beautiful wife, but he had loved Bess. "What do you need?"

"I would have them away from court," I said. "I have arranged passage to the west country, leaving tomorrow, but I cannot get the funds in time to pay their way."

"They'll not take it from me," he said. "She might, but not him."

Tom would not take money from his wife's lover, even to save his family. "I will take credit, if they ask, and I'll repay you within the week."

He clasped my shoulder. "No repayment necessary. Just see her safely away."

Cromwell traveled back to London that evening, but I made an excuse to stay on. One of Hawkins's men brought me a purse near midnight, and in the morning, I delivered it. No young men this time; this was a deed I needed to accomplish myself.

"Quite a hasty departure." The man counted the money and shoved it in his purse. "Is there a price on someone's head? Not that I care," he said, smiling expansively. "You've bought my silence."

I wanted to bash his face in. "The lady is a friend," I said, "and there have been some unwelcome attentions."

"Ah. Well, at least I'll have the company of a comely lass on the road."

"Along with her husband and their young son." I gleefully punctured his fantasy.

His face fell. "It's always the way, isn't it?"

I hadn't lied to him. If things kept going the way they were, Bess or Tom could become the subject of very unwelcome attentions. I would do what I could to prevent that.

Tom carried a pack and a canvas bag containing his lute. Bess had her small harp and her son by the hand. Young Harry was tall and thin for his years, with black curling hair and Tom's eyes, bright with intelligence.

"You're going on a journey," I said. "Are you excited?"

"I've never been anywhere but here." His voice was normal, showing no sign that he had inherited his parents' extraordinary talents.

At six, I'd been trapped in Hawley, and the court was unimaginable. "There's a whole world outside this place. See as much of it as you can."

"Don't encourage him, Robin." Bess's voice held laughter. "You were always eager to leave, and yet you came back."

"I go where I am of use." I looked at the things they carried. "Is this everything?"

"I brought a trunk down earlier," Tom said. "This is the last of it."

Bess looked around. "It's not just Harry. This is the only home I've ever known."

"We can make another." Tom took her hand. "We've always worked well together, you and I."

She made a sound between a laugh and a sob. "You're right, of course."

"Think of the music." I knew that, reunited with Ewan, the three of them would play until the stones fell from the walls.

Darting forward, Bess embraced me. "Thank you. Starting over won't be easy, but—"

"It's better than the alternative." I shook Tom's hand and tousled Harry's curls. "I will write you care of the abbey."

"Another favor?"

"If I can."

"I didn't tell Edith," she said. "I didn't want to put her in a position of knowing, should there be questions. But once we're safely away, if you could let her know where we've gone…"

Mistress Edith watched over the Music, mothering the small children, tending the sick, and keeping everyone in line. She had been a good friend to them both since childhood.

"I will tell her."

The courtyard was a bustle of wagons and carts being loaded. Space had been saved for them in the back of a wagon.

Tom added the last of their belongings, then swung his son up among the parcels. "I thank you, Robin, for your care."

Bess climbed up to join Harry.

While she was busy with the boy, Tom turned to me. "Perhaps I should stay," he said. "I might be able to speak on Mark's behalf." I resisted the urge to shake him. "Smeaton is already dead. If you speak up, you'll be dead along with him, and then what will happen? You can't save everyone, Tom. Save the people you love."

"They would be safe with Ewan."

"You know she'd come back for you." Tom closed his eyes, imagining what Bess might do, and when he didn't move, I said, "You've had a second chance. Do you want to lose this family too?" I flinched at my own cruelty, but it was necessary.

"You could try to be kind."

"I want you to see sense." I shoved him toward the wagon. "I will speak," I said, to give him comfort. "Coming from one of Cromwell's people, it might make a difference."

"We're off now, Rob. Are you coming?"

"I thought I'd get some work done." I hadn't intended to witness the executions; I had lost my taste for such matters as a boy when I saw the Duke of Buckingham's trip to the block.

Ned's eyebrows raised. "We're *all* going."

I took his meaning. Of course, they were going. Cromwell had worked tirelessly toward this for months. He would be in front, in his rightful place in the proceedings. My absence would be noted.

"I'll be right there." Part of my hesitation was a strange sympathy for Smeaton. He'd gotten his start in Wolsey's choir, transferring to the Chapel Royal on the cardinal's fall from grace. From there, he found the queen's favor and moved to her household, where, by looks, talent, and breathtaking stupidity, he encompassed his own end.

I hadn't spoken up for him, of course. What I said to Tom was true—Mark was already dead, and I had no desire to join him in that subterranean chamber with the maiden and the rack and the thumbscrews. Being one of Cromwell's men would not save me.

The five men who died that day were guilty, though not of the charges brought against them. They were guilty of the crime of getting in the way of Thomas Cromwell.

I was torn. I liked Cromwell. He was a man like myself or Cardinal Wolsey: born low and achieving greatness by sheer, stubborn hard work. He was arrogant and rearranged facts to suit his intentions, but I would not condemn a man for my own faults.

"All of them married men," Ned said hoarsely. "With children."

"The king will not punish them for their father's misdeeds." I was almost certain of that, for Cromwell had worked with Wolsey and had only risen after his master's death. If one was useful, King Henry looked away.

Smeaton died last, after the gentlemen, and worst. He was carried to the platform, the rack having done its evil work on his joints. When he saw the block slick with blood and the sodden, mucky straw beneath, he cried out and twisted away, so the crowd jeered.

Two days later, Anne Boleyn met a similar end. That execution I did not attend, having given myself no time the day before to complete some necessary task for my master. I had never been fond of her, but I could not bring myself to watch her die; if I did, I would have to write that to Bess.

She was given the favor of a French sword, instead of an English ax. Her black hair was tucked up under a plain coif, and once her eyes were covered, the swordsman struck a clean blow.

The king was rid of his troublesome second wife, and he celebrated by announcing his betrothal to Jane Seymour the very next day.

Chapter 43

TONIGHT WE WILL REST in Cambridge town, at a house formerly owned by one of Cromwell's men, now inhabited by Samuel Cuthbert, loyal to Mary. "I know the place," I say, wishing it were still held by Matthew Doran.

"Are you acquainted with the current owner?" Hawkins, by this point, assumes I know everyone in England.

"No."

"I will keep close tonight, Lewis. There will be no repetition of Kenwood."

I smile crookedly. "There is only one Jack Darlington, may God be thanked."

"May I ask…what happened to your friends?"

The question surprises me. "I tell you of the execution of a queen, and you ask the fate of a pair of minstrels? Is it curiosity alone, or does your mistress have some hitherto-unknown sympathy for musicians?"

"I am curious," he says. "I feel I've gotten to know them through your stories. And it's personal—my father, after all, did help get them away."

"True." I am fixed on Mary. "I've heard the court is a dour place, with music in its rightful place in the church and all merriment supplied by the queen's dwarf."

"That is not true." The stiff tone is back.

"I am glad of it." I follow this with a question he will not like, but he is not the only curious one. "What is the state of the queen's womb? Were the rumors true, that the babe burgeoned only in her mind, and she delivered nothing but disappointment?"

His face reddens. "Damn it, man, that's the queen you speak of. Have respect!"

I bow my head. "I've angered you. I'm sorry."

He reaches out a hand as if to touch my arm, then withdraws it. "We weren't speaking of the queen."

"No. You wanted to know of my friends. Well, they made it and spent several years in Wales. Beyond that, I know not, as my own situation soon became unsettled. They may have returned to England, or they may still be there. Wherever they are, I hope they are happy."

Chapter 44

UPON THE ADVENT OF Queen Jane, a semblance of calm settled over the court. She was a placid, sensible young woman, though she possessed a family as ambitious as the Boleyns. I hoped for all our sakes she knew how to handle her father and her strong-willed brothers.

She knew how to handle the king: she got pregnant. The king's hopes had been dashed before, but he was certain that this queen, quiet, submissive Jane, would not disappoint. She *would* deliver him a son.

It was during this period that I received a letter. It was not delivered direct, but handed to me by Ned, with a packet of other papers. "Something in there for you."

"For me?"

His expression was unusually cautious. "Think you that our correspondence is not read, as any other subject's might be?" He laid a finger on the edge of a page that rose a hair's breadth above the rest. "Take care, Rob."

The page showed signs of rough handling, whether in delivery or in reading after the fact I could not tell.

Dearest Robin,

We have arrived. It is strange to see my father's country, all these years later. It is wild and beautiful and totally unlike England.

We arrived in Ludlow after ten days' hard travel. After a brief rest, Tom located someone heading for Shrewsbury, and we arrived at the abbey within a week. The monks sent word to Ewan, but before he got there, I was delivered of my child.

Her name is Jenny, and she is the bonniest mite I have ever seen. She has Tom's hair, though it may darken. She is our good little Welsh baby. Ewan brought us to his master, who was delighted to add two minstrels to his household.

Here we are, and here we shall stay. I thank you again for all that you did for us, and pray for your safety.

Please let us know how you fare, and give news of our friends.

With greatest affection,
Bess

I was glad to know they had reached their destination, but I was not pleased to discover my letters were being read, and my part in their disappearance was now known—by whom?

Ned was often absent doing Cromwell's bidding around England as I did his bidding closer to home. I made a trip across the narrow sea to France, carrying diplomatic missives, and though I had my usual joy in escaping the confines of my life, my dark thoughts never left me.

Had my involvement in my friends' disappearance harmed my prospects? Had I disapproved too visibly of the Act of Supremacy and the acts which followed? I did not regret informing Cromwell of my discomfort with the monastery program, and I found the French work interesting, but it was not at the center of things, and I wanted to bask in the heat of important goings-on.

The slam of the heavy front door echoed through the building. I looked up from my reading, my ears attuned to the very particular sound of my friend's return. His boots thudded on the stairs, and in a moment, our door banged open, bouncing off the wall behind and leaving a dent in the plastering.

"You could try not to disturb the entire house," I said by way of greeting. "They would know you were here soon enough."

He threw off his cloak and stretched, reaching over to tousle my hair. "I like to make an entrance."

I shook my head to repair the damage. "You're quite good at it."

"No one will ever mistake me for you. I don't slink around, trying my best not to be seen or heard."

"I don't slink."

"I am turning into you in one respect," he said, dropping his pack on the floor and sinking down on the bed. "If you'll believe it."

Closing my book, I inquired, "And what might that be?"

"I've brought you a book." He sat up and nudged his pack closer to the bed with his foot. Rummaging inside, he produced a square leather-bound volume. "Here."

"What is it?" The worn leather was soft as flesh under my fingertips.

"It's a record of the last eighty years at Wardlow Priory." Ned dropped back on the mattress, scratching his chest. "They didn't have much of a library, but as we were cataloging its contents, I came across this."

I spoke with difficulty over the pressure in my chest. "Did you read it?"

"No."

"You didn't look inside?" The book was suddenly heavy, containing as it very possibly did the names of my parents. At the very least, there would be mention of my surrender to Wardlow.

"I didn't," Ned said. "Because I knew you would ask me. And because I don't want to know unless you want to tell me."

The book weighed as much as a man. Possibly even a priest. I put it on the table and turned to my friend. "I don't know if I should thank you or not."

"I don't care if you thank me." His voice was muffled by the pillow. "Look at it, or don't. The choice is in your hands."

That was the problem. My parents had been a mystery all my life. Did I want to know who they were? If the rumor was true, there was no pride to be found there. If only one parent was a religious, it was no better, for I had still been left as a foundling.

I shoved the book aside and reached across, slapping Ned's leg. "How about a drink?" I asked. "The Swanne has missed you."

The evening ran late, and when we finally returned to our lodgings, Ned staggered up the stairs and fell across the bed like a tree.

Frugality and self-control kept me from his level of indulgence; I was tired but not drunk, and I regretted it, watching his noisome slumber. My thoughts would not allow sleep until I dealt with his gift.

The battered volume, resting on a stool, looked innocent enough, but inside its worn covers could be the answers to my lifelong questions. It might say nothing. It might say everything. It might contain names, dates—I might discover my actual birth date. I might discover my mother and my father.

I brought it onto my knees. The leather was warm to the touch, the hands of generations of monks rising to greet me. This—this book—was my provenance, my history.

I grasped it in both hands and threw it into the fire.

Watching as it smoldered, I felt a momentary pang at my recklessness. I would never know now.

Father Gideon's words came back to me. *Forgiveness is as much for your benefit as for the person who has wronged you.* I hadn't completely forgiven my parents, but knowing would not change who I was, who I had become with no help from them. It was not for me to know.

I took a deep breath, let it out. The leather had burned away, and flames licked at the boards. Before long, the pages would be alight. Shedding my clothes in the uneven glow of my history, I rolled Ned to one side and crawled into bed.

"May I borrow a quill?"

Taunton tossed one from the next desk. "What happened to yours? You always have a supply."

I looked at four neatly sharpened quills, all snapped into pieces. "An accident." It was the second such accident that week, and before that, my inkhorn was empty when I'd filled it the night before.

The culprit was obvious. Darlington's schoolboy tactics were more annoying than dangerous, but I prided myself on my preparation, and he knew it. He wanted to make me look bad, and that was a danger in itself.

I'd not been disliked for so little reason since I was a boy. Even then, there was reason, for I'd no idea how to comport myself and offended simply by breathing. Darlington was an adult and should have his own ideas of comportment. Perhaps he did, but they didn't involve any fellow-feeling toward me—even before the dressing-down I'd given him at Morden.

He could not accept that I outranked him, and his antipathy, carried out in gibes and trickery to make my associates laugh and lessen their respect for me, was genuine. I tried my best to ignore it. He would behave as he would; I could only control my own reaction.

I got on with him because I must. Cromwell permitted no dissension in his ranks, though there were plenty of less-than-cordial relationships. Loyal Ned did what he could to make Darlington's life miserable, giving him unpleasant assignments or sending him out in bad weather, just for his own satisfaction.

"I'm glad he's on your side of things." I met Ned outside the wall of Austin Friars when our day was complete, and we repaired to the nearby tavern. "He has no interest in France, so his meddling would be caught out much sooner."

Ned drained his ale with a satisfied smacking of his lips and waved his mug for a refill. "I'd like to catch him out," he said. "Catch him out and put him under a bridge. Beat him like a drum."

His fancies were more extreme than mine. For a moment, I relished the picture of Darlington's blond locks strewn like seaweed on the muddy bank. I would settle for Cromwell noticing his antics and putting him in his place.

The maid refilled our mugs and giggled prettily as Ned toyed with the corner of her apron. He had a way with girls, though he appeared as eager for marriage as I was. Despite his light ways, he was intent on building a career at court and could be as serious as a magistrate when required.

There was shouting at the door, and a half-dozen men entered, jostling and carousing as if they were already drunk. One head, gleaming gold, stood above the rest.

"Can we not even escape him here?"

Darlington and his band tended to frequent taverns closer to the river, establishments with more whores and sailors and less talk of business.

"Drink up," Ned said. "I'll be right back." He took off after the barmaid, twisting his way through the noisy crowd.

I nursed my ale, my thoughts turning dark. I was a man of thirty. Having a boy of twenty-two attempting to bring me down was ridiculous. Worst of all, I had no idea how to stop him without making myself look contemptible in the eyes of my betters.

They shoved their way in and commandeered a table, pushing off the men who were seated there. A scuffle erupted, but a coin was thrown, and the men went off satisfied.

"Lewis," one of them called. "Drinking alone?"

I looked away. Where was Ned?

"His bitch is here somewhere," Darlington drawled. "He doesn't stir without Pickering yapping at his heels."

They burst into laughter, and my face burned at the accusation contained in those words. A man was not required to marry, and no one truly cared what he did in the privacy of his bed, but a public accusation of sodomy would be damning. No one wanted a practitioner of such a vice on their staff. Cromwell would draw a line simply because of the number of young men in his household, and the questions it would in turn raise about his tolerance.

Ned shouldered his way through the throng, throwing an arm about my neck and reclaiming his mug. When the neighboring table jeered, he made a rude gesture in their direction. "We'll finish this one and be off."

I drained my mug. "I'm ready."

Hoots and whistles followed our exit. When the door shut behind us, the dark street, even with its layer of filth, seemed a place of peace. We struck off toward the river to find a wherry.

"We won't be seeing Jack tomorrow," my friend said as we

climbed into the small vessel.

"What do you mean?" I caught hold of the side of the boat as it dipped sharply.

"Nothing." Ned sat down hard and began to laugh.

We did not see Darlington on the morrow. When he finally appeared at Austin Friars, on the day after, he was in a more subdued state than usual, and with most of his visible skin mottled with bruises.

"Cutpurse," he said when asked how he came by the beating. "I went out back for a piss and they grabbed me."

"How many were there?"

"Did they rob you?"

The questions came thick and fast, and Darlington brushed them off. "Two or three, as far as I could tell. They came at me from behind." He winced when his split lip began to bleed. "They can't look any better than I do, because I gave it back."

I drifted toward my desk, listening to their conversation. As the story was repeated, the number of attackers grew. I wondered that there was a cutpurse living who had not felt the sting of Darlington's fists.

By late afternoon, the novelty had worn off, and the chambers were silent again. I left early and waited at the doors of Westminster for Ned to emerge.

"Have you seen our friend?" His smile told me all I needed to know about the impetus for the attack.

"Beaten by a band of cutthroats. I wonder how that happened?"

He gave me a puckish smile. "I wouldn't know. I only gave the barmaid enough to hire one man."

Ned and I had agreed to disagree about the closures. A firm believer in reform, he was pleased when Cromwell gave him my duties, and I truly wished him well, glad there was someone involved in the matter who was a good man.

I tried to avoid listening to the rumblings from the north, but they became too loud. Lincolnshire, and soon Yorkshire, rose up against the king and in support of the monasteries. They banded together: monks, nuns, villagers. Even a few brave nobles lent their support—and their armies—to the rebellion.

It would not end well. I knew that before Ned went north with the king's commissioners to deal with the uprising.

We didn't see each other for some weeks. When he at last returned, he stumbled into our chamber, threw his pack on the floor, and collapsed on the bed, closing his eyes.

"Are you well?"

"I am sick," he said. "Sick in my soul. The king and Cromwell between them have destroyed something of great value."

My eyebrows raised. "I thought that monks were leeches, living off the delusions of the poor?"

He propped himself on an elbow. "Perhaps some are. But what I've seen, Rob—men and women thrown out with no warning, no explanation. With nowhere to go. There were nuns walking barefoot, wearing nothing but their habits. One carried a babe left at the convent—no provision had been made for those poor souls either. She used her veil as a sling to carry it, but the boy froze before the gathering was broken up."

"What happened to them?"

"I don't know." He fell back, the ropes squeaking their disapproval of his weight. "The king and Cromwell are killing innocent people to enrich themselves. You were right in wanting no part of it."

It grew worse. Robert Aske, a lawyer who had become the figurehead of the Pilgrimage, was brought to London at Christmastide in the cause of negotiating with the king. When it was over, he was sent back to York, but it was not long before he was on the city wall before the remaining pilgrims, having been hanged in chains.

Their king had betrayed them and could not even be bothered to hide it.

Chapter 45

WE ARRIVE VERY LATE, though this time, Hawkins has sent riders ahead to warn of our coming. Rather than disturb the Cuthbert household, who are about their business in the hall below, we are directed upstairs to our chamber, and soon a manservant arrives with a jug of ale.

Hawkins thanks him. "We'll require wine, if you please."

The man bows and reaches for the ale.

"You can leave that."

He bows again and retreats.

I look at Hawkins.

He shrugs. "It's been a long day."

"This is a rather nice chamber they've given us, don't you think? The fire well-laid, the bed nicely curtained. We shall be quite snug when we go to our rest."

"There's no need to make me feel guilty. I said I was sorry about last night."

I seat myself opposite him. "It was a comment on the room, no more."

The wine arrives, and Hawkins pours a cup, pushes it toward me, then serves himself. "About Kenwood—I didn't think they'd have the nerve to touch you."

I sip the wine, though I want to gulp it down, and more, to dull the ache in my ribs and knee. "He's never been short on nerve."

To hell with it. I drain the cup and push it back for a refill. "I'm thankful they only toyed with me, else you'd have to drape me over the saddle to get me to London, and I'm near enough to that from the ride."

The door opens again, this time to Seb bearing a tray with our supper: richly-scented stew, a bread, and a block of hard cheese. I smile my thanks, and he retreats.

We eat, talking little, both of us tired. He still feels bad, I can tell.

"This is nice," I say, savoring the stew. It has an interesting flavor, unfamiliar but very tasty.

"Mmm." He wipes the last of his bowl with a scrap of bread and stretches.

"Tired?"

He gives me a look. "Just of riding." He takes a mouthful of ale. "You may tell me more of your story, if you like. It passes the time well enough."

It does, indeed. If only I could prolong the tale. I can do only so much. I will either live or die, and nothing I do at this moment will change the outcome. "Do I dwell overmuch," I ask, "on this most heinous, far-reaching event of Henry Tudor's career?"

"You certainly like to talk about it."

Spoken like a young man who's only been exposed to information he agrees with. "Do you realize just how many houses there were when it began? More than five hundred were closed in a mere four years—not just closed but demolished. Wrecked, in some cases, their cellars packed with explosives and the entire structure blown to bits."

"I'd heard about that," he said. "Wasn't one of them taken by Cromwell?"

It had been, but he'd paid for it, in a manner of speaking. "Not only were the religious deprived of their way of life, but the people around them were deprived of land, work, education... The ends did not justify the harm done, and it damaged the new religion for many who might otherwise have come to believe over time."

Cromwell believed an English Bible in every church would make up for the loss of the men and women who prayed for all the souls of England, but he was wrong. It would take more than a generation for that feeling to come to pass, and it was still not well settled.

"My father has some sympathy for the new religion," Hawkins ventures. "My mother kept to the true church."

I note this and wince at a stabbing pain in my side. Had they broken a rib? "In the best instances, people were left to fend for themselves. In the case of some who participated in the Pilgrimage of Grace or who refused to sign the oath of supremacy, they often received a death sentence, and not usually a swift death either."

"Hanging for those who refused to sign the oath, wasn't it?" Hawkins looks uncomfortable, shifting in his seat.

"But not until they were dead," I point out. "The whole point of the exercise was to draw their bowels out while they lived. Then they were quartered and beheaded and their parts spread throughout the kingdom."

Such business is not unusual, but it still turns my stomach. I have never yet crossed London Bridge without fearing to look up.

A knock, and Seb and Hawkins's servant enter to ready us for bed. Seb clears the table, noting with particular interest the cleanliness of our bowls. "Was the supper to your liking, master?"

"Rich but good," I say. "Did you not eat from the same pot?"

He shakes his head. "We ate with the servants."

Hawkins is ready before Seb starts with me. He does not avert his eyes as I am undressed, noting the livid bruises on my person. "Are you in much pain?"

"Not as much as he would have liked," I say, "but I won't heal as quickly as a lad your age. I was able to ride, you'll notice."

"You did well." A flicker of discomfort crosses his face, and he returns to our earlier conversation. "What about the monasteries? I thought they were supposed to be beds of sin, and yet you make it seem that they were unjustly closed."

"Some lies live longer than the people who tell them." I debate going to bed and instead seat myself before the fire; there is still wine left in the jug. "Some places had fallen below the standard expected of men of God—some of them very far. On the whole, though, they were goodly places of learning and contemplation, which are necessary to the life of a country. They could have been repaired, but their wealth was required elsewhere, so they were destroyed instead."

The king made a fortune from the closures, and yet when he died, his treasury was near to empty. His marriages and his wars and his extravagance pissed away the monasteries' money, and left the country without a soul.

"Many of the abbots became bishops in the new church, didn't they?" Hawkins closes the shutters and leans against them. "They took care of themselves."

"I don't begrudge them their lives; my own relationship with the Almighty has been somewhat flexible. They believed in God and the king, and then they believed in the king and God. A simple reversal of priorities."

Chapter 46

THE KING GOT HIS heir at last. The boy's christening procession was as elaborate as a coronation, involving nearly every noble in the kingdom and causing both the king's daughters to be returned to court. What did their illegitimacy matter now? Then, just days later, Queen Jane died, leaving the king to mourn the wife who had given him what he wanted and departed before the shine could wear off.

What would happen next? Henry did not need to marry again, but our king was a man who liked the attentions of women, and the discussion of candidates began immediately at Austin Friars. Cromwell's only job was to give the king what he needed, often before he knew he needed it. Remarriage was mentioned right after the funeral—it was best to get an idea in the king's ear before he got one of his own—and while official mourning continued, so did my master's quiet search for a queen more suited to his own purposes.

Too, another wife would be practical. Young Edward was stronger than his mother, but he was a babe, and babes were known to die of every passing fever. A spare prince, a Duke of York, would not go amiss. The king, after all, was a second son himself, never intended to rule.

Many expected Cromwell to put forward a French princess, and there had indeed been much tiresome correspondence on the matter. But France and the Holy Roman emperor were talking peace, and it was decided to choose a bride from a region that would give England support in the event of an alliance against her.

At the turning of the year, rumors abounded of Christina of Milan, the emperor's niece. Beautiful and biddable, with a connection to not only the emperor but to Sweden and Denmark, she would be a good candidate.

But again, France. Marie de Guise, widow of the Duc de Longueville, already claimed by the King of Scots. Why should he get such a prize when our king was in need of cheer?

A portrait of Christina swayed the king; reports of Marie's

red hair pulled him back. And all the while, Cromwell labored on. There were frequent meetings with the French and Imperial ambassadors, Castillo and Chapuys. If the ambassadors arrived smiling, they left dejected; if they drooped in, they danced out.

Cromwell, expressionless, kept going, and we with him.

I was summoned one evening as I was about to depart. He sat behind his enormous desk, barely visible behind stacks of correspondence, a teetering pile of books, a jug, several apple cores, and his black bonnet. He looked up. "Lewis. Sit yourself down."

Seating myself on the edge of a stool which bore a similar burden of paper, I wondered what he had in store. Usually, Cromwell's orders filtered down; it was rare to be called into his office.

"How do you feel about France these days?" He looked tired. I couldn't imagine what his days were like—no personal life to speak of and having to dandle the king on his knee to keep him sweet-tempered.

"Fine, sir. No matter if we like them or loathe them, there is always much to be done with them." I tilted my head. "And if we marry them, there will be even more."

That got a brief smile, but he returned immediately to his purpose. "We will soon be entering into a new endeavor on the king's behalf," he said, his tone deliberate. "I think you've had enough time in France. How do you feel about the rest of the continent? What languages do you speak, Lewis?"

"French, Italian, Latin. A bit of German and Spanish."

"You've been to the Low Countries?"

"Not since 1525," I said. "I worked for a merchant after I left Oxford."

"Good." He looked up from his reports. "You know, of course, of our conversations with France."

I did. I knew far more than I wished about the attributes and habits of several French princesses. "Yes, sir."

His hands—the hands of a laborer, no matter how long he'd been in service to the king—fiddled with a piece of parchment bearing the royal seal. "The king needs a wife, and it would not hurt us to look outside France and the Empire."

A party of German ambassadors had visited during the summer. They were well received, and though they were obviously Lutheran in their beliefs, the king met with them and had nothing bad to say. "The Prince of Cleves has two sisters who are of marriageable age." The parchment furled and unfurled. "I'm going to send a delegation to open negotiations, and I'd like you to be a part of it."

Somehow I conveyed my acceptance while concealing the fact that I was ready to dance for joy. A break from the French; a trip across the narrow sea; a visit to Düren, a place I had not yet experienced.

I tidied my desk and made my way toward London Bridge; I needed to talk to Ned.

The old hall at Westminster was dark in all its corners, branched candles on the desks doing little to alleviate the gloom. Each scrivener squinted and scrawled in the man-made twilight, their black coats and caps floating like dark clouds in a gray sky.

I made my way down the central aisle, searching for Ned in the ranks of near-identical clerks. He was toward the back of the hall, near a securely shuttered window, his desk covered with an untidy mountain of paper held down by several small caskets.

"Ned."

He looked up, at the same time licking his quill before finishing his sentence. "Rob!"

"You look like one of the Boleyn's spaniels," I said, marking the trail of ink at the corner of his mouth. "It's like the pit in here. Can't you get some light through these windows?"

"No." He rubbed at the ink, making it worse. "There's too much that can't be seen. You had trouble getting in?"

The guards had examined me closely, and I only made it through because Layton passed by and confirmed that I worked for Cromwell. "Yes."

"Look around." In the dim room gleamed objects looted

from the monasteries, there to be catalogued before fulfilling their purpose of augmenting the treasury: gold pyxes and chalices, the glint of a glass-fronted reliquary, silver candlesticks that would do better duty on Ned's desk than piled in a corner. "We're grave robbers." His tone was quiet, as befitted a man criticizing his own line of work. He looked up at me, and his face brightened. "Congratulations, by the way."

"On what?"

Ned made the face he always made when I was being obtuse: brows raised, eyes wide, trying to will a response from me. "On the trip to Düren. You'll get the first look at the Princesses of Cleves."

Was there a pipeline that ran direct from Austin Friars to Westminster? "I only just found out myself."

"You know me, ear to the ground." He wiped his pen. "Do you want to get a drink? I'm done here." Straightening a stack of papers covered in rows of numbers, he weighted them down with a small metal box. Catching me looking, he said, "You'll believe, of course, that this contained the finger bones of St. Peter."

"The very finger that touched the key to heaven?" I hated what the Augmentations men did, but even as a Catholic, I'd never been a believer in relics.

"The very same." Ned pushed back his stool and said a flurry of goodbyes to the clerks still at their desks. "Drink?"

We traced our way back through the hall and into the courtyard, planted with all manner of flowering herbs. It reminded me of the garden outside Austin Friars, and it occurred to me that Cromwell was no doubt responsible for even this small thing.

"I have an invitation to the Bonnato house, if you'd rather." I would rather, but I hadn't seen much of Ned recently, so I left the choice to him.

His smile, which had been less merry since he joined the Augmentations men, broke forth. "Lead me to Chelsea, and let the lady feed our minds and our bodies," he declared. "Signor Vincent, he can supply the wine."

When Cromwell had approached me about being part of the German delegation, I assumed it was a diplomatic enterprise. The addition of Master Holbein was a surprise, though it shouldn't have been: King Henry wouldn't marry a woman of unknown appearance. Despite his own deteriorating beauty, a pretty face was still a requirement in a royal wife.

In Düren waited two princesses, sisters, of adequate birth and, more importantly, of useful connections in the king's eternal disputes with the pope, the empire, and France. They were currently Catholic, but that was of no matter. The new queen would not be entitled to her own opinions on religion; indulging Anne Boleyn had cost the king dearly, and he had not yet recovered from the rebellions during the reign of Queen Jane.

I knew something of the sisters of Cleves from reading the briefs prepared by Cromwell—and, of course, from Ned's eavesdropping. Princesses Anne and Amalia were in their early twenties, unmarried, unpromised, unused to being in the public eye. They sounded perfect for a king who feared to find another man's fingerprints on his wife.

"Are you looking forward to returning to Germany?"

Holbein was lingering, again, at Austin Friars. I think he was hoping for one of Cromwell's good suppers, and it was likely he would get his wish if he stayed long enough. "Not so much," he said. "I have a wife and children there, but not in Düren. I will not be able to see them."

Why were they not here? I wanted to ask, then reconsidered. There were many reasons a man might not want his family with him. I knew nothing of Holbein's personal life; he kept such things to himself.

"I saw the portrait of Christina." Accompanying Cromwell two days past to the king's privy chamber, the portrait had been on prominent display, though it seemed her star had fallen in the royal estimation. This week, at least. "It is—she is beautiful."

"Beautiful women are everywhere, Lewis." He scribbled on a piece of paper, looking up at me for a moment. "I did not start out as a portraitist, you know. In Germany, then in Basel, I made religious paintings. Madonnas." His voice lowered reverently. "I did a beautiful dead Christ in the tomb."

"That's not how you've kept yourself fed here." I had made it my business to see many of his works by this point, in preparation for our journey.

Holbein shrugged his heavy farmer's shoulders. "In England, men want to look at themselves. I became a portrait painter."

His first portrait had been of Thomas More's family. I remembered the painting, and Holbein working on it, when I visited the Chelsea house early in my days with Wolsey. It was like no English picture I had seen. The level of detail in the figures, in their skin tones, in the crush and luster of the velvet—this was something totally new. Holbein did not see like an Englishman.

He returned to Germany shortly after, but rumor held that he would come back. How could such a talent exist anywhere outside of Henry Tudor's England?

It was always politic to say that the world outside England was a small, dark place, not the glorious flowering of art and culture and religion that it truly was. King Henry was the center, even if the center was a small island to the west of everything that mattered.

Holbein returned in 1532 and made the acquaintance of Thomas Cromwell. After that, he went from strength to strength, painting at first his fellow Germans in the Steelyard community, venturing soon after into English society. His portrait of the king, a colossus astride the world, was so like the original, I expected the canvas chest to move in and out with the king's breath.

Cromwell was sending a delegation, including myself, to negotiate and interview and document, but for the visuals, he was sending Holbein.

"Lewis." Thomas Wriothesley stood in the doorway, his elaborate bonnet in his hand. He'd become attached to Cromwell's hip when Ralph Sadler began to spend more time with the king. Wriothesley was affable and canny, and I didn't quite trust him.

"What is it?"

"The lord chancellor has reorganized the delegation to Düren," he said. "Petrie is going in your place."

"May I ask why?"

He spread his hands. "I was just told to pass on the news."

I knew better than to question Cromwell's decision, but this was hard to accept. My inclusion in the delegation had shown me I was still useful to Cromwell. My removal meant the opposite.

I continued to work, preparing documents that would go to Düren in hands other than my own. Hands that belonged to a dear friend of Jack Darlington.

Was that it? The news of my trip had reached Westminster before I had. If Ned knew, Darlington would have known as well, and as Ned congratulated me, Darlington, in his turn, could have begun to work against me. Legh and Layton, both in Augmentations, were close with him. They could have influenced a change in personnel easily enough.

It didn't make me feel any better to know who was behind my removal. It simply meant that Darlington was able to successfully work against me, and this was something I would have to continually be aware of in my future.

The whole thing made me tired.

Before I left Austin Friars for the day, Holbein sought me out. "Lord Cromwell isn't here yet," I said. "I believe he's with the king."

"I can wait," the German said, settling himself. "I hear I will not have the pleasure of your company on our journey."

"News spreads quickly."

"There is no understanding the minds of these men." He gave me a wry smile. "It only hurts your head to try." Reaching into the leather bag on the floor beside him, he brought out a small piece of card. "Since I will not have you captive on the voyage to make more studies, I bring you this."

It was a small portrait, no bigger than the palm of my hand but startlingly accurate, as all his work was. He had not colored it, but from the sprinkling of freckles across the long nose, any viewer would correctly assume the color of my hair. The rest—thin lips, deep-set eyes, a chin now decorated with a Henrician beard— all rang true. I had been rendered in all my imperfections, for no purpose other than Hans Holbein's amusement.

Chapter 47

A PAIN IN MY gut wakes me, like a cord tightening from my breast to my tailbone. I sit upright, gasping, and find Hawkins out of bed, standing at the window. "What is it?"

"Sick," he says and then turns away and vomits on the floor.

The scent reaches my nose, and my stomach rolls. I lean over the side of the bed and bring up my supper. "Seb!" I call, hoping that he is, as usual, sleeping outside. Suddenly I am both hot and cold, sweat streaking my face and turning to ice. "Seb!"

He bursts in with a rushlight and takes in the situation. Leaving the light, he dashes out again and returns with Hawkins's man, each of them bearing rags and basins.

I ease myself into a chair, curling around the pain in my stomach. Seb tucks a blanket around me and stirs up the fire. Hawkins joins me as our men clean up the mess, whispering to each other.

"Gods," he says, pulling his blanket tight. "I feel like I've been drenched."

I am too busy shivering to respond. Is it a fever or just a reaction to whatever illness has attacked my guts? Ever since Italy, I have feared a relapse of that malady.

Seb is fussing at me, his face full of concern. "I'll go and wake someone," he says, "see if there are any herbs downstairs that will settle this."

"Please," I say through gritted teeth and reach for the basin.

No light filters through the shutters; it is not yet dawn. I shut my eyes, and the room sways. How am I dizzier with my eyes closed than open?

Hawkins's breath comes quickly; he's almost panting. "I hate puking," he says, then does it again. "It's why I don't drink wine; it always comes back up."

Had he drunk any wine this night? I certainly had, but he'd

stuck to his usual ale, as far as I knew. "Is it bad?"

"You tell me." He gestures at the basin. "Whatever this is, it's got both of us."

Seb returns bearing two steaming cups. "Cook boxed my ears," he says cheerfully, "but says this will fix you up." He hands a drink to each of us and watches like a doting mother as we try to swallow. "Drink it all, he says, else it won't work. And I'm to come back for another dose near ten."

The stuff is disgusting, as most herbal remedies are. I drink it down and hand back the cup. "We'll be on the road by that point."

"We will not." Hawkins holds his nose and tips the cup back. "I can't ride in this state, and I doubt you can either."

I see Seb's expression, its rapid change. He is relieved. As am I, of course—but he was hoping for this. "Put another log on the fire, Seb," I say. "I think I'll do better sitting up."

Hawkins agrees. "I can't lie flat, not right now."

The fire crackles companionably, but my companion is deep in his thoughts, and I am equally deep in my discomfort. We have been sick several more times, and it seems there can be nothing left to come up, but I still have sharp pains, and Hawkins's arms are wrapped around his middle.

"Darlington ruined your chances in Germany," he says out of nowhere. "What a bastard."

I force a smile. "Well, you knew that," I say. "In the end, perhaps it was for the best. The queen obtained through that trip was part of Cromwell's downfall."

I'd been at Austin Friars when the delegation returned. When he heard the tumult, Cromwell emerged from his inner chamber and was presented with a sheaf of signed documents. They disappeared into his office. I was not alone in straining my ears, but the doors were thick in Thomas Cromwell's world.

Later, the men talked. We were told that the princesses had no interest in music or dancing. They played no instruments and spoke no language but their own. Their chief amusements were cooking and needle work. All told, they were perfect yeoman's wives but would not do for the king of England. And yet—

"The king will take a princess of Cleves to wife." Cromwell drummed thick fingers on the marriage contract. "They will learn each other's ways and be happy."

The room swims, and I pull myself back to the present to hear Hawkins's question. "Was she so ugly, the Flanders mare?"

I wince on behalf of poor Anne of Cleves. "I think she was not what the king expected," I say carefully. "As I am sure he was not what she expected." Wiping my brow, I continue, "I saw Holbein's portraits."

Hawkins has beads of sweat on his upper lip. "What were they like?"

The paintings were beautiful, like tiny jewel boxes, but unlike Holbein's sketches, which dug deep into the character of the sitter, they lacked any sense of the sisters' personalities. The costumes worn by the princesses of Cleves were rendered down to the last fold, pearl, and encrustation, but Holbein, for all his skill, had painted them as beautiful, empty vessels. Which was, for all intents and purposes, what they were.

"Anne was fair," I say, inadequately. "Serene. Her sister was dark, with a sharper face." She reminded me of the Boleyn. "The king always liked a fair maid, so Anne was chosen."

Cromwell showed us the portraits later, after the king had been informed of his bride-to-be. "Princess Anne is twenty-five, a good age for the king. If the marriage is conducted by the new year, that will give her time to produce several strong sons."

It amuses me yet that Cromwell—or any man—could speak so glibly about the production of strong sons when we were so little involved in the process. And the king had, by that point, sired a good half-dozen sons with his three wives and mistresses, and it appeared to be no one's fault that only Prince Edward survived.

Except fault there always was, and fault never rested on the royal head.

Chapter 48

THE PLANS FOR THIS new marriage moved quickly. I was involved in the paperwork—the endless letters and copying—but beyond that, I was left out, having fallen out of favor in some unknown way. I was no longer a part of Cromwell's most vital projects: the monasteries were almost completely dismantled, the king was well on the way to marital bliss, and matters with France and the empire were their normal state of unsettled.

Ned was more often in London, and we talked it over, but he had few ideas beyond shooting the bridge with Darlington and dropping him into a whirlpool. His ideas were picturesque but impractical.

"Maybe a better question, Rob," he said over breakfast one morning, "is whether you are still happy being part of this world?"

I chewed that idea over with my bread. "What else is there?"

"You know people now," he said. "You could hire yourself out as clerk to some illiterate noble with a heap of correspondence. Or some highly-placed merchant so you could go back to traveling." He swallowed the last of his pottage, jammed his bonnet over his sandy curls, and snatched the last of the bread from the table. "I'm off to Westminster."

"Have fun in the dark." I remained at the table for a bit longer, having less of a journey to work, and much to think about. Clerking for a noble or a merchant felt like going backward; working for the lord chancellor was the highest position I was ever likely to hold.

"How long have you been with the court?" Cromwell placed his quill on the blotter before him.

"I joined the cardinal's household twelve years ago."

"And before that?"

What was he getting at? He knew my history. "Before that, I

was at Oxford as a reward for my years in the Chapel Royal, and before that, the cardinal's choir."

Cromwell nodded. "That is as I have heard. Where did the cardinal find you?"

"At Hatton Priory, in Yorkshire," I said, beginning to understand. "I was a student there."

He picked up a sheet of paper from the rubble on his desk and scanned it before tossing it impatiently to one side. "Do you keep up an acquaintance at Hatton?"

"Not as such," I said. "I haven't been there in many years. Not much changes in a monastery, so I imagine most of the brothers I knew are still there."

Again, the slow nod. "And you believe your future is here at court?"

"I would like to believe that." There was always an assortment of educated, ambitious young men around Cromwell. I was on the outside compared to men such as Ralph Sadler, who was nearly family, and lately, the odious Jack Darlington, who had insinuated himself into the charmed circle. "I was a foundling," I told him. "I wanted a place where I could be of service and rise above the station into which I was born."

"Well, you've done that."

"It is not difficult to rise above the station of foundling, sir."

"True enough." He looked at me from beneath his heavy brows. "But you're ambitious. Close-mouthed, not many friends."

Was that how people saw me? "I have friends," I said carefully. "But my work is paramount."

"I have need of someone like you," he said. "More aptly, perhaps, I have need of more people like you. People who will not be distressed by doing…things that some might deem unpleasant."

My first thought was that Cromwell had an abundance of men who were happy to do unpleasant things on his behalf. "What is it you would have me do?"

"You grew up in the monasteries. Tell me, what value do they have to the crown?"

That was a fine question to ask three years into the dissolution. "That depends," I said. "Do you want me to answer from a spiritual standpoint or an economic one?"

He leaned forward, steepling his fingers under his chin, a pose he often adopted when listening. "Start with the spiritual."

"The faithful take honor from having a monastery in their midst. They like knowing that the monks—or the nuns, for that matter—are engaged in perpetual prayer on their behalf."

"Nonsense," said Cromwell. "Man needs no intermediary between himself and God."

"No one has yet convinced *all* Englishmen of that," I said. "Many believe it improves their standing in the eyes of God if they support a religious house with their alms."

"Their alms would be better off in their purse or given in taxes to the king."

I shifted in my seat, brushing up against the hard spine of a book. "Shall I continue to the economic side of things, sir?"

An infinitesimal movement of his head.

"A religious house is embedded in the life of the community— shelter, employment, education. They produce food and livestock. Monasteries near the coasts support the fishermen." Cromwell had all these facts, and more, at his fingertips. He was looking for something specific. "I cannot imagine, in truth, how some communities will manage without them."

Cromwell smiled, a stretching of his lips that chilled me through. "Alms given to these corrupt religious do nothing more than support their debased lives. They hoard treasure in their chapels or locked in the abbot's residence. This is theft, depriving the king and the crown of their rightful due."

This was the logic put about when the dissolution was begun. There were, of course, pockets of corruption and small houses that would benefit from closure but the widespread corruption and licentiousness of which Cromwell spoke was, for the most part, an excuse created to raid these houses for the treasury.

"There must be a way to manage this without causing so much

injury to the people. They have relied on this system for centuries."

"They are being given a new religion," Cromwell said, "with King Henry as its head. He will deliver the kingdom from its slavery to Rome."

I thought of the gentle men who raised me and recognized none of them in the words of my employer. "Every new idea takes time to be accepted," I said. "It will be hard to bring people around when they are homeless and hungry and their sons have no chance of education."

I looked at him across the desk. "Without the monasteries, I would have grown up in an alehouse, beaten for every infraction, and like as not, I'd be dead by now. The system is not perfect, but it does much good. Is there not a way to direct some of the money toward education and the raising up of those in dire poverty?"

Cromwell's face changed. "You sound like Anne Boleyn," he said. "She had no objection to the dissolution, but she pleaded for funds to be allocated to the benefit of the people."

"As a queen might do." I didn't spend much time thinking of Anne Boleyn, but her zeal for education had been a rare instance where we were in agreement.

"As a queen might have done if she had not spread her legs for every man in her vicinity."

Cromwell had drafted the charges against the queen, but he believed them no more than the rest of us. The charge of incest was ludicrous, and one charge of adultery downright impossible, as the queen was still in confinement after the birth of her daughter when it was to have occurred.

"I'm going to send you north," he said abruptly. "There are still houses in Yorkshire which need to be cleaned out."

"And you believe I am the best candidate for this job?"

"I do." Cromwell pulled a slip of paper from an untidy pile on his desk. He shaved a fresh point on his quill and dipped it into the ink. He signed his name, a tidy signature with just the right amount of flourish, and waved it delicately in the air. "You will not be alone," he said. "I'm sending Joseph Weston and a collection of young men eager to make names for themselves."

We were to ride north, evict the remaining monks from five establishments, inventory and pack up the valuables, and return them to London. He mentioned the monastic libraries as a special point of interest, and told me to look out for volumes that would enhance the king's collection. We had six weeks, nearly two of which would be spent in travel, so great feats were to be accomplished in a short period.

"You're not enthusiastic," he observed. "Why?"

I bit my lip. "Because I am a product of the monasteries, sir."

"In your own words, you have no attachments there."

I had an attachment to the monastery system, but I couldn't explain my reluctance beyond the words he already refused to comprehend. "I don't believe I'm the best person for this assignment."

The black brows rose again. "When you began your career under the late cardinal, could you imagine a time when he would not be the king's most trusted advisor?"

"No."

"And can you now imagine a time when I won't be the king's most trusted advisor?"

I began to see where this was going. "No. But…"

"Exactly." Cromwell's hands beat a brief tattoo on the tabletop. "You need to be seen as more than just as another of my promising young men if you're to stay on."

"But, sir—"

He cut me off with an upraised hand. "You need to be seen as loyal to a policy larger than the work you do for me."

By asking me to do the thing I least wished to do, Cromwell was protecting me. The dissolution was his brainchild, to please the king, but pleasing the king was the goal, even more than the destruction of the religious houses. If I pleased the king, that would be remembered over any particular loyalty to my master, as Cromwell's work for the king had sloughed away any lingering stench of his attachment to Wolsey.

"I understand." I thought I understood.

"And you'll do it?" His hands, never still, were sorting papers again.

"I will." I would figure out how to live with myself after.

He looked up, our interview clearly at an end. "Good. You'll be notified when the plans are completed." He smiled faintly, a personal smile this time, not the one that chilled my bones. "You're a good man, Lewis. You'll go far if you don't let your principles get in the way."

A few days later, we left for the north. Joseph Weston was in charge of the expedition, and with us we had a half dozen young men and the budget to hire as many more as we needed to carry out our task.

It was October, and I was looking forward to seeing Yorkshire at its most beautiful. It was perfect traveling weather, besides, and we approached the city of York in three days, a near miracle that depended on dry roads and bright skies.

"Someday there will be a king who puts roads first," Weston grumbled, swinging back up into the saddle after checking his mount. The horse had stumbled into a hole and thrown him, but both were unhurt.

"And then the final trumpet will sound, and we'll all be taken up to heaven without ever having had time to enjoy them." I gazed between my gelding's ears, looking for more hazards. The afternoon sun tinged the landscape with gold; beautiful to look upon, but it did not make it easy to see details of the terrain.

Weston laughed. "Then I'll enjoy the view from above." He sobered. "You're a northerner, aren't you, Lewis?"

"I was." I allowed my horse to carry me on before continuing. "I haven't lived here since I was a child."

He dug his heels in and jerked his head for me to follow. We soon left the boys in our dust.

"What is it?"

"I wondered if you had any connection to any of the places we're to finish off," he said. "It's been done before as a test of loyalty, making a man close down the priory that served his family. Paul Mattison, down in Cornwall, had to evict his own brother, who'd been with the Benedictines since boyhood."

"I've no family," I told him. "I've some connection to a monastery up here, but it isn't on the list of houses we're to visit."

"What's this business he's asked you to take charge of?" Weston had not learned of my presence on the trip until the last minute. If it were me, I wouldn't be happy, not knowing.

"Books," I said, and saw his expression clear. "Because of my familiarity with their libraries, the lord chancellor wants me to select books the king might appreciate."

Weston burst out laughing. "Break up the monasteries but take their books for the king to read on his close stool!"

I kept my counsel on that one. Rumor had it that books were indeed part of the king's lengthy morning ritual, the result of his infirmity and rich diet. "I have no argument with what becomes of the monasteries, but I would prefer to be kept out of it, if at all possible."

"That's good, then. I want this to go smoothly." He pulled his collar snug to his throat. "I don't like the black monks, but this is a bad business."

Like many people, Weston was hedging his bets; he was happy to be seen as a reformer, but wary of angering his Maker unnecessarily with cruelty to men whose religion had been his own but a few years ago.

As we approached Whitby, my breath was shallow, and my heart pounded erratically. I slowed its pace using the exercise taught me by Master Cornysh to fend off nerves while performing. At least my training still had some purpose.

I did not like our errand, but I would do it. Many of the monks from this abbey had been involved in the Pilgrimage of Grace, and it was surprising that its many buildings were still standing, much less that there were holdouts among the members.

Weston spoke sharply to the abbot, as was his manner, and

soon the remaining monks were gathered in the courtyard. He informed them they had one night to gather their belongings and make provision for their future.

"But what are we to do?" This from a monk so old, he seemed part statue. "I have not been outside this gate these fifty years."

"That is none of my concern," Weston said. "You may ask the court for a pension, if you like. If you've done good by the town, I'm sure they will help care for you."

Leaving Weston and the others to debate with the monks, I took one young man and went in search of the library. "Find a crate or chest for me, Dickon," I said. "I will put the valuable books to one side."

The library had already been picked over, significant gaps showing in the collection. Had the monks taken them, or had someone been here ahead of us? The remaining books were choice, and I was sure to find something to please the king, but I wondered at the missing volumes.

On a low table beneath the arrow slot window were several large books which undoubtedly contained the monastery's records. I generally included these with the volumes sent to the court, in the hopes that someone would keep them for future reference. It was a shame to lose these local histories—though I had readily destroyed such a history in throwing Wardlow's ledger on the fire.

The door banged open. "I found a few likely chests, Master Lewis," Dickon Talbert said. "Is there anything here worth taking?"

"There's always something," I said. "Start over there, and bring that stack to the table. I'll show you what to look for."

As the day wore on and there was less fun to be had in tormenting the monks, other young men joined us in the library. Dickon repeated my instructions, and they appeared to listen, though I had little confidence in their ability to choose a worthwhile manuscript.

Returning from the jakes, I was met by rowdy laughter in the hall. My heart lurched. The young men were clustered around a book, laughing. One had a bit of paper crumpled in his hand. Bright colors and bits of gold were visible between his fingers.

"Stop it!" The despoiler and the others looked askance, and I hastened to explain. "These may have no value to you, but someone may want to purchase them. The lord chancellor will not be happy at this destruction of property. Pick them all up and return them to the table. Now."

They muttered as I left the library. I didn't care. Breaking up the monasteries was bad enough. This wanton destruction of centuries of learning—that I could not tolerate. Having witnessed Brother Anselm's painstaking work on an illuminated manuscript left unfinished by some long-dead brother, I knew the labor involved. I knew the dedication and the skill. I knew the mysteries and wonders inside those bindings.

There was nothing I could do to derail the dissolution, but this—this might be an area where I could rescue something and not risk myself.

"It is Alexandria all over again," I said to Weston when we met that night at the inn. "I had to stop them from tearing apart books today."

"Let them have their fun," came his response. "What's the harm?" It was the justification of a commander who turned a blind eye to rape and pillage after a battle.

I thought quickly. "Those books are valuable," I said. "Whitby's library alone must be worth fifty pounds, possibly more."

His eyes lit up. "They've been burning them in the south," he said. "I know some have been selling them to merchants so they can break the bindings and use the paper. Wasteful to just burn it."

I would as soon see a book burned as wrapped around a piece of fish, but I held my tongue. "I could look into that," I said. "Whether there would be some nobles or men of means—loyal to the king of course—who would nevertheless be interested in the monastic libraries."

"We've a job to do here." He hesitated, thinking no doubt of Cromwell's reaction when I informed him of the waste of money. "Very well," he said, clearly misliking the idea. "It's to be done on your own time, mind."

"Understood." How much money did I have with me? How much could I find, quickly, and under whose name could I make the purchases? I fully intended to buy the books myself, or at least as many of them as I could afford. Others, I would simply cause to disappear until I had space for them.

"Today is Hatton," Weston said over breakfast. The lodging house we had chosen was clean as inns went, but the food was dull. "Only one more after that, and we can return to London." He belched and leaned back against the wall. "This stuff doesn't agree with me."

"Hatton?" The blood drained from my head. "That wasn't on the list I was shown."

"It was a late addition. Cromwell's man, Darlington, said it must be added."

Hearing his name was like a blow to my gullet, and I thought what I would like to do to him. It far outpaced leaving him in a ditch like Ned's paid bullies. He would never let me be, and it frightened me that he knew enough of my background to know of my attachment to Hatton. It was no secret, of course, but it was past, and a man's past was unnecessary in Cromwell's world unless it could be of use.

Darlington had learned that much.

Dickon Talbert stood in the doorway, his expression uncertain. "There's a problem."

"What is it?"

Hatton was deserted when we arrived. Weston, cheered that his plan was not much derailed, had gone on with most of his men for our last stop at Middlesbrough. I was the highest-ranking man left.

He edged further into the library. "There are several...men left in the building. Monks," he said hastily. "I tried to tell them they had to go, and they threw me out."

This was the last thing I wanted to deal with. It was bad enough I was ransacking Hatton's library, but if there were actual brothers left, I would not be able to cope. "Can't you handle it?"

"They threw me out bodily," he said. "I'm not going back in. You're in charge, sir."

I was, but I didn't like it. I followed his directions, realizing they would lead me to the infirmary. The door was closed, and when I pushed, it refused to budge. I knocked on the panel with my fist. "Open the door!"

Silence. I knocked again, this time more gently. "Open in the name of the king."

A voice on the other side of the slab said, "Is the king here?"

I recognized that voice. "Brother Rufus?"

There was a murmured conference, and the door opened a crack. The eye that peered out at me did indeed belong to Rufus. "What are you doing here?"

I met his gaze, looking away when I saw no warmth there. "I am here on behalf of the king."

"Your people have been and gone." He turned to speak to someone behind him.

Noting an opportunity, I pushed into the warm, light-filled infirmary, the sanctuary for the sick and the dying. I had a momentary flash of Santa Giustina—

No.

Several figures clustered around a bed. None of them looked up, concentrating only on the figure under piled blankets.

Rufus made an exasperated sound. "They were here," he said, "the king's fools, and they put us out, but some of us returned."

I did not appreciate Cromwell's men—and by extension, me— being called fools. "We are enforcing the king's law. It would not be good for you to be found here by anyone but me. You must leave, Brother Rufus."

"Look at that bed, and tell me we should leave."

I approached, and the monks parted. The narrow cot contained an ancient monk very busy in the process of dying. He also happened to be Brother Anthony.

I dropped to my knees. Looking up, I asked, "How long has he been like this?"

"A few days," said an unfamiliar monk. "He's been dying for years."

"As are we all." Another familiar voice. I greeted Brother Anselm, but he looked away, less happy to see me even than Rufus.

How could I manage this? The building must be declared empty and the monks moved along, but no matter the cost, I could not put a dying man—especially *that* dying man—out on the road.

I directed my words at Rufus. "I cannot stop this from happening, but I will find a way to delay it." Anthony's wasted figure, the uneven rattle of his breath, told me it would not be long. "When he is gone, you will have to go, but you are safe until then, if I have to put my body between you and the king's men."

I found the uncertain Dickon hiding in the library. "One of their own is dying," I told him. "They ask our indulgence to stay a day or two longer until he meets his God."

"We don't have instruction for circumstances like that," he said. "Best we should just put them out anyway. If his God is so powerful, he will find him on the road."

"What if it were your grandfather?" I fixed him with a look that would cow any underling, and indeed, the boy crumbled.

"I would not want him disturbed," he said slowly. "But…"

"It will be a matter of a day or two, no more." I looked around the library and considered the young man. Was he upright, or could he be swayed? I pointed at a set of candleholders, not valuable, but solid pewter pieces a young man would be proud to display. "It is no longer theirs to give, but the brothers asked that we take something for our trouble. I have no need of these myself."

His hands closed around the metal, making the decision against his better judgment. I would remember him for it.

"I didn't see them," he said. "Is that good enough?"

"That will do." I looked around; our work was nearly done. "You may take the others and join Weston at Middlesbrough. I'm almost finished here. I'll get one of the young brothers to help me load the cart." I met Dickon's eyes in a show of bravado. "It's the least they can do."

"True enough," he said. "And the wastepaper dealer will be here in the morning for the rest."

I hated thinking about any book being called wastepaper, but I could only do so much. The most valuable books were crated, marked for the king, and there was a modest pile which would come with me. The rest, unfortunately, would be used as wrapping paper or firelighters.

The others rode off within the hour. Dickon had the candleholders pushed deep in his bag, so there were no suspicious bulges. I watched them out of sight before returning to the infirmary.

The door was not locked, nor was it fully open. I took it as meaning to enter at my own peril and did so. It was the time of tierce, and the brothers were standing around the bed, heads bowed, singing the afternoon service.

After a moment, I joined them, my voice rusty from lack of practice and the Italian fever. They looked up but were too well disciplined to break off and reprimand me.

I continued to sing, wishing for the first time since leaving the court that I still had my old voice, which had been a glory to God. The only glory I could offer to God at this juncture was to let one of his most faithful servants die surrounded by his loved ones, in his own bed.

"You've no right to do that," Rufus said afterward. "You're not one of us any longer."

I closed my eyes. "Brother Anthony is my family." I looked around. "So are you and Anselm, for that matter, and these other brothers, whom I don't know. If they are your brothers, then they are mine."

"You profane this place." Anselm spoke for the first time. "You work for the heretic, Cromwell, destroying our way of life, a way of life which raised you, and you call yourself our brother?" He dragged me away from the bedside. "Go back to picking our bones. I'll not have you near him."

I shook him off. "I will stay with him until he is gone." I loved Anselm, but his ungentle handling reminded me of his other life before he became a Benedictine. "If you do not like it, you may leave." I joined the two unknown brothers at Anthony's side. "For here I stay."

Anselm stalked out, but he would return. I turned to the brother nearest me. "What happened to the others?"

"Some left before the king's men came here the first time," he said. "Father Nicholas refused his pension but took a priesthood in the new church." At my surprised expression, he shrugged. "The pension was not much. I suppose he preferred a church—any church—to nothing."

I was surprised that more had not chosen this option, but not everyone had my flexibility toward religion. Joining the new church as a priest or becoming a schoolmaster were the two of the few options open to monks, besides beggary.

There was a great rattling from the bed, and I crouched, catching Anthony's hand in mine. His eyes opened. For a moment, he did not see me.

"Anthony, can you hear me?"

His hands were like claws, the skin paper-thin, the bones almost pushing through. His eyes opened wider, and there was recognition there. "Robin, my boy. Have you come back to say your farewells?"

There was no point in dissembling; he knew as well as the rest of us that he was dying and was better equipped to meet his maker than most men I had known. "I have," I said, my voice catching. "Is there pain?"

"Life is pain," he said with the tiniest of smiles. "Perhaps I have been a bad Christian because I have found so much joy despite it." His face was drawn with illness and that most Christian pain, but I could still see the joy there. It was what I loved most about him.

"That cannot be," I said. "For your faith always increased mine."

He did not wake again that night. After compline, when the great silence was upon us, I slipped down to the chapel. It had been stripped of its candles and plate, all the trappings of Rome, but I could still feel God in that space. Perhaps He was simply embedded in the stones, from the hundreds of years of prayers that had been offered under the vaulted ceiling.

I knelt at the rail and prayed as I had not prayed for years. I prayed for Anthony, of course, for an easing of his pain and a quick transition to his Heavenly Father. I prayed for the other monks, that they would be strong in this time of trial. I prayed for Cromwell and the king, that their hearts would be turned away from the cruelty of the dissolution. Selfishly, I prayed for forgiveness, and for strength to someday make amends for what I had done.

Shortly after dawn, a cart rumbled through the gates. I was waiting and had warned the monks to stay away while I dealt with the paper seller.

He and his boy jumped down, and I showed them to the library. "All the crates along this wall," I said. "Do not touch the ones on the table—those are meant for the king, and it will be your hides if they are damaged."

"Very good, sir," the man said with a tug of his forelock. "I've already settled with Master Weston. Did he tell you?"

The boy hefted one of the crates onto his shoulder. "These books—you may be able to get money for some of them. There's bound to be a bookseller in York who would cast an eye over them."

"I've been well paid." The man shoved one of the boxes with his boot. "I don't have the time to be hunting down no bookseller."

"Perhaps the boy could do it," I said desperately. "Really, some of these would have a value far beyond what you've been paid."

The boy was back, hoisting another box, staggering under the weight.

"He's got enough to do. And who would want this popish rubbish, anyway?"

I gave up. This was a man who would not have valued books no matter their content. I had saved what I could, and the sooner he was gone, the sooner I could return to Brother Anthony.

214 • *Karen Heenan*

The death watch continued for the rest of the day. Anthony regained consciousness several times but only briefly. When awake, he joined in the prayers of his brothers, of whom I was one, despite Anselm's objections.

His life drained away with the daylight. As the room darkened, his breathing grew shallow and irregular. One of the younger monks slipped away to light a candle, and Rufus stopped him. "Let him go into the darkness."

From the small oblivion of sleep into the great oblivion of death.

Rufus, as the eldest, gave him extreme unction. I remembered that he and Anselm were ordained choir monks: priests in all but name, for everyone was equal in a monastery. We continued to pray as Anthony faded away.

A breath. Silence. Another hitching breath. A longer silence.

"He's gone." Rufus got up stiffly, crossed himself, and pressed a kiss on Anthony's forehead. "Go with God, brother."

We followed his lead, and then a light was struck. "Shall we do what needs to be done?" asked Brother Philip.

Rufus nodded. I stayed behind for a few minutes, but the two young brothers did not require my assistance. They gently stripped Anthony and washed his body. A fresh habit had already been set aside to dress him for burial. I backed from the room and encountered the other two in the hall.

"We can't leave until he's buried," Rufus said, forestalling any remark I might make.

"Of course." I knew the succession of events involved in the death of a monk. "Will he stay in the dead room, or shall we bring him down to the chapel?"

"Don't bother yourself," Anselm said roughly. "I'm sure there's a bed in the dorter where you can keep yourself until the burial tomorrow, unless your people have taken the beds."

"I would stay with him in the chapel." Tradition said that two monks should kneel at the feet of the dead man, and that they should be kin, or as close to kin as possible.

"That is for us. You have no place there."

Anselm was angry. I understood, but I would not allow him to deprive me, or Anthony, of my prayers for his salvation. "Nevertheless," I said, "I will be there."

Any further interaction with the brothers would take place during the silence, and they could not forbid me the chapel. I returned to the library, occupying myself until they had time to move Anthony's body. It gave me an opportunity to clear my mind, and hopefully, it gave Anselm time to accept that I would be present to see Anthony to his rest.

When the taper burned down a few fingers, I closed the book and made my way to the chapel, navigating the building by memory. Anthony, dressed for his journey in habit, cowl, and boots, lay before the altar, surrounded by candles.

Brothers Rufus and Anselm knelt at his feet.

I took a deep breath. They would not welcome my presence, but I must be there, for Anthony's sake and for my own. He was assured of heaven; while I would pray for him, I would also pray for forgiveness for myself. One did not destroy their family home and eject their relations simply because they were ordered to do so.

Refusing would have done no good in the end. Hatton would have been emptied, the monks displaced, but I would not have been part of it. I would not have had to see disappointment in the eyes of men who had cared for me, and who now, no doubt, wished me in the darkest pit of hell.

I removed my shoes and padded silently down the aisle. Kneeling behind the brothers, I bowed my head and began to pray.

The stone floor was cold and painful under my knees during that long night. The familiar prayers never left me, but they were interspersed with more personal, reformist pleading. *Accept him, O God, for he is the best man I have known. Hold him in your arms as he held me, as he held many a stranger come to this place. Grant him eternal peace, O gracious God.*

There were tears on my face, as I contemplated a world without

Anthony. It did not matter how many years it had been since I'd seen him; I knew he was there, praying for me. It was a more personal version, I understood, of how people felt when they had a religious house nearby, with the brothers there in permanent prayer for their souls.

I no longer knew what was right. I had a connection to the new religion, but I understood the benefit of collective prayer. I would be poorer without Anthony's prayers, as we would all be impoverished without the prayers of the monasteries. What would become of us without them?

What would become of me without this place? In an itinerant life, this had been my true home, taking me in twice when I was in need. These brothers had been my family, and now they were not. Rufus and Anselm would never forgive me.

I didn't blame them; no one was to blame here but myself. The king and Cromwell would do what they would, but I did not have to be a part of it. I did not have to forfeit my soul to enrich the king.

Catholic or evangelical, the end would be the same. Heaven was achieved by good deeds, by faith, by ardent prayer, and by care of one's fellow man.

By any definition, I had failed.

Brothers Philip and Jerome joined us for matins. It was strange, but I could feel an increase in the holiness of that space during our combined silent prayer.

The vigil passed. I had no clear memory of how the hours went by, but when the dawn bell rang, I rose from my aching knees and joined them for the morning prayer.

"We have dug the grave," Philip said to Rufus. "The ground was hard; it took both of us."

Jerome chimed in. "There was no time to make a coffin."

"A shroud will do," Rufus said. "It is the burial itself, not material things, that matter."

Brother Anthony was sewn into his shroud while Anselm

led us in the prayers for the dead. Tears ran down my cheeks as I contemplated the differences between my life and that of the dead man.

I went ahead to open the gate to the graveyard where the monks of Hatton had been buried for centuries. I had attended several burials and always found the graveyard to be a place of peace. This day, despite the high feelings among us, the same peace descended as Anthony was carried out to the yawning hole dug during the early hours by his young brothers.

"*Réquiem ætérnam dona eis, Dómine; et lux perpétua lúceat eis.*" Eternal rest give to them, O Lord; and let perpetual light shine upon them.

As I made the automatic responses and sang the dies irae, my mind was occupied with what came next. If Dickon Talbert kept silent, all would be well. If not, there would be questions, and men would return to Hatton to drive the monks away. This must be conveyed to Rufus, but I dreaded having that conversation.

Anselm gave the final benediction and stepped back from the grave. Philip took up a shovel, but I stepped forward. "Allow me," I said. "I can do no more for him than this."

He surrendered the shovel and backed away. Anselm cast me a look of loathing before joining him.

Rufus stayed at my side for a moment. "Do this as well as he deserves." He paused, then said, "I do not wish to see you again in this life."

The earth was wet and heavy. It took a long time to fill the grave, and I tamped the soil to make an even surface. Looking around, I spotted a bush of rosemary growing against a marker so old, the letters had disappeared. I apologized to the unknown brother and dug up the rosemary, placing it at the head of Anthony's grave. *Rosemary for remembrance.* He would have no stone, but this bush would grow, and I would know it was there.

I returned to the priory and was met with a profound silence. It was a monastery—it would be silent—but this was different. This was the silence of spirit drained from the very stones.

The brothers were gone.

Chapter 49

"I LOOKED FOR THEM." I close my eyes as a wave of nausea sweeps over me. There can't be anything left to bring up, other than my lights. "I climbed to the top of the bell tower, cast my eyes in all directions, but it was as if they had been swallowed by the earth."

Hawkins's chin is on his chest: is he sleeping? No. He blinks and says, "Your absence would have been noted, even if Talbert kept your secret. Questions would have been asked."

"Exactly." I'd wanted to find them, Rufus and Anselm especially. I wanted to apologize, abase myself, ask for some kind of penance. "I packed up my books and joined the others at Middlesbrough."

Nothing would have changed their opinion of me. I could not go back in time and work for someone other than Thomas Cromwell. Even now, thinking about that day makes my head ache—or is it this illness?

"Oh, God." I look up. Hawkins's expression is that of a man faced with something most disagreeable. "Dennis!"

His servant appears at his elbow. "Sir."

"Get me out of here. Get me—" He doesn't have to finish; his servant manhandles him from the chamber toward the jakes. I say a prayer that he makes it before Dennis has another mess to clean up.

I say another prayer that I am nearing the end of my own affliction.

"How do you feel, master?" Seb has arrived without my hearing him.

"Like death." I search his face. "How is it that you're not sick?"

His brows raise. "We ate with the servants."

"And is the family also sick?" I lift the sweaty band of my shirt away from my neck. "Seb?"

"They are not." He wipes my brow with a wet cloth. "It's a miracle, I'd say."

The cool cloth feels good against my fevered skin but not so good that I don't fix Seb with a suspicious look. "Is it?" I grasp his wrist. "Or was this done on purpose?"

It is difficult, but not impossible, to see a black man blush. His head drops, and I can't hear his muttered words.

"What?"

"Holly berries," he says softly. "I put some in the stew."

"But why?" Holly berries are poisonous—fatal in the right amount. He has to know this. "Do you want us dead? You could have at least only poisoned him."

He kneels before me. "That would have been too obvious, master. It had to be both of you. When we stopped yesterday, they said the queen is near to death. If the news has reached this far, she may be dead already." He looks up, his eyes pleading. "We need more time."

And now we had it. If Hawkins has reached the next stage of the poison exiting his body, we won't be riding in the morning. "You could have told me."

"I didn't want you to starve for fear of getting sick," he says. "I know how you feel about illness."

Chapter 50

HAVING BEEN GIVEN PERMISSION to rescue the libraries, I wasted no time. While the young men stripped the valuables from the Middlesbrough chapel and loaded them up to be taken to London, I scavenged several crates and began a gentle, personal pillage. The books were out of order due to previous ransacking, but they had not done much damage.

For this, I thanked the God who undoubtedly was looking down with a jaundiced eye as the monastery was taken to pieces around me.

I found several damaged books and put them aside with regret. It would be difficult enough to remove books without being detected; like the book that had been torn at Whitby, I could not waste my resources on volumes that needed repair, however much it hurt to see them discarded.

The shelves and tables groaned with the weight of the knowledge they bore and with the fate that awaited them. I began with the histories, pulling volumes in Greek and Latin and the priory's own history of England and the surrounding region. I wondered if the brother in charge had noted the Pilgrimage of Grace before his removal.

In the quiet of the library, my thoughts returned to Anselm and the others. Where had they gone? It hurt to think of them, especially as there was nothing to be done. I couldn't rescue monks; skimming books from the library was risky enough, and as yet, I had no place to store them.

I came upon that solution with relative ease, paying a tavern keeper several shillings to conceal my crates in his attic. "I shall be back for them shortly," I said. "I am looking for a house nearby."

The man's brows raised. "What sort of house?"

"Not large," I said, "and far from the town. I would like a place where I could work away from the court."

He chewed his lip, deciding whether or not to trust me. "Has your lot been to Whitby yet?"

"To the abbey?"

"Nay," he said. "Winterset, just below the town. Rumor is the Preston family plan to take a ship for France. The old man is a staunch papist, and his sons were involved in yon pilgrimage. One of them escaped capture, but the king killed the other one."

"The king killed no one," I said, hoping the man took my meaning. I cared not what he thought, but it was dangerous to blame the king, even in passing.

A look of disgust crossed his face. "Aye. Well, then, Lord Cromwell killed the Preston boy. You'll not find much sympathy here in the north."

I spun one of the shillings that lay on the bar between us. "I care not for sympathy," I said, "but not everyone is willing to overlook such words. You would be wise to be more circumspect."

I rode out alone later in the morning, heading toward Whitby. I knew the abbey, and thus the town, but I was not familiar with the families thereabouts and asked at the inn where I might find Winterset. I was directed to follow the cliff road for several miles. "You can't miss it," the innkeeper said. "It's not a big house, but it's fine enough."

Not only was it fine, I judged, seeing it rise ahead of me, it was isolated. Winterset was a small manor, of such a size that two would fit in the kitchens at Hampton Court. I didn't mind that. I needed only space for myself and my books.

I liked the elevation; it would afford me a view of anyone approaching. After my time with Cromwell, I wanted nothing more than to be left alone to immerse myself in the new learning and forget that things such as courts and kings existed.

Now all I had to hope for was that the rumor was true and Preston wished to sell the place.

I rode through a modest stone gate and into a flagged courtyard. The house loomed, two stories of local gray ashlar, with a steep tiled roof. There were chimneys at both ends, and thin drifts of smoke issued from them.

A row of narrow windows flanked one side of the round-topped door; on the other side, the house jutted out, giving some relief from the sea wind. I raised the large bronze dolphin and let it fall, hearing the sound echo through the house.

A few moments later, a servant granted me entry and asked my business with the master. "My name is Robert Lewis," I said. "I am with Lord Cromwell's men."

He blanched. "My master may not be at home."

"I'm here on my own behalf." It disturbed me, the reaction people had to Cromwell's name—loathing or fear. He was never popular, but when had it become this bad? I would have expected his involvement with Anne Boleyn's fall would have increased his popularity, but it had done nothing. He raised her up and just as easily brought her down. Who would trust such a man?

"You may tell the lord chancellor there is nothing here for him," a voice said behind me.

I turned. Sir Ralph Preston was lean and gray-haired, with the leathery skin of a man who spent most of his life outdoors. Though I had been at court off and on for twenty-odd years, his face was unfamiliar.

"I am not here on his behalf," I said. "I heard in the village of your loss, and I offer my condolences for your son."

"And yet you work for he who killed him." His expression did not change; he was watchful as an old hawk, with an aquiline beak of a nose that did nothing to hamper the resemblance.

I had nothing to say to that. Finally, I inclined my head. "I have come, sir, because I was informed in the village that you and your family plan to relocate to France."

There was a momentary crack in his composure. "Is that against His Majesty's laws as well? Do I have to swear an oath of residency?"

I ignored his anger; it would do us no good to tread that path. "I was told your wife has family lands in Normandy. It might be best to go there until the situation here becomes more stable."

Sir Ralph's eyes narrowed. Without speaking, he led me into an inner chamber. A moment later, the same servant appeared with a jug and two pewter cups. "You're in an interesting spot, aren't you?"

I pressed my lips together. "I don't expect it will be like this forever, but what I don't know is how long it will last or what comes next. The pope will not be welcomed back in His Majesty's lifetime."

"I fought for this king and for his father, but I can no longer live in a country that will tear my son to pieces for doing what he believed was right."

The chamber was of middling size, with a small table and two chairs placed to take advantage of the fire, a cheerful sight on this dull morning. Across the room were a pair of diamond-paned windows, which appeared to be curtained on the outside with cloud. It was mist, I realized; this side of the house must be close to the cliffs. The long wall facing the window was bare, but for a small cupboard and a painting of a Preston ancestor—the beaked nose and narrowed eyes were near identical, though the costume was from a century past.

"What is it you want, Secretary Lewis?"

The time for dissembling was over. "I want Winterset," I said. "I have always been quartered at court, and I would like a place away from there to do my work. I have a substantial library and would like to finally see it. I want a home."

"You want *my* home." A muscle twitched in his jaw.

"I do." I had known it from the moment I walked in the door. Like the first time I stepped into the Bonnato house, this place had surrounded me, comforted me. I wanted it for my own.

But could I afford it? It was far better than what I'd intended to purchase. Sir Ralph might well ask more than I could afford. Desperate to leave the country though he was, Winterset was a fine house, and he knew it. He also had no reason to like me or to do me any good.

"What if I don't want to sell?" He looked at the painting: a forebearer who would sit in judgment of his flight or his surrender of their ancestral manor. "As you say, the current troubles may not last forever. I may not live that long, but I still have one son, and this should be his when he returns."

"If he chooses to return. How old is he now?"

"Seventeen. My first-born, my Ralph, he was twenty-six." His eyes closed. He looked much older in his grief. "We have two daughters in between, both married and gone. One is a believer in the new religion. She sent us a letter after her brother's death and said she would pray for him but that he brought it upon himself."

"Some say religion is the cause of all the world's ills." I took a sip of beer and allowed the rich barley taste to warm me and to loosen my tongue. "I say it is those who believe too fervently, no matter the religion they espouse."

Sir Ralph laughed, a rusty bark of sound. He'd not had much to laugh about in recent years, I was sure. "You work for Lord Cromwell, with that tongue in your head?"

I could not explain, even if he would listen, the multi-faceted Thomas Cromwell, a man who held so many opposing beliefs, he should have been dizzy: a man who both outlawed the translation of the Bible into English and paid for its printing in another country. "You see why I might want a place away from all that."

He drained his cup and set it down hard on the table. "I'll not sell," he said. "Not right away. But I'll lease it for five years."

That could work. But— "What happens in five years? Do you return, or does your son come and put me out?"

The bark again. "Well, you'd see how it felt, wouldn't you?"

"I know how it feels," I said, taking his meaning. "I was raised at Hatton."

That silenced him. He turned the cup in long fingers, his eyes moving about the room. Saying goodbye to the house where he'd lived his entire life and had expected to die.

"Five years' lease," he said, "and before that is up, we can discuss whether my family will return." He looked at me squarely. "That might give you time to afford it."

We shared dinner in the hall with plump Lady Margaret; their son, Walter, a sullen young man still grieving his brother; and a small girl named Margaery, who was their dead son's child. Preston and I came to an agreement over the meal, interrupted only once by Walter, who did not relish the idea of leaving.

"Winterset is ours!" He overturned his cup in his passion. "Why should he have it?"

Sir Ralph stared him down. "Because I would like you to live to see twenty, boy."

I would lease the house, and only the house, for the next five years. The steward, Jasper Fowler, would stay on, paid by Preston, to continue running the farm, handling the sale of crops and grain, and seeing to the shearing. Two additional servants would stay with the house, to make certain it was kept up to Preston's standards; I could hire others, if I wished, but his servants would have precedence.

"Do you intend to leave any furniture behind?" I cast my mind about, wondering where I would acquire the necessary items.

"I won't leave you an empty house," he said. "I'll have a bed moved into the great chamber. I imagine you'll want to sleep there, and my wife will not leave without her bed."

"I certainly will not," she said, waking up to the conversation around her. "It's enough that I have to leave my home."

He inhaled a sharp breath. "You know why, Margaret."

"I do not have to like it." Her eyes were pink-rimmed, whether with upset over their upcoming relocation or continued grief for her son. "And I will not leave my bed. It is too much to ask."

"I understand." I was looking forward to a bed to myself, something which had happened so rarely in my life it was as alluring as that chamber on the other side of the hall, which I intended to turn into a library as soon as I was able to call myself master of this house.

"What's wrong with your voice?" little Margaery asked. "Was it always like that?"

I smiled at the girl, who looked like her grandfather with her beaky nose and dark eyes. "No," I said. "When I was your age, I had a beautiful voice. I sang for the king of England."

"What happened to you?"

Oxford—Gregory—the Low Countries—Padua—Salvatore. So many thoughts rushed at me that my head swam. I blamed Sir Ralph's strong beer. "I got sick," I told her. "It's never been right since."

She seemed satisfied. "Do you like dogs? I'm taking my dog with me. You can't have him."

"I've never had a dog." Would I get a dog? It might be nice to have a companion who wouldn't expect me to speak, who would curl at my feet as I read in the evenings.

"Did you think you could buy this whole place?" Sir Ralph appeared more kindly now, having eaten and arranged the situation to our mutual advantage. "Did you not think about the size and all the responsibilities that come with it?"

"Do I look as if I have experience in owning property?" I knew one could not just buy a house of this size, set on substantial ground, without the responsibilities of tenants, livestock, and staff. Sir Ralph had done me a favor in his agreement to let me be leaseholder. "I just want a place away from the court."

"There is no place away from the court if it reaches out to you."

I hastened to Chelsea to share my news. Bianca was still the first person who came to mind when good fortune struck. She was alone, and happy to see me, and we spent the day together in her chamber, knowing Vincent would join us in the evening.

"I will be sorry to see your books leave." She rolled over, resting her head on my shoulder. "It gives you a reason to come here."

Her hair tickled my nose, and I smoothed it away with the arm not pinned down by her body. "I need no reason to come here but you," I said. "The books were an excuse; you know that."

She was silent for a moment. "Perhaps. But I was younger then."

"You are ageless."

It was true. I couldn't imagine the girl she had been when she came to England; I could only see the woman she was now. The years of our acquaintance had passed with few changes to her face or figure; only when she was undressed could I see the silver that ran through her dark hair, the slackening of once-firm skin.

"And you, my Robin, are ridiculous." She circled her fingers through the scant hair on my chest. "Someday, you will appear with a young and beautiful bride, and you will see me for what I am."

I trapped her hand beneath mine. "You know that I shall never marry. It is not in me to want it." I brought her fingers to my lips. "But you still heat my blood. No young bride would do that."

Her hand strayed lower. "Young brides can be taught many things," she murmured. "Do not forget, I was once a bride."

"I prefer you as you are now." I struggled to frame coherent words. Gilbert Turner might have had a short tenure as her husband, but his lessons were long-lasting.

Later, when Vincent returned. I told him my news and accepted his condolences on my departure. "I will visit," I said. "I've told Bianca, my feelings for the two of you go far deeper than your capacity to maintain my library."

"How did you find this place?" Vincent asked. "And why so far away?"

"The family is on their way to France." I explained about Preston's son and his worries about Walter. "I believe he wants to get the younger one away before he ends up in similar straits."

"As might we all." Bianca's earlier lightness had fled. We spoke little of current events during our time together, but she and Vincent were Catholic and not likely to change their beliefs for the king's convenience. Their situation could become precarious at any time.

"I keep my head down," Vincent said. "A man's business can be affected if his beliefs are too loud."

It made me glad that Bianca rarely left the house, though I did not know how much longer a priest would be able to come and say mass for them.

"Should London ever become untenable, please consider Winterset as your own." I smiled to blunt the seriousness of such potential circumstances. "You would at least have no shortage of reading material."

We stayed long over wine, discussing the future. Bianca retired at eleven, and I stood to wish her good evening. In a surprising display of affection before her brother, she took my hands in hers and kissed my cheek. "Be well, Robin," she said. "And be careful. Your world is a dangerous place."

The door closed behind her, and I resumed my seat.

Vincent looked at me, one eyebrow raised. "Everyone's world is dangerous these days."

I had always wondered if he suspected what was between us, or if he cared. The business was his, through her husband, but if Bianca had chosen to remarry, Vincent might have had to find his own wife. I believed he was as much the marrying kind as I was, preferring to have his world made comfortable by someone for whom he had an uncomplicated affection.

"I meant it," I said. "Should it become unsafe for you, I want you to come north."

Vincent refilled our glasses. "It's not like you," he said, "sticking your neck out."

"I wouldn't make the exception for everyone."

Winterset called to me: its comfortable rooms, the nearby cliffs, the sea. Though it was impractical, given my limited funds, when I received Preston's message that they had gone, I decided to take myself north. Some opportunity would present itself; something always had.

I took myself to Cromwell's office and requested to leave his service. "It is beyond time, sir. I am no longer happy here."

Outside his chamber was the never-ending murmur of ambitious young men trying to rise. I had been part of them but never one of them. I would not miss them, save Ned.

"You are well compensated," Cromwell said, assuming financial discontent. He pressed his lips together. "I could perhaps raise you up a bit."

"It's not that, sir." I struggled to put it into words. "It's the dissolution, sir. You know my feelings about the closures—"

His deep-set eyes regarded me. "And I advised you it was in your best interests to go along with the program."

"And I did." It had taken me to Hatton, where I had done things unforgivable by men of God. "Perhaps if I'd gone to any place other than that where I'd been raised, I might feel differently. But it is done, and there is nothing for it. It is best for me to leave before I find myself in a worse situation."

He eyed me with a mixture of surprise and curiosity. "I never took you for a moralist."

"Neither did I, sir. But it appears that I am one."

Once I told Cromwell, my departure was effected with all speed. I had a surprisingly sad parting from Ned.

"I should have expected this," he said, watching from the bed as I gathered my things. "You haven't been happy. You should have let me drown Jack like the rat he is."

"I don't need to be happy," I said. "But I do need to be able to live with myself. As do you, so no drownings, please."

He rummaged among his own wardrobe, coming up with a shirt of mine he'd forgotten to return. It was unwashed and smelled mightily of beer-and-prostitute, his favorite cologne. I bundled it in with my other things, hoping the scent would fade.

"I will miss you," he said. "There's not another man in Cromwell's lot like you."

I closed the chest. "You'll find a new friend," I said. "Willing or not, as I once was."

His face reddened. "You remember everything," he said, cuffing me lightly. "It must be all that reading." Sobering, he slung an arm around my neck. "But you'll be all alone with your books from here on out. What do you say to one last night at the Swanne before you abandon us?"

Chapter 51

As DAWN LEAKS THROUGH the shutters, the sickness begins to recede. I no longer want to hurl up my guts every few minutes, but I'm bone-tired, and my legs are weak.

At some point, I will have to deal with the fact that Seb poisoned us. I understand his desire to delay the journey, for wasn't I thinking the same thing when we arrived? I just hadn't planned on facing—or at least feeling like—death to achieve that end.

Hawkins dozes by the fire, wrapped in two blankets, a basin at his feet. His head tilts back, and he snores like one of the lions in the king's menagerie. He hasn't been sick for several hours. Perhaps the worst is over.

I close my eyes and let exhaustion take me.

"So you decided that abruptly to leave the court?"

My captor is awake and curious again. I open one eye. "I did."

"Was it the house?"

How to explain it? "It was the house," I say, "but also what happened at Hatton. Being a part of the dissolution was bad enough. Confronting the men from my childhood was more than I could bear. I could not reverse what I had done, but I could cease to be a part of it."

There had been other reasons, not so easily articulated, and one of them was cowardice. I did not want to be at court when Henry met the princess and found her not to his liking, as he very soon did. What had he expected? A man of nearly fifty, his beauty gone, presented with a girl of twenty-five, who shared none of his interests, spoke none of his languages, and who did not even dress herself to tempt him.

Hawkins senses the truth. "You missed the wedding."

"I did and shed no tears for having done so. 'I like her not,' he apparently said. I hope he didn't say it to the poor girl's face. Even if she had no English, the king could make himself understood without saying a word."

Stories of cast-off Katherine and beheaded Boleyn had spread throughout Europe. The queen knew the risks, and when Henry suggested she might agree to an annulment, she showed herself to be, if not the prettiest, then certainly the canniest of all his wives. She was happy to pretend her marriage had never occurred, and she was happier still to stay in England, with a considerable pension, and be called the King's dear sister and live happily ever after without having to be bothered ever again with marriage.

"It was a good deal," he says. "A house, a pension, her head."

"Cromwell's reputation with the king never recovered from matching him with the wrong wife. He died because of it. There were other reasons, an entire faction who wanted the old religion back or who just hated him because he was an upstart. None of that was new. But the king's dissatisfaction was enough to make it matter."

I was glad not to be in London then. Hearing of Cromwell's execution sickened me; he was no saint, but most of what he did was to please his master, and with such a master, it took just one misstep to erase decades of dedicated work.

"Henry was a monster," I say. "Let no one tell you otherwise."

Chapter 52

As promised, Sir Ralph left a curtained bed in the upstairs chamber, but there was very little else in the way of furnishings. I did not mind; I prowled the empty house, admiring its bones, deciding what I needed and where it would be situated. It was a new experience and one I liked very much.

Winterset had been built by a Preston ancestor, a yeoman farmer whose son bettered himself and whose son after that—perhaps the beaky man of the now-missing portrait—expanded the house and added the fine stone frontage. The back of the building was rubble stone, more than likely the original material. It merged nicely with the landscape, making the manor seem as if it had grown from the rocky soil.

I furnished the place with little trouble or expense. After spending a few days in spacious emptiness, I inquired of a man I'd met during the monastery project who'd been in charge of disposing of ordinary goods and furnishings. With his help, and in short order, I obtained benches, tables, and painted wall hangings with which to make the house comfortable. None of it was new, but it was good, plain stuff, gently used by the vanished brothers. I bought a bed for the second bedchamber, should I ever be so fortunate as to have guests.

Slowly, it became a home. I awoke every morning to the sound of the sea. Rather than the great chamber at the front, where the bed had been left, I chose a smaller room on the side of the house. Its windows looked past the stables to the edge of the property, where the land ended abruptly and tumbled down toward the shingle below.

I walked the cliffs at all hours, drawn by the ever-changing sea. Some days, it was clear and dark blue; others, the waves were rough, and the horizon a blur that melted into the wide sky. I'd always been drawn to the sea, and now I lived on the edge of the world.

It was some time before I found the route down to the beach, concealed as it was in scrubby trees: a set of meandering, uneven steps cut from the rock. They stopped and started, with several jumps, ending just above a semicircular cove. A small boat hung from a hook pounded into the cliff face, the perfect size for rowing out to meet a larger vessel. Had Sir Ralph, that upstanding Yorkshire gentleman, done business with smugglers?

I visited the shingle until frequent use made the steps come easier. Desk work had made me soft, and my body began to change as I rode and walked the grounds each day.

The dramatic moorland of the North Riding was another country from the Yorkshire dales of my childhood, though they were separated by less than a day's ride. In love as any new landowner, I spent the first few months exploring my world. I avoided the hulking remains of the abbey, but every other town, village, and lonely cliff path called to me.

Indoors, each time I opened the thick oak door to my library, it thrilled me to see the books in their chests, and more especially, the ones I had been able to leave open on the broad, slanted table that served as my reading desk. I had left papers about in Cromwell's offices, but I'd never had a place of my own where I could just get up and know that my things would be left undisturbed until my return.

I expected to miss my work and my friends, but exploration and the organization of my books kept me occupied, and the days passed quickly.

Jasper Fowler, the steward, was a blunt, straightforward man, who grew to like our situation when he understood that I would not interfere in his management of the estate. He joined me for dinner most days, his company making for a pleasant change as I experienced solitude for the first time in my life.

I did not mind being alone. I had been a solitary child and a solitary adult as much as was permitted in the crowded places I had lived. But this was different. I knew none of the neighboring families, and they knew me only as a Cromwell-supporting interloper who took advantage of the departing family.

The servants were a silent few. In addition to Fowler, the Prestons had left behind their cook, who refused to set foot on a ship, and a young girl who cleaned and served at table. Never having had servants, that seemed sufficient, but now I realized more help was required to keep the house running properly.

"We need to take on some people." The maid had just brought in a steaming joint of mutton, her thin arms straining with the burden of the platter. She hurried back to get the other dishes before they grew cold.

Fowler cut himself a thick slice of meat. "Was wondering when you'd come to your senses," he said. "Would you like me to ask in the village?"

"If you would. I think another girl, to help with the cleaning and the laundry, and a young man." I didn't need much in the way of service myself, but I stayed up late and did not like to call for food or drink because the maid had to be up before dawn. A male servant would also be able to be an escort, should I need one while traveling.

"I'll ride in today." He raised his pewter tankard. "People will be glad to see you're taking on help like a normal landlord."

"Do they talk?" I cut another slice of mutton and blessed the cook for her dislike of travel—and her presumed liking of Fowler.

"It's a village. Everyone talks." He wiped his graying beard with a napkin and placed it on the table. "I'll be off now, by your leave. I'll tell anybody interested to come in the morning."

"Morning is best," I agreed. After dinner, I tended to retreat to my books or walk along the cliffs if the weather was fine.

A new maid was easily acquired—I took on the first likely girl who appeared, and the cook and the other maid were happy to have her—but none of the young men who straggled up from the village were right. Considering I didn't really need a servant, it was ridiculous to be so particular, but this would be a young man with whom I would spend significant time. He couldn't be one of these uneducated, loutish boys who did nothing but laugh at my books and leer at the maids. I didn't mind if he was uneducated; I required nothing more than a respect for learning and the female servants left unmolested.

A few weeks after the maid had been installed, I received a visitor. He looked familiar, and when he introduced himself as a representative of the lord chancellor, I recognized him as one of the newest generation of Cromwell's promising young men.

"Lord Cromwell sends his greetings," he said as we sat down over beer. "He hopes you are well and enjoying your life here."

"I am." Cromwell would not send a man all this way simply to inquire about my health and happiness. "What does Lord Cromwell require of me?"

The fellow looked abashed and took a deep draught before responding. "He sent me with this." He pulled a letter from inside his coat. "Though it be sealed, I know it to be an offer of a royal appointment."

An appointment? I opened the letter and confirmed it was thus. I had been awarded the clerkship of the town of Whitby, a position formerly held by Sir Ralph Preston. It was a position that required very little effort on my part but would give me a small but adequate salary.

I had left with no plan in mind for my future, hoping only that the Lord would provide, and the Lord Cromwell had.

I tried to avoid riding directly into Whitby as it caused me to pass the ruined abbey, but it was the least circuitous route, and I wished to make myself acquainted with my new position before it languished vacant for too long. I knew well enough that a void asked to be filled, and I didn't wish to extract anyone from the clerk's duties.

There was very little I needed to acquaint myself with as it turned out—the men who had been delegated to do the work for Preston were more than willing to continue—and I did no more than ascertain that they were honest, with no extreme opinions, before thanking them and preparing to take my leave.

The door to the town hall had not closed behind me when an uproar reached our ears. "Come," I said to the men who had escorted me out. We followed the sound, which came from several men energetically beating a boy in the market square. There was a crowd gathered around, but no one intervened.

I mustered up what authority I had, and shouted, "Stop!"

Nothing happened, other than that one of the men knocked the boy down and kicked him in the ribs. Either they did not hear, or they put as much weight in my authority as I did.

I waded into the melee and got between the boy and the man who'd been kicking him. "What is going on here?"

"Little bastard stole a pie." The man, heavy-shouldered and fat, was panting with effort. I recognized him as the owner of the cookshop.

I looked at the boy, taking in his surprising brown skin and matted hair. "Did you?"

He shrugged. "I was hungry." His nose was bleeding freely, and I thought one of his eyes would soon be black.

"He's been hanging about here for a week. I won't have thieves ruin my business; I'm an honest man."

"And a violent one," I said. "Let the boy go. I'll take responsibility for him."

They knew where I lived, though perhaps not that I was their new town official. I prepared to press the issue, but the merchant turned, kicking the boy one last time so that he curled into a ball at my feet.

"That's right," he said, kicking up dust to mix with the blood. "Beg him for mercy, for you'd get none from me."

I waited until they had gone back inside before turning to the boy. "Are you all right?"

"Yes, sir." He wiped his nose, smearing the gore everywhere, and got to his feet, staggering a bit. "I'll go now."

"Come with me." He was older than I'd first thought, possibly sixteen, but gangly and underfed. I walked him to where my horse was tethered. "Can you ride?"

"I'll walk alongside."

"Get up behind me." I swung my leg over the saddle. "And don't bleed on my coat."

We rode in silence for a mile. The boy's breath bubbled, and several times he spat red into the ditch. I hoped they hadn't broken his ribs.

"Do you have a job?"

"No, sir."

Fowler could find him work doing something. "Do you need one?"

"No, sir," the boy said again. "I'm going to sign onto a ship. Sailors don't mind people like me."

"Are you certain?"

"Yes, sir." His voice thickened, and he cleared his throat and spat again. "My pa was a sailor."

I slowed at the place where the road split, the left road leading toward Winterset, and the right heading for the port. "This will take you there, and you can avoid the town center."

He slid down and tugged off his cap. His nose was definitely broken and swelling badly. Blood tracked down his neck and into his shirt. "Thank you, sir."

"Good luck to you," I said. "If you change your mind, you come to me. A house called Winterset, just south of the abbey."

He bowed and crossed himself. "Bless you for your kindness, sir."

I turned the horse and rode away, wondering what had possessed me to invite the boy to my home, glad he was too sensible to take me up on the offer.

There was a scratch on the door, and the new maid looked in, bobbing a curtsy. "There's a boy, sir."

"A boy?" I looked up from my book. "What boy?"

"I don't know, sir. He's here about the job."

Closing my book, I pushed it to one side. "Do you know him?"

"No, sir."

"Are you sure?"

Her eyes widened. "I'd have noticed him, sir. He's not from the village."

This was interesting. "Bring him in, and bring a jug of ale as well."

The girl bobbed again and returned with the pie man's victim. It was obvious someone had seen to him; he showed signs of washing, with little evidence of his beating other than the bruises on his face. He snatched off his cap and bowed. "I thank you again, sir, for your care the other day."

His clothes were in tatters and had not been good when new. Either they belonged to someone else, or he'd had a growth spurt; his shirt sleeves ended above his wrists, and his coat strained across his shoulders. He had an open, friendly face, with full lips and hazel eyes, shadowed now with bruises.

"'Twas no matter," I said. "Did you decide against the sea?"

He shrugged. "It decided against me. I applied to several captains, and none would have me." His mouth twisted. "Then I saw one of the men from the market, and I left."

At least he'd gotten away in one piece this time. "What's your name?"

"Sebastian." He smiled, then rubbed his jaw.

"Just Sebastian?" I gestured for him to seat himself on the bench before my desk and noted that he carefully shifted a book so as not to sit upon it.

"Sebastian Black," he said, using one of the common surnames given to his people. "I prefer Seb." He ducked his head. "Until recently, I was Brother Jonas, of Middlesbrough."

"You were released from your vows?"

"I had not professed my final vows," he said. "Two months more, and I would have been a brother for life, but now, I don't know what to do with myself. I've been wandering on the road with a few others, but that leads nowhere. I made my way to Whitby because of the port, but… I didn't go there straightaway, as you know."

The maid returned with ale, and I sent her away, pouring the tankards myself. "Why didn't you return to your family after Middlesbrough was closed?"

"I joined the brothers to get away from them." He flushed. "Not just for that, sir—I had a vocation, but I wanted to get away from home as well."

I understood that well enough. "Your nose will never be the same."

"I never intended to live off my looks." He shoved his fingers through his thick hair, which had been trimmed and a comb tugged through it. "Nor my wits, as it may be. I've never stolen before."

Whether it was true or not, I chose to believe him. As a child, I had been saved from theft only by the fear of being caught. I liked this boy; perhaps fortune had thrown him in my path for a reason.

"You may not know," I said, "but I was formerly in the employ of Lord Chancellor Cromwell and was involved myself in the dissolutions."

His face fell. "They said you were from Hatton."

"I spent part of my childhood there," I said, "before I joined the household of Cardinal Wolsey. Later, I worked for Secretary Cromwell, and this past year, he sent me north to deal with the last of the smaller houses."

Sebastian took a healthy gulp of ale. "I'm not sure I can work for you, sir."

"I'm not sure I could, in your place." At his curious glance, I elaborated. "While I believe in the new religion, I did not agree with how Cromwell and the king dealt with the monasteries."

"Yet you did their work."

I raised a brow. "If the abbot gave you an order, would you have argued?"

"He would have been speaking for God."

I smiled. "And Thomas Cromwell spoke for the king, who is head of the new church."

"You had no choice, then?"

It was my turn to drink while I found the words. "A man always has a choice, Sebastian. It's whether he faces up to it and whether he can live afterward with his actions." I set the mug down on my desk. "I chose to keep my head on my shoulders and my bones in their sockets. I chose not to think too hard about the brothers who are now homeless and hungry because of me." I met his gaze frankly. "I do think of them. Every day. They were the kindest men I have ever known and gave me my first home."

He closed his eyes. When he opened them, he had come to a decision. "I'll stay, if you'll have me."

Seb fitted into the household as if he'd always been there, taking heavy work from the maids, turning the stables inside out in a whirlwind of cleaning, and tagging along after Fowler when I had no need of him. At night, he slept on a pallet in the upstairs hall, outside my door, though I told him repeatedly there was space in the attics and he needn't sleep on the floor.

"I'm here to serve you," he said. "I will be where you can find me at all times."

He wouldn't talk about Middlesbrough, but it was easy enough to learn his past before he'd joined the monastery. He'd been raised in the port town of Hartlepool, not far from the priory. His mother was English, and his father was a sailor, a black African come from Spain as a young man.

"Why did you not go to sea?" I asked. His wistful tone made me wonder.

"My pa died when I was five," he explained. "My mum remarried, a farmer she'd met at the market. He took us too—me and my sister—but he wasn't happy about it."

"Because of your color?" It was an easy guess; people outside of the larger towns weren't accustomed to such folk, and there were many who disliked taking on another man's children, before the added complication of them being dark-skinned.

Seb nodded. "He got another boy on my ma straight away, and made it clear I was welcome to stay only until I could survive on my own."

"How did Middlesbrough come about?"

"It was close by," he said. "And I spent so much time praying to God to get me away from my stepfather, it seemed natural." He smiled faintly. "I did love it there. It was quiet, and everyone was so kind."

It was what I'd loved about Hatton; the more I knew this boy, the happier I was that I'd run across him. To my delight—and it shouldn't have been a surprise, for most monks were literate—he had an interest in books. When I saw him looking at an open volume on the table, I asked if he would like to borrow anything from my library.

"Do you have a book of maps?"

"What's your interest in them?" Seb was a constant surprise.

"Just like them." He shrugged. "I guess it was listening to my pa's stories and going with him to look at the ships."

I had a vivid memory of going with Brothers Nicholas and Anthony to greet an abbot visiting from France. They'd had to pry me from the pier, so fascinated was I with the many vessels at rest in the harbor. "I have an atlas you can look at," I said. "A whole book of maps. And there's a globe, besides, put away in the cupboard."

He brightened, and I knew that I had a like mind to talk to and that my quiet life at Winterset need not be so quiet.

Chapter 53

"So CROMWELL LOOKED AFTER you," Hawkins says. It seems to rankle; he'd been thinking better of me until my old master reappeared in a positive light.

"It must have been one of his last acts." When the news of his execution traveled north in the summer, I could scarcely believe it and yet was not at all surprised. "He said more than once that as Wolsey had fallen, so could he, but I hadn't believed it." Despite his missteps and his inability to obtain the divorce, Wolsey never believed Henry would turn on him. "Cromwell was a student of human behavior, of royal behavior. He knew the king's volatility could encompass his end if he failed to please him."

Hawkins eases himself up from the chair where he's spent most of the night. He tries his legs, finds them somewhat lacking, and sits himself down again. "Do you really think the king killed him just because of a marriage?"

Even Thomas Cromwell did not know the workings of Henry Tudor's brain; I could not begin to hazard a guess. "I doubt his only crime was the provision of an unsatisfactory wife," I say, "but the people were accustomed, by now, to the king's marital foibles. It would not have seemed implausible to execute a valued minister, a man he'd just given a barony, for such a reason."

My opinion was that Anne of Cleves was a perfectly adequate wife for a man of Henry's age and history, but not an adequate mate for the vision still held within the royal head. Perhaps Cromwell's choice was a mirror, showing the king his reflection.

Seb knocks, bidding us a good morning. "You both look on the road to recovery," he says, handing us our stinking herbal drinks.

"If not the road to London," Hawkins says sourly. He gulps the liquid, this time without the nose-holding routine. "Do you think eating will kill us, Lewis?"

I consider. My stomach is both achingly empty and fearful of another bout of sickness. "Something bland," I suggest. "Pease pottage, if there is any, Seb, and some bread."

He bows his way out, my loyal poisoner, and I look at Hawkins. "Are you curious about the Howard girl?"

His mouth twists. "I shouldn't be, but you've had me tied up in this tale for a week now. You might as well continue on."

I smile to myself. "She was the most inappropriate wife of all, and the most tragic, I believe. Henry called her his rose without a thorn, but she'd already been pricked by Thomas Culpepper when he met her."

Prurient interest lights his eyes. "It was true she cuckolded the king?"

"Undoubtedly, but she was a child, maneuvered by her family into marrying a sick old man. Who could have blamed her?"

Hawkins snorts. "The king."

"True enough, when it was brought to his attention." I think back on the letters I'd received from Ned, well away from court himself by this juncture. "Do you believe in spirits?"

"No." He leans back, allowing Seb to set up our breakfast on the small table.

I take a tentative sip of ale. It goes down easily, and I tear off a piece of bread to accompany it. "I didn't, at your age. Now that I'm older, closer to meeting the God I haven't served these many years, I'm not so certain. If there are, I believe the shade of Kat Howard will haunt Hampton Court until it is dust."

As we eat, I think of Kat Howard. I could have seen her; she had come north with the king in the autumn of 1541, after another bout of unrest. Ned tried to persuade me, but I refused, wanting no more of kings and queens.

Hawkins pushes back his food, half-eaten, and tries his legs again, walking to the window and back. Looking at his boots, he says, "I'm sorry you had to encounter Darlington on my watch."

"My bruises have been overshadowed by this latest discomfort, I assure you." I hoist myself to my feet and join him in his pacing. My legs feel like jellied comfits, quivering when they should hold firm.

As always, Seb appears at the slightest need, sliding his arm beneath mine.

"I can walk," I say crisply. "I need to be able to stand on my feet, Seb."

"I'm just trying to be of assistance." He takes a step back.

"You're fortunate you didn't eat our meal," I said, "else you would be in this same state."

He retreats, clearly wondering if I will expose him. I will not, but after all these years, I would expect him to warn me before he administered poison. I'd trained him better than that.

"You may go," I say, raising an eyebrow. *No more of your foolishness.*

Hawkins is peering into a clouded glass, inspecting his face. "I look like my father," he says. "My cheeks are sunken."

He does not look like his father. Not on his worst day did Nick Hawkins look like this ordinary young man. I humor him. "We're both a bit worse for wear—though I'm sure the others have enjoyed the rest we've given them."

"He's been with you nearly twenty years?" he asks. "Your servant?"

"Yes. He's the closest I will ever have to a son." I can't imagine myself with children.

"What will become of him, once you're…" He tapers off, clearly no longer anticipating my demise. "Then."

"I wish I knew. I've tried talking to him, and he refuses to listen." I would send word to Ned, if Hawkins allowed. Ned could take charge of him or send him back to Winterset to look after—

"You're thinking of your wife," Hawkins says, looking closely at me. "I couldn't let you stay there long enough to greet her, man, you must understand. We're already beyond the time I promised to have you in London."

I sigh. "I was thinking of her, yes. And I do understand, Hawkins—"

"You can call me Will," he says. "It may not be appropriate, but we've gone through enough together, and I can safely say I've learned as much from you as from my father."

"Will." That was a step more than I expected. "Then, I shall return the compliment, and you may call me Rob."

Chapter 54

"I STILL DON'T UNDERSTAND," Seb said, commencing again a conversation we'd had many times. "Why would you work for Cromwell?"

"I've told you." I made a note to have a carpenter come up from the village to help with the new storage room behind the kitchen. "And told you."

"You grew up at Hatton. How could you do it?"

I put down my pen. "I joined Cromwell years before the dissolution." I tried to explain what a good situation it was for someone like me, but Seb closed his ears. In all other instances, he took me at my word, this boy who had attached himself as firmly as I'd once attached myself to Brother Anselm. "You don't understand—"

"He hated the Catholic church," Seb said. "And you came from it."

I sighed. "I was no longer Catholic by then, and he knew it, as he knew my discomfort with the dissolution. In the end, though, I did as I was ordered."

Like the child he had been not so many years ago, Seb wanted this story repeated at regular intervals: perhaps until he understood why I had done it. "But Hatton was your home."

"As Middlesbrough was yours, but it was not your whole life."

He looked down. "I still miss it sometimes."

There were times when I still missed Hatton, but it did no good to think along such lines any more than it did to think of Anselm. "Do you know what happened to the brothers there?"

"Why would I know?" Seb busied himself with tidying my desk, moving smoothly around me as I tried to stop him. "Just because I was one of them, doesn't mean I know where every last monk has gone."

I gave up. He was a compulsive tidier, and I wasn't an untidy man to begin with.

"I didn't say you did," I said, "but you were on the road a good long time between leaving Middlesbrough and washing up here. I'm surprised you didn't run across any of them."

A shadow passed the window, a man on horseback. "That's Fowler," he said. "I'll go look after his horse. He never brushes them well enough after a long ride."

"There's food missing from the larder," Fowler said as we sat in the hall over a splendid meat pie. "I've questioned the maids. Both claim to know nothing, but there's an entire cheese gone and several loaves of bread."

"Have you spoken to Seb?" Fowler knew how I'd found him, and had probably heard other rumors in the village.

The steward shook his head. "He's yours. I can't imagine the boy would steal, though—he's got it better here than the abbey, and if he were a thief, things would have gone missing afore now."

I retired to the library. Within the hour, Seb would bring wine and a piece of fruit, a final repast before bed. Promptly at nine, his soft knock sounded, and the door opened.

He placed the tray on the table and put the glass by my hand. "Is there anything else?" he asked. "If not, I'll go up and ready your chamber."

"Sit for a moment," I said. "Fowler gave me some bad news this afternoon."

His forehead creased. "What is it?"

"The women have been selling food out of the larder. Tomorrow, I shall have to let them go. We may be on light rations for a few days until they can be replaced." I looked at him keenly. "Can you cook?"

His face flushed. "They would not steal from you, master. The cook has been here since the time of the Prestons, and both maids are good girls."

"Someone is stealing, and it's not the steward," I said. "His men rarely come indoors, and he vouches for their honesty as I have vouched for yours. It must be the women."

Seb's hands knotted together. "Don't punish them. I'm the thief."

"Don't take the blame," I said. "If they've stolen, they should bear the punishment. You haven't done anything wrong."

He paced back and forth in front of the fire. "But I have, master."

I made sure he didn't see my smile. "What have you done, Sebastian?"

He swung around. "Remember when you asked if I knew what happened to any of the brothers?" At my nod, he continued, "I don't know where they all are, of course—most of them scattered when they were put out—but there's a Brother Rufus, from Hatton, concealed not ten miles away."

Brother Rufus! My rush of pleasure faded almost immediately when I recalled my last meeting with my old schoolmaster. "Why concealed? He was released from his vows."

"He's not alone." He was unable to keep still. "There's nearly a dozen of them. Some are considered criminals."

"What do you mean?"

"There are three from Whitby," he explained, "and one from another house. Many were involved in the pilgrimage."

"Charges were dismissed against all but the ringleaders." I remembered what happened to the ringleaders—the scapegoats—and then tried not to remember.

"Brother Terence was accused of stealing treasure from his house to support the pilgrimage. Those charges were not dismissed, nor were the ones against the Whitby monks, on the same grounds."

I was not surprised that some monasteries had used illicit funds from their treasuries to support the pilgrimage, but it did surprise me that all those monks had not been discovered. Cromwell's death would not have stopped the hunt, and the men who took over his duties, Richard Rich and Thomas Wriothesley, among others, would have no more sympathy for theft than their master, or the king.

"How long have they been there?"

"Almost two weeks. They move frequently, not wanting to get anyone into trouble."

"So Fowler taking an inventory of the larder has disrupted their schedule?"

"I just wanted to help them." Seb dropped to his knees in front of me. "Please don't turn them in, master. I'll tell the brothers that we've been found out, and I'll go with them. I won't take anything else, but I can't allow them to be arrested because of me."

"I can't allow them to be arrested because of you either." I gestured for him to get up. "I have no animus toward these monks, especially the ones involved in the pilgrimage."

It couldn't go on. Though the ground was clear and hard at the moment, soon enough the snow would come, and a band of underfed, possibly elderly, men would starve or freeze. Something had to be done.

There was no safe place for them in England. On a larger estate, a few might be taken on as servants; a single man could be stashed away as an eccentric relative, but what did one do with a dozen men?

"Fowler is riding to York tomorrow," I said. "Take the cart after he leaves, and get them here without being seen."

"But master—"

"I'm not going to turn them in," I snapped. "If that were the case, I would simply have the barn raided." I grasped Seb's arm. "You and I, we're going to get them out."

"Out?"

"Out of England," I said. "I'm not sure how yet, but we're going to get them safely away."

Fowler rode out at dawn, and within minutes, the cart rattled off in the opposite direction. One of the maids brought my morning ale and cheese in Seb's place, knocking brightly on my bedchamber door.

"Come." I was already up and dressed, following his journey in my mind as I tried to come up with a plan to dispose of a dozen retired monastics.

The girl placed my tray on the table. "Is there anything else, sir?"

"Not at the moment," I said. "But tell the cook we are expecting guests later today. She should prepare supper for at least ten."

"Ten?" She goggled at me, unable to conceive of ten visitors to Winterset when we'd not had that many since my arrival.

"Tell her it doesn't have to be elaborate. But they will be hungry, and they will be staying for a few days, so you should ready the other rooms."

"I will, sir." The girl curtsied and fled, clattering down the stairs to spread the news of our imminent invasion.

After breakfast, I rode into Whitby. My business took the better part of the morning, and when I returned in the afternoon, the covered cart was in the rear courtyard.

I stripped off my cloak and my wet gloves and went straight to my library. Seb would do what Seb did best: arranging the lives of others. He would know I was back, and he would come to me when he was ready.

Sounds of activity echoed through the house, but I remained closeted, letting him get our guests sorted into their chambers. I hoped that fires had been laid in the rooms; the day was chill, and the men were unlikely to have had a fire anytime recently.

It was nearly supper time when he knocked on the library door. "Are they here?"

"They are, master." He looked pleased with himself. "There are four each in the guest chambers."

"Weren't there twelve?" It wasn't like him to be inaccurate.

"Ten," he said. "But one is sick, and his friend wouldn't leave him." I didn't waste time in argument, just gave them food and blankets, and brought the others here. I'll go back tomorrow and not take no for an answer."

I pushed back my chair. "Are they well enough to join us at table?"

Seb smiled. "I believe they are." Sobering, he asked, "What is your plan? I hated not being able to tell them when they asked me."

"I will reveal all over supper."

While in the village, I had stopped at the clerk's office, checking on my surrogates and repeating a rumor of monks arrested in Lincolnshire for participation in the pilgrimage. Their response confirmed that the crown was still looking for all such men. It would not be as straightforward as I had hoped to get Seb's monks out of England.

But as always, there was a way, and the price was within my grasp.

I took in the unusual sight of a full table, going immediately to Brother Rufus and taking his hands. "Welcome, brother," I said. "Welcome to this house. You and your brethren are safe here."

Rufus was clean and neatly dressed—they all were—but far thinner than when I had last seen him. His tonsure was grown out, making his face, which still bore the expression that cowed many a boy, somewhat unfamiliar. "How is that?" he asked. "How are we safe under your roof when you evicted us from ours?"

They all began speaking at once, and I raised my hands to quiet them. "I mean what I say. You are safe here. I can't undo what was done or change my part in it, but I can make amends now. The king's men are still looking for some of you, so I intend to get you to safety."

I looked from man to man, meeting eyes that were blue or brown, steady or watery, but all filled with some degree of skepticism. I explained the plan simply, ending with, "You have every right not to trust me, and if you choose not to take my offer, you will be given food and coin and allowed to leave under your own power. There are several days before the ship departs, and I would ask you to take that time in prayer and discussion. Decide for yourselves what is right."

I walked to the head of the table and sat down. "Please, partake of my hospitality, and know that you are welcome here." I looked at Rufus. "Would you say the blessing?"

The meal was quiet, the habit of a lifetime difficult to break. The maids brought in dish after dish, twittering with excitement to have company in the house. The cook herself brought in the final platter, curtsying and smiling at the motley collection of men.

When the trenchers were empty, I rose from my seat.

"I will leave you now," I said. "Please consider the house as your own. If you need anything, Seb will accommodate you."

Instead of reading as I normally would, I pulled several sheets of writing paper from a leather box and sharpened a quill. It had come to me during dinner where I could send the monks to guarantee their safety, but it involved writing a very difficult letter.

After a few false starts, I had it.

> *My dearest Brother Salvatore,*
>
> *It has been many years since we parted, but you have been ever present in my mind and my prayers, as I hope I have been remembered in yours.*
>
> *You will have heard, even in the peace of Santa Giustina, of the turmoil that has befallen my country and the harm which has come to many religious folk because they hold to Rome.*
>
> *The bearer of this letter is one such monk, and more than that, he was my teacher. I told you of him in a letter I once wrote, and of the love of learning he instilled in me. He and his brethren are no longer safe here. I remember my time with you as a time of sanctuary, and I would grant that same peace to these men who have suffered much because of their beliefs.*
>
> *Brother Rufus will tell you of my part in their losses. He will speak the truth, and he will no doubt be kinder than I deserve. Your oca has strayed from the path of righteousness. Sending these men to you is part of my work to regain that path.*
>
> *I thank you for taking in these worthy men and for being*

the most worthy man of my acquaintance. You will be in my prayers until my last breath.

> *Yours in this life and the next,*
> *Robert Gideon Lewis*

I dropped my head into my hands, tears stinging the corners of my eyes. It was true that Salvatore had a place in my prayers, but I tried not to think of him otherwise, even after fifteen years. Part of me still craved his voice, the touch of his hand, the commonplace moments of our friendship.

I remained in my library until bedtime, unwilling to show myself again and quite happy, for the moment, that none of them had knocked on my door.

"Did our guests sleep well?" I cut a slab of cheese and put it on a wedge of bread. Sliding my knife into the thick crust, I held it over the fire, deeming it ready when my skin started to prickle with the heat.

"They did and broke their fast downstairs," he said. "They aren't comfortable with the maids fetching for them."

I savored the hot melted cheese. "Are you returning for the other two?"

"Yes. Brother Francis is coming along to help convince them."

"Should I accompany you?"

Seb looked shocked at the suggestion. "You are too noticeable, master."

I cocked an eyebrow. "And you are not?"

He looked at his brown hands. "I look like a worker, and Brother Francis can pass as one. You look like a gentleman."

"It has only taken thirty-odd years for anyone to say that to me."

Coming downstairs a while later, I was met with a familiar sound. The monks had discovered the chapel on the other side of the hall. I looked in and saw that Seb, Fowler, and all the other servants knelt there.

I retreated, shutting the door behind me. It was not my place to be there, but it seemed fitting that, in this house whose people had been driven off by the Pilgrimage of Grace, mass was again being heard.

Chapter 55

"DIDN'T YOU CARE?" WILL Hawkins asks.

"Care?"

"That they were Catholic."

It is an odd question from someone who follows the Pope. "Why would I care? I was born a Catholic. Everyone was Catholic then; we didn't think much about other religions. There were Jews in London, of course, and the Crusades taught us of the Moslems that Christianity tried—and failed—to exterminate. They value their religion as much as we value ours."

Those strange religions have always interested me, but there was never any time to speak at length to any of the faithful, and what I wanted to learn was not always contained in books, a lesson that took decades for me to learn.

I give Will Hawkins the benefit of more of my knowledge. "The world would be a more peaceful place if everyone could just accept each other's faith. God is God, no matter what name you use or how you dress Him up."

He looks shocked. "Now you sound like a heretic again."

"I never said I wasn't." I take a careful sip of ale. Untainted, it tastes like the freedom I shall soon experience: freedom, at least, from this house. "The reformation took away the Latin so everyone could understand the Bible and the mass, and I approved of that. Everyone should understand. It also took away the rote prayers, on the theory that coming up with our own words deepens the experience. I'm not so certain of that, though I am certain that most people prayed to God in their own words all along, in addition to whatever prayers they'd been told to say."

Will shakes his head. "I've never heard it explained like this."

"If you have any personal connection to God, you speak to him." I exhale deeply, wishing I could release this tired conversation as easily as air. "I've been deep in conversation with Him these many years. Penance is a tricky thing."

Chapter 56

FINDING A WAY TO save the monks was part of my penance. The books were one thing; saving the libraries was a good deed, but as much as I loved them, books weren't men. To restore the damage I had done, I needed to get these monks to a place of safety.

Seb and Brother Francis returned. I went out to assist them and was shocked to find that the brother who would not leave his sick companion was none other than Anselm.

Unthinking, I embraced him. He was stiff in my arms, and I drew back. "Welcome, brother."

He looked around. "Working for Cromwell has been profitable."

I saw the house through his eyes. "I no longer work for the court."

"Help me get him out." Seb had rigged a litter for the sick man, and I reached in and grabbed the end. He weighed almost nothing, swaddled even as he was with rags and blankets.

We got him indoors, and I said, "You can put him in my room."

Seb stopped. "But, master—"

"I can sleep in the library," I said. "This man needs warmth and a good bed."

"I'll not say no to that," came a faint voice from the swaddling, and Brother Anselm elbowed me aside to put his hand on the old man's head.

"You are safe now, brother," he said softly. "I am with you."

A bony hand issued from the blanket, and Anselm caught it. The raw affection between the two made me uncomfortable, and I gestured to Seb to gather the sick man up and carry him to my chamber.

I retreated to the library and shifted things about so there was an open space before the fire. This would serve as my bed until the old monk either passed on or recovered.

A knock raised me from my reading. "Enter."

Like the others, Anselm was dressed in secular clothing. He still looked like the man I had known, just thinner and worn down. He glanced with approval at my books. "You have done well here."

I shrugged. "There was only so much I could do." I closed the book I was reading and turned to face him. "They were burning them or selling them to fishmongers as wrapping. I sent the most valuable books to the king, who would appreciate them, but many others made their way here."

"Why would the king appreciate anything from our libraries?" Anselm asked. "He is excommunicate; our books should mean nothing."

Excommunication, although painful, had not caused the king to lose his faith or his appreciation of beauty. "He is a mystery," I said. "He can believe two things at once and find nothing strange in it."

Anselm's brows arched. "He can cause offense to God, destroy our way of life, and still appreciate a good bit of illumination?"

I shook my head; I could not explain the king. "How is your friend?"

"Dying," he said bluntly. "But now he will die warm and indoors, surrounded by his brethren, as you allowed Anthony to die."

I did not wish to think about that. "Was this brother at Hatton?"

"Not when you were there." Anselm turned to look out the window, toward the sea. "When his priory closed, only the prior was given a new placement. Brother Levi was handed a few shillings and left to fend for himself." His palm struck the window frame. "He is near eighty. What did they think would happen? One of our farmworkers found him in a ditch."

"You have done well by him," I said. "And I will continue your work." I explained that I had found a captain willing to take the monks as far as Antwerp. "The ship leaves in two days. Sebastian and I will care for Brother Levi until his death. We will give him a Christian burial here on the property."

"That is kind," he said, "but I will stay with him. Let the others get to safety. I will make my own way after Levi is gone."

I knew better than to argue. Anselm had always been a decided man; I remembered his clashes with Prior Richard on matters of obedience. "It is perhaps best; I'm sure he would like a familiar face by his side."

"How do you intend to get them out?" Anselm drifted to a table and opened a volume. "Bringing a score of unfamiliar men into Whitby will not be easy."

It would be next to impossible. I had looked into it, and there was no way to get that many letters of transport without explanation. "They do not travel as passengers; they go as cargo."

At his look, I explained further. "You see the cliffs outside the window? There is a small beach below, and on that beach is a boat which can be rowed out to the ship. They will drop anchor, and Seb and I will row them out to the ship."

"You've taken to smuggling?" There was a tinge of laughter in his voice.

"Not until now."

My words fell on deaf ears as Anselm took up another book and gasped. "This is from Hatton."

It was a history of the area, begun by the Hatton brothers in the thirteenth century. I took it because of my connection to the place; Anselm's ties were even deeper. "It was yours," I said. "It still is. Please, take it with you when you leave."

He held it to his breast. "It may be safer here," he said. "But I shall take it up and read it to Brother Levi." He reached out a hand, and I took it. "It is a strange path that has brought us together, Robin, but I thank you for your care of these men."

"There is no one left to give me penance," I said. "I have chosen this myself. It is not yet enough."

Seb pushed his way into the library after Anselm had gone. "Don't worry," he said, swinging the crackling cloth bag down from his shoulder, "I left the feather bed for Brother Levi, but you can't sleep on the floor, master."

"It wouldn't be the first time. I slept with a cow when I was a boy."

"At Hatton?" His eyes were wide.

"No, long before, when I lived in Hawley. She was warm as a feather bed, that cow, but she didn't much like having me in her stall."

Wrapped in a blanket before the dying fire, I remembered the Wythes' shed. When I was sleeping there, cocooned in straw and stealing warmth from animals, I would have laughed at anyone who told me I would someday live in a house with more beds than people.

The scent of lavender, clean and calming, reached my nose through the tight-woven bed. It was one of the tricks of housekeeping that I appreciated without understanding how it came about.

In the morning, Seb brought a basin and a body cloth to the library, and I rubbed my face and neck until the skin stung with the cold. My beard prickled but was not yet long enough for him to wield his razor to any effect. Standing before the fire, I pulled on a fresh holland shirt and my customary black hose and allowed him to tie my points. "Are the brothers awake?"

"They've been up since dawn. They've already sung prime, you slug-a-bed."

I cuffed him affectionately. "You've become far too familiar, young man. I may send you to Antwerp with them, if you're not careful."

That afternoon, the men learned to navigate the cliff stairs, with varying degrees of success. They'd not all been active men, and their strength was curtailed by hunger, so they did not have an easy time. It was soon obvious that all but the two eldest would be able to manage. Both men could walk, but they were unsteady on their feet, certainly not capable of the descent. Seb and Rufus volunteered to carry them, hoisting the men on their backs to practice.

There was a sense of excitement in the house. The servants, including Fowler, had been brought in on the plan; it was difficult to keep them in ignorance of what was going on. Fowler offered to take Rufus's place carrying the monk. "I've climbed that cliff for all my life, and you've done it what—twice? You'll drop yon old man and kill yourself trying to save him."

Rufus did not object and turned instead to check the packs that had been assembled for each man. I called him aside and gave him the letter I prepared. "You may not need this," I said. "The Low Countries are very welcoming of refugees from England. But if you—any of you—feel the need to go further, this letter is for a monk at Santa Giustina in Padua. He is an old friend and will make you welcome."

He took the letter and slid it inside his surcoat, which had been fitted with pockets for carrying letters and such. The hilt of a knife was visible, and I wondered how many of these men carried steel near their hearts.

"You've done God's work," he said, "helping us."

"I did the king's work first," I said. "You wouldn't need my help now if I hadn't."

Rufus made a sound of disgust. "You always were a self-important little bastard. This is no more your fault than it is the kitchen maid's."

Levi and Anselm stayed close in my room. The old monk was failing rapidly, despite his comfortable conditions; he was weakened by his travails and looked peacefully toward his end. Anselm was not so accepting, but he did not let his friend see his anger, going out and walking the cliff during the periods when he would allow me to sit with Levi.

"He's a good man," the old monk said as we sat together in the fading winter light. "Just impatient with the world."

"Most of us are." The fire was built up, and the curtains drawn close around the bed, with only an opening near the pillow so we could converse. "Brother Anselm was good to me when I was a boy."

Levi's eyes opened, bright with life despite his pain. "He told me of you—of your boyhood at Hatton and of your return."

I looked down at my hands. "I regret my return. I was not strong enough to refuse."

His hand crept from beneath the covers and touched mine, light as a bird. "If it hadn't been you, it would have been someone else." He continued, wheezing, "You were there for Brother Anthony, he told me."

"Yes." That was another regret I would live with for the rest of my life. "He brought me to the priory as a child and saw me come back as a destroyer. How he must have hated me."

"Why would he hate you?" He barely finished the question before a paroxysm of coughing took him.

I sat on the edge of the bed and put my arm around his frail shoulders, holding him until the spasm passed. When it did, we were both shaking. I gave him a drink, and we returned to our prior positions.

"How could he not hate me?" I responded as though there had been no time between question and answer.

"Anthony died surrounded by those who loved him—including you." Levi dropped back against the pillow, his strength failing him. "That is all we can ask for."

The snow started at daybreak, a lazy, drifting of flakes which would not delay the departure of the ship. I looked around at the group at the table. "You'll have to wear everything you own," I said. "Between the climb and being rowed out to the ship, you'll be chilled through."

"We'll manage," Rufus said. "You keep safe here. It won't do to have it known what you've done."

I didn't tell them that word had already spread of their presence; when I circulated my false rumor of monks in Lincoln, I was told of a group in Yorkshire. They had enough on their minds without that extra worry.

We sent the first group—the able-bodied—down near ten in the morning. They could get the boat ready and light a fire on the shore. Seb went down with them and returned quickly.

"They're all right," he said. "The wind is fighting any chance of a fire, though."

It wasn't necessary, but it would have helped to keep them warm while they waited. I looked at the remaining four men. "We should start."

We made our way through the trees to the edge where the steps began. Seb bent down, and we got Brother Oswald on his back. "This will take some time, brother," he cautioned. "Let me know if you need to rest."

I took the lead, with Seb behind me and Rufus in the center. Fowler was behind him with Brother Jeremiah, and Anselm followed up the rear. He wouldn't leave but insisted on seeing his brethren safely on board the ship.

It was slow going. The first steps were steep but wide, and after I attained the first ledge, I turned and guided Seb to flat ground. Despite the cold, he was sweating heavily. Was it strain or fear? Brother Oswald's eyes were closed, but his grip was still strong. After a few minutes, Seb was rested, and we continued.

Behind me, I could hear Fowler and Rufus negotiating the cliff. I couldn't see them over Seb, so I had to pray they were all right.

I was not the only one praying. "*In nomine patris, et filis, et spiritus sancti…*" came from behind me, and gradually we all joined in, reciting the paternoster as we made our painstaking way to the beach. It gave us something to focus on besides the biting cold and the stones skidding underfoot.

At the halfway point, I stopped again. "Is everyone all right?"

"Still here," Rufus said. He was visible over Seb's shoulder, ruddier than usual but seemingly all right.

"Here, sir." Fowler sounded a bit out of breath. "Are you doing well back there, brother?"

"I haven't seen the sea since I was a boy," said Brother Jeremiah. His voice piped like a child's. "I could have run these steps then without a care."

"Anselm?"

A pause. "I'm here."

I couldn't see him. "What's wrong?"

"Hate heights," he said. "That's all. I'm fine.'"

The wind buffeted us, and I leaned against the rock face. "Stay here," I suggested. "We'll join you once the ship's off."

"No." There was determination in his voice. "I want to see them off from the shore. You might need me, and I'm not staying on this blasted rock alone."

We continued our descent. The last steps were narrower and involved an open area where some rock had fallen away. I braced myself, and Seb crossed it with my assistance and a push from Rufus. The process was repeated for Fowler and Jeremiah, and there was a thud and a spray of pebbles as Anselm landed heavily behind them.

The prayers started again, and as I dropped the last few feet onto the shingle, I was immediately surrounded by the other monks.

I exhaled.

We had done it. All that remained was for the ship to appear and Seb and Fowler to make two trips with the monks in the small boat.

The monks had gotten a small fire going. Brother Francis was feeding it with scrub from the dune, and we clustered around, letting the old men stand closest to the flames. Anselm hung back.

I joined him. "Fear of heights, and you came down here?" I asked. "I had trouble with it in the beginning, and heights don't bother me."

"Going back up won't be as bad." He was white around the lips. "Once I know they're safe."

"But you're not." What would become of him after Levi's inevitable passing? "Have you thought about that?"

He looked toward the sea. "Not yet. One thing at a time."

The boat was brought down from its anchorage. Two pair of oars lay neatly inside. There had been but one before; Seb had made further provision to ease the trip out.

The snow was harder now, and the waves battered the shore with greater power. It was still possible to row out to the ship, but every moment we waited would make it more difficult.

Seb approached. "I think we should take the old ones out first, master. Get them aboard and warm."

"How many do you reckon you can carry?"

"Four, plus two to row. You and Brother Anselm stay on shore."

"Why must I stay ashore?" I bristled at being safe on land while my servant risked his life; his attachment to the monks was no greater than my own.

"Because Fowler and I are more fit," he said. "You're a good man, but you get out of breath saddling a horse. I can't be worrying about you when I need to worry about them."

"I could manage." My tone made me flinch; I sounded like the young, petulant Robin who wanted to do something forbidden.

"You could." His voice softened. "But we can do it faster, and speed is more important than good intentions."

He was right. I looked up, scanning the horizon, just as Fowler said, "There. Coming round the headland."

There was a flurry of excitement as the ship approached. A lantern swung on the port side, in case there was any question that this was the vessel we awaited.

I handed Seb a purse. "When you go out with the first four, let them know that you'll bring this with the second lot, so they'll be sure to wait." A ship's captain was always willing to add to his tally for the voyage.

The two elderly monks were put into the boat. Anselm and I approached, receiving blessings from each. Rufus and Donald joined them, and Fowler climbed in and took up a pair of oars while Seb made ready to push off.

Rufus pulled me in close. "I wasn't happy about coming here," he said, "but you've likely saved our lives with this scheme. I thank you, Robin."

"Don't thank me," I said. "Pray for me."

He smiled. "I always have."

The boat slid into the water, Seb splashing alongside and jumping in when they were afloat. The rest of us remained on shore, watching the boat pitch and bob, disappearing from sight a few times as the waves grew higher. The wind picked up. My muscles ached with sympathetic strain, imagining how hard it was to move forward—and they would have to do it again.

"There." Anselm was at my side. "They've dropped the ladder."

Squinting, it was possible to see the old men being carried up, the younger ones scrambling behind. The rope swayed in the wind, straightening as Seb dropped into the boat and they began the return to shore.

The fire was dead by the time they grew close, and the four remaining men embraced Anselm, blessed me quickly, and ran out into the surf.

"They'll be frozen." Anselm shivered in the stiff wind.

"Almost as bad as Seb and Fowler." I met his eyes. "You should go back to the house and tell Brother Levi and get warm. I'll wait for them."

"Levi is in good hands." Anselm was right. The cook and the maids fluttered over the ancient monk; he would want for nothing in our absence.

The second journey took longer, the water increasingly rough. Anselm and I prayed aloud; I knew not whether our prayers reached heaven, but they concentrated our minds and calmed us when there was nothing to be done. Several times, they were blown back, their strength insufficient to the waves, until the monks took the oars. With two men to each oar, they grew closer and closer until they were at last within reach of the ladder. One man jumped, climbed, was pulled up. Then another and another. Finally, the fourth man made his ascent. Before he cleared the rail, the boat pushed off.

Rowing with the wind was easier, and in no more than ten minutes, I was able to run into the waves to pull the boat onto the shingle. Both men were drenched, their fingers stiff on the oars. We helped them out, and I pushed Seb toward the steps.

"We'll handle this," I said. "You need to get in front of a fire."

They ducked their heads into their collars and trudged away. Anselm and I dragged the boat to safety and returned it to its hook.

As we approached the cliff, I could see the other two were nearing the top. I looked at Anselm. "Ready?"

He pulled his coat tighter. "As ever I'm likely to be."

I would let him set the pace. "You first."

We started off well, climbing steadily despite the snow. Anselm's breathing was loud. Now that we were alone, his fear was palpable. I was surprised he'd concealed it so well on the descent. He paused at the second stopping place, leaning hard against the rock.

I joined him, touched his arm. "Stretch your leg across," I shouted. "It's not as far as it looks."

A thick gray eyebrow raised. "Maybe I should climb on your back?"

I bit back a retort. It wasn't easy for him to show weakness before me, who had once been a child at his elbow. "Take your time, brother, I'm only worried that the snow will make it hard going above."

That stirred him, and he accomplished the transfer to the other side in one smooth move. I followed, and soon we were on the final section which had, as I feared, gotten slippery. We inched along the icy surface, step by step, until we were within reach of the top.

Seb's head appeared over the edge. "Grab my hands, brother," he called. "Almost there."

With Anselm safely up, I quickened my pace and hit a patch of ice. My feet went out from under me, and I fell, sliding toward the edge and the swirling flakes beyond. I clawed at the rock and threw myself down so I wouldn't go over, and a bolt of pain shot through my knee.

"Master!" Seb scrambled down, squatting on the step above me and raising me up. "Are you hurt?"

"My knee." With his strong hands holding me steady, I was able to climb the last steps. Never had I been so glad to be on solid ground. I leaned against him and looked out to sea. The ship was barely visible in the mist. "They're safe," I said. "That is what's important. I'll mend."

While Seb waited for us, Fowler went on to alert the servants of our return. We stumbled into a hall made snug with a roaring fire and the cook and maids bringing platters to the table.

My face stung with the sudden change in temperature, and as much as I wanted a drink and a full belly, I also wanted to retreat to my chamber and sleep away the sudden shaking that enfeebled my limbs. Because of my own clumsiness, I had nearly undone myself.

I couldn't retreat to my chamber; Brother Levi was still in residence. But the rooms vacated by the other monks were available. I turned toward the stairs. My knee stabbed again, and I stopped, gasping.

"Clothes," I said to Seb. "We need dry clothes, and I don't think I can manage the steps."

"I'll fetch them." He took off with Anselm while I swayed before the fire.

The cook crept up to me. "Are they all off, sir?"

"They are."

"God be praised." She pressed a cup into my hand. "You're a good man, sir, and no mistake. You saved them."

I drained the cup, leaning against the mantel and staring into the flames, feeling my knee throb in time with my heart. Seb joined me with a dry shirt and hose, and I leaned on him as we walked to the library. There was no fire, but I was warm with beer and exhaustion. I stood as he stripped off my wet things and manhandled me into dry ones.

"I'll take care of these," he said. "Jasper and Anselm's clothes are drying in the kitchen. They've been cooking all afternoon to celebrate."

I sat down with Fowler and Seb. Anselm joined us shortly after, having spent a few minutes with Brother Levi, sharing the good news. We dug into our trenchers like starving men, exchanging not a word. There was nothing left to say. If it wouldn't have upset the women, we would have gone to bed. Once supper was cleared away, we remained at the table with more beer, too tired to move.

"Did you hear something?" Seb turned toward the window.

"Just the wind."

"No," he said, and was interrupted by a pounding at the door. Now I could hear what his sharper ears had picked up, the sound of hooves on the cobbled courtyard.

"Open the door." I pushed myself up and found Anselm at my side.

Seb slid back the bar, and men crowded in, pushing him back. They were heavily armed and dressed for the weather. They filled the hall, spilling over onto the stairs.

"What is the meaning of this?" I strode forward, ignoring the pain in my fear. "What business do you have here?"

A man stepped forward, shaking snow from his cloak. "Beg pardon for the intrusion, sir. Is this your house?"

"It is." Over his shoulder, I saw familiar, malicious blue eyes. I was dizzy with exhaustion and pain, and now rage that Jack Darlington would enter my house with ill intent. "As I am sure your companion here is well aware."

The man looked around, then returned his gaze to me. "My name is Alfred Gowan. There's a rumor of renegade monks in the area, and the former owner of this house had popish sympathies." He was repeating information he'd been given. "You are Robert Lewis?"

"I am. As your companion is well aware."

Darlington drew himself up in a way I remembered, a peacock spreading its tail when challenged. "Every rumor must be investigated if these men are to be rooted out."

"The previous owner of this house fled the country," I informed Gowan, "because of such sentiment. The house has been in my possession these two years."

The men were milling about, trying to see past me. Darlington edged forward, and I blocked him. "Many in this part of England still sympathize with the old religion."

"They will be found out in the end." Disappointment had not been kind to him. His habits had begun to show; he was not as pretty as he once had been. Drink, I assumed. Women, undoubtedly, though they didn't show on the face.

"They could still be here," he said. "I'll have this place turned upside down."

Gowan, in charge of the expedition, elbowed him to keep quiet.

I smiled, knowing my calm would infuriate him. "Master Gowan, your companion has any number of reasons for wishing me ill. Perhaps not sufficient reason to bring armed men to my home in the dark of night, hoping to catch us unawares or to perhaps make a move that could be misinterpreted so someone could be hurt." I spoke to Gowan, ignoring my nemesis. "Ask him his motives."

"He's a papist sympathizer, same as Preston." Darlington's face, red from the cold, flushed further with anger.

Again, a bland smile directed at the leader of the party. "With my—our—history with Cromwell, you should know I'm not likely to be harboring monks."

Darlington continued to bluster, but Gowan heard me. "Who are these men, sir, if you please?"

I gestured. "My servant, Sebastian Black, whom you nearly knocked down. Jasper Fowler, my steward. And—" I looked at Anselm "—Gideon Lewis, my uncle."

"Are there others here?"

I swung my arm wide. "Feel free to look. There are three women in the kitchens, and possibly a few of the land workers, hiding from the weather." Anselm's fingers tightened on my arm. "My grandfather is abed upstairs. He is ill, and I would prefer he not be disturbed."

Several of Gowan's men headed for the kitchen, and I heard shouts of feminine outrage.

"I must look, sir," Gowan said. "I have my orders."

Seb spoke up. "My master has an injury; he cannot accompany you. I'll show you the rooms. Please do not alarm the old man."

Gowan alone followed him. I remained with the rest, listening to their footsteps overhead. "Would you like to check the rooms down here?" I asked. "Uncle, please show them the library, the chapel, and the storage rooms."

"You have no family," Darlington said when we were alone. "These are just more of your lies."

"Even a bastard has to spring from somewhere," I said. "It was during the dissolution that I found them—not my parents, but these two. Finding kin late in life is better than finding them not at all."

The party returned from the kitchen, looking over their shoulders as if fearing the cook was still behind them. They were wet and unamused by their errand and cast disgusted glances toward Darlington, who still circled me.

I pointed toward the hearth. "Warm yourselves," I said, "whilst they investigate."

They did not need to be told twice, and when Gowan returned with Seb, only Darlington remained by the door. The others were arrayed before the fire, their wet wool stinking powerfully of sheep.

"Come along," he said. "There's no one upstairs but the old man. Where are the others?"

The remaining two emerged from the library, shaking their heads. "No one in there, sir."

Fowler spoke for the first time. "You'll be wanting to search the barns and the storage sheds, I suppose?" He reached for his coat. "You might want to warm yourselves a bit first; there are five or six likely buildings where they could be hiding."

A variety of expressions crossed Gowan's face, chief among them a desire to be in front of his own fire, with his own beer. "I will bid you good evening," he said. "It is obvious we were mistaken. I'm sorry to have disturbed you."

Darlington wouldn't give up. "We should check the outbuildings," he said. "He could have them concealed anywhere."

"I'll not be out in this for a moment longer than I must." Gowan looked down his nose. "And you'll not come back here on your own either. Robert Lewis is the appointed clerk of Whitby; he could have you in irons."

I wasn't sure if I had that much power, but I tried to appear as if I did. The door closed behind them, and they circled the courtyard and rode away. Soon all that remained of their visit were puddles on the wide planked floor.

"Whew." Seb reached inside his codpiece and brought out a rosary. "This might need to be blessed, Brother Anselm. I was able to catch it up, and there was nowhere else to put it."

Anselm's lips quivered, and he began to laugh. Exhausted and relieved, we all joined in, tears streaming down our faces as we released the stress of the long day.

"I think they're as blessed as they need to be," he wheezed. "You saved them from those heretical bastards."

His words stopped me, but I let them go. I was a heretical bastard, but this was neither the time nor the place to remind him. We had gone through a lot together this day and prevailed: that was the important thing.

"Another drink?" I suggested. "And then to bed."

Chapter 57

WE ARE MUCH MENDED, but when Cuthbert invites us to partake of dinner in the hall with the family, Will Hawkins declines. "I think we are best here," he says, "with some lighter fare, and perhaps more bread."

Bread did seem to soak up the poison in our systems, and I am happy enough to stay in our chamber. Seb has taken our sweat-soaked shirts to be laundered; even if I am to face the fire or the headsman, I would prefer to go in a sweeter state.

"I'm still trying to understand how Darlington managed it," he says at last.

I stand before the open shutters, looking down at the grounds of the house, at the long hedge leading up to the door. "He's always been able to get around people."

"But he's accused you of heresy, of working to spread the English Bible, of destroying the monasteries, when he's done the same things himself."

"As I said, he's always been able to get away with things." He'd married a Catholic heiress, despite his Protestant pedigree. "And the accusations against me are true, balanced as they are against one good deed." I turn from the window. "Perhaps your queen might not want me roasted quite so badly if she knew about that particular episode, but it wasn't for public knowledge."

Chapter 58

I SLOWLY RECOVERED FROM my injury. After the monks' departure, the household servants, who until then had looked askance at my assumption of Winterset, treated me as a favored son. I was inflicted with every remedy the cook knew, and Seb packed my leg in ice to decrease the swelling, but a nagging pain remained, and the joint was never the same.

Brother Levi lingered until spring, coughing and wheezing in his featherbed. Anselm nursed him, and when Levi at last expired, he wept and prayed over his body. A grave was dug in the Preston family plot, and the local priest said all the right words. Anselm, Seb, and I had a separate service over his grave later, to make sure Levi was sent to his maker with the correct Catholic prayers.

Anselm stayed on. With nowhere to go and no one to take care of, he assumed the persona I had given him, that of my uncle, and settled himself in a small room above the library. We were still tender with each other, but in time we might achieve the relationship we pretended.

Life settled down; time passed. When nothing disturbs the peace and quiet of your life, it is easy to see time as a river.

The river ran smoothly until the death of King Henry, by which time I was firmly settled at Winterset, Ralph Preston having extended my lease indefinitely. Thanks be to God he'd had a son, else the country would have been split apart between one contending princess and the other. Believing in the succession, as I did, the rightful princess would have been Mary; I feared her Catholic zeal and was pleased to hear from Ned that young King Edward was a likely boy, intelligent, compassionate, and strong for his age.

He was without flaw, but that he was nine years old. Child-kings have always been a problem in England—as recently as Henry VI, whose care so many had the mismanagement of that it brought about the war between Lancaster and York. It was never the child-king himself, but those who would protect and serve him, who generally served themselves at the same time.

A council was selected, headed by Edward Seymour, Queen Jane's older brother. Seymour was a dour fellow, straightforward as a courtier might be, but his younger brother, Thomas, was a roistering sort. I prayed for the young king and for his council to choose good sense over ambition.

For myself, I would stay in Yorkshire and watch from a distance. News made it north in less than a week; I would never be uninformed unless I chose to be.

The courier arrived before dinner. I relieved him of his message and sent him to eat with the servants.

It was a brief note from Ned, announcing his presence in Lincolnshire and his imminent arrival at Winterset. I couldn't help myself; I broke into a smile at the idea of seeing him again. We exchanged letters of course—fat, gossipy letters on his part, brought by private courier—but I had not seen him since I'd left London.

I set the maids to getting a chamber ready and made sure we were fully stocked with Vincent Bonnato's best wine. His goods were still imported into England, even though he and Bianca had recently returned to Venice, and I had become the northern distributor for his excellent wine.

Two days later, drowsing in my library—the rosemary hedge doing nothing at all to keep me awake and alert—I was startled by riders in the courtyard. It was Ned, with two men at his heels. I hailed him from the window and was outside before Seb could open the door.

Ned's embrace nearly knocked me off my feet, and sent my cap sailing into the hall. "Jesu, you're like an overgrown pup," I sputtered, picking it up and jamming it back on my head. "Have you not aged at all?"

He had broadened, both in face and girth, and his clothes were of better quality, but he was the same irrepressible Ned. I brought him inside and led him into my library while his things were taken upstairs.

"Wine?" I pushed him toward a chair when he appeared ready to examine every corner of the room. "Sit, Ned."

He sat, stretching out his legs before the unnecessary fire. "This is nice," he said. "I can almost understand why you shun the world."

I handed him a glass and put the jug on the table between us. "I don't shun the world," I said. "Avoid would be a better word."

Seb brought a tray of suckets and retreated, leaving us to our reunion.

"It's beautiful country." Ned took a handful of sweets, and through bulging cheeks said, "I can't imagine living this close to the sea."

The cliff was visible from the window today, with the endless blue of the North Sea beyond. "It's one of the reasons I chose this place."

"How goes the clerkship?" He sprawled, a glass of wine in his fist. "Still keeping that watchful eye?"

"Most of the work is done by delegates," I assured him. "I prefer not to leave this place if I can."

Ned looked around again and pointed to a painted hanging of which I was particularly proud. "It is nice enough, but it lacks a woman's touch." He took a deep swallow. "Never thought I'd say it, but I highly recommend marriage."

I refilled his glass. Depending on the length of his stay, Vincent's stock would decrease dramatically. "I knew you'd fall eventually. You're too merry a man to be alone."

"What about you? Haven't you become a merry man in your later years?"

"I am the same man I have always been," I said with a smile. "It suits me."

Age notwithstanding, Ned could still produce the baffled face of his youth. "What do you do with your time?"

I waved a hand at the books that were stacked and scattered

everywhere. "I'm translating Plato's *Symposium* from the Greek, if you'd like to read any of it."

"I've forgotten any Greek I knew," he said. "You sound like Ascham and Cheke."

"I will take that as a compliment." They'd had, until recently, the education of the young king in their care. "I've corresponded with both of them."

"Of course you have." He changed the subject. "You always claimed to want a wider world, and yet I find you here cloistered away as securely as any monk. What happened?"

"Nothing happened." The crow that roosted outside the library window set to making such a racket that I reached over and closed the casement. "The wider world was not all I had imagined. I find enough of it in my books."

He shook his head disbelievingly. "I am here to offer you the world again," he said. "Do you know William Cecil?"

I considered the name. "I don't believe so. Why?"

"He reminds me of you, but with less sincerity: he goes with the prevailing wind, and right now, the wind is blowing from the land of reform." Ned stared at me when I shrugged. "You must know him. He married Cheke's sister, does that help?"

It did not. What correspondence I had exchanged with John Cheke did not concern sisters or marriages. "What of him?"

"He's been aligned with Edward Seymour for the past few years. Somerset is the lord protector, and Cecil will rise with him."

I pushed the plate toward Ned; he was eating them all anyway. "What of it?"

He shot upright, scattering crumbs everywhere. "Is that your response to everything? 'What of it?'" He leaned in close to my face. "What of your future? You can't stay hidden in Yorkshire forever."

"Why not? I am content. I have my position, so long as it remains mine."

"It most likely shall; the Seymours will have enough to do without worrying about minor appointments. No offense meant," he said, raising his glass.

"None taken." I recounted to Ned the raid on the house, without mentioning the monks. "Darlington hung about Whitby for some time; Seb kept an eye on him. How is our old friend? Do you have occasion to see him?"

"You've not heard?" Ned asked. "He got himself contracted to Francis Morefield's daughter, and someone—no one knows who—informed him that Jack had been one of Cromwell's men."

"No one knows?" I asked, seeing Ned's imprint all over the deed.

"Well," he said, "no one can prove it. But the point is, the engagement was ended, and Jack skulked away in disgrace. Morefield died last year, and before he was cold, Jack married pretty Peggy and took ownership of all that Morefield had."

That sounded cold, even for Darlington, and I said as much.

Shaking his head, he said, "There's no leash on the dog now. Jack Darlington would do well to remember you have powerful friends, and so would you. You should come south."

"I don't want to return to court." There were no words for how much I did not want to return. There was nothing the court could offer now that I did not already possess. I no longer feared Jack Darlington—he had his bride and her inheritance; I was no longer important enough for him to bother me.

"At least come and stay for a bit, meet Joan and the children." Ned's face flushed with excitement. "I'll introduce you to Cecil, let him know we have a man in Yorkshire on the side of the king."

"There are many men in Yorkshire on the side of the king," I said. "Just about everyone, even the Catholics." The country had waited so long for a legitimate male heir that even those of the old religion accepted Edward's succession. "I don't believe there will be any trouble from this quarter."

"There's always trouble," Ned said. "It's good to be seen as being on the right side."

It took ten days to reach Ned's home in Surrey, during which we renewed our friendship and he shared more court gossip than I thought possible for one man to contain.

"Shall we visit your Italian friends while we're in London?" Ned leaned over to nudge me. "Pay our respects to the fascinating Signora Turner?"

"She and her brother have returned to Italy." I dug in my heels and cantered ahead of him.

He soon caught up. "Was it getting uncomfortable?"

I remembered her distressing letter. "Her brother had been attacked in the street."

"Shame." Ned looked perturbed. "And you needn't call her Signora Turner, you know. I figured out years ago what was going on."

That didn't surprise me. After several visits, Bianca let her formal manner slip, and Ned always had a bloodhound's nose. The only surprise was that he'd never mentioned it.

"All that time I tried to get you to come out whoring with us, and you had a mistress. You!"

"Is it that surprising?" I asked. "I do have the same urges as you mere mortals."

Shouting with laughter, he said, "You wouldn't know it." He gave me a sideways glance. "My Joan will be about introducing you to every unmarried girl in the county while you're with us."

My horse jogged along while I considered the prospect of an endless stream of marriageable girls. "She does realize we're the same age, doesn't she? A girl would be quite inappropriate."

"Forty is not too old for a young wife," Ned told me. "My Joan's only twenty-five, and we're as likely a match as you'll ever meet."

That might be, but I cringed at the idea of marrying a girl. Me with a young girl—it was as ludicrous as my long-ago sister Dorcas being married off to her old brewer. "I'll never marry, Ned. You can tell your lady and save her the trouble."

"It's no trouble," he assured me. "She will be only too happy to find you a wife. I'll tell her no one under thirty if that makes you feel better." He shortened his reins, and I stopped with him.

Taking off his hat, he waved it toward the scene below. "That's it, Rob. That's my house down there, with my brother's estate over the hill. You'll meet him as well."

I was beginning to feel exhausted from all the socializing, which had not yet occurred. "It's beautiful," I said honestly. The vivid green of the low-lying Surrey fields was vastly different from Yorkshire but lovely all the same.

We started down, Ned still talking. "If I don't have you contracted in marriage and back at court within the next two weeks, I've lost my touch."

I was welcomed to the Pickering house by sweet Mistress Joan, who, although young, was indeed a fit mate for my boisterous friend. She calmed and teased him in equal measure, treating him like a larger version of their two boys, who were miniature Neds with mischievous eyes and curly brown hair.

She looked at me with a calculating eye until Ned said, "Rob doesn't want to be married off, my darling wife." He kissed her neck and made her giggle. "We will have to convince him of the benefits of matrimony."

"You may do that," she said, shoving him off. "I'll be taking care of your household and the fruits of our matrimony." With a curtsy, she said, "Master Lewis, you are most welcome. Will you take a drink with us while your man unpacks?"

We strolled the gardens while Seb carried on with his tasks. The boys ran ahead, playing some game comprehensible only to them, diving in and out of the flower beds until their mother took them in hand. She and Ned each took a child by the collar and continued on as if nothing had happened, and I marveled at this sort of parenting, never having experienced it before. I might not be sold on matrimony, but I did appreciate seeing parenthood that did not consist of shouts and blows; these boys were allowed to be children but also knew when it was time to allow themselves to be reined in.

I spent an enjoyable week in their company, though, as warned, Mistress Joan invited many county families—and their daughters—to dine. The daughters were nice enough, ranging in age from fourteen to forty and from virgin to widow. I conversed with them all, danced with a few, and asked none for their hand, to general Pickering disappointment.

"I told you I wasn't in the market for a wife." Joan had gone to bed, disappointed in my continued bachelorhood, leaving me and Ned in front of the fire. "I'm happy as I am."

Ned's forehead creased. "But Signora Turner…the other rumors weren't true, that much I know. So why?"

"What other rumors?"

"That rubbish Darlington tried to circulate. None of us believed it." He spread his hands. "So I don't understand. Marriage has much to recommend it, Rob. And the children—I love them dearly, though I think I shall like them better when they're older. You're missing out on so much."

"I should have let you deal with him." Darlington hadn't succeeded in damaging my reputation with his lies, but he had tried.

"Who?"

"Darlington."

Ned blinked. "Why do you care what he said all those years ago? We're talking about your future, not the past."

They were one and the same to me. Darlington's accusations were as true now as they were then, which was just true enough to ruin my life with the sort of people to whom it would matter. Such as a priggish, reform-minded royal council. "No, Ned."

"It would also lay any rumors to rest." His tone had changed. "Isn't that worth something?"

I blew out an impatient breath. "I'll not marry some poor girl just to bury a rumor. Besides, I'm so far from the world now, rumors mean nothing."

"What if you decide to work with Cecil?"

"I won't." I had already made my decision; I remembered the

brothers Seymour with no affection and less trust, and did not wish to spend the next decade watching them grapple for power.

"But if you do," he insisted.

"Then I shall swear to him that I am a monk, not a sodomite, and I have no need of a wife." I fixed my friend with a glare. "Leave me in peace."

Ned leaned forward, picked up the branched candleholder. "I give up. At least for tonight."

There was one last dinner, this time with a Pickering cousin and Joan's widowed sister, both brought in with some haste as final temptations before my departure. I was seated to Joan's left, with her sister Isobel to my right and cousin Molly across from me. It was quite the largest number of women of whose attention I was the sole focus since I'd sung for the king.

It was also the most personal. Every time Molly smiled at me with her girlish version of Ned's face, I started to itch.

Isobel Trent was easier. Tall and quiet, she had foregone black but still wore her grief like a veil.

"You have a child?" It was one of many facts Joan had thrown at me earlier.

"Yes." Her eyes were focused on the table. "A daughter."

"How old is she?" Why was I even asking? This woman was as interested in me as I was in her; at least the exuberant Molly wanted my attention.

"Three," she said. "She lives with my husband's people. It was his wish."

"I'm sorry." That was harsh to remove a child from her mother.

Her eyes flickered sideways, acknowledging my words. "He was ill for a long time and made plans. He said it would be easier for me to make another marriage without a child. Men don't often wish to raise the children of other men."

I cut a piece of mutton from the joint and offered it to her, cutting another for myself. She spooned some of the mustard sauce over both our portions. Chewing my meat, I considered her words.

"Perhaps it might be easier for your husband, but what about you? Don't you miss her?"

"Of course," she said. "But I have no recourse. His family keeps her close."

I leaned to one side as a servant refilled our cups. "I hope you are able to see her, mistress."

"Hope is a dangerous word for a woman." With that, she turned to her right and began to speak to Ned, and I was left with Joan and Molly, who had been following the conversation with some interest.

When the meal was done, we retired to a small bright parlor where one of Ned's men played and sang for us. Brought up as I was with high musical standards, this was painful, and I was even more affrighted when Joan asked Molly to give us a song. She flushed and fluttered but took the lute with a familiar grasp and proceeded to give us a sweet-voiced, competent rendition of "Greensleeves."

If I'd wanted to match myself with any of Joan Pickering's candidates, the last two were the most interesting: Mistress Molly for her singing, and Isobel Trent for her mysterious remarks.

But again, I was not in the market for a wife, and I waved both women off as they left in Joan's brother's coach.

"No?" He eyed me behind his wife's back.

"No." Ned had always been one to enthusiastically recommend anything that he enjoyed; wedded bliss was no different.

Chapter 59

Sunday, November 16, 1558
Cambridge

"BUT YOU DID MARRY," Will interrupts.

I incline my head. "I acquired a wife, yes, but it was none of Joan Pickering's matchmaking that brought it about."

We have ventured forth to the gardens to clear our heads and allow the servants time to remove all evidence of sickness from our chamber. I give a baleful glare at the holly hedge as we pass. "We'll get to her in good time; you can't rush a tale of this length, my friend."

"I'm beginning to understand that."

Chapter 60

THE NEXT DAY, WE left for London. I said my farewells to Mistress Joan and the boys. "You are more than welcome to come to me whenever you wish. My house is not so comfortable, but I like to have guests."

"We might." Joan kissed my cheek. "If young Ned turns out as bright as I think he will be, perhaps we'll ask you to take charge of his education."

"Uncle Rob's college for extraordinary boys." Ned kissed his wife with enthusiasm. "He looks like me, my dear, so let us hope he has your brains."

London was achieved with only one night at an inn, Ned and I sharing a room with Seb and his men on the floor. I had forgotten how crowded inns were near the city; already I longed for the clean Yorkshire air.

Seb was astounded by everything, from the size of the Pickering house to the number of horses in their stables to the worn grandeur of the wayside inn.

"If this is how you feel now, you'll not survive London. It's ten times the size of York."

His mouth fell open, and for a moment, he looked like the young ex-novice who had stumbled into my life nearly a decade before. "How do people live that close together?"

"You'll soon see," I said. "If you like Ned's men, get them to take you out some evening to see the sights." I would take him myself, but the likelihood of escaping Ned's affectionate clutches was unlikely.

Once settled in Ned's London house, a small place not far from Austin Friars, he made arrangements to present me to William Cecil, currently employed by the Duke of Somerset. Cecil was younger than both of us, but he had that perpetually-worried expression civil servants often wear, especially when their masters are as demanding as Edward Seymour.

"Pickering tells me you're interested in coming back to the court." It was a bright spring day, and Ned had tempted him out-of-doors into the garden at Somerset House.

"My friend overstates the matter in his zeal," I said. "I had my fill of court life under the late king; I am content in Yorkshire and would be happy to keep my appointment as clerk there."

We walked for a bit while Ned collected gossip. I admired the placement of Somerset House, right on the Thames, with access to the city on one side and the river on the other. Such could have been mine, perhaps, if I had played my hand differently, but the longer I stayed in London, the more I knew that what happiness I would ever find would be in the north, away from men such as these.

"Ned did tell me that your late wife was the sister of John Cheke," I ventured during a lull in the conversation. "I've corresponded with both Master Cheke and Roger Ascham these many years; their letters bring the world to the north."

"John's not about," he said, "but Ascham will be in London on the morrow before he takes up his new post. Would you like an introduction?"

Cecil was true to his word. Two days later, I received a summons to dinner. Accompanied by Ned, who feared missing anything of importance, we journeyed to meet Roger Ascham.

Beneath a luxuriant dark beard, he was fresh-faced and younger than I expected—or else I was older than I realized—but we connected easily and continued the conversation contained in our letters with no interruption.

He was as excited as a boy about his new opportunity as tutor to the princess Elizabeth and her cousin, the Lady Jane Grey.

"It's a shame about Grindal, of course," he said, referring to his predecessor, dead of some plague. "Poor man. I've never known a finer scholar. But the princess and the Grey girl are both possessed of brilliant minds, and my brief is to continue their Latin and

Greek education."

"How old is the princess now?" I recalled the tiny flame-haired mite who was the wrong sex to save her mother's life.

"Fourteen." Ascham smiled. "The perfect age, really. She's been studying her entire life, but she is close enough to adulthood to now comprehend the more abstract new learning while keeping up her languages."

The princess spoke French and Italian in addition to Latin and Greek, and Ascham shared that she was even conversant in Spanish and Flemish, thanks to her governess.

This was a student after my own heart. Of all the things I'd learned, at Oxford or elsewhere, languages remained my favorite and had stood me in good stead throughout my life. "I would be honored to meet the princess someday."

"I'm riding to Cheshunt the day after tomorrow," Ascham said, "to take up my post. You are welcome to accompany me. I cannot promise you overnight lodging, but I can arrange an introduction to the princess."

Cheshunt was less than five leagues from London; the return could be made easily enough. I accepted his invitation with alacrity.

We continued to discuss his plans for the princess's education over dinner. Cecil chimed in occasionally, but he had other guests in addition to Ned and left us to our own interests.

"Wasn't the princess here in Chelsea until recently?" I cut a slice of beef from the joint between us and offered it to him.

"She was." Ascham accepted with a nod. "The dowager queen decided it was time she had her own household."

That wasn't what I'd heard. The night before, Ned related a scurrilous tale of the young princess being pursued by Tom Seymour, the dowager queen's new husband and Somerset's brother. From what I recalled of Seymour, he was entirely capable of such behavior. Poor Kathryn Parr, only just rid of a sick, elderly husband, and now matched with a man who, when unable to marry the princess himself, tried to have her by other methods.

"That is perhaps best," I agreed. "Far less distractions to study."

We left at dawn two days hence, Seb and I riding to meet the royal tutor at his London lodgings. Ascham waited for us on a beautiful black gelding. I knew from his letters that he valued horsemanship only slightly below archery as gentlemanly pursuits. He had two servants with him, and there was also a small cart, loaded, I could only assume, with books.

Seeing me, he stood in his stirrups and waved his cap. "What a day for a journey!"

I trotted to his side. "Indeed it is. Thank you again for allowing me to accompany you."

Excited by the opportunity I was being given, I'd spent the day before at the booksellers, trying to find an acceptable gift for a princess who already translated Latin and Greek. I settled on a small volume of Tacitus, beautifully bound, with an embossed leather cover. It was superior to much of my personal collection, but I considered it a necessary expense and perhaps a form of insurance for my future.

Sir Anthony Denny emerged from his house as we arrived. Ascham he greeted as a friend, and when I was presented, he bowed with a courtier's politesse, welcoming me. "Having the princess in my household is honor enough," he said, ushering us inside, "but if we shall have a constant influx of scholars, I shall be overwhelmed."

I believed this to be a polite way of expressing his dismay at the appearance of an unexpected guest, and I assured him, in equally circular fashion, that I had simply accompanied Ascham to his destination and would be leaving after I had paid my respects to the young princess.

The cart arrived in our wake, and Denny watched from the hall as several chests were unloaded. "Where shall those be brought?"

"That one"—Ascham pointed—"goes to my chamber. The others are for the princess's education, and they may be brought to whatever chamber we will be using."

We followed Denny to a wide, airy room on the ground floor. "This is Grindal's schoolroom. Does it suit?"

Ascham looked around, a smile breaking across his face. "Very nicely, Sir Anthony."

"I shall leave you to settle your things," our host said. "Please ask my people if you require anything further. We will meet again at dinner."

Ascham ranged around the room like an excited schoolboy, looking at everything, his smile growing broader by the moment. From the diamond-paned windows flecked with bits of colored glass to the tables waiting for his books, all was in order.

I left him to his arrangements and looked out the windows. The schoolroom was on the side of the house, overlooking meticulously maintained gardens and, beyond, what appeared to be an orchard. Men were busily working there; it was a domestic scene, and I suddenly missed Winterset.

A door closed somewhere above. Light footsteps followed, and Princess Elizabeth spun into the room in a whirl of skirts. "Mistress Ashley told me you had arrived!"

She was a slender girl, dressed in a plain dark gown with no embellishment—still in mourning for her father. Her vivid hair was restrained, and only a bit of it showed, sunset-bright, at the front of her pushed back French hood. She appeared to be a quiet, intellectual princess who would never trouble anyone.

Ascham and I snatched off our caps, clutching them to our chests, and bowed deeply. "Your Grace," he said, "I valued our correspondence, but to be in your presence again is a true delight."

Pale as she was, a blush stained her cheeks like roses. "That was a lovely pen you sent, Master Ascham. And now you will put me to using it."

He looked pleased. "Indeed I shall, Your Grace."

She continued her small talk. "I hope your journey from London was uneventful."

"It was very easy," he said, "and I had company for the journey."

The princess noticed me as if for the first time. "Please, Master Ascham, introduce me to your friend."

Ascham presented me, and I bowed again. "My condolences on

the loss of your father and your tutor, Your Grace."

"I thank you, Master Lewis. Losing the king was a loss for all of England." Her eyes brightened. "But the king, my brother, is able and just, and I pray he becomes an even greater king in his time."

We murmured our agreement, and the princess's attention was caught by the several chests, which were being brought into the room. "New books?" she queried, running a hand over the heavy lock.

"Yes, Your Grace. I shall have them unpacked, and tomorrow you may explore to your heart's content."

She clapped her hands like a child at the prospect. "Excellent, Master Ascham. I have exhausted Grindal's supply."

I remembered my errand of the day before and reached behind me on the table. "Your Grace," I said, "knowing that I would have the honor of meeting you today, I brought a small token."

She took the packet and neatly undid the cloth wrapping. "Tacitus!" She turned the book over in her hands, admiring the binding. "What a lovely volume, Master Lewis. I have not yet read—nor translated—this particular bit of his writing."

I bowed my head. "Then I hope it gives you great pleasure." I risked being deemed inappropriate to say, "I once worked for Cardinal Wolsey. I saw Your Grace several times when you were just a small girl."

She looked at me, and I experienced a shock of recognition. Despite her resemblance to her father, there was a touch of Anne Boleyn about her eyes. "I would not remember that," she said, "and it is to my regret. Do you stay to assist Master Ascham?"

"I regret that I cannot." I did regret it; Ascham had an enviable assignment in training the mind of this most excellent princess. "I have been visiting friends in London, but I live in Yorkshire. I will be returning there within the week."

"Then I wish you a safe and easy journey." Elizabeth turned again to Ascham. "I must go to Mistress Ashley, or she will be cross. We will continue our conversation later." Her manners, while youthful, were those of someone who expected care to be

292 • *Karen Heenan*

paid to her words.

Ascham bowed over her hand. "It will be my privilege, Your Grace."

"I shall depart before then," I said. "It has been an honor to meet Your Grace. I quite envy Master Ascham his employment."

The princess laughed. "Do not, Master Lewis. I am not always so easy."

Partly from curiosity, I helped Ascham to unpack his books. Before the job was complete, Sir Anthony appeared in the doorway. "Dinner will be served shortly," he said. "Master Lewis, you are welcome to join us if it does not delay your return to London."

I hesitated but a moment; while I wished to continue my visit with Ned, spending more time with Ascham and the princess was irresistible.

Dinner was six courses, with wine, and not only were we joined by Princess Elizabeth, but her younger cousin, Lady Jane Grey, was seated to my right. She was a slight dark-eyed girl, who, when she discovered I had corresponded with Ascham, launched into an enthusiastic discussion of his *Toxophilus*.

It was dizzying to be surrounded by this level of intellectual discourse. I hadn't discussed books in such depth since my early days with Bianca and occasionally—if he was in the correct frame of mind—with Anselm. This loud, energetic discussion of the new learning, of philosophy, of Erasmus, carried out in rapid-fire Latin and Greek, interspersed with the occasional French phrase, made me realize just how much my self-imposed exile had cost me.

It was four of the afternoon before Seb and I set out for London, and I was replete with food and words.

"Was it worth it, master?"

I thought of the princess: her sharp, intelligent gaze, the way her long fingers wrapped themselves around the volume of Tacitus. "It was," I said. "It was."

Ned wheedled industriously, but I refused his blandishments.

While his invitations were tempting, they were not enough to keep me from my home and my library. I did not trust the men surrounding the young king, nor did I wish to be part of their intrigues. I had survived my years with King Henry, Wolsey, and Cromwell by being on the periphery; I had no wish to rise higher and risk more.

The reign of the young king was notable for its rigid enforcement of the new religion. King Henry had given up Rome, but his version of the new faith still had all of its trappings and most of its ceremony. Edward stripped the churches as Cromwell had stripped the monasteries: statues, candlesticks, stained glass, incense. None of these things were necessary for prayer to reach God.

That may have been true, but they made the experience damnably pleasant, and I, for one, missed them. I attended the church in Whitby as an official of the town, but I also frequented Anselm's mass in the house chapel, still attended by the servants and assisted by Seb.

What was not known would not hurt us.

I heard from Ned as the situation at court again grew dire: Thomas Seymour was found outside the king's chamber with a loaded pistol and was executed for his pains. Soon after, his brother, losing his grip on the protectorship, all but abducted King Edward to Windsor. When he was extracted, he, too, paid the price. Queen Jane died as a result of birthing the king; her brothers died in self-service instead of serving their nephew.

Once the Seymours were gone, it became more unsettled. Ned's wife gave birth to a daughter, and he used her slow recovery as an excuse to remove himself from court. It was not stated in his letters, but I knew he was still in contact with Cecil. He would no doubt return once Joan had improved and Edward was older and had taken control of his council.

That never happened.

In the spring of 1553, news traveled north that the king had been ill since Christmas. There was talk of recovery, then relapse. In July, it spread rapidly across the country that King Edward

294 • *Karen Heenan*

was dead, just short of his sixteenth birthday. The great hope of England, for whom Henry had discarded one wife and executed another, did not live long enough to rule as an adult.

His Catholic sister, Mary, was the rightful heir—or so we believed. It was then announced that during his decline, Edward had signed a document invalidating his father's plan of succession, naming his cousin, the Lady Jane Grey, as his heir.

Once again, Princesses Mary and Elizabeth were declared illegitimate.

Jane was Edward's age, the daughter of Henry Grey, Duke of Suffolk. I remembered the quiet, dark-eyed girl I'd met at Cheshunt, and it surprised me to learn she'd been married to Guildford Dudley, the youngest son of the Duke of Northumberland.

Northumberland had been responsible for the overthrow of Edward Seymour, and he certainly hadn't done that out of a sense of principle. He looked at the throne, envisioned it empty, and found a way to place a child of his upon it—even if it meant marrying him to a girl with a lesser claim, who had at first declared she had no wish to be queen.

She was convinced, in one way or another. I'm sure it involved making her understand what Mary Tudor would do to her beloved Protestant faith and those who practiced it.

It couldn't last, and it didn't. Northumberland, the power behind the plot, set out to capture Princess Mary. Forewarned, she eluded his grasp and rallied her own support. After nine days, Jane's own privy council switched sides and acknowledged Mary as the rightful queen, and Jane was imprisoned, along with her husband.

Northumberland was brought to justice swiftly, but Jane, her husband, his brothers, and Archbishop Cranmer were all charged with high treason and tried at the Guildhall in November. They were found guilty, all of them, but Queen Mary showed compassion in the beginning. Jane was contrite, and it appeared the rebellion was over.

Jane's supporters backed away to their manors far from

London, hoping Mary wouldn't be as harsh on the new religion as they feared. But she was, and to make it worse, she was soon contracted to marry Philip of Spain, a confirmed and enthusiastic heretic-burner, who wanted all Protestants rooted out before he would set foot on English soil.

Men rebelled. Thomas Wyatt, son of the poet who had loved Anne Boleyn—and not half the man his father was—raised an army, along with others who also feared the Spanish marriage or supported Princess Elizabeth. He was joined by Henry Grey, Jane's father.

The rebellion ended before it was begun, and it was the end of Jane as well.

It was nearly the end of Princess Elizabeth; she was summoned to London, ostensibly for her own protection, but also so she could be watched, as the rebels had fixed on her as the next queen. Either way, Jane was cast aside, but under Elizabeth, she might have kept her head.

Chapter 61

SUPPER IS EATEN IN the hall with the Cuthbert family, who are concerned about our illness and recovery—and grateful, I imagine, that Seb seasoned only our dishes and not the household pot.

Cuthbert is an amiable man for all that he supports the queen. "Word is that Her Majesty is still poorly," he says, crossing himself. "We pray for her each night, if you would like to join us."

"God hears all prayers," I say, glancing at Will Hawkins. "I am not averse to praying for Queen Mary."

Our host looks at me. "You, sir?" He appears surprised out of all comprehension. "Aren't you a noted heretic?"

Will speaks up. "Master Lewis is many things, but I can assure you, he is a man of God."

After the meal, we are ushered into the Cuthbert chapel. It still bears all the marks of Rome; somehow, it survived Edward's reign unscathed. As did the priest, who holds a fully Latin mass, complete with enough incense to make my eyes burn.

I watch as the assembled company genuflect and make all the responses which were mine for the better part of my life. I cannot join them.

Instead, I let my mind drift. Has the delay given me enough time, or am I still Tower-bound on the morrow? With good weather, and if Hawkins pushes, we might reach London by nightfall.

The Tower is at its worst at night. In the day, with blue skies over its stone walls, it is not forbidding. But after dark, the shadows, the plashing of the moat, the reflecting torches, all remind me of the bad days with Cromwell and the executions I witnessed.

I do not wish to witness my own execution.

When mass ends, I leave with Hawkins.

He grasps my arm. "I must thank you."

"For what?" He puzzles me.

"You could have escaped while I was ill—I know you were too, but your man could have gotten you away. I thank you for not attempting it."

It hadn't occurred to me to try; Hawkins was sick, but his men were not, and Seb was better at small cunning, not taking on some half dozen men, no matter how much he'd cultivated them on the journey.

"I'll take my chances," I say, turning toward the stairs. "Are you fit to travel, do you think?"

He nods. "I am. You?"

I feign shock. "Would I be permitted another day of bed rest, Will?"

My use of his name surprises him, but he had given it to me. "No."

"Well, then." My legs do not like climbing yet; between my knee and the remaining exhaustion, I sink down onto the edge of the bed when we reach our chamber. "That does not leave much time to conclude my story."

Will takes a seat at the table, not yet ready for sleep. "I thank you for it, Rob. You've done more than you ought, by making this pleasant for me. You needn't have, you know."

"I know." I think about the many reasons I've told this story, and in truth, it's not all Shahrazad's inspiration. "It's done me good, remembering it. If I die, my mind will be at rest, if not my conscience."

"What would it take to quiet your conscience?"

I laugh and join him at the table. "I have no idea."

We sit quietly for a bit, watching the fire and contemplating our separate futures.

"Are you all right?"

"Just marshaling my thoughts." I settle further into my seat. "We've come now to my head, and my sentimental attachment to it.

"In the spring of that year, a letter reached me from London, carried by Ned's private courier. I had been named as a supporter of Wyatt's ill-advised rebellion against the crown—accused, of course, by my old friend, Darlington, whose wife was one of the queen's ladies."

Hawkins snorts. "No wonder you've no fondness for the man."

I raise an eyebrow. "He has none for me either, since it's taken more than four years for his plan to come to fruition."

The letter suggested that I get myself out of England at the first opportunity, either to the Low Countries or a visit to Bianca in Venice. "Ned did not put it in writing," I say, "but the courier said men were already on their way to seize me."

He sets aside the cup, pressing his fingers to his temples. "I think I need to lie down."

I am more than ready for sleep, but I dread the morning. "I shall join you; it's no fun to drink alone, and we have an early start." We set aside our things and ready ourselves for bed. "Aren't you tired of the sound of my voice?"

"No," he says. "And I'm curious, how you manage to believe some of the things you do."

He was not the only one; sometimes I wondered how I managed it. "It's simple, really," I tell him. "I have Catholic sympathies and friends, no matter my personal beliefs. I knew the queen when she was Princess Mary. It was hard to warm to her, even then, scarred as she was by her father's inconstant love. I knew she would have little pity for those who supported the new religion."

Will Hawkins nods. "And she does—have no pity, I mean. I've heard things—"

I cut him off before he says something he will regret. "People just want to know that their prayers will be heard. It was difficult when they lost the benefit of the monks' continuous prayers. The trade-off was the Bible in English and a more direct connection to God."

Stretching, Hawkins says, "Was the new religion that widely accepted?"

I shrug and snuff the candle, speaking into the darkness. "Whether or not everyone believed, they had grown accustomed to it by the time Edward died. Mostly they wanted peace. England couldn't withstand another civil war. That fear was part of what made Henry so mad to get an heir."

"But he did," came his reply, "and Mary was Edward's rightful successor, not a cousin brought forward by Northumberland."

I had been disappointed by Jane's fall; I knew Mary would bring disaster with her immediate martyring of Protestants, and I was not wrong. I wish I'd been wrong.

I drop back against the pillow. It's an old argument, and I am cursed to see both sides. "The fear was that Mary would not only re-establish the bond with Rome but attempt to repossess the monastic lands which were distributed to nobles all over England." I turn to him. "I believe your father got some of those lands, didn't he?"

There is an uncomfortable silence, and Will rolls over so that all I can see is the hump of his shoulder. "Yes," he mutters, finally.

Smiling, I continue, "In Mary's eyes, Protestants are heretics, and heretics are burned. If there's one thing more unpleasant than losing one's head, it's the anticipation of being burned alive. "You may take that as fact. It has, as you imagine, been much on my mind during our journey."

Chapter 62

IT TAKES A LONG time to plan a journey, but an escape can be executed in a remarkably short period. I called Anselm, Fowler, and Seb into the library and informed them of Ned's letter. "I fear he's right, and there's no time to mount a defense if Jack Darlington is behind the accusation."

"We should have buried him behind the barn," Fowler said, looking to Seb for agreement.

"I thought of that," he said, "but I wasn't sure Brother Anselm would hear our confessions after." Looking from Fowler to me, he asked, "What's to be done, master? How soon must we leave?"

"We?" I glanced down at the list I had begun on the back of Ned's letter. "You're not going anywhere."

"I am," he said emphatically. "You're not leaving here—especially if someone wants your head—without me to watch over you."

The others immediately backed him up, and I gave in more quickly than I should. I could always send him home, but in the meantime, I was glad to have company on a journey of undetermined length.

Fowler offered to book our passage. "I'll ride north to Hartlepool," he said. "They're less likely to look for you there." I left the destination up to him, only that the ship did not put in anywhere else in England. He left with a purse, promising to be back by evening with our passage.

Anselm spoke for the first time. "You needn't worry, Robin. Fowler and I will look after the house in your absence." He looked around the room. "Perhaps I'll do a bit of reorganizing in here while you're gone."

My books! It was bad enough to leave them behind, but even if I were gone, there was proof of my heretic sympathies on every shelf. "We've got to put some of these away."

He glanced around. "Where can we hide them?"

"Seb?" He rose from his seat and lifted another one of the

painted wall hangings that everyone decried; beneath it lay perfectly innocuous paneling, except that one panel was hinged and concealed a cavity in the wall. "This should hold them all."

"What did the previous owner get up to?" Anselm asked. "Or was that your addition?"

I shook my head. "A lucky find," I said. "Preston didn't mention its existence."

For the rest of the day, Anselm and I sorted through my books, wrapping the objectionable ones in cloth and putting them inside the wall. The cook brought our dinner into the library so we could continue, and Seb joined us after he finished packing.

"Just a small trunk, master," he said, "and a pack for each of us."

"You can leave the trunk," I told him. "Shove a bit more in our packs; I'd rather travel light as I don't know where we'll end up."

Anselm picked up the Tyndale Bible as if it were covered in something noxious. "This one definitely goes into the wall," he said, wrapping it tightly. "For my sake and for yours." He smiled to show that his words were at least somewhat in jest. "What about your friend's suggestion—Venice?"

"It may come to that." I hoped we would not be away long enough to justify a trip of that length, though I would love to see Bianca again.

Fowler returned while we were at supper. "Antwerp," he said shortly, handing me the papers. "They sail at noon tomorrow. You might want to leave tonight, though, just to be safe. I've arranged for you to stable your horses at the Crown."

I thanked him. My plan had been to go as soon as he returned, so Seb and I hastened to finish our meal. "Anselm, will you be all right?" I asked.

He raised his brows. "And why would I not?"

It was difficult to find the right words. We'd shared Winterset for the past dozen years without having a conversation about my part in his lost life; it appeared that this would not change. "You won't be lonely?"

"I've Fowler and the servants if I am," he said. "We're alike in that, Robin—once settled, it would take a threat of bodily harm to move me again."

Seb was an engaging traveling companion, interested in everything and apparently tireless. As we crossed the bucketing North Sea, he glanced over at me. He was braced against the rail, one hand clutching his hat. "I should not be enjoying this!" he shouted. "I feel guilty."

For the first year, we lived an itinerant lifestyle, traveling where the ships and our inclination took us. From Antwerp, we turned east, and I visited Bruges for the first time in thirty years. I recalled to Seb my youth and my excitement at being away from England that first time.

Once the attractions of the Low Countries were exhausted and the news from England had not improved, we shifted to France. I debated visiting the Prestons at their house near Lisieux, but decided against it. I notified Sir Ralph that I had temporarily vacated Winterset, but I did not wish to remind him by my presence that Catholic Mary would welcome his return. I hoped to be able to return soon enough myself.

Amiens. Rheims. Four months in Paris, a lively city, much like London, with beautiful buildings, thriving markets, and enough booksellers to make my heart happy. Seb complained about the food, but I sent him off to explore the city, and he returned enchanted and spoke no more of unfamiliar dishes.

It became obvious that I would have to follow Ned's advice and accept Bianca's frequently issued invitation. Without an income from my appointment in Whitby or the Bonnato imports, I could not afford for us to travel indefinitely. We needed a base, preferably an inexpensive one, for the duration of our exile.

When I first came to the continent all those years ago, Venice had been my dream. I could not imagine a city built on water. I passed through, briefly, on leaving Italy, but I could not recall what

I had seen; my pain was so great that I single-mindedly got on a ship and ran away.

We spent a few nights in Milan at a monastery guesthouse, and I sent a courier ahead to Venice with news of our coming. I hoped the message would reach Bianca before we arrived on her doorstep.

Across Italy we rode, a man, his servant, and far more books than Seb deemed necessary. Riding alone was dangerous, so in each large town, we attached ourselves to a party traveling in the right direction. Milan led to Verona. From Verona, the only town of any size before Venice was Padua. I inquired and found another place where we could stay and avoid Padua entirely.

It was perfectly safe to enter the city, of course, but I couldn't bring myself to do it, nor could I explain my refusal to Seb, telling him only, "I was ill in Padua. I have bad memories of the place."

Eventually, we reached the edge of the world, a wharf that looked out onto a misty blue nothingness. Somewhere across that span of water lay Bianca and a respite from our travels.

There were boats of all sizes at the docks, and I began to search for one heading into Venice. Seb was no help; he spoke English, Latin, and some French, but no other. My scattered Italian verbs and phrases returned as the language swirled around me.

I arranged our passage, and that of the small trunk of books acquired during our travels, on a craft scheduled to leave in the late afternoon. We waited at a dockside tavern, drinking raw Italian wine and eating something delicious and unfamiliar.

"You will be at San Marco in time for vespers," the captain assured me upon our return.

Another vespers arrival. My comings and goings had always been marked by the divine office.

"Do you know how far that is from Rio Malatin?"

He shrugged. "Not too far, not too far. You can find a gondola at the piazza to take you there."

I stayed on deck, close to the prow, watching the vast expanse of water split before us. The sun began to fade, and before long, a scattering of islands appeared in the distance. Was this Venice?

"Outer islands," Seb whispered. "There's apparently a lot of them."

There were. Some were barren, some sparsely populated; some bore churches nearly as large as the ground on which they stood. Everywhere, light reflected on rippling water.

I closed my eyes. It was suddenly too much—leaving England, the endless travel, knowing that I was hunted by my own countrymen. I wanted to reach the shelter of Bianca's home and sleep for a month. Seb's comforting shoulder bumped against mine. "Soon, master."

"Soon," I agreed. "I am sorry, Seb, to have dragged you through all this with me."

"And where else do you think I'd be?"

My eyes still shut, I said, "You could have stayed with Anselm."

"He is happy to have your library to himself," he said. "When we return, he'll have it completely rearranged."

There was no one I trusted more than Anselm. I hoped it would not be long before I saw him—and my books—again.

We bumped against a dock, and the oars were put up. I opened my eyes to a broad plaza, filled even at this time of the evening with a mass of people, surrounded on three sides by beautiful Eastern-style buildings.

"Just look at it." The scent of the lagoon reached me, pungent, different from the Thames but certainly no worse.

We disembarked, carrying our few possessions, and one of the oarsmen pointed me toward a cluster of sleek black boats. "Gondola," he said. "They will take you to your destination."

I approached one, and the boatman sprang out. "Where do you go?"

"Rio Malatin," I said. "The Bonnato house. Is it far?"

"No, no. You get in." He handed me down, and I seated myself, reaching for Seb as he joined me. Our parcels were settled, and the boatman took up his own station, reaching for the long pole that moved the boat almost silently through the water.

We turned from the great lagoon down a canal, then another

narrower one. Once, the boatman had to squat to get under a low stone bridge. We passed other similar boats, and the boatmen hailed each other. Their voices echoed in the high stone passages.

It was nearly dark and darker still between the buildings. Snatches of purpling sky were visible at the end of the canal and above the rooflines with their odd funnel-shaped chimneys.

This was no good. I wanted to *see* Venice. I wanted to see our arrival so that I could remember it always.

We passed a larger boat, then maneuvered between two other gondolas. One of the boatmen reached out and slapped ours on the shoulder. "My brother," he said, not turning around but beginning to pull us in toward the side of the canal. "You are here."

"Here" was the blank front of a stone house with barred windows overlooking the canal and an enormous wooden door. "Could you?"

He hammered on the door with the bronze ring, and the sound echoed up and down the waterway.

I waited impatiently and, truth to tell, somewhat nervously. What if my letter had gone astray? What if it had arrived, but Bianca was not there? It was dark, and we were in a very strange place. I could feel Seb's concern beside my own.

My worry was for naught. It took some time, but the door creaked open, and then swung wide. "Signor Lewis?"

"*Sì!*" I got up so hastily that the gondola rocked beneath me, and Seb grabbed my calves. "Is Signora Bonnato at home?"

"Of course."

After the trip through the lagoon and the gondola ride, the marble floor swayed beneath my feet, and I took a moment to steady myself. "You were expecting us?"

"Of course," he said again. "Every day. Your room is waiting. Allow me to bring you to the signora."

From the canal entrance, we moved to a hall with a central staircase. "Follow me," he said and started up.

My knee gave a twinge as I ascended. I put it out of my mind; I did not want to meet Bianca while feeling like a decrepit refugee.

Upstairs was far more elegant, with patterned marble floors and warm plaster walls, interspersed with more stone and marble. We were led through one chamber after another until we reached a door. The servant knocked and waited for a word audible only to his ears. "You may go in."

The open door showed nothing but the glow of candles and wide windows whose shutters were open to the darkness outside. I stepped across the threshold.

"Robin."

Her voice was the same. The honeyed tones I had found so seductive, the hint of an accent—stronger now that she was back among her own people.

Despite my aching joints, I crossed the room and knelt at her feet. Taking her hands in mine, I pressed them to my lips. "My lady."

"Do get up, Robin." The words were tinged with laughter.

The rest of her had changed as little as her voice. I looked at her in the mellow light. Older, obviously, with her dark hair gone silver, but still slender and gracious, elegant as a queen in her black silk.

"You look glorious." I kissed her on both cheeks.

"And you speak nonsense." She tilted my chin with a finger. "I'm not certain how I feel about this beard. I like clean-shaven Robin best."

"You've known me with a beard," I protested. "I've had it nearly thirty years."

She waved me toward a seat near the window. "I know. I prefer to think of young Robin, the barefaced boy who came to borrow books from my brother."

I did not like to think of that barefaced boy; he embarrassed me. "How is Vincent?"

"He died earlier this year. Still shouting." She smiled faintly. "Despite being a disgrace to my family, I am the only one left. On my death, the house will go to a nephew in Bologna."

There was a scratching at the door, and a different servant

brought in a tray with two glasses of wine. Accepting one, I admired its sinuous shape. "These are even more beautiful than the ones you had in London."

"Glass is easy to come by here." She raised her glass to me. "When you have rested, I wish to hear what has happened that finally brought you to me."

I took a sip, and the complex flavor flooded my senses. As tired as I was, it would take no more than a single glass to finish me. "The same thing that caused you and Vincent to leave," I said. "A change of monarch, a change of religion."

"Well, now you are here, and you are safe."

After finishing the wine and being shown to my chamber, I allowed Seb to undress me, and I fell into the softest bed I had known since leaving England. He snuffed the candle and settled himself on the trundle. The night was eerily silent, the only sounds the lapping of waves and an occasional boatman's call. Reflections danced on the ceiling above my head, and I fell asleep watching them.

Breakfast arrived on a tray, and Seb kept a vigilant eye on me as I ate. He was bright-eyed and already dressed. "You should stay in bed, master," he said. "The lady has given orders to bring you food until you are ready to come downstairs."

"I'll get up now." I did not want to be treated as an invalid by a woman two decades my senior.

"You will not," Seb said firmly. "You are worn out from these last months on the road." He picked up the tray and gave me a stern glance. "I will be back to make sure you are asleep."

The weariness was deep in my bones. Just another hour, and then I would get up. When I next opened my eyes, afternoon light slanted across the floor, and I was fully recovered.

Because of the water, light had a strange quality here. The canal below my window was empty, an opaque green that resembled no color I had ever encountered. Opening the casement, I leaned out, listening to the sounds of this new place—the calls of the boatmen, a cacophony of church bells, the abundant gulls circling overhead, busy as the birds of prey over London.

There was a basin of water and a cloth on the cupboard, and I stripped off my tired shirt and washed myself thoroughly. My clothes had been neatly put away—Seb needed less recovery time—and I pulled out my best linen and least travel-stained hose and stocks.

Seb returned when I was almost dressed. He wore unfamiliar clothing, borrowed no doubt from a Bonnato servant, and he immediately scolded me for the state of my points. "You think you'd never dressed yourself before." He redid the ties at my back. "You'd look like a plowman before suppertime. The lady wants to see you, but not that much of you."

"Where is the lady?" I allowed him to shave me and considered asking him to remove my beard.

"Downstairs, in the chamber where you saw her last night." Seb got me into my black doublet, pulling at me as if I were being presented at court. "Supper will be served in about an hour, but the lady would see you first."

There was awe in his voice; Bianca had worked her magic on him. Speaking to her last night seemed like a dream; between wine and weariness, I could hardly remember our conversation. An hour would not be enough before I had to share her with others. "Am I presentable?"

He eyed me critically. "You'll do. But you'll need new clothes if we're to stay here any length of time."

I caught my reflection in the window: not so very different from the boy she'd known or, for that matter, the student I'd been before that. If I hadn't changed by near-fifty, I would be long-boned and awkward all my life. "This will have to do."

Bianca's face was turned toward the window, watching the world go by. It reminded me of the way she'd withdrawn in London, and I startled her by saying, "I hope you go outside now."

Turning, she gave me the full effect of her dark eyes. "I do, now that I am home again. But I still like to observe; I spent too many years that way to change completely."

I sat down beside her. It was a slightly different view from my upstairs room, further along so that I could see the turning of the canal. "I'm sorry I slept so late."

"Don't be," she said. "Your man told me how long you've been traveling and a little of the reason. I'd like to hear more about that later."

"But for now...?"

She inclined her head. "For now, I'm simply happy you are here."

"As I am happy to be here. I thought we'd never stop traveling." My desire for a wider world had evaporated, and all I wished for was my snug library at Winterset, a few books, and the people I cared about. Barring that, the Bonnato house on Rio Malatin would do well enough, seeing it contained Bianca and Seb. In a city such as Venice, I was sure there were books to be had.

Our silence stretched comfortably as we waited for supper. Bianca broke it at last with a surprising statement. "I wonder that you never married."

"What do I have to offer a wife?"

Bianca looked at me with affection. "You were such a sweet young man."

A wave of mortification rolled over me; her view was far different from my own. "I have never been sweet, and am no longer young."

"You've never been able to see yourself. You have much to offer a woman." Her smile curved slyly. "Beyond the obvious."

All the blood in my body rushed to my head. "I always wondered that you let me touch you," I said, my voice hoarse with embarrassment and remembered passion.

Her delicate hands lay still in her lap. "You saved my life. I would have died in that house if someone hadn't been able to see me."

Again, the difference in our views was astounding. "Anyone

could have seen you and been a more appropriate match than I was," I said. "Looking back, I was a boy, and a callow, unattractive one."

She placed her hand over mine. It was as pale and finely grained as parchment but still beautiful. "I was afraid to be seen." Smoothing back the silvery hair that strayed from beneath her veil, she went on, "You got past that—perhaps because you were young. I did not think you would be a threat to my peace of mind. I did not think someone your age would find me attractive."

But I had. In her widow's garb, she had been formidable, but once we spoke and I encountered the mind beneath the stern exterior, I saw the true Bianca. After we became lovers, I could never see her any other way. Her age did not matter. Even now, at seventy, she was desirable in my eyes.

"I will always be grateful. You brought me back to myself."

I caressed her hand, admiring a gold ring with a fine purple stone. "Why did you never form another attachment?" I was not a suitable husband, but the merchant community teemed with candidates. "You could have remarried."

She shook her head. "It was unnecessary. When Gilbert died, I was young. I spent the years between his death and your arrival almost frozen. I had not been able to see myself as anything but his widow. You broke that spell."

A gondola glided past the window, the boatman singing a bawdy song at the top of his lungs. We stopped to listen, smiling.

"You're a good man, Robin. You should find a wife."

It was like sitting with an attractive female version of Ned. Why did those closest to me refuse to understand my feelings? Seb was the only one who did. "I'm a bastard with no family and no connections, currently exiled from my own country. I'm quite the catch."

She ignored my sarcasm and continued, "You're well educated; you've worked for the king of England. You may not have family, but you have plenty of connections. You've got a lovely house—"

"Which is not mine."

"You have a lovely house, which you can afford to lease. You have many good and influential friends."

These were all good arguments, applied to anyone other than myself. "I'm not good at letting people close," I said finally. "You were the last physical relationship I've had."

"Sweet Robin. You have deprived yourself of so much."

"You have said yourself that you've made no new connection."

"I am older than you, and I've been married, borne a child. It might not have lasted, but it was enough. You've not let yourself have that."

A few days later, Seb woke me before dawn.

"What is it?" I muttered, pushing myself upright. I had been dreaming of Winterset.

"The lady wants you." His tone told me it wasn't the first time he'd said it. "She says to dress warmly."

"I always dress warmly." I hadn't expected Venice to be cold, even in summer. The damp settled into the stones, and then my joints. I'd not ached this badly since my fall on the cliff ten years past. "I'm going back to sleep."

Seb blocked me. "You are not. The lady is expecting you downstairs."

I opened the shutters, but there was nothing to see. A thick fog blanketed the canal, moving like smoke between my window and the house across the passage.

Dressed, I ventured downstairs but found Bianca's parlor empty. One of the silent servants entered. "The lady is downstairs, signor."

Downstairs? I went down one more flight and found Bianca waiting at the canal-side door, already wrapped in her cloak. She reached out her hand as I approached. "Did you see?"

"See what?" I was still so sleepy that I could barely see her.

"The mist." She looked delighted, and I remembered the story she'd told me, when we first met, of escaping into the mist.

"But it's cold," I said, realizing immediately how childish I sounded. She lived in this damp place without complaint. I could handle an early morning boat ride.

"Silly man." Her expression was fond but imperious; I was not permitted to go back to bed.

The gondola bobbed outside the door. Bianca was handed down, and I joined her under the wooden felze, pulling a fur-lined blanket closely around us.

"Where would you like to go, signora?"

"Just row," she said vaguely. "I'm taking Signor Lewis to see the mist."

The boatman dipped his oar in the canal, and we moved off, retracing my arrival until we reached the Grand Canal.

The fog was absolute. How the gondolier managed, I couldn't imagine. Not only sight was decreased, but hearing. Each sound was simultaneously deadened and magnified, bouncing off the stone walls so the source could not be identified. I found it disconcerting in the extreme, but Bianca was glowing.

"Isn't it wonderful?" I could feel her energy in the slender arm that curled through mine.

"I've never experienced anything like it," I said, trying to quell my disquiet. I liked sailing, but this was a very small boat on open water, and unless the boatman possessed vision keener than a bird of prey, he was rowing blind.

There were other boats around us, voices coming faintly from all sides, oars splashing, the calls of the gondoliers—already recognizable after only a few days—but they were invisible.

"It feels haunted." It was the only word I can think of to describe the sensation.

"Yes! That's what I've always loved. When it's like this, Venice could be a city of the dead, and no one would be the wiser."

I did not find this comforting. I had no belief in ghosts, but if they existed, they would live in Venice, over a thousand years old and like no other place on earth.

Bianca's head rested on my shoulder, and I leaned back in the seat, prepared to enjoy this trip for her sake, if not for my own.

The magic crept up on me. After perhaps a quarter-hour, the mist lifted slightly so that the green-blue water was visible alongside the gondola.

Sounds still appeared and disappeared from nowhere, but I was more certain that the boatman might be able to see where he was going. "How does he do it?"

"Instinct," she said. "Venetian boys learn this lagoon in childhood. He knows the currents of the air and the water and can judge his location by how sounds echo from the buildings." She smiled, a touch of pride lighting her delicate features. "I was able to do it when I was young."

"You were a brave child." I imagined the child Bianca, alone in this mist, and shuddered. Though their solution had been extreme, I sympathized with her parents' worry. "A brave, mad child."

She laughed softly. "And look at me now. No madness, no bravery."

"I disagree." Church bells boomed out, bouncing across the water like cannonballs being skipped by giants. Seven bells, picked up almost immediately by the surrounding churches; we were caught in the crossfire of their ringing. When it finally stopped, the air shivered around us. "I think it took much bravery to live your life in London and to return here when it was time."

"It was, perhaps, madness to take a young lover."

I interlaced my fingers through hers. "Not mad." My mouth close to her ear, I said, "You said the other night that I saved you. You saved me too. Without you, I would have stayed shut inside myself."

"That would have been a shame. You have much to give." She raised her voice to the gondolier. "You may take us back now; the mist is rising."

It continued to dissipate so that by the time we slipped past San Marco, I was able to see flashes of gold through the last streaks of fog. "I must see the basilica," I said. "Will you come with me?"

"Perhaps." Another gondola passed, and she shrank back under our protective covering. "On a day when I feel up to it."

Chapter 63

"I SHOULD NEVER HAVE started listening to you," Hawkins says. "Aside from feeling bad about my role in this, you've made me discontented with my life. I don't want to ride about the country hauling in prisoners who may or may not be guilty."

I note his wording with interest. "How did you end up doing this? It doesn't suit you."

"My brother got me the post," he says, "since I hadn't shown any initiative to find my own place."

My perception of him has changed during this very strange week. Now I see a man, young for his years, perhaps, but able to see beyond his upbringing, able to be brought along the right path, as it were.

"If I were the man Ned Pickering wanted me to be—influential, with a place at court—I would find a spot for you, Will."

He laughed. "Why would you do that?"

"You follow direction, but you know when to think for yourself." I put a hand on his arm. "You're a better man than your father," I say. "Or you will be in time. The bones are there."

Will blinks, touched somehow by my criticism of his father. Just days ago, he struck me for a similar statement. "Let us not go there, Rob."

"We're reaching the end of my Italian journey," I say, no longer wanting to torment him. "Shall I go on?"

Eager as a boy at his mother's knee, he says, "Yes."

Chapter 64

DESPITE HER FAMILY'S HISTORY in the city, Bianca did not have a wide circle of acquaintances. "I fear you will be lonely here." We sat at her window as we did every night. "I have never minded it."

"I did not come here to meet people." I allowed my voice to soften. "I came to see you."

"And to avoid arrest," she said, smiling.

"And to avoid arrest," I agreed. "But it is enough that you have given me shelter. I require nothing more."

Nevertheless, she used her limited resources to find occupation for me. In addition to her own small library, she obtained access to a larger collection owned by a distant cousin to the former doge and invited him to dine one autumn evening.

Earlier in the day, she had the servants go through her brother's wardrobe, and Seb staggered into our chamber, his arms full of slightly-out-of-date but very elegant Venetian finery.

I looked at myself in the ornate gold-framed mirror, wearing Vincent's black velvet doublet with its decadent carved buttons, my new linen shirt poking through the discreet slashes in the sleeves. "I look quite distinguished," I said, turning this way and that. "If you disregard my head." Black hose and shoes in soft Italian leather made me feel like a gentleman who could mingle anywhere—even the English court.

"Your head is why we're here," Seb reminded me. He stepped forward and tweaked my sleeves. "Now you're fit company for the lady, and whoever it is who is coming to dinner."

Piero Grimani was a petite, brittle-looking fellow in the most elaborate clothing I had seen on someone not a king. Velvets, furs, and feathers notwithstanding, he possessed a sharp mind, a quick tongue, and a collection of books that stopped my breath.

His library was not a large chamber, but he'd had shelves built along the walls to store his books vertically, an innovation I'd seen only once before. It was stunning, being surrounded on all sides by books, and it made me yearn to rebuild my library in its image.

Seb did his part as well. With no Italian but immense goodwill and his novice's Latin, he made his way to the Benedictine monastery at San Giorgio Maggiore, an island across from San Marco. He spent so much time there that I worried he'd resumed his vocation.

When asked, he laughed. "I will not abandon you, master. I think that has been established. But the brothers have the best library I have ever seen. They do not often allow outsiders. I was lucky to be received myself, but I told them what happened to me in England, and they took pity upon me."

I raised my eyebrows. "Well, they're not likely to take pity on me."

"Perhaps not, if we are truthful. But I have told them that I am traveling with my dear uncle, and they will allow you access to the library on that basis."

Seb and I looked as much alike as a hawk and a hen, but his open expression appeared incapable of falsehood. If he told me we were related, I would want to believe him.

"You are a marvel," I said, shaking my head. "Truly, Seb, I don't know what I would have done without you this last year."

"Where would I be, if not with you?"

"I don't know," I said. "England, with a plump wife and several children?"

He wrinkled his nose. "That is no more my future than it is yours."

"Then we are fated to wander the world together." I could think of far worse fates, and by appearances, so could he.

To Seb's disappointment, I found the library at San Giorgio Maggiore—and the brothers—not to my taste. They sensed my Protestant leanings, looking at me as if I smelled bad. I left him there and visited my new friend instead.

Despite his outlandish appearance, Grimani was a man to be

reckoned with. I understood from Bianca that politics in Venice were a serious matter and that a complaint to the Venetian senate could make a man disappear. The Doge's palace was a pink-and-white marble fantasy, but it contained dank and isolated prison cells behind its beautiful facade.

Grimani was no doge nor even a senator, but I had become attuned to the risks of befriending powerful people. When he asked me to dispense with Signor and call him Piero, I hesitated.

"You *Inglese*," he said, "you topple the Church of Rome, yet you are too timid to use a man's name."

We *were* an odd lot, alternating between shoving ourselves into everyone's business and then tiptoeing about on lesser issues. "I am sorry, Piero," I said. "I will try to rise above my people."

He winked at me. "Good. I like having visitors who appreciate my books."

I visited him frequently, often going on foot, though it took far longer than using Bianca's gondola. When I exited her house on the land side, the tall chimneys of the palazzo Grimani were visible from the tiny piazza, but there was no direct route, I soon learned as I went down passages and over small bridges, only to arrive back at my starting point. Traveling in circles maddened me, and I vowed not to leave until I could find my way around the city, something that made Bianca laugh. "Many of us don't know the whole city, at least not by foot."

Nevertheless, I would do it. Seb was intrigued by the project, though he was equally interested in learning to maneuver a gondola. On the days when he was not on the water or hidden away at the monastery, he accompanied me on my walks, and in the evenings, he would add to the map he was drawing on the table in our chamber.

It was a remarkably detailed piece of work, with the Bonnato house at the center and canals, streets, and squares drawn in as we encountered them. Churches were denoted by crosses, and the large piazza San Marco was filled with minute figures.

"You've quite a talent." I wondered that he could produce such detail from memory. "You've been hiding this."

He ran a finger over the Grand Canal, where he had inked a small, wide-eyed sea monster. "You just haven't noticed. I made a small one when we were in London, just the bits of the city that I saw. I'd like to draw a whole city someday, but I would have to be there and walk it and get to know its dimensions." There was passion in his voice. He had been deprived of so much by his attachment to me.

"Seb," I said gently, "you may return to England whenever you like. If you went to Ned, he would take you in. You could learn the city, make your maps, have a life that isn't based around me. Make something of yourself."

Seb looked up, methodically cleaning his quill and stoppering the ink. "Master Pickering might take me in, but I would not have this life you speak of."

"I can only imagine—" I began.

"You can't imagine," he said firmly. "You think yourself an outcast because of your birth and your lack of status, but physically, you are no different than the people who look down on you. Your difference can be concealed with the right coat or sufficient coin." He fixed me with a glare most unlike him. "I am who I am—what I am—forever."

One afternoon in Piero's library overlooking the Grand Canal, he produced a book written in his own hand. "You might find this interesting," he said. "I no longer have the original, but I doubt you could read it—it was written in an Arab tongue, which I learned in my merchanting days."

I admitted to having none of those languages. It thrilled me to know there was an entire canon of knowledge which had not yet been translated into Latin, French, or English.

"It's a book of tales," Piero said. "Odd, Eastern things, but interesting. The framework is laughable. A sultan—a doge of the East, if you will—is given horns by his young wife, and he vows to never again trust a woman. He marries a new virgin every day and executes her with the dawn." A cackling laugh. "A bit like your late king, eh?"

His description was uncomfortably apt. "Go on."

"One day, he marries a woman who brings her young sister into their chamber. I am assuming this was after the rites of marriage, else the sultan could have gotten two for the price of one."

I let him laugh, though my mind had immediately flown to King Henry and the Boleyn sisters. At least he'd not had them at the same time.

"The wife has a final request, knowing she will die in the morning. She wants to tell her sister one last story. The sultan agrees, and she spins a tale which, very shrewdly, is not finished at sunrise. The foolish sultan wants to know how it ends, and instead of forcing her to tell him, he lets her live another day."

"Does he kill her when she finishes the story?" A tale in which a woman got the upper hand, even briefly, was something new and different.

"No!" Piero exploded with laughter. "She goes on and on and on, weaving her stories together, until finally the sultan is so in love with her that he lets her live."

I riffled through the pages. Piero's handwriting was as eccentric as his wardrobe, and I had not attempted an Italian translation in some years. "May I borrow this?"

Translating the tales of Shahrazad, the clever young wife, took all winter and the better part of the spring. When I showed the book to Bianca, she was so intrigued that she offered to work with me, a repetition of our earliest days.

Winter in Venice was not as cold as England, but it was damp in a way England could only dream of, a raw chill that worked its way through the heaviest wool to lodge in neck and knees and back.

"How do you bear it?" I hobbled into Bianca's morning chamber like an old man. My knee had ached for days and had decided, that very morning, that it did not wish to bend.

"I was born to it." I noticed the fine woolen wrap around her shoulders and wondered, for the first time, if it had a purpose beyond the decorative.

We alternated reading and transcribing the tales, laughing helplessly at times over the antics of Ali Baba and his inept thieves and other strange and fantastical characters.

"I believe this is more than what Grimani says. He may have translated it from a Syrian volume, but these tales are too inconsistent to have come from one culture." The idea had nagged for days: the stories ranged far and wide, their inhabitants as varied as the birds of the air. The East was a vast place, and this only hinted at its riches.

"Do you mean that the stories have been collected and fitted into a frame of the storyteller's choosing?" Bianca's fingers tightened on the pen. "I have questioned some of the references throughout. It makes sense."

It was a joy, after a few hours of work, to have a glass of wine and discuss our thoughts, speculating what the stories had meant to the original audience. Undoubtedly they were as meaningful to them as biblical tales were to the ancients, and their meanings just as impenetrable to a modern reader.

It was an entertaining way to pass the cold months when we rarely stirred outside except for mass and my weekly visit to Piero. Once, a heavy fog blanketed the islands, and I was the first to wake and call for the gondola.

Seb disappeared to the monastery for weeks on end, returning each time somehow more vivid but still assuring me of his intention to stay in secular life. I questioned what called to him so strongly, then stopped: if there was one thing I understood, it was a man's tangled relationship with his God.

Letters trickled in from England. Ned, away from court but never far from a source of information, wrote that Queen Mary lived up to every fearful expectation, hunting heretics with a zeal that would have made her father proud and doing her best to

A Wider World · 321

restore Rome to England's churches.

The Archbishop of Canterbury had been arrested before I left, and in April, 1556, a letter arrived telling of his execution. Cranmer had recanted—which did not surprise me, as he was fond of life—but upon learning that Mary intended to burn him anyway, he renounced his prior words and went to the fire with his convictions intact.

I'd met Cranmer many times, at court or at Austin Friars. He was a pliable man, as were all survivors of that place, and news of his death struck me hard. Who was I to be safe when, all over England, men no different from me were being tried and executed?

Ned's discreet letters, arriving five or six times a year, told me enough of the truth that I resolved to stay in Italy, despite my worry for those I'd left behind. Was Anselm safe with Jack Darlington still at large in the world? He could always reveal himself as a former monk, I supposed, but he was unlikely to do that; he'd inhabited his role as my uncle for many years.

Beyond Anselm and Ned, there weren't many people for me to worry about. How had I reached such an age with so few souls who laid claim to my heart?

I understood, after this period of travel and the long respite in Venice, that I was lonely. Twenty years hence, I did not want to be like Bianca, alone in a large house, with only servants for company.

Unless I heeded Ned's advice and returned to court when Mary died, as would surely happen, that would be my future. I loved Winterset, loved my life there, loved Seb and Anselm, and had much affection for Jasper Fowler, but they had never seen the other life to which I had been exposed.

My choices were thus: the court, with its attendant intrigues and friendships, or Winterset, with little contact beyond the few men who shared my home. Neither was right. Neither was enough.

I refused again the offer of Piero's gondola. I wanted to clear my head from the long afternoon in his library and the abundant wine he pressed upon me.

The first few times I had walked from the palazzo Grimani, I became lost within minutes. Now it only happened if I failed to pay attention or deliberately set out to lose myself in the web of tiny streets.

There was no time for that today; I had overstayed my time, drinking and listening to his stories. At times, he reminded me of a smaller, more excitable Ned in his love of gossip.

I walked a stretch of cobbles along a wide canal, then took an abrupt right into a crowded piazza. A market was taking place, and I circled around so as not to return with an unnecessary purchase.

I traversed through an arch, and the shining water was abruptly at my feet. A left turn this time took me to a bridge. I walked quickly up the shallow steps and stopped, for a dizzying moment, at the apex. The lack of rails always made my head swim as I pictured buckling at the knees and disappearing into the green water below.

It would be so easy.

I shook my head and continued down the other side.

Exile, despite the luxury of Bianca's home and the acquaintances I made in Venice, was a prison. I was not accustomed to idleness.

My life had been, for the most part, about work. I looked always toward the next thing, dropping my past like an outgrown coat when it no longer served. I shaped and accommodated myself to each job, each master, never wondering what versions of myself had been sacrificed along the way. Each life eclipsed its predecessor: school, court, Oxford, Cromwell.

Another narrow walkway led through a long passage and then into a sunlit square, blinding after the brief darkness. At this time of day, it was nearly deserted, only a few stragglers lingering at the church door.

I leaned against the central wellhead, the stone warm beneath my back. A cat wandered past, sprung onto the cover, and pushed insistently at my shoulder with its head. I scratched it absently, then brushed its white hair off Vincent's short mantle.

I'd hurt people with my ambition, my constant forward motion, and when I'd had enough and walked away, what had that done to pay my debt to the world? What did I gain when the only thing I'd ever tried to escape was myself? I thought to escape pain by avoiding relationships, yet my life was inexplicably peopled with those I cared about: Bianca, Ned, Seb.

I had done myself no good at all and much harm. Enough, I thought. I was but fifty-two; there was still life to be lived if I had the courage to face it.

The church bell rang, jarring me from my thoughts. The cat jumped down and stalked away, tail high.

It was time, I knew, for the cat and I to go home.

My head hurt from too much introspection, and an untimely hunger growled in my belly. Calling for Seb, I proposed a trip over to a tiny cantina we had discovered near the fish market. It served raw wine and inexpensive fish and shellfish in small portions. I had come to appreciate the taste of Venice's many sea creatures, so unlike plain English eels or fish. Seb's opinion was not so positive, but he was happy to drink wine, eat abundant bread, and sample small bits from my plate.

"It is not right that we are out like this," he said. "You need friends here other than Signor Grimani."

I chewed a piece of calamari, which was tasty but had a most disconcerting texture. "We have been out like this since we left England," I pointed out. "Why such a tender conscience now? Would you prefer to be with your own friends?"

He looked shocked. "Of course not," he said. "But you are a gentleman, and I am a servant, and everyone can see that."

I pushed a coin at him. "Then get us more wine, and let me remind you again that I was born no better than you."

As Seb fought his way to the counter for our refills, the tiny, crowded space closed in around me. Several hundred years old, it was a snug, dark tunnel, with vessels hanging from the ceiling, barrels of wine waiting to be tapped, and a constant crowd of men sneaking time from their market boats and stalls.

It reminded me of the parts of London I frequented with Ned, and I was abruptly swamped with nostalgia. I missed my friend. Boisterous and annoying though he could be, he was one of the kindest people I knew, and he had never given up on me.

His most recent letter pushed for my return. Queen Mary was certain to die soon, and then Princess Elizabeth would take her rightful, Protestant place on the throne, and the world would be safe for men like us.

It would be safest of all, of course, if I returned not to the north, but to London, and aligned myself with William Cecil, who would surely have a position in Elizabeth's court. I didn't dislike Cecil—I respected his ability to survive during Mary's reign—but my days of being an ambitious young man were long past.

Perhaps, if there were a place for a moderately ambitious, middle-aged man with a bad knee, I would consider it.

Seb slid the glass in front of me. "You were far away."

"I've had another letter from Ned."

"His letters always make you thoughtful."

I shouldn't be surprised that Seb noticed. After fifteen years, he knew more about me than anyone. "He thinks it's time for us to return."

His face brightened. "Is it safe?"

"Not yet, but soon." It was August, and Venice was not at its best. "Why don't we start for England by the end of the month?"

I poured the last of my wine down my throat. I would miss Italian wine in England. "Let us go. I must break the news that we are leaving."

"Do you think the lady doesn't already know?"

Bianca was not surprised by my decision. She arranged a dinner for the few friends I had made while in Venice, exhausting herself in the process. I ate with our guests and visited her afterward in her chamber, concerned that my departure had upset her.

She assured me otherwise. "I am just tired."

"Are you sure? I don't wish your failing health to be upon my head."

"Your head is fine." Her voice issued faintly from the depths of her brocade-swathed bed, but I could hear her smile. "It is such a serious head, full of serious thoughts."

I laughed and came to sit on the coverlet. "You've always seen a different version of me," I said. "May I have anything brought up for you?"

She smiled at me. "No. I am sorry for not attending your party. I could not face it."

I understood. She had never put herself into society, and on my account, she had invited near-strangers into her sanctuary. "It wasn't necessary," I told her. "I would have been as happy dining alone with you."

"We have dined alone every day for three years." She pushed herself up against the pillows, her silvery braid falling over one shoulder. "I thought I could make the effort now that you're leaving, but I cannot."

A thought occurred. "Would you come back to England with me? There are few enough people at Winterset, and I believe you would enjoy Anselm's company."

Her fine-boned hand clasped mine. "Venice is my home, and sooner or later, I shall die here." She closed her eyes. "I do not dread death so much as a party."

Kissing her forehead, I left her to her rest and went back to my chamber, where Sebastian had created chaos while attempting to make order.

"We're leaving with far more than we arrived with," he informed me, staring at the accumulation of exile. "Where did you get all this?"

I wasn't certain where it had come from: books and more books, Vincent Bonnato's clothing and my own, Sebastian's smaller lot of possessions, a few securely-swaddled pieces of glass for Winterset. I didn't care how much luggage we had, only that it was all heading in the direction of England.

Chapter 65

WE RIDE THROUGH THE gate of the Cambridge house a different party than we'd entered. Will Hawkins is no longer just my captor; I see him as a man, and I believe he sees me the same way, which makes things difficult for both of us.

When he helped me dress this morning, Seb murmured in my ear, "The steward says the queen is dying."

That was a brightening thought, and not just because it might save my life. How many others would be spared the wrath of her warped religious fervor? "I wish she'd hurry up about it."

Chapter 66

THERE WAS ONE BIT of unfinished business before I could leave Italy. Delivered from Venice to the mainland, I found an inn near the port. "You will stay here with our baggage for a few days," I said. "I am—I have one last thing to do before we return to England." I could barely articulate my plan to myself, much less to my inquisitive friend.

"Our things will be safe without me," Seb said. "Wherever you're going, I'm coming along."

"You're not," I said decisively. "I'll be back in a day or two."

"No, master." He folded his arms. "It's not safe for you to ride alone. Who knows what sort of brigands are looking for a red-headed Englishman?"

Seb had a point, but I was insistent, and eventually, he remembered that I was his employer and consented to stay at the inn and work on his Venetian map. Early the next morning, I rented a sturdy gelding and turned toward Padua.

I hadn't intended to visit Santa Giustina. It had come upon me as abruptly as the decision to go home, and I could no more easily ignore it. Padua was only a few hours' ride from Venice; I had been so close, and for all that time, I had resisted the urge to see him again. Why now?

It had been more than thirty years since we parted. How could I ride the wide road to Padua with my heart in my throat like a green boy? Some men did not live as long as I had carried this love inside me.

The memory of Salvatore, of the time spent with him, the intensity of our conversations—his beautiful eyes—had never left me. As I kept myself aloof from others, his importance had only grown, and I knew I would have to see him to release myself from the power of that memory. It was the unspoken part of my conversation with Bianca, about why I had never married—while there was much truth in the argument that I had little to offer a wife, there was also this.

The flat Italian landscape with its distant blue hills passed quickly. Padua seemed larger than I remembered, but I had seen nothing clearly then, sick with either love or heartbreak. Perhaps it was the same; perhaps it was smaller. There was only one memory of that time that I could trust.

The Basilica of Santa Giustina, with its attached monastery, was just the same. I had grown so accustomed to seeing the picked-apart shells of monasteries in England that to see a vital, bustling house of religion brought a flush of something like happiness. Even now, I could not separate my past and present religions.

Circling the church, I made my way to the monastery entrance. The young monk at the gate sized me up and greeted me in halting English. His eyes widened at the fluency of my greeting, and he relaxed into his own tongue. "God's greetings, *signore*, and welcome to Santa Giustina. How may we assist you?"

I swung down from my horse, feeling my knee protest at the landing. "I was a guest here many years ago when I was recovering from illness." I handed my reins to a boy, and the beast was led away. "I find myself in Italy again, and I wished to pay my respects to the brothers who nursed me if they are still here." It occurred to me, suddenly—horribly—that perhaps Salvatore was not here. He would be sixty now; men in such marshy areas often developed tertian fevers from the bad air.

The monk inclined his head, his hood completely shading his face. "I will bring you to the sub-prior, *signore*, and we will see if it may be arranged."

The room where I was placed was spare but comfortable, and a servant soon brought me a drink and asked if I required food. The idea of food made my already tense stomach turn over. "No, *grazie*." I sipped my ale and waited for the sub-prior, letting my mind drift in the peculiarly monastic quiet which surrounded me.

So tranquil was the atmosphere that I did not hear the soft footsteps until they stopped at my shoulder. "God's grace be upon you, *signore*," the voice said. "How may we serve you?"

I sprung from my seat and beheld the object of my journey. "Salvatore!"

"*Oca!*" His face lit up, and he clasped me to him in a brief, rib-cracking embrace. Hands on my shoulders, he held me back to look at me. "How is it you have come here?" His eyes were the same. Deep brown, sparkling with wit and kindness, gazing at me in a way that made my knees weaken.

"I found myself in Italy," I said, stumbling over my words. "I had to come."

He pushed back his hood and took my hands. "I am glad you did. I have thought of you often over the years."

I met his eyes squarely. "I have thought of you as well."

I could not say what was in my heart. The words pressed upon my chest like a weight, but I could not utter them to this man who was Salvatore and yet so unlike him.

The man who stood so close to me might be Salvatore in his depths, but his exterior was firmly and obviously that of the sub-prior of the monastery of Santa Giustina. He was older, but that was no surprise. I was no longer the *pettirosso* of our first meeting either, and the damp weather of Venice, followed by the early-morning ride, left me feeling every one of my years.

Salvatore's curls were a mix of black and white strands framing a face still far too attractive for my liking. The fine skin around his eyes had thickened, but the creases there, and bracketing his mouth, showed that his happy nature was the same.

"What brings you to Italy?" He seated himself on the bench and gestured for me to join him. "Whatever the reason, I am glad your travels have brought you here."

I gave a brief recital of those travels, leaving out the fact that I had been driven from my own country. "I have been in Venice for some time, staying with a friend, but I could not leave Italy without seeing you."

His expression tightened for a moment as the meaning behind my words struck him. "I have thought of you often, as I said." He put a hand over mine. "You have caused me much prayer and contemplation over the years."

"As have you." I could not determine his meaning, but the feel of his palm resting on the back of my hand made my entire skin come alive.

He noted my empty cup and called for a pitcher to be brought to us. At my raised brows, he said, "With position comes some privilege, my friend. I am but offering hospitality to a guest of this house."

"That is true." I smiled. "And your guest would be uncomfortable if you did not join him. You are the sub-prior now?"

"I am." He sighed. "I still spend more time than I should in the infirmary. That is where I am happiest, but it is not where I have been called to be. I still have trouble accepting God's plan."

I could not imagine a calling more genuine than his. From the moment I opened my eyes in the infirmary, I was comforted by his presence. His years at the abbey undoubtedly caused this promotion, but it was a loss to their patients.

"I've never known God's plan," I said. "Even after all these years, I still wonder."

"Have you a family, Robin?" He filled our cups and placed the pitcher on the table. The high, narrow window left a bar of light across the tabletop.

"No." Bianca's words and my response echoed in my mind. I could not repeat these things to Salvatore.

He lowered his eyes. "I am sorry."

I took a mouthful of ale. "Why should you be sorry? It is not your life."

Salvatore's laugh was soft, rueful. "Ah, my prickly friend. Thirty years, and you are still the same."

He remembered how long it had been since we'd parted. Perhaps it was not all one-sided? I should not even think this way. "And how much have you changed?"

"Not much." His hands rested on his black-robed knees. They showed his age more strongly than his face, blue veins standing out on their backs, the knuckles thicker. "I love my God. I love my fellow man. I still struggle with obedience, despite the fact that I monitor the obedience of the novices."

"Who better," I asked, "to understand their struggle?" I remembered my offer to join the order and his firm truth-telling. "If I had become a Benedictine, you would have been my superior."

"No, *Oca.*" He shook his head. "My promotion is but recent, and I would never consider myself your superior." A long pause, followed by another sigh. "It was the fact that you were my equal which made it difficult to send you away."

It rolled over me then, the wave of my love for him. For decades it was, if not dormant, at least safely contained. Now, confronted with the reality of the man, I returned to that stammering twenty-year-old boy. "Leaving here was the most difficult thing I have ever done."

"And telling you to leave, those were the hardest words I ever said." For a moment, Salvatore's face showed pain, and then it cleared, becoming placid again. "But it was for the best. I have made vows before God, and you, my friend, you made those vows difficult. Perhaps not in the way that you had hoped," he continued. "I do not find my vow of chastity burdensome. But you lit a spark in my mind; you made me think things that were not safe for a Benedictine to think. You made me see—and feel—outside myself."

"And all I wanted was to make that vow of chastity burdensome," I said. "You know how I felt. How I still feel, even after all these years."

Salvatore brought out the truth in me. "I have had relationships," I said. "But I have never married, have never wanted to. Part of it is because I have nothing to offer a wife. I have gained some position in England by my work, but it is not enough. Beyond that, my entire heart was never there to give." This time, it was my hand that covered his. "I left a part of it here, all those years ago. I came back to see if you had kept it."

The mask dropped from his face. I could see that he did love me, as much as he was able, but he would never allow himself to feel what I did.

I brushed my fingers along his cheek. "It is all right that you don't love me. It is enough that I can tell you I do."

He was very still. My fingers remained on his cheek for a moment, and then I dropped them, knowing to keep them there too long was to risk disappointment or exposure. We were, after all, in a room with an open door.

"I cannot." Salvatore's voice was hoarse. "You understand, I think."

"I don't like it, but I do." I took a deep breath. "Tell me, has anything happened in the last thirty years?"

He laughed in spite of himself. "You are good for me." Pushing himself up, he said, "We have time before sext. Walk with me?"

The wind was brisk, whipping our garments as we slowly traversed the cloister. Salvatore moved with some stiffness, and I was glad that my own halting gait would not be noted.

"I wrote you a letter," I said. "Did you ever get it?"

"We don't often get letters here."

"This would have been delivered by hand." I explained about the monks I'd sent from England. "I don't know if they would have come this far, but I said they would be welcome here."

"And so they would have been." Salvatore paced along beside me. At some point, he had taken my arm; I had not even noticed. "Has it truly been so bad in your country?"

News of the dissolution had spread, even to this isolated place; it was church news, not just a secular happening. How did I tell this man what I had done? To not tell him was impossible. Along with my love, he deserved my honesty.

"It has been very bad," I said. "All the houses have been closed, and their members scattered."

"But your queen, she is Catholic, no?" He turned his face to me. "Has she not re-established the church in England?"

The weight of Mary's reign dragged at me like a sodden cloak. "She has," I said, "and it has been as bad—or worse—for believers of the new religion. She is more occupied with rooting out heretics than rebuilding monasteries, I fear."

From beneath his hood, Salvatore looked at me. "Are you a heretic to be rooted out? Is that why you are in Italy?"

I closed my eyes. "It is," I said. "I supported her cousin, Jane, because I feared the strength of Mary's faith. There are some in the government with very long memories, and it became necessary for me to leave." I squeezed the arm linked with mine. "The smell of roasting meat is all well and good until it's your own carcass."

"You cannot turn hearts and minds toward God through fear."

I did not tell him that hearts and minds could be swayed more easily than that—that they could be purchased with a grant of land or a marriage contract or a blind eye turned to questionable behavior. Despite his age, there was an innocence in Salvatore that I could not bring myself to shatter.

"Did you not say you were returning to England? Will you be safe?"

I began to walk again. Standing still made me want to take him in my arms. "I have received word from a friend that the queen is unwell, possibly dying. I wish death on no one, despite the charges brought against me, but if this is indeed the truth, then I will be safe with her sister on the throne."

"The sister is of your faith?"

I nodded. "She is, though she has observed the Catholic faith for her own protection."

"Then she will come to power and burn Catholics," he said. "It will never end."

"I pray that is not the case." I told him what I knew of the young Elizabeth, of her education and her breadth of mind. "I think she is not so damaged as her sister and perhaps will not lash out at every perceived threat."

"I pray you are right." He turned at the sound of the bells. "It is time. Will you come with me, or is that an insult?"

"There is no insult where you are concerned." I followed him to the chapel and sat toward the rear, closing my eyes. My ears would never tire of this sound. It was impossible that I had ever sung these words, made these sounds, believed with all my heart that my voice would reach God.

I no longer truly believed that my prayers reached anyone outside myself. This was heresy in either religion, but I had, over time, come to believe it. How long had I prayed—how much had the brothers at Hatton prayed—to no avail? If anyone listened, they were not in the habit of granting requests.

When the service was over, Salvatore rejoined me, accompanied by several monks whose faces were vaguely familiar. I remembered them as his contemporaries during my prior stay.

"You will have dinner with us?" he asked. "I have things I must attend to before then, but Brother Zio, who has taken over from Brother Ludo, would like to show you his latest acquisitions."

I accepted happily and spent two hours perusing their excellent collection of books. Brother Zio was friendly and knowledgeable, and I shared with him the reading I had done in Venice from Piero Grimani's library.

"It is the only time I think of the world outside," he said. "There is so much knowledge that will never make it inside these walls."

"And there are many things inside these walls which do not make it outside," I told him. "You may be the better for it."

I was treated as an honored guest at the monks' table, though the meal, as always, was silent. Whenever I looked up, Salvatore's eyes were upon me.

The issue of whether I should stay the night or return to Sebastian was resolved as soon as the benches were pushed back. "You cannot travel at night," Salvatore said. "I will have a guest chamber made up for you."

I should leave, even if it meant taking a room at an inn. There was no point in my staying. I had seen him and told him of my feelings. There was no point in my staying. "I would be honored to accept your hospitality," I said. "Just for one night."

The hours between dinner and vespers were spent in the

company of Salvatore and Brother Zio. I was shown some improvements to the infirmary, and from the window, Salvatore pointed to the herb garden, which had been enlarged since my previous stay. "I work there when I can," he said. "I find time, even with my other duties. Having my hands in the earth brings me closer to God."

I remembered helping him in the garden, and the light on his face as he spoke of the healing properties of the herbs. It seemed unfair that his seniority had promoted him away from the work of his heart.

Dusk fell, and the church was dim for vespers, only a few candles lighting the enormous, airy space. The monks were joined by a full choir of boys, and the unearthly sound of their voices lifted me as close to heaven as a skeptical man could be lifted.

I was left to my own devices after that and chose to return to the library. Benedictines did not eat supper in the summer months, and my rumbling stomach would remain unappeased until breakfast.

Far too soon, the bell rang for compline. Before we entered the chapel, Salvatore turned to me. "The great silence begins after this," he said. "Do you remember?"

"Of course, I remember." I was piqued that he would think I'd forgotten such a basic principle. "I will speak to you in the morning."

He brought up his hood to cover his laughter and disappeared into the quire.

After compline, the monks disappeared to their cells, where they would stay until called to matins, in the deepest part of the night. I followed, a bed having been reserved for me in the dorter. The hosteller had ceded to my request because of my history with Santa Giustina and my friendship with Salvatore.

"I was raised in a place such as this," I explained. "In England, the monasteries are no more."

"Of course." He showed me to a small cell at the end of the row. Besides a low cot, the only things in the room were a stool, a shelf, a hook upon which to hang a habit, and a crucifix.

Despite several years of Venetian luxury and my comfortable existence at Winterset before that, this cell was comfortable. A man never truly gets over his childhood.

The great silence permeated the building, broken only by faint sounds from the other cells as the monks readied themselves for bed. Despite my belief that my prayers reached no one, I got on my knees beside the bed; it felt disrespectful to do otherwise in this place.

The silence grew deeper. My eyes remained stubbornly open, despite the exhaustion brought on by the emotions of the day.

Somewhere in the dorter, close by or at the other end, lay Salvatore. We were separated by more than walls; despite my impulsive words, his feelings for me were no more than brotherly regard. I would have to accept that.

Shuffling footsteps echoed in the hall. It was the privy watch—the bed check carried out nightly to make sure that the monks were abed and not about any sinful activities.

Not likely, I thought. The sub-prior could check all he pleased and not find anything—

The sub-prior. The soft-soled presence making its way down the dorter, blessing each cell with a sprinkling of holy water, was Salvatore.

I held my breath. The footsteps continued, paused, and moved on. They stopped again outside my cell. The pause stretched out, far longer than any blessing. I sat up in bed.

One step forward, into the room. Then another.

Throwing off the blanket, I swung my legs over the side. I moved forward, step by step, until I encountered an obstacle.

The obstacle was warm, covered in a layer of light wool, and had hands that gripped my shoulders. The aspergillum dropped to the floor, spattering my bare feet with holy water.

Salvatore's warm breath was on my face. I leaned forward and rested myself against the length of him, learning the shape of his body through his habit. His grip loosened, his hands moving down my back.

We stood there, just inside the doorway, pressed together. My blood was thick, moving sluggishly through my veins, when all I wanted was to be able to swiftly capture his face between my palms and kiss him.

His hands at my waist were large and warm, trembling slightly.

I freed one of my own hands, cupped his face, leaned my forehead against his. Our noses bumped, and I turned my head, dipping lower to brush his mouth with mine.

A moan, completely without sound, escaped his lips. I froze, stunned at the enormity of what I had done, waiting for him to push me away or break the silence to call me all the names I deserved.

Instead, he moved closer, raising a hand to my head, pulling me in and kissing me with a depth of passion that shook me to my core.

It is difficult to conduct such business in total silence. Breath that wishes to be loud and ragged must be stilled; moans of pleasure must be stifled. Shirts and habits, once removed, must be dropped without becoming entangled in feet that stumble toward the cot. It creaked loudly under our combined weight, and we rolled to the floor.

Grappling like wrestlers, mouths and hands seeking what eyes could not see, we were shocked into stillness by a cough in the next cell. The cough was followed by the sound of a body rolling over, and a gentle snore.

I got to my knees and drew Salvatore up to face me. I could see nothing beyond his barest outlines; I wanted nothing more at this moment than to see that entirely beloved face before I kissed him and helped him to his feet.

But the darkness was absolute. I could not see him, nor could he see me.

I found his habit by touch and helped him pull it over his head. I tied his belt and settled his cowl, drawing up his hood so that his face was even more concealed. He stood like a statue, allowing me to dress him. He quivered at my touch, and his breathing was still shallow, but he made no move to touch me.

When he was fully dressed, I took his face in my hands and kissed him lightly. He returned the caress and made the sign of the cross on my forehead before backing out of the room.

I stayed where I was for a long time, letting the cold torment my skin. Eventually, I put on my shirt and got back into bed, knowing I would not sleep.

The bell tolled for matins, and the monks stirred and flowed downstairs to pray. I remained where I was, feeling waves of hot and cold shame wash over me. I'd tempted a man vowed to chastity into my bed, or at least onto my floor. And I had allowed him to leave with our desires unconsummated, out of fear of discovery and because I knew he would never be able to forgive himself if we'd gone further.

Whether I would be able to forgive myself was another matter.

In the morning, I dressed slowly, noticing the marks of rough handling on my arms and wondering if I'd left similar bruises on him. As I reached for my boots, placed side-by-side beneath the crucifix, I caught a glint of metal and retrieved the aspergillum, kicked aside in our passion. I slipped it into my bag to return to him—somehow—before I departed.

I arrived late to breakfast and listened as the rule was read out by the lector. Salvatore did not meet my eyes. He ate with his head down, listening to the reading, as if I were not there.

While the monks were at their chapter meeting, I walked along the edge of the marsh, noticing with surprise the number of geese in the high grass. When I got close, a large goose plunged at me, hissing a warning, its white wings spread wide.

"Careful." The boy emerged from the marsh, wiping his bare feet on the grass. "They don't like strangers."

"Where did they come from?" The boy's sudden appearance flustered me as much as the bird's threat. "There were no geese here before."

The boy squinted at me. "They've been here as long as I have," he told me. "They belong to Brother Salvatore. They protect the basilica."

Brother Salvatore's geese? I began to smile.

A few black-clad figures strayed into the cloister; chapter was complete. I bade the boy farewell and hastened back to the monastery.

I retrieved my bag from the refectory and went in search of Salvatore. Not surprisingly, he was in the room where we'd met the day before. I knocked on the frame and waited for him to admit me.

"Robin." He looked up from his papers. "Come in."

Robin. Not *Oca*. I tried not to read too much into his use of my name.

"I came to say goodbye." I wanted to draw him from his seat and embrace him, but I could not move. "And to thank this place for its hospitality once again."

"Safe travels," he said. "And safety beyond, in England." He looked up, and I imagined I could see another Salvatore inside.

"Thank you." I reached into my bag and brought out the long, mace-like aspergillum. "Also, you'll need this again tonight."

He tucked it into the pocket of his habit. "I'll try not to drop it again."

I attempted a smile. "I hope you are not caused to drop it again."

Emotions warred on his face before his essential nature won out and his eyes crinkled in a smile. It was a wary smile but nonetheless real. "It will not happen again, *Oca*. So long as you are leaving."

My heart turned over. "I am, and with more regrets than before. I should have stayed in the guest house."

Salvatore came out from behind the table. "And I should have blessed your door and moved on. No, my friend, you should have no regrets." He took my hands, and it was a simple gesture with nothing else behind it. "Although what happened will never be repeated, I feel no regret. It is something I will pray over long after you have gone."

I exhaled. "I was afraid you would not speak to me this morning."

His smile was wearier than it had been the day before, his innocence not quite as evident. "I cannot blame you for my own carnal feelings."

"You would not have felt them if I hadn't pushed you." I would take responsibility for the matter if it would make it easier for him.

"If I am capable of that sort of desire, it is a flaw within myself." He took my arm. "Come, I shall accompany you."

We walked in comfortable silence out to the courtyard. Seeing us, a servant ran toward the stables.

Beneath his hood, his eyes were bright. "I am glad you came back. I would not wish to spend the rest of my life not having seen your face again."

The servant approached, leading my horse by the reins.

"I return home a different man because of you." I looked at him now as the man he would be to me in future. "May I have your blessing?"

Salvatore touched his fingertips to my forehead, murmuring a blessing. "May you become the man you were meant to be, Robin Lewis, a man in full, deserving of love and life."

Before I slid down from my horse, Seb scrambled through the door and relieved me of my bag. "Are you all right, master? Have you eaten?"

I was filled with a warm benevolence at his care. "I've eaten, but I have a mighty thirst. Turn in the horse, and have a jug of wine brought up to our room. Then you can tell me what you've gotten into in my absence."

My sleepless night caught up with me as I mounted the stairs, and by the time Seb returned with the wine, I was sprawled across the bed, fully dressed. His entrance made me open my eyes, and I rolled to an upright position.

"Are you well?" He peppered me with questions as I drank, curious as to my whereabouts and the cause of my exhaustion.

"What can I do?"

"Nothing at all," I said, draining the cup. "I'm going to take a nap, and then we'll go and investigate ships' schedules."

Seb removed my doublet and set about dealing with the rest of my clothes. "I've already done that. There's a list on the table for when you wake up."

"I'll look now," I said, but he pushed me toward the bed. "I was thinking we might visit the Prestons."

Seb spiked his fingers through his hair, making it stand up. "On the list," he said. "Ships stopping in Normandy, Brittany, and the Low Countries. Just in case."

My eyes were closing. "You are a marvel," I murmured before sleep claimed me.

Chapter 67

"'A MAN IN FULL,' Salvatore said. What do you think he meant?" I'd had no idea, though the truth had been coming to me for some time.

Will considers the question, his horse jogging along close to mine. "Well, you did get married after that, I assume?" he asks. "At some point, you acquired a wife, and there's not much left to tell."

"True." It was that but more than that. A man in full, allowing myself to be open to the thought of marriage for the first time but also opening myself to others, letting them in, something I had resisted my entire life. Born from nothing, I succeeded on my merits. What need I had was for recognition of my abilities.

I had never let a deeper need take root.

"Do I get to hear about her?" Will asks. His tone is careful—he will not ask rude questions, no matter now prurient his interest, nor how confused he must be after I told him of my reunion with Salvatore.

"It is not yet time."

Chapter 68

OUR HORSES' HOOVES STRUCK sparks on the stone flags of the courtyard of the Preston house. Before my boots touched the ground, a child ran up and took the reins. Sebastian dismounted and followed as they were led toward the stable. The wide front door opened before I could knock. A liveried servant led me to a gracious chamber off the main hall. "M'lady will be right down."

I waited, admiring the room's appointments, which were luxurious without being lavish. Somehow, despite the difference in architecture and furnishings, it felt like Winterset. I wondered how it came about, the talent for making a home. I had made improvements to the house, but it was not this comfortable.

The door swung open, but instead of Lady Margaret, a young woman strode into the room. Taking no notice of me, she peeled off her gloves and flung them on the table.

"Good afternoon."

She whirled. "Good afternoon, *monsieur*." Her eyes narrowed. "I know you."

"You do?" I remembered her: the small daughter of the slaughtered Preston son. "You were very young when we met."

"You took our house." Her eyes were her grandfather's, sharp and canny; she'd grown into the nose at least. "I'm not likely to forget."

I attempted a smile. "It was an arrangement with your grandfather to keep you all safe."

Her mouth curved into a smile as sincere as mine had been charming. "If by safe you mean bored to death."

"Good afternoon, Master Lewis." Margaret Preston was in deep mourning, but her round face wore a genial expression. "How wonderful to see you again. Margaery, Master Lewis is our guest."

Brows like slashes of ink rose to her hairline. "And has been these many years."

"A moment, sir." Lady Margaret marched her granddaughter from the chamber, and I listened to the rise and fall of their voices outside the door. She returned, her hands clasped at her breast. "My granddaughter is not much in society. Her manners are appalling."

"I found her refreshing."

"Like cold water to the face," Lady Margaret said. "Please, come through to my parlor." Another pleasing room, this one more feminine but with comfortable chairs and an inlaid table before the fire. Lady Margaret put aside an unfinished bit of embroidery so our refreshments could be set out. "Tell me, how is Winterset?"

"Well, when last I heard," I said. "It's under Fowler's care at the moment, as I've been traveling. He reports to you?"

"Most regularly." Lady Margaret sipped her wine. "But he doesn't live there, and you do. I miss my house."

After eighteen years, Winterset felt like *my* home. "I've been very comfortable there. I regret I've had to be away so much these last years."

She gazed into her cup. "It's time for us to return to England."

"For me as well." I explained the queen's failing health, and her having—at last—made Princess Elizabeth her heir. "But if you plan to return, I'll send word to Fowler to start packing my things."

"Let us see how it goes," she said. "We will not make a quick removal. Stay in the house for as long as you require. And until you are ready to take ship for England, you must be our guest."

"It will only be a few days," I said. "I have already arranged passage on the *Unycorne*, leaving from Honfleur on the sixth of November."

The chamber I shared with Seb was snug and comfortable, imparting an immediate sense of ease. "I almost wish we hadn't booked passage; it's very pleasant here."

"You don't need pleasant. You need to go home."

Seb was always cautious on my behalf, often with good cause. My life was made easier, and safer, because of his vigilance, but sometimes he took it too far. "We'll be on our way soon enough,

Sebastian. Let us appreciate this bit of civilization while we may."

After years of wandering, I yearned for Winterset, and this brief interlude in Lady Margaret's household was a taste of the comforts which awaited me in England, where my house—my books!—were as I had left them.

If the Prestons returned, I could find other accommodation. I was happy at Winterset, but there were other houses. I would like to stay in the north, far from the court and all its intrigues.

I encountered Margaery Preston in the courtyard the next morning, returning from a visit to the stables. At supper the night before, she had kept her eyes down and spoke only when addressed, still feeling the effects of her grandmother's lecture. She bid me good day, her manner still distant. By her costume, she was intending to ride. I returned her greeting, and we fell into step.

"I apologize for any disturbance my presence may have caused."

A shrug. "You can't disturb a tomb."

It was quiet here; I liked that, but it was not an appealing life for a girl her age. "Is it just you and your grandmother?"

"Yes. I stayed on as her companion when my grandfather died." She looked at the sky. "Do you think it will rain?"

It was cloudy, but it did not feel like rain, and I said so.

"Good. I dislike riding in the rain." She fiddled with her gloves; the edges were neatly ornamented with blackwork. Was she the embroiderer? "My mother has married again; did grand-mère tell you?"

Talking to her was like playing tennis. "I'm surprised you do not live with them."

"Grand-mère needs me." Her pointed chin challenged me to disagree. "With Uncle Walter gone, I'm all she has left."

I remained silent, thinking of what Lady Margaret told me about her daughter-in-law's new husband, a minor French nobleman who spent much of his time at court, begging for scraps of royal attention.

"And they want to marry me off."

"That is what parents do." It was surprising that a match hadn't already been arranged.

"Did yours?"

The path split: the stables were to the left, while the right path curved around the back of the house toward a walled garden. I turned toward it. "I didn't have parents."

She frowned at me comically. "Everyone has parents."

A scrolled iron gate let us into the garden. As we walked, I sketched my origins: Wardlow, Hawley, Hatton.

"I've been threatening to join a convent," she said. "Do you think they'll accept me?"

"Do you have a vocation?" I tried to imagine Margaery Preston taking the veil. Stranger things had happened—women ended up in convents for reasons above and beyond a love of God.

"Of course not," she said, kicking at the gravel path, "but it would be easier to fake that than enthusiasm for Jean Rigard's choice of a husband. You should see the men he's paraded in front of me."

"Ah." She had been her grandparents' darling for so long; she wasn't likely to accept her mother's husband in control of her future. "I'm not sure a convent would welcome you without a vocation."

"Grand-mère will give me a dowry," she said. "And I'd rather marry God than some fat old man who only wants a broodmare."

I ignored her language, even though I agreed with the sentiment behind it, remembering Dorcas and her brewer. "Do you want to be a nun?"

Her eyes glinted. "What I want is to be left in peace."

"That's not going to happen." No one who wanted peace ever had it for long; I had learned that lesson over and over in my life.

Margaery ran her fingertips over the flowers, dusting her gloves with the drying stalks. "Then it's the nunnery."

"You'll have to profess vows of poverty, chastity, and obedience."

"Obedience is the only hard one."

Even during our few interactions, I had been struck by her forthright manner; this was not a girl who would take easily to the bridle. "You will have to give it to someone," I said, "whether it's God or your husband."

"Why? I'm happy with grand-mère. I don't want to marry anyone—especially if it benefits my stepfather."

"Perhaps Lady Margaret could find a more acceptable match?" She had been twenty years in France and had family here besides; surely, she could find someone her granddaughter could tolerate.

"I don't want a more acceptable match." She crossed her arms. "I don't want a match at all."

"Marriage is a fact of life."

"You aren't married."

"I'm a man." I admired the view of the house from this angle; the garden had been laid out to take advantage of every view. "It's not the same."

"Why did you want my grandfather's house, then? He assumed you had a family; I remember he was surprised to find you intended to live there alone."

Margaery asked very probing questions. "I'd never had a home before." I gave her the look that cowed my underlings in Cromwell's offices and, occasionally, Seb. It did not seem to bother her at all. "Hasn't your grandmother ever told you it's rude to ask questions?"

"Yes, but I didn't listen."

"I can see that." I tried to conceal my amusement.

"Wait." She stopped and was still for so long that I turned around to see what was wrong. "Master Lewis."

"What is it?" She looked like she'd been struck by lightning.

"I think you should marry me."

"What?" Perhaps I was the one struck by lightning.

"You should marry me," Margaery repeated with growing conviction. "I'm an heiress. You could own the house you've been living in all these years. It would solve both our problems."

Margaery left on her ride, and I noted with satisfaction the downpour that started immediately thereafter. I retreated to the house and, after some deliberation, looked up Lady Margaret in her parlor. She bade me be seated, putting aside the letter she was writing and waving toward the silver pitcher on the cupboard.

"Your granddaughter is a remarkable young woman," I said, pouring wine for myself. It wasn't much of a conversation starter, but I was still unsettled.

"I have done my best." She smiled fondly. "She has been a great comfort to me since my husband's death and the death of my son."

"I didn't know until Margaery told me," I said. "I will pray for him."

The older woman closed her eyes. "We left England to keep him safe, and he was carried off by a fever. The will of God is a strange thing."

"Indeed." I had begun to believe the will of God was as random as a coin toss. "About your granddaughter."

"She is full of ideas," Lady Margaret said. "She's had a bit more education than a girl should have. Don't let her bother you."

I rocked on my heels before the fire. "I see no fault in an educated woman, but she just suggested that we marry."

The surprise on Lady Margaret's face vanished quickly, replaced by her usual agreeable expression. "Did she? How did you respond to such a proposal, Master Lewis?"

The flames blurred. What did I have to say? "I have no need for a wife," I said carefully. "I have never wanted one."

"Do you find the idea repulsive?" she asked. "Or is it simply something that has never occurred to you?"

The nose was her grandfather's; the tendency to probe was from her grandmother.

"More the latter," I said. "Marriage is not repulsive, only unnecessary. During these last years, I have been happy to be unencumbered."

She absorbed this, pressing her lips together. "A man needs a wife. I guarantee Winterset is not in the same state as it was when I left it."

I was offended. "It has been nearly two decades," I reminded her. "I have made certain changes."

"And one of them is an insufficient number of servants," she returned. "Fowler tells me things."

I spent a moment thinking about what I would say to Fowler if he were in front of me. "I am one man. Fowler has his men, and there is the cook, two maids, and my servant, Sebastian. He does everything I require."

Lady Margaret sipped her own wine and continued with her line of thought. "An estate does not run itself. Winterset needs a master."

"I am returning within weeks," I said with a flash of annoyance. "I will see how things stand and rectify any defects."

"A wife would be able to do those things and leave you time for your own pursuits." She looked down, twisting the marriage ring on her left hand.

Was her surprise feigned, or had she been a party to Margaery's proposal? I believed it was the girl's idea, not the grandmother's, for she had more to lose by marrying. But how on earth was I any more to her taste than her stepfather's choice?

"Do you think Mistress Margaery would make me a suitable wife?"

"I think you would make her a suitable husband," she said. "If you married my granddaughter, Winterset would be yours for the duration of your life." She had learned much from Sir Ralph in their years together. "If you have children, the estate passes to them. If you do not, and you predecease her, Margaery will undoubtedly remarry, and Winterset would go to the issue of her second marriage."

The Preston women were sharp; perhaps Seb was right to worry.

Still, I could not deny the benefits to myself. Lady Margaret spoke of returning, and while I could find another house, another library, I didn't want to lose Winterset. Did I value my comfortable existence enough to disrupt it with a young and not very retiring wife?

"I would return with Margaery," she said. "To guide her in running the estate, and as her companion. I would not want her to impose too much upon your solitude—I understand that is why you chose the house."

My cup was empty. When had I drunk the wine? Seeing my look, Lady Margaret gestured to the pitcher. I refilled my cup and topped off hers.

"It is an interesting proposition," I admitted. "I do not know if it is in your granddaughter's best interests to be married to a man twice her age. One of her objections to her parents' plan is that she does not wish to marry a fat old man."

"Well, you're not fat," Lady Margaret said drily.

"Gluttony has never been among my flaws." I was beginning to feel quite bowled over between the two of them and the wine.

"What are your flaws, then?" She was getting down to business, questioning me like a prospective employer.

I ran through the capital vices in my mind as I paced again before the hearth. Of gluttony, wrath, and sloth, I was not guilty. Of lust...only for books. "Pride, greed, and envy, in some small measure," I said. "Most of those add up to ambition, which has put me in a situation of having to flee my own country. I think a little sloth might do me good."

Lady Margaret joined me before the fire. "Master Lewis, I may be an interfering old woman, but I love that child, and I want her to be happy." She put her hand through my arm. "I disliked your dealings with my husband, but I bear you no ill will. It was an arrangement between men, and the feelings of women do not enter into such things."

The conversation I was having, though, was mostly about the feelings—and the plans—of women.

I was expected to accept her offer, and I felt a fool for not immediately doing so. "You honor me greatly," I said. "And it is not that I find your offer—or your granddaughter—unacceptable, but I have been a single man all my life. Changing my life at this age requires much thought and some prayer." I placed my cup next to hers. "You will have my response by Saturday dinner."

"Very well." Her smile had much patience in it. "If you require conversation with either myself or Margaery before then, please seek us out. Otherwise, we will leave you in peace to make your decision."

The tiny chapel at the back of the house offered a quiet place to think. I knelt on the floor and fixed my gaze on the colored glass windows on either side of the altar. It shouldn't be a difficult decision. Marriages were, for the most part, contracts, and I was behaving more like an unwilling bride than a man who would acquire not just a young, attractive woman, but all her worldly goods—and a house that he already considered to be his own.

Was it Margaery or the idea of marriage that I balked at? I had been alone for so long and had grown to accept solitude, to enjoy it.

I wanted to go home. I wanted to walk into my library and close the door on the world. If there was a woman on the other side of the door, backed by her grandmother, what chance would I have of peace?

Lady Margaret's plan of inheritance disturbed me. I didn't care to whom the estate passed after my death, but my experience with children was limited to having been one, and I had not found it enjoyable. But a married man, particularly one blessed with a young wife, was expected to turn her belly into a ripe melon in short order.

It was ludicrous. Me—a married man! A husband. A father?

I did not want women in my household. I did not want feminine chatter at my dinner table or the prattle of children at my feet while I tried to read.

And yet...on entering the Preston house, I immediately remarked on its comforts. These, too, were the result of women. I had not the knack, or the interest, to make such a home myself, but I appreciated it.

Was that shallow of me? Bianca made a sweet and pleasant home, but her mind was as sharp as my own. Gender had nothing to do with brains, and certainly, Margaery was a bright young woman, perhaps more than bright—without knowing if her intelligence was acceptable, she might be hiding it under the guise of girlishness.

On second thought, I doubted that. Mistress Margaery seemed incapable of hiding anything.

I looked at the situation from her angle. I was educated, not poor, and possessed some useful friends. Those things were of little value to a woman. I'd never been attractive, and I didn't know how to play the courtship games that endeared a man of my sort to women. I could not imagine having to constantly watch my words so as not to wound someone of more delicate sensibilities.

It was better to be alone.

The rain had stopped. I took myself into the countryside to see if exercise helped any more than prayer. It was dark by the time I returned. The lighted windows guided me as I crossed the fields, and as I grew closer, I expected Seb to burst out from every tree to attend to my needs.

My needs were thus: wine and a good supper and a solid night's sleep, in the hopes that in the morning, I could come to some resolution. My walk had not given me the hoped-for mental clarity; I was as muddled now as when I'd set out.

Seb lingered in the courtyard. "You've been gone for hours, and the ladies knew not where. Are you well?"

"Just tired," I said, "and with much on my mind. Give them my apologies, and bring my supper to my chamber."

Upstairs, in merciful privacy, I stripped off my coat and boots. Seb had lit the fire, and I sat before it in my shirt and hose, letting the warmth seep back into my bones.

With a knock, he entered with a laden tray. "The ladies hope you are well." He looked at me searchingly. "And Mistress Margaery asked if you had any questions for her."

I ignored his curiosity as I ignored her query. "That will be all," I said. "You may take the tray later."

The needs of my body were addressed with warmth, ample wine, and several thick slices of spit-roasted beef. Lady Margaret's

French cook was as adept as the one left behind at Winterset, and I again considered the skill required in the making of a home.

I shook myself. I was not meant to be thinking of Lady Margaret's comfortable house or her granddaughter's uncomfortable offer. I was simply eating my supper in front of the fire and considering with which book I should while away the evening.

Because England's harsh return to Catholicism was much on my mind, I chose one of Calvin's biblical commentaries and tried to lose myself in its pages, but my mind stubbornly returned to Santa Giustina.

Even after all these years, my heart clenched at the thought of Salvatore. I was glad I'd made the visit, gladder still I had not found him changed or dead. For three decades, he had lived in my memory, a beautiful young man full of joy and grace and love for the world. The reality was better, and yet I was able, finally, to let him go.

I turned the page. A man could not help whom he loved or why. It was best to just offer it up to God and do the best one could.

A light tap on the door heralded Sebastian's return. When he did not immediately enter, I called, "Come."

Instead of Seb, the intruder was Mistress Margaery. She performed a neat curtsy and approached. "Your manservant is rude," she said. "I told him I would retrieve the tray, and he tried to block me."

"Seb is protective." I raised my book as she cleared, brushing crumbs into the napkin and placing everything on the tray.

"Should I leave the wine?"

I nodded. I was not in a frame of mind to talk.

She peered over my shoulder. "Is that Calvin?"

"It is." I tilted it so she could get a better look at the page.

"No wonder the queen wants your head." Despite my presumption of her Catholicism, she was scanning the page intently, her lips moving.

"It is but the word of God."

354 • *Karen Heenan*

Margaery straightened. "Not Queen Mary's God."

"They are all the same." I was weary of this discussion. "Even the infidels' God is still God."

She gave me a sharp look. "It would be interesting to be married to you."

I closed the book. "Your grandmother promised I would have peace."

"I'm not good at taking direction." Margaery's voice held a smile. "Perhaps I shouldn't tell you that. It doesn't recommend me." She picked up the tray, then put it down again. "I will go, but first—is there anything you would ask me, anything that would inform your decision?"

"I do not believe so," I said. "You have given me your reasons for marriage. Your grandmother has furthered them. It is simply a matter of deciding whether or not I wish to change my life in such a fashion."

Margaery walked to the window, her dark gray skirts brushing my leg as she passed. It struck me that I was in my chamber with a young lady while in a state of undress. It was enough to compromise her, if her family were more traditional.

"Men should marry, don't you think?" She turned to face me. "For appearance's sake, if nothing else."

"That's not enough reason."

"I wouldn't bother you," she said earnestly. "I'd leave you to your books or whatever else makes you happy. I could learn your ways. I don't believe you would hurt me or lock me away if I said the wrong thing."

Her directness was equal parts appealing and horrifying. "But I don't want a wife."

"Do you not like women?" She straightened her coif, from which strands of dark hair had escaped. "I know there are such men."

The speed and direction of her words left me breathless. How did she know of such things? "I do but perhaps not as much as I should if I were to marry."

"What if you were to marry someone who did not mind? Someone who wants the freedom that comes from being Mistress Lewis more than the rest of marriage."

"Rather than being Lady Margaret's granddaughter?"

Her narrow shoulders raised. "Lady is but a word. Our dairy-maid is more of a lady than some who bear the title."

I was intrigued in spite of myself. "I'm also thirty years your senior. What will happen when I die before you, as I surely will?"

"I'll be a rich widow."

I gave in. The lure of owning Winterset was too strong, and Margaery had grown on me. I did not mind Lady Margaret in the slightest, whether she stayed in France or returned with her grand-daughter.

When I told Seb of my plan, his expression darkened. "This will change everything."

"It will change nothing important," I assured him. "The ladies will assume the running of the house, and my life—and yours—will go on as before."

He brushed lint from my shoulder and tied on my sleeves. "Women cannot help themselves. They get into everything."

"It has been a long time since you've been around women—as long as it's been for me. Perhaps they've changed."

"Not likely." He made certain I was presentable and went off, muttering.

"I know your inclinations lie elsewhere," Lady Margaret said, "but we are still Catholic here in France."

"It is but God's blessing on a contract." She was not alone in her practicalities.

The wedding took place in the late afternoon. In addition to Seb and Lady Margaret, Margaery's mother and stepfather had been summoned from their nearby estate. They glowered at me, the ruination of their plans, but nothing could be done. Lady Mar-garet was their daughter's guardian, and I was, more or less, an acceptable match.

My bride—shocking word!—wore a gown as blue as the Virgin's robe and looked impossibly young. She offered a shaky smile as we met before the priest, and I attempted one in return.

Afterward, Father Laurent congratulated me. "I will be sorry to lose Madame Marguerite and the young lady," he said, "but I wish you all God's blessings and many sons."

There was a sound that could have been a snort, and I turned to see my bride hiding her face in her hands. She emerged, smiling in restrained fashion. "I'm sorry," she said, "it is an emotional day."

"Try for the correct emotion."

How did a man extract himself from his own wedding supper? My bride solved the problem by yawning enormously, drawing her grandmother's attention. "Child," she said, "you're about to fall asleep in your plate."

Margaery blinked. "It has been an eventful day, grand-mère. Only this morning, I was a girl, and now I am a wife."

"Not yet." Her mother had been drinking steadily throughout the feast, and she looked at her daughter with something like malice. "Let us escort the bride upstairs. Master Lewis, please take another glass with my husband while we ready my daughter for you."

Nothing could be less appealing than another drink with the sullen Jean Rigard. As the women departed, he refilled our cups, carelessly splashing wine on the table. The dark red liquid settled into the cloth, and I had discomfiting thoughts about what lay ahead.

"*Monsieur.*" The maid was at the door. "They say you may come up."

Rigard said something behind me, his voice low, and the maid giggled. When I reached the landing, Lady Margaret and her daughter-in-law waited outside the door to my chamber.

"All my blessings," Lady Margaret said, kissing me on both cheeks. "May you and Margaery be very happy."

I thanked her and bumped into Frances Rigard, circling around from behind. "Felicitations," she said. "May you have much pleasure in my child."

I opened the door with trepidation. My bachelor chamber had been transformed since morning, my scattered possessions put away, my books placed neatly on the window seat. The table was centered before the fire, and a silver jug and two cups stood ready, the firelight flickering on their gleaming surfaces.

The bed, with its blue curtains, was the same, but in the center was a wide-eyed Margaery, her dark hair arranged over her shoulders.

We stared at each other for a long moment.

"I hadn't planned for this," I said.

She relaxed just a bit.

"I suppose I should have."

"It does show a lack of forethought." Her voice was slightly unsteady, but the tone was purely hers.

"It feels very uneven." I gestured at my fully-dressed self and her obviously chemise-clad person under several layers of covers. I picked up her night robe from the chest and held it out. "Why don't you put this on, and we can talk for a bit."

"Don't look."

The robe shifted as she slid her arms inside. I waited a moment longer before asking, "May I open my eyes?"

"If you must." She was pouring two cups of wine. The flames cast a glow on her skin, and her hair shone a deep umber.

"At least you had assistance getting ready." I raised my cup to her. "Your womenfolk seem to have scared Seb out of the house."

"With any luck, he's safe in the stables," she said. "I haven't had this much speech with my mother in five years." She had on a brave face, but there was something bruised about her.

"Recriminations?"

"Grand-mère stopped most of it." She dropped her head in her hands, and her words were muffled. "How could I do this? Do I realize the harm I have caused to her husband? Do I understand they could have found me a rich man, one who did not need to be

358 • *Karen Heenan*

bribed to take me?" She laughed. "The same conversation every girl has with her mother on her wedding night."

Did girls talk with their mothers before the wedding night? Margaery surprised me with her knowledge that men might prefer other men, but that did not mean she understood the mechanics of marriage.

Come to think of it, I didn't understand the mechanics of marriage, only the act that might in time produce children. The rest of the relationship was as mysterious to me as the dark of the moon.

Margaery stood up, drawing her robe close about her. "What would Sebastian be doing if he were here?"

"You do not need to act as my body servant." Something in me cringed at the idea of her being that close.

"I am your wife, and your servant is absent." She came around my chair and stood behind me. "Please, allow me this. I feel far too undressed while you still wear your entire wedding costume."

I drew in a breath and stood up, loosening my surcoat. I untied my points and allowed her to draw off my sleeves. She removed my doublet and draped it over the chair.

"Now we are even," she said, "for this is what you were wearing last night."

I ducked my head. "I hoped you hadn't noticed."

"A nice young lady would have chosen not to see or else run screaming from the chamber." She shrugged. "I am nice and young and a lady, but perhaps not all at once, because those choices seem silly."

"You are an interesting creature." The fire and the wine warmed me, and I found myself looking at her, not as a bridegroom, but as a man who has just had something unexpectedly wonderful fall into his lap. "I don't know how you wish to conduct this marriage, Margaery, but I will do nothing to hurt you, I swear it."

Her eyes softened. "Thank you for that, Master Lewis."

"Rob," I corrected. "Or Robin. I'm your husband, after all. You should call me by name."

"Robin." She put her hand on my arm.

I could feel each individual finger through my lawn shirt, and I placed my hand over hers.

"I thought you did not like to be touched?"

When had she noticed that? "I don't if I'm not comfortable with the person."

"We are not so well acquainted yet." She leaned forward so that her head rested against my chest.

I looked down at the delicate white parting in her glossy hair. An unexpected wave of desire rolled over me. "We are not," I agreed. "And our acquaintances may take whatever form you prefer and however long you like."

Desire for Margaery Preston—Margaery Lewis now—was unexpected but not totally surprising. I'd learned long ago that what was necessary for desire was intellectual stimulation. I could have that in abundance with my wife, if I chose.

"They will be expecting the marriage to be consummated." She looked away, toward the bed. "Even my grandmother said so."

"The seal on a contract."

"Exactly." It was said with a touch of bitterness. This match was her idea, but it was only the best of several unsavory options. She could not have what she wanted, which was the independence of a man. "A nice blob of red sealing wax."

I reached into the cupboard for my satchel. Bringing out the small knife I carried when we traveled, I made a small cut on my forearm. When the blood welled up, I pressed it to the sheet on her side of the bed.

Margaery's lips parted as she watched. When I stood up, she pressed her kerchief to my arm. "You didn't need to do that."

"They have their proof," I said. "Let them fly it from the window if they wish. You and I know the truth, and if there is ever another bloody sheet, it will be when we have agreed to it."

She stood on her tiptoes and kissed me, her lips lingering for a moment longer than necessary. "You are making marriage very agreeable," she said, "and I would love to talk to you all night, but I am exhausted. Is that terrible?"

The combination of exhaustion and nerves made me so heavy, I could barely stand. "I'm not surprised. You were yawning at supper."

She giggled. "I just wanted to get this over with. Otherwise, we would have been there all night."

"Would you like me to braid your hair for sleeping?"

Margaery looked at me. "If you wish."

"I have a few husbandly skills." I divided her hair into three parts and produced a neat braid, then realized I had no idea what to do with it. Keeping hold of the braid with one hand, I pulled one of the points from my doublet and tied it off.

She flipped it over her shoulder. "I did not imagine a man capable of such things."

"Are you not capable of riding as well as a man?" I recalled our earlier discussions. "You argue as well as a university student."

She shed her night robe and got under the covers, carefully avoiding the blood. "Put out the light."

I pinched out the candle, inhaling the scent of wax. In the darkness, I removed my hose and got into bed on the other side.

We lay side-by-side like tomb sculptures until at last her hand crept across the space between us. "Thank you," she said softly.

"For what?" I asked, equally soft.

"For agreeing to this. For your patience. For your...for your blood." She took a deep breath. "This is not what either of us would have chosen, but I pledge to make the best of it if you will."

"I give you that pledge." I clasped her hand in mine. "Now let us sleep."

We were man and wife for four days before Sebastian and I left for Honfleur. I was unexpectedly sorry to leave. Our union was still unconsummated, but in conversation, we had become very intimate.

"I do not wish to go." I braced myself as she flung her arms around my neck, to delighted cackles from Lady Margaret. "Not yet."

"Such a demanding husband." She kissed my jaw. "Go back to Winterset, and make ready for my return. And Sebastian, if you please?"

"Yes, madam?" Seb still looked askance at her and avoided coming to our chamber for fear of seeing her in deshabille.

"Could you please shave my husband before I reach England?" She rubbed my beard. "I think there's a nice face under there, but I cannot be sure."

"If there is, I will be surprised," he said. "But I shall shave him clean as a babe."

I looked between them. "It's my face," I protested. "And I like my beard."

Margaery raised her chin. "My husband will be clean-shaven."

As we rode away, I looked at Seb. "I suppose you'll spend the entire voyage sharpening your razor?"

"It will be as my mistress wishes," he said. "Women know what they like."

Chapter 69

"AND THERE YOU HAVE it," I say. "My life up unto this point. I had an easy voyage upon the *Unycorne*, landing at Hull, whereupon I made my way to my house, was greeted by my servants, had a good meal, got drunk, and had but one night's rest before you hammered on my door."

Will looks abashed. "I do feel bad about that." He calls to the innkeeper for more ale; our dinner has grown long, and several of his men are drowsing where they sit.

"I hope the queen pays you well for your services," I say sourly. "Do you think we shall make London by nightfall?"

He looks into his empty cup. "It is possible, if we push."

"Then I'd prefer that we not push." Strangely enough, I am not looking forward to the loss of his company; after a week, I've grown attached to him. He's as awkward as I was but far more brash. With proper training, something could be made of him. "I hope my tale has been informative. I wish I'd known more of the workings of the human heart when I was your age."

We finish our drinks and gather ourselves, Hawkins rousing his men. "Get up, you fools!"

Seb is at my shoulder. "No news," he says quietly. "I went out to piss and asked the ostlers if they knew anything."

"We're not in the Tower yet." It's true, but I'm beginning to sweat a bit. Between the weather and our extra night in Cambridge, something should have happened by now.

I swing up into the saddle and land hard, jarring every aching bone in my frame. "Oof."

"Are you well?" Hawkins asks, probably fearing a recurrence of our mutual debility.

"It's nothing." I wait until we're away from the inn and Seb at the rear before speaking. "I would ask something of you. Will you see that Sebastian goes back to Winterset to serve my wife?"

"Of course," he says. "There's no warrant for him, though I imagine he'll want to stay with you until…" His voice fades away as he visualizes what Seb will stay to witness.

I have an idea. "You're unmarried. Perhaps you should ride back with him and present yourself for consideration. Margaery will be a well-off young widow, and your father has been remiss in not providing you with a wife."

He turns so swiftly, I can hear the bones in his neck snap. "How can you say that?"

"A man your age should be wed," I tell him. "Even if his inclinations don't lean that way, it makes life easier."

"Watch your mouth." Will's ears are flaming.

"I wasn't inferring anything. You're obviously a virile young man, attractive to—and attracted to—the fair sex. You shouldn't protest. It makes people wonder."

With a snort, he kicks his horse and rides ahead. I drop back to ride with Seb, who is telling the guards an involved tale about a Venetian prostitute. I listen for a while, interject, make them laugh. When it becomes rowdy, Hawkins reins his horse. I wait for him to shout at us, but he is standing in his stirrups, looking south.

I join him, straining to see what he's looking at. "What is it?"

"Riders on the road ahead," he says shortly. "A fair number of them."

My heart thuds in my chest. "I do hope it's not more of the queen's men, stealing your thunder by capturing me from you."

He laughs but looks again at the road.

"Are we stopping?" I ask. "My seat is getting a little worn after this many days in the saddle."

He ignores me, one hand on his sword, the other shading his eyes. "Damn," he murmurs. "I can't tell the colors."

Seb appears behind me. "How they do come on. At least a dozen, I'd say."

"Armed too. I can see the sunlight on their weapons." I can make out their numbers now. I look at Will Hawkins, who appears distinctly uneasy. "If this is the end of our journey, I will make my thanks now. You could have made this far more arduous had you really wanted to get me to the Tower."

"What do you mean?"

"Look at the man at the head of the riders," I say. "The one waving. Do you know him?"

"No."

I smile full in his face, watch the confusion bloom in his eyes. "I do."

The rider, on a gray horse, comes toward us at speed. He stops, raising a cloud of dust that set us all to choking. Jumping down, he approaches, takes my reins in his hand. "It's been a long time."

"It has indeed, Ned."

"What is the meaning of this?" Hawkins sputters.

Ned gives him the wide, disarming grin that for years deluded people into thinking him less than serious. "Haven't you heard? The queen is dead, long live the queen, and your prisoner is to join my escort as we ride to Hatfield."

Hawkins blinks. "Dead? When?"

"This very morning, God rest her soul." My friend crosses himself in all sincerity. "Though I disagreed with her, I will let God dispose." He drops my reins, slapping my thigh. "Are you ready to ride, Robin?"

I sigh. "I've been doing nothing else, Ned. You might have gotten here a little sooner."

His expression, viewed between my mount's flickering ears, is all fond impatience. "I couldn't come before she died, man—I'd have ended up in irons alongside you, and I've worked very hard these last five years to let myself be seen as a mild, no-trouble sort, happy to work toward the restoration of the true faith in England. Just very slowly and inefficiently."

He mounts, and we join the others. I see Anselm in their midst. I've never before seen him on horseback; he said his years of soldiering gave him a distaste for it. "How is he here?"

"He's the one who sent news of your arrest," Ned says. "He sent a courier from York and only just met up with us last evening."

My heart cracks open. No man of Anselm's years would ride such a distance to save someone he'd not forgiven. I look forward to spending a few quiet moments with him once we are on solid ground.

One question nags. "What about Darlington?" I ask as we turn our horses south. "He still has to be dealt with."

"I think not." Ned grins. "He's been such a vocal supporter of Queen Mary's anti-Protestant policies that he'll never recover. And if you join the court, or are at least seen as well-connected, he can't touch you."

It was a weight off my mind, knowing that the pointless years of hostility were ended. I would still look over my shoulder if I heard his name, but in changing his coat to serve the prior queen, he doomed himself with this new one.

We ride toward Hatfield, toward the future of England. I spare a backward glance at Will Hawkins and his men, talking amongst themselves. At last, Hawkins shakes his head, spurs his horse, and they follow.

"What sort of captor is this?" Ned asks. "Is he giving in, or does he hope yet to collect his reward?"

"I'm not certain." I look back and take in Will's set expression. He has his father's temper but Elinor's softness. "I think he feels the wind blowing and has seen fit to follow it—something neither you nor I can criticize."

We would not make Hatfield before dark, so Ned sent men ahead to arrange lodging—for all of us, as the two parties have merged. Our host is stunned when more than twenty horses clatter through his gate, but he opens his hall and makes two chambers available for our rest.

We sit down for supper, and I look at Ned, who is wrapping our host in a net of words. "My friend here," he says, gesturing in my direction, "was on his way to the Tower."

"Surely not?" The man looks distressed. "How fortunate you were able remove him from his unworthy captors."

"Indeed." Ned looks down the table at Will, who is eating steadily, his color high. "Very fortunate."

Anselm and Seb are across from me. Seb is so happy to see him that he is almost incoherent. Eventually, I catch Anselm's eye. "May we speak, after?"

He spares me a glance. "Of course."

Venturing into the darkness, we walk in the walled herb garden behind the house. Most of the plants have gone brown, brittle to the touch. I break off a sprig of rosemary, roll it between my fingers. The familiar scent reminds me of Winterset, where I had planted a hedge of it beneath my library window.

"I can't believe you rode all that way," I say. "You hate riding."

"If I'd walked, you'd be dead." His voice is as astringent as the smell of the herb.

"True." I stop in the center of the garden, where an elaborate knot pattern can still be made out. "And I will never be able to thank you enough. Another failing to add to my list."

"You are a man," Anselm says. "A man can make mistakes. It is how he responds that shows his measure."

I bow my head. "No matter how many times I've told you I'm sorry, I—"

Anselm's knotted fingers clasp my shoulders. "It's what you've done to remedy your mistakes that's important. Saving my brothers—saving Sebastian, for that matter—shows who you are."

I close my eyes, memories flickering past: every regret, every wrong word and false step. "Not enough."

His grip grows stronger. "Are you so arrogant that you refuse absolution when it is offered?"

Arrogant? He might well have slapped me. "That is not what I intended," I say, the words coming slowly. "But I've done—"

He sighs. "I know what you've done, or enough of it. But I didn't jar every bone in my body so you can waste your life on regret." He shakes me ungently. "You've been given a second chance, Robin. Use it. Live your life." He turns away. "Or don't. I'm going back to Winterset in the morning."

I watch him, this man who has taught me and judged me and, against all logic, loved and forgiven me. "I'll send Seb with you," I say into the silence. "Perhaps you'll reach home in time to welcome my wife."

That stops him. "Your what?"

I offer a crooked smile, thinking of Salvatore's words. *A man in full.* "Apparently, I was hoping for that second chance."

Chapter 70

IT HAS BEEN TEN years since I met the young Princess Elizabeth. During that time, she grew into herself and into her father's grandeur. Still slight, she appears larger than she is, seated on the dais in Hatfield's great hall, surrounded already by a legion of supporters.

She offers her hand—white, long-fingered—and I bow low, brushing my lips above it. "You supported our cousin. You are fortunate to still have your head, Master Lewis."

"I respected your sister's place in the succession," I say, "but my fear of a return to Rome, and what it would mean for people like me, was greater."

Elizabeth rises. How does such a slender girl embody such majesty? "I will make no windows into men's souls." There is a lifetime of experience in her youthful voice. "A man's religion is his own, unless he tries to supplant me, and then he will find me as fierce as any king."

She has survived her childhood, attempts at murder and marriage, and a stay in the Tower. I look forward to seeing her grow into her full powers, surrounded at last by those who want her on the throne and who would work to keep her there.

"Will you come to court, Master Lewis?"

I feel the pull of Winterset, my library—but also toward this young woman, in whom I had seen something long ago. "Your Majesty," I say, "we have met once before."

A small smile. "I remember. You came with Master Ascham and brought a book. Tacitus."

"It pleases me that Your Majesty remembers." She appears ready to dismiss me, and I speak again. "I served the court during the reign of King Henry." I cast my eyes down and prepare to doom my future. "I would have you know that I once worked for Thomas Cromwell."

The queen stills, taking my meaning: I had worked for the man—for the men—who killed her mother. "Do you swear to serve me and no other?"

"I do, Your Majesty." I feel again the pull of Winterset and remember, suddenly, Margaery. This pull was irresistible and would not like to be resisted. "If Your Majesty would grant me a brief reprieve—I have just married, and I would like to return home to welcome my wife."

She inclines her head. "You may do so, Master Lewis, and then bring her to court. I will give her a place among my ladies."

I back slowly away to be replaced by another supplicant. Still facing the dais, I join Ned at the door. "She's asked me to come to court."

"Good. Cecil wants you with us."

We exchanged greetings in the outer chamber. Cecil looks old for a man still in his thirties, but that is the way of it. Dancing to the tune of inconstant masters is wearing; perhaps now, with stability on the throne, we might all relax, take a breath, and enjoy the world we have made.

Author's Note

THIS BOOK WAS UNINTENTIONAL. When I finished my first novel, *Songbird*, I thought I had written the only story I wanted to tell about the life and times of the Tudor court.

Oh, Robin. He had other ideas. After *Songbird* was on the way to publication, I started working on another novel, set during the Great Depression. (It will be finished someday, I promise.) It was going well, but I kept hearing this voice that had nothing to do with the 1930s and far too much to do with the time period I thought I had finished with.

Robin wasn't the most likeable character in *Songbird*, and apparently, he had a few things he wanted to set straight. I humored him and listened and then listened some more. This book is the result.

While I began *A Wider World* knowing a fair amount about Henry VIII and the events of his reign, I didn't know a lot about the dissolution of the monasteries, which turned out to be a major event in Robin's life—and in the lives of all English people at the time. I understood the dissolution in theory (Henry broke with the Catholic church and made lots of money by dissolving the monasteries and taking their lands), but I'd never thought about it in terms of what happened to the people. Not just monks and nuns, but ordinary people who relied on the monastery system for everything from employment to food to medicine to constant, intercessory prayer. The system took centuries to build, but Henry and Cromwell destroyed it all in four years.

There are two schools of thought on Cromwell: he was evil, and his downfall was deserved, or he was Henry's man, doing acting on the king's orders. I tried to find a middle ground, because while I'm sure Cromwell did what the king wanted, he had his own beliefs, and there are instances where he led the king to the conclusions he wanted him to reach.

Those who know more about the dissolution than I did when I began will note the lack of John Leland. Leland was a scholar and historian who was sent by Henry VIII to inventory the monastery libraries; this happened prior to the dissolution, and when it became known that the monasteries would close, Leland wrote to Cromwell and asked him to rescue many of the books, resulting in a reorganization of the royal library. Including Leland, and his book project, would have taken my plot too far afield, so I gave Robin a job which relates to Leland's mission: book rescuer (and occasional pilferer).

The religious houses personally connected with Robin are my creation; the larger ones—Middlesbrough and Whitby—did exist. Nothing remains of Middlesbrough, but the ruins of Whitby Abbey are an amazing sight, which I hope to visit someday. I could have placed my fictional characters in real places but decided not to because, sometimes, a real place constrains me to write about real events, and while the dissolution happened as written—and far more dramatically in some spots—Robin, Ned, and even Jack Darlington, were not there.

Readers of my first book will recognize Bess and Tom, and I hope you're happy to get a bit more of their story. At first, I was hesitant to give them too much time (although I really do love them!) but in the end, it was about the story, and my placement of Robin in Bess's life meant that she had to be there for parts of his. I was glad I'd dropped so many breadcrumbs in *Songbird*, because it was fun to find them later and figure out how to build this new story with what I'd left behind.

For those who wonder about Robin's translation project, while the tales of Scheherazade hadn't made it to Europe in his lifetime, there were bits and pieces of it floating around, including a 15th century Syrian translation I saw mentioned in an online source. It was plausible enough that his merchant friend could have come across them in his travels and translated it into Italian for his own library. When facts aren't available, plausibility is the historical novelist's best friend.

There is (at least) one more story left to tell in this series of Tudor-court-books-without-much-royalty. The royalty quotient may increase, because the next book features Margaery Lewis, still reeling from her abrupt marriage and appointment as a lady-in-waiting to Queen Elizabeth I. (I think that's what's going to happen. It's marinating.)

I like to joke that if *Songbird* were a child, it would have been accruing college debt by the time it was published. *A Wider World* took much less time, but Robin was a precocious child.

Acknowledgements

This is where I thank all the usual suspects, starting with my husband, Mario Giorno, who now knows more about Tudor England than he ever wanted, finds Tudor-themed documentaries for us to watch, listens to me ramble about story arcs, and knows most of the major players, both real and fictional.

Huge thanks are due to my Twitter writing clan: Marian L Thorpe, Eva Seyler, Bjørn Larsson, Laury Silvers, and Annie Whitehead, who are always there to work out plot snarls or talk about our characters as if they're real people (they are to us). Dianne Dichter, reader of multiple drafts, has my undying gratitude. Thanks also to Jennifer Summerfield, not only for her friendship and support, but for reading the audiobook for Songbird and giving Bess a voice.

Lastly, I'd like to thank my readers. (I have readers!) Writing may be a solitary activity, but it needs people at the other end. Thank you.

About the Author

As an only child, Karen Heenan learned at an early age that boredom was the ultimate enemy. Shortly after, she discovered perpetual motion and since then, she has rarely been seen holding still.

She lives in Lansdowne, PA, just outside Philadelphia, where she grows much of her own food, makes her own clothes, and generally confuses the neighbors. She is accompanied on her quest for self-sufficiency by a very patient husband and an ever-changing number of cats.

One constant: she is always writing her next book.

Other Books by Karen Heenan

The Tudor Court Series
Songbird – Book I
A Wider World – Book II
Lady, in Waiting – Book III

Follow her online:

Twitter: @karen_heenan
Facebook: @karenheenanwriter
Instagram: @karen.heenan

Or sign up for her mailing list on her website:
www.karenheenan.com

Printed in Great Britain
by Amazon

18762357R00219